I0595840

Miss Mary Investigates
Book One

Death of a Clergyman

A Pride and Prejudice Mystery

RIANA EVERLY

MISS MARY INVESTIGATES BOOK 1

DEATH OF A CLERGYMAN: A PRIDE AND PREJUDICE MYSTERY

*Copyright © **2020 Riana Everly***

All rights reserved.

*Published by **Bay Crest Press 2020***

Toronto, Ontario, Canada

No parts of this publication may be reproduced, stored in a retrieval system, or transmitted in any form or by any means, electronic, mechanical, photocopying, recording, or otherwise, without the prior written permission of the copyright owner.

This book is sold subject to the condition that it shall not, by way of trade or otherwise, be lent, resold, hired out, or otherwise circulated without the publisher's prior consent in any form of binding or cover other than that in which it is published and without a similar condition including this condition being imposed on the subsequent purchaser. Under no circumstances may any part of this book be photocopied for resale.

This is a work of fiction. Any similarity between the characters and situations within its pages and places or persons, living or dead, is unintentional and co-incidental

Cover design by Mae Phillips at coverfreshdesigns.com

ISBN-13: 978-1-7771504-2-6

Dedication

For Jyl, who shone too brightly and left us too soon.
I hope that wherever you are, you know I could never have done
this without you.

Contents

Acknowledgements

I am an unfaithful reader. I cannot commit myself unshakingly to a single genre. As a teenager and young adult, I flirted shamelessly with science fiction and fantasy, and then developed a more mature love for mysteries. Jane Austen has always held a special place in my heart, but I strayed, and often, to other women: Agatha Christie, Ngaio Marsh, P.D. James… I just could not stay true. And then I discovered I did not have to. I could revel in my love for Austen and also for those writers who kept me up late into the night, trying to figure out whodunnit. And this is the result.

I have so many people to thank for helping this book see the great wide world. Mikael Swayze is my keenest critic and best friend, and his editorial skills are second to none. I would like to thank my beta readers and ARC readers. To Anna T and Melissa R and Donna K, you rock! Marion Joseph was of particular help in shaping this story, and I cannot thank her enough. Thanks to my children, who sat patiently for far too long as I mused, "should I call him Alexander? What about James? Fred?" They still love me.

Thanks also to Hadassah Swayze for her work on the silhouettes, and, as always, to Mae Phillips for her beautiful cover art. They say not to judge a book by its cover, but having something eye-catching and beautiful on the front never hurts, does it?

Cover design by Mae Phillips at coverfreshdesigns.com

Prologue

The small stream threaded its way through trees and brush, across the landscape of gently sloping fields, past hedgerows and under bridges, until it entered—and a scant distance thereafter emerged from—a thickly wooded area near a small town. Swollen from several days of unusually heavy rains, the stream nonetheless kept mostly to its muddy banks, bubbling cheerfully over the stones and pebbles that formed its bed, splashing at the larger rocks and tufts of earth that interrupted its headlong flow. In the spring, the higher banks would be a riot of wildflowers, glistening under a gentle sun. Nearby trees would present pink twigs to the crystal blue sky, proudly offering delicate green buds and fragrant white blossoms to the world. In summer, the leaves would darken to various shades of emerald and pine, and the fields would colour the earth with the golden shades of ripening corn. Even in winter, the weak sun would yet illuminate the pristine blanket of white snow lying protectively over the fertile land, shimmering and perfect in its icy embrace, the bare trees standing as sentinels until the earth awoke once more to bestow its bounty upon its inhabitants.

But it was yet autumn, and the flowers had long since faded and the harvest mostly brought in for the year. The trees stood bare, but for a few stray leaves that had yet to relinquish their hold upon dormant branches, the colours of autumn's glorious palate now faded into browns and duns. The sky on this day lay leaden and heavy, for the rains – although they had ceased for the moment – had not yet passed, and the brown mud was tinged with the grey that preceded the advent of winter. Through all this, the stream yet flowed, cheerful and insistent, carrying on its conversation with itself, though its waters were dark and grey, mirroring the sky above.

And yet there was still some colour to brighten the burbling waters. A delicate trickle of bright red eddied in the water as it swirled around a protruding stone, spiralling in the flow before gradually spreading out into the rush of the current and disappearing from view. A dog from one of the local farms sniffed at the unaccustomed odour of the water and followed its interest some feet upstream, where the origin of the red trickle could be found. Step by step, the dog sniffed at the water as the red trickle skirted a black shoe, so inappropriate for the rural scene, flowed blithely over a submerged knee, and decorated the prone torso with a delicate pattern of droplets and streaks. The decorations meant little to the beast, for they carried no further distinctive aroma to tempt his nose. Far more interesting was the weakening flow that originated so very close by, only inches away, beckoning to the sensitive canine nose.

The dog sniffed once more at the body. It cared not that the man lay half submerged in the rippling brook, one hand flung outwards as if in supplication to a god who no longer cared, a leg bent at an unnatural angle, eyes wide and unseeing; only the unexpected presence and the tang of blood in the air captured the dog's attention. A more critical observer would soon realise that it was not the cold waters or the broken limb that seemed to be the cause of the man's demise, but rather the slit in the side of his neck, from which the bright red blood oozed to decorate the currents. The dog sniffed once more at the vacant face and the outstretched hand, and then at the blade with the decorated handle that lay so close, and with a low growl and a whimper, returned to the brown boot upon which he had been chewing with such contentment.

Chapter One

An Unpleasant Morning

Mary Bennet sometimes wondered whether she had been born on a full moon, or on some day sacred to the pagan druids, or whether she had been cursed in infancy with some hex, for she seemed to have been granted the dubious gift of invisibility. Neither her parents nor her sisters, or even the household staff, seemed to notice her comings and goings unless they somehow interfered with or otherwise interrupted some planned activities. Or, she considered, perhaps her invisibility was a skill developed during her eighteen years as part of the Bennet family, a trait to ensure survival, or an attribute to mirror her personality.

Mary had always been called the quiet one. Being the third of five daughters, she had much competition for her parents' attention and had learned, consequently, to rely on herself for amusement. Jane, the eldest, had a disposition that was all sweetness and kindness, and was blessed with a face and figure to match. Next to Jane in age and beauty was Elizabeth, whose slight deficiency in physical perfection was more than compensated for by her quick mind and her sparkling wit. Whilst Mary had few doubts about her own intelligence, she could not match her sister in the art of sharp repartee or uttering *bons mots* that would astound the room. It was usually best to remain silent when Lizzy was around.

Nor did Mary have much patience for the childish games played by Kitty or Lydia, her younger sisters. She had no desire to chase after red-coated officers or redo the same bonnet for the fifth time. These were inane activities, so unsuited to a young woman of sober and serious thought such as herself. Her time, she considered, was far better spent improving her mind or practising her scales and etudes at the keyboard. And it was only at these times, when the clattering of another sonata or the recitation of the advice from the books or sermons she often read impinged upon the attentions of the other members of the Bennet household, that she was noticed.

Today, however, Mary was not unhappy to be ignored and left to her own devices. The entire day had been one of upheaval and chaos, almost from the moment she arrived downstairs for her tea and bread. The family had slept late after the revelries of the previous night's ball at Netherfield. Mr. Bingley, who resided at the neighbouring estate, had certainly put on a grand affair and his sister Caroline had outdone herself in ensuring that no detail was overlooked. Miss Bingley's motives, Mary was certain, arose more from wishing to assert her own superior taste over that of the society of Meryton than from a real desire to please her guests, but the results of her efforts were commendable. There had been food and wine and music aplenty, and of excellent quality as well, and it was not until long after midnight that the Bennet family carriage rumbled back along the lanes, carrying the tired family to their home at Longbourn.

The sun had risen too early upon the household this morning after the ball, and with aching feet and tired eyes, the family had emerged from their bedrooms. Mary had been the first awake and downstairs, but she had not taken two sips of tea when her mother's voice had penetrated the fog of her sleepiness.

"Where is my shawl, Jane? Did I have it when we returned last night from Netherfield? I was certain I had it, but now I can find it nowhere. But never mind that. Jane, you must tell me once more. How did he look at you? Did his eyes wander to seek out other ladies, or did he keep his regard entirely upon you for the entire dance? Did he look at his feet, for that is very bad form, although it is excusable should he be taking special care not to step on your foot or damage your gown. What did he say to you after supper, before the next dance? You must tell me again, Jane, or I shall not be easy and you know how my poor nerves cannot abide uneasiness. Where is my shawl?"

As Mama and her eldest daughter entered the room, Mary willed her gift of invisibility to shield her from their view. She quite expected her mother to prattle on all the day about the ball, about the great riches Mr. Bingley must surely command, and about the inevitability of Mr. Bingley finally offering for Jane's hand. Mrs. Bennet seemed determined not to disappoint her middle child.

"And he danced with you three times, Jane. Three! You must know what that means, for a gentleman does not raise such expectations unless he is determined upon a path. What colour was his waistcoat? I did not see it so closely as you did. Was it white? My missing shawl is white, with green embroidery. It is a custom in my family to wear white when one is contemplating a proposal..."

Jane laughed and poured her tea. "No, Mama, his waistcoat was grey, but it was everything proper and most becoming. And I have never heard of such a custom, not in our family or in any other. Where did you last see your shawl?"

"But what of his eyes, Jane? Did he take your hand to lead you in to supper, or merely offer his arm? These things matter!"

Mary sighed. She seemed, once more, to have been forgotten. And so the morning continued. Kitty descended the stairs with red eyes, followed by Lydia, face triumphant, clutching a shawl that Mary knew had been given to Kitty the previous summer, the silent remains of a bitter argument still fomenting between the two. Then Papa walked in from his study, took a cup of coffee and a small plate of toast and eggs, and without more than a nod and a curt "Morning," to his family, returned whence he came. At last, Elizabeth entered the breakfast room as well, although not from the stairs. She must have been outside walking, for the clouds were lighter than they had been in many days and promised a short respite from the succession of rain. Her cheeks were rosy from the cool autumn air and she wore the air of resplendent health from her exercise. Now only one person needed to appear before the company was complete.

The tea was cooling in its pot when the final resident of the house found his way to the breakfast room. Mr. Collins was a tall, heavy-looking young man of five-and-twenty, a cousin on Mr. Bennet's side of the family and the heir to Longbourn. He had imposed his presence upon the family in a sort of peace offering to atone for a rift between Mr. Bennet and his own father and had further proposed to soften the blow of his position as heir by taking one of the Bennet sisters as his wife. To that end, he had fawned and simpered and made every attempt to ingratiate himself into the good graces of Elizabeth, who had shown not the first sign of reciprocated interest. Even the previous night, when

Mr. Collins had claimed his dance with his fair cousin, Mary had observed Lizzy's carefully contained expression of dismay and distaste at his clumsy dancing and poor conversation.

Lizzy was too well bred to display her sentiments openly, but Mary knew her well, as sisters are wont to do, and was a keen observer of the world in which she participated but little. It had not been a chore to scrutinise Lizzy's expressions, after all. Mary had not danced, but had sat silently, invisibly, amusing herself with her own games, in which she drew inferences from the subtlest details of what she observed. Compared to some, Lizzy's carefully schooled features were as an open book. She resented every moment she was forced to spend with Mr. Collins, and to be honest, Mary did not disagree with her.

Mary had thought, at first, that Mama would have steered Mr. Collins towards her rather than to Lizzy. It ought to have been clear that Lizzy and the parson would never suit, but Mama seldom looked beyond her own needs and desires. Mary ought, at first blush, to have been a more appropriate choice for a young clergyman. She was always reading her sermons, after all, and spouting words of censure and inspiration from the Good Book to all who would listen. It was, she admitted, easier than finding some other subject on which to speak, for she had little talent for falling into the witty repartee of her older sisters or the inane babblings of her younger. She was certain her mother figured Mary as the ideal candidate for a clergyman's wife.

Mary had even, for a while, considered that her older sisters thought her to be a good match for their cousin. Mary stifled a giggle at the thought! First, she reprimanded herself, refined ladies do not giggle; it is most immature and unseemly, almost as bad as rolling one's eyes. Second, it would not do at all to call attention to herself. There were times when her ability to melt into the walls was something she appreciated and being in Mr.

Collins' presence was one of those times. The man bored her! Yes, he had been subjected to an education of sorts and was of a bent that lent itself to her pious inclinations, but he was a fool! An educated, pious fool! He could recite pages on end from Fordyce, but had little understanding of the words he parroted so freely. He could sermonise and pontificate but could not discuss the material he had so clearly committed to memory, for he comprehended not a word of it. No, with his high sense of self-importance and his low intelligence, he might be amusing for an afternoon or two, but Mary would never have him as a husband. Lizzy seemed to understand that, for after the first day of Mr. Collins' visit, wherein she attempted to include Mary in every conversation, she ceased her efforts completely, offering her sister a wry smile in place of a tempting question.

And thus it was that she felt her eyes dart this way and that as Mr. Collins settled himself at the breakfast table and asked after the tea pot. It would be most impolite to stand up and leave without good reason, but she had little desire to remain and listen to his prattlings and meaningless compliments, strewn as straw before swine.

"I believe the tea is cold, Mama," she spoke quickly, drawing the eyes of all at the table to her.

Lydia blinked, as if noticing her sister for the first time that morning. Kitty snickered into her napkin, and Mrs. Bennet voiced her surprise. "Oh! Mary."

Yes, Mama, I have been here all the while. You choose not to take any regard, but I am here. The thoughts raced furiously through her brain, but she kept them unvoiced, replying with simple tones. "I shall ask cook at once to fetch us a fresh pot for Cousin Collins. Please excuse me." She stood and curtseyed once, and then with all haste vanished in the direction of the kitchens, most grateful for her escape.

What to do next had been a simple decision. The one room into which neither her mother nor her cousin tended to enter was the small salon at the back of the house. Too small for the entirety of the Bennet family to sit comfortably and too far from the kitchens for real warmth in the winter, it provided a welcome retreat where Mary often hid herself to read, undisturbed, for an afternoon. There was a chair by the window that was mostly obscured from the door, upon which a warm blanket often lay waiting to warm a young lady's toes, and it was there that Mary hid herself. It was also directly across the hall from the front parlour where Mrs. Bennet and her daughters often sat and provided an excellent place from which to overhear conversations from that room.

As she sat and considered her book—a shocking and most edifying treatise on the rights of women to an education by Mrs. Wollstonecraft—a most uncommon sound reached her ears. Mary heard her mother hustle Kitty out of the parlour and close the door upon whomever it was that remained within. No! Could it be that Mr. Collins had decided to press his suit? Oh, poor Lizzy! How would she refuse him? With a gentle word and a sympathetic smile, or with a sarcastic eye and a string of words that stung? Mary allowed her book to close, and she sat perfectly still, listening for any sound that might reach her ears from the sequestered pair inside.

Her efforts were soon rewarded. The door was pushed open, slamming against the wall behind it, and Elizabeth's voice could be heard, tight and angry. "To accept you is absolutely impossible. My feelings in every respect forbid it. Can I speak plainer? Do not consider me now as an elegant female intending to plague you, but as a rational creature speaking the truth from her heart." Then she ran, as quickly as her upbringing would allow, upstairs to her room to escape her unwanted suitor.

"You are uniformly charming!" Mr. Collins cried up the stairs after her. Mary caught herself before her laugh became audible. Did the man not understand that he was being abused by this "charming" Miss Bennet? No, it seemed not, for he continued, "and I am persuaded that when sanctioned by the express authority of both your excellent parents, my proposals will not fail of being acceptable." He shuffled his feet loudly enough that Mary could hear each motion, and she could imagine the looks Mrs. Hill would cast upon him if she caught him so damaging her polished floors. There was no reply from above, and Mary wondered if Mr. Collins had given up his ill-fated suit. But then, in a resolute voice, the parson called out, "Mrs. Bennet, Mr. Bennet, I must talk with you at once!" and his footsteps disappeared in the direction of Mr. Bennet's study.

Mary heard little else that morning, save for vague rumblings of discontent throughout the house, punctuated by Mrs. Bennet's agitated cries of "Elizabeth Bennet!" and "Lizzy, this will not do." After some time, the shouts ceased and Mary imagined her older sister had left the house, all the better to escape the demands of both parents and erstwhile lover in the brief respite from the rain. She nodded in approval. Escape was exactly the course of action she herself would have taken. Satisfied, she crept out of her hiding place and ventured to the kitchens, where she procured a tray of chocolate and muffins, before disappearing once more into her secluded den where her book awaited.

The treatise was fascinating and the chocolate drink warming and the hours passed as if they were minutes. A later foray into the kitchen in the early afternoon proved the house to be unnaturally quiet. A quick chat with Mrs. Jackes, the cook, revealed that Lizzy had indeed left the house in a hurry after a short but tense interview with her parents shortly after the failed proposal, and that Mr. Collins had stormed off shortly thereafter, but not without waiting for a basket of cakes and fruit to be prepared for him. Mr. Bennet had not emerged from his study since the interview with his daughter, and Mrs. Bennet had retired to her rooms in a fit of nerves, demanding that her remaining daughters attend her at once! Returning to her chair and blanket, Mary tried to read further, but she was warm and well fed and her eyes grew heavy and she soon fell asleep.

The sun was well past its zenith when she awakened to the sound of a slamming door. Her little salon, being towards the back of the house, was proximate to the servants' door and the door to the back garden, through which Lizzy was known to come and go as the mood took her. Mary could see nothing from her nest, but heard everything. Her ears awake before her mind, she was aware of the reverberation of the heavy door as it swung on its hinges, of the sound of wood against wood, metal upon metal, as it was closed again with great force, and of her sister's footsteps— for she most certainly recognised each sister by her unique gait— as she passed into the house and towards the stairs. But... something did not seem right. They were Lizzy's footsteps, to be certain, but there was a slowness to them, some dragging quality that pulled Mary from her chair. She rose and moved to the doorway and gasped at the sight of her sister.

There, in the dim light of the hallway, stood Lizzy, barely standing upright, skirts streaked in mud and shredded about the hem, her petticoats in disarray, her boots unrecognisable from the mire in which they were encased. But these were nothing compared to the look on her sister's face. She seemed stricken, her complexion ashen, her lips white. The sparkling eyes were vacant and the accustomed impish expression replaced by one that bespoke sheer horror. And when she turned in Mary's direction and held out a hand, begging for help, that hand was scratched and injured and covered in blood. The same blood, Mary could now see as her eyes grew accustomed to the unlit hallway, which covered the front of Lizzy's dark green walking cape.

Eyes still wide with shock, Lizzy turned to her younger sister, mouth open as if to speak, but then turned away immediately and ran up the stairs towards her bedroom. Too stunned to move, Mary stood in the hallway, wondering whether to go after Lizzy or to leave her in peace, until there came an insistent knock at the front door. It was too late for unexpected company, and no guests were due for dinner or cards. It required only a few short steps from where she stood for Mary to have a good view of the door, and within seconds she was at the corner of the hallway from which she could observe all.

Mrs. Hill, the housekeeper, opened the door and stepped back unsteadily. "Sir William," she curtseyed, her voice unsteady. "Is Mr. Bennet expecting you? I had not been informed, but I shall set another place—"

"That will not be necessary, Mrs. Hill," the man replied. "I am not here on social matters, but on ones of business. I am here in my position as local magistrate." He stepped inside, followed by two large men whom Mary knew worked at the smithy and functioned as constables on the rare occasions that they were so needed.

Mrs. Hill stepped aside, mouth agape. "Sir William?" she asked, as the master of Longbourn rounded the corner from his study.

Without a nod or greeting to his friend, Sir William intoned, "I am here to arrest Miss Elizabeth Bennet on suspicion of murder."

Chapter Two

Overheard at Netherfield

Sir William Lucas's words echoed in the foyer of Longbourn. For a moment, he was met with utter silence, and then, all at once, the house erupted into a cacophony of shouts. "What are you on about?" Mary's Papa demanded from his position by his study door, whilst Mrs. Hill gave a soft cry and rounded on the two burly constables, who growled their own warnings at her to stand back. Mama must have heard the banging at the door and left her rooms, for she stood on the landing halfway up the staircase to the upper storeys and screamed. Meanwhile, Jane attempted to calm her and Kitty and Lydia scurried around, crying, "Mama, what has happened?" and "Is something interesting going on? Shall I change my gown?"

At last, after a minute of this chaos, Mr. Bennet bellowed a command for all to cease their infernal noise. Mary gasped and took an involuntary step back. Never in her life had she heard her father use such a tone of voice. "Now what," the gentleman demanded, "is going on? This is preposterous, William. You cannot mean it!"

With a grimace, Sir William puffed out a great breath of air and relaxed his shoulders. In a lower voice, he sighed, "May I please come in, Thomas? This is a serious matter." His friend shook his head in resignation and wordlessly gestured for the unwelcome visitors to enter the house.

"Now tell me," Papa asked again, "what in heaven's name this is all about! Surely you are making a poor joke."

Sir William turned to his constables and whispered something to them, and they stepped back towards the door, easing their threatening stance. He sighed once more. "Your guest, your cousin Mr. William Collins, was found dead about an hour ago in the stream that runs through the field by Oakham Mount."

This was met with a flurry of exclamations of horror and astonishment, but Sir William stayed them with a hand. "Your Lizzy favours that locale, does she not?"

"Yes," Mr. Bennet agreed, "she does. But what is this nonsense about murder? Did the man drown? The way he dances, one should not rely too much upon his steadiness of foot. He must have fallen into the waters."

"That might be a plausible conclusion," Sir William conceded, "were it not for the fact that the man died with a knife in his throat. Mr. Jones," he mentioned the village apothecary, "has looked at him and has summoned a doctor from Hertford, but it seems that the man had no time to drown, for he was mostly dead by the time he was damp."

"But what has this to do with Lizzy?" Mama had recovered herself enough to form a coherent sentence. "Whoever would want to kill Mr. Collins? It can hardly be believed. It must have been a vagabond passing through, looking for any sort of decent man to kill and rob!"

"Perhaps, madam," came the reply, "this might be the case. For indeed, who *would* want to kill Mr. Collins? But the knife we discovered by Mr. Collins' body was most certainly Elizabeth's."

Mama screamed again, sparking a new flurry of activity around her, which took some several moments to settle. She collapsed into Jane's arms, and when Jane protested that she must see to her beloved sister, her mother insisted, "No, attend me, Jane! My nerves cannot take this!" At last Jane led her to a chair at the bottom of the stairs, where she collapsed in a most inelegant manner, her face alternately pale and red, her eyes fluttering, as her fingers clenched and unclenched ceaselessly.

"Mama!" came a new voice from the top of the stairs. "Mama, are you ill? I heard you cry out!" The voice was raw and hoarse, but it was unmistakeably Lizzy's. Mary took a small step out into the main hallway to try to see her sister.

"Miss Elizabeth, please join us." Sir William's words were a command. Lizzy began to demur, but obeyed. Mary watched as she descended the stairs. She had changed her torn and blood-covered dress for a clean one and had put up her hair, but her face was white with a blue stain forming around one eye, and she could not conceal the wealth of scratches and cuts upon her arms and hands.

"Lizzy!" her mother exclaimed. "What have you been up to? What happened to your eye?"

Sir William stood still, his eyes taking in every detail of the young woman's appearance, his head nodding slightly.

"When did you last see Mr. Collins?" he asked, his voice more gentle in the presence of the injured girl.

Lizzy blinked. "Mr. Collins? Why do you ask about him?" Her voice was a quaver and if anything, her face drained even further of colour. Mary stared at her sister; this was not the headstrong Lizzy she had grown up with.

Disregarding the question, Sir William spoke, "He is dead. Murdered, so it seems, and we have evidence that you were with him. We have evidence that you killed him. Now what do you say to that, Miss Elizabeth?"

Lizzy swayed on her feet, and Mary dashed out from her place in the darkened corner to steady her. "Lean on me," she whispered. "I won't let you fall."

Lizzy's eyes closed and her head drooped on her neck. "I didn't... I could never... You must be mistaken..." Her sentences all died half spoken.

Sir William took a breath to speak once more, but before he could let out a sound, the door blew open behind him and his daughter, Charlotte, rushed into the house. "Oh, thank heavens," Mary spoke aloud for the first time since the unwelcome arrival of the men. Charlotte was Lizzy's closest friend besides Jane. Sensible and intelligent, Charlotte would know what to do! Lizzy sagged in relief into Mary's arms at the sight of her friend, and Mary had to struggle to prevent her from falling.

Charlotte noticed and took a step towards Lizzy, but then stopped and turned on her father. "Papa, I will not allow you to do this!" she insisted. "I heard the men who brought the news to you, and I refused to believe a word of it! I still refuse." Her voice was steady and firm where Lizzy's had been so weak, and Sir William took a small step back at the sound of it. Mary fought the inclination to smile.

"Now what is your evidence, Papa?" Charlotte demanded. "You cannot seriously entertain the notion that Lizzy—our own dear Lizzy—could have the first thing to do with this matter, can you?" Her voice and manner insisted that he had better have no such notion indeed. "Tell us what little you have, so we can show that

Lizzy is guiltless!" She kept her gaze fixed upon her father, daring him to speak against her. Mary sighed slightly in relief. If anyone might take charge of this awful situation, it would be Charlotte.

Sir William nodded and closed his eyes for a moment, not abandoning his position near the doorway. "Very well. As Mr. Bingley was taking his leave before returning to London on matters of business, two farmers came by the house, knowing I am the magistrate. They were out checking the stream for flooding after the rains and found Mr. Collins dead in the brook. One man's dog had smelled the body and led them to him. He had a large knife wound in his neck and Miss Elizabeth's knife was in the stream, mere inches from the body, and a satchel containing her monogrammed handkerchief and a book with her name in it were then located in the field a short distance away. And now look at her—scratched and injured and in shock! Killing a man would certainly send any woman into shock. Who else can it be?"

Charlotte settled her hands upon her hips and huffed. "Papa, must you ask this? Anybody might have taken Lizzy's satchel! I know she keeps her knife in there for peeling fruit and cutting twigs. She has rescued many of my skirts in such a way when we have been out walking in the woods. Her knife might be guilty of this crime, but not she! She might have dropped the bag, or forgotten it by a stile, or had it stolen from her. You cannot arrest her for a crime we all know she could not have committed." Her eyes dared her father to contradict her.

He looked diminished under his daughter's glare, but would not cede the argument. "Look at her, Charlotte. She has been in a brawl. Speak for yourself, girl." He turned to Lizzy.

Lizzy blinked back tears and Mary reached into her apron pocket for something with which to dry them. Her fingers found a piece of cloth, which she handed to her sister. Mopping her eyes as she spoke, Lizzy replied in a whisper, "We did argue. He approached me and I shouted at him, and then I ran off. But he was alive when I left him. I did not kill him." Mary cocked her head. She did not think her sister to be lying, but something seemed wrong. There was something in Lizzy's voice, something uncertain. She would puzzle it out later; right now the important thing was to assert Lizzy's innocence.

"What of your injuries, then?" Sir William stared at the scratches on Lizzy's hands and on the bruise darkening on her face.

"I... I was upset at the confrontation. I ran to the woods, to the small clearing where I sometimes read, and scratched myself on the branches, for I dared not slow down to avoid them. I thought..." she took a deep, shuddering breath, "I thought he might chase me." Her voice was barely audible, a mere whisper in the air, but Mary could see her father's eyes widen at this statement.

"Did he hurt you, Lizzy?" Papa's voice carried an edge of warning for a man who was in no condition to heed it. "If he hurt you..."

"No, Papa. He did not. I managed to get away. But I left him alive, I swear it! I will swear it on the family Bible, in the church, anywhere. I did not kill him!"

"Papa?" Charlotte stared at her own father. "You are the magistrate for the area. You have the duty to decide who bears enough of the stain of guilt to be charged for such a heinous crime as murder. Are you prepared to assert that there is enough to point towards Lizzy—my dearest friend!—as the perpetrator? I cannot believe you will!" She narrowed her eyes and Mary felt her lips twitch into the smallest semblance of a smile at Charlotte's determination.

"Well, my dear," Sir William began, "who else could it possibly be? A crime like this must be punished." He wavered under his daughter's glare. "Very well. I will take some time to consider the possibilities. Miss Elizabeth, I shan't arrest you yet, but I must caution you not to leave the grounds of Longbourn until this matter is resolved one way or another. I shall consider a breach of this injunction to be an admission of guilt and I shall act accordingly. A doctor is arriving shortly from Hertford to examine the body, whereupon I shall make my next determinations."

Charlotte greeted this with a terse nod and a grim smile, and Lizzy sagged further in Mary's arms. As the remaining company began to murmur their relief at this decision, Sir William spoke up once more. "But Miss Elizabeth—I will have the frock you wore today, for it is surely not the one you have on now. Call your maid immediately, for it must not be washed. I shall wait. And you might pray that another, more suitable suspect is found to answer for this crime against God."

At that he stepped backwards to the door where he stood between his constables, an assurance that justice might be delayed, but it would ultimately be served.

Sir William and his entourage left shortly thereafter, although Charlotte lingered a while to sit with her friend. Confident that she was leaving Lizzy in good hands, Mary relinquished her sister to her friend's ministrations and crept back to her chair in the cosy salon. Her thoughts were awhirl, and nothing made sense. She had heard the end of what had clearly been a poorly offered and more poorly received proposal, and then had witnessed the aftermath of what must have been an unsatisfactory discussion between Lizzy and their parents. Mama, Mary surmised, must have insisted that Lizzy accept her oafish cousin, and Papa must have refused to echo his wife. That would certainly have sent

Lizzy outside for the duration of the day in an attempt to escape the inevitable haranguing and arguing at home.

It would also explain Mr. Collins' somewhat later departure. He would have petitioned Mama, rightly reckoning her ear to be the more sympathetic to his cause, and thereafter would have settled in for a conversation with Papa. He would have supposed it to be a negotiation of terms for the marriage settlement, but it would have become, rather, an affirmation of Lizzy's refusal. Crossed and vexed, Mr. Collins would have wished for distance from Longbourn, hence his own departure (with a packed luncheon) from the house.

This all seemed straightforward to Mary; indeed, it involved very little conjecture. What followed, however, was less clear. She resolved to talk to her sister and find out the truth of the matter. However, her thoughts would not be stilled. Perhaps, she mused, Mr. Collins followed Lizzy. He was not a man who seemed taken by long walks, and Oakham Mount was a fair way away, but if he had a purpose, he would not baulk at the distance. He must have followed Lizzy along the route he knew she favoured, and upon finding her, started up some argument. Did he chastise her for her refusal? Did he threaten her somehow? Whatever his deeds, a disagreement ensued and Lizzy fled, leaving her satchel and knife behind.

But this, too, seemed not quite right. Lizzy was not one to flee from a quarrel. She thrived on argument and debate, and could certainly hold her own against a mushroom like their cousin. She had not lied to Sir William, Mary was certain, but neither had she told the entire truth. Now was not the time to talk; there was too much of anxiety and distress in the air for that, and they did have a short reprieve. But soon, Mary knew, she must find the truth and save her sister from arrest—or worse, conviction and execution!

Alas, Mary's musings were shortly interrupted as her mother entered the room. Bother! This was supposed to be Mary's sanctuary. "Oh, there you are, Mary. I have been looking for you this age. Why must you always hide yourself away so when you are needed? I need you to return to Netherfield to ask after my shawl, the green and white one that goes so fetchingly with my best gown. I cannot find it anywhere, and I must have left it at the ball. I would send Susie, but she is needed in the kitchen, and you have nothing useful to do. If you ride, you may be there and back before the sun sets. Off you go."

Arguing was useless; Mama always had her ideas and would not be put off from them. Still, Mary made an attempt. "Should we not all be here to comfort Lizzy? She is horribly upset, and my books of sermons have words of comfort that she may well require. May I not sit with her instead? You can send Lydia, or Kitty. They can retrieve your shawl as well as I can."

"Enough with the sermons, Mary. No one wishes to hear those words of chastisement. And your sisters may not go. They will be distracted by the first man in a red coat they see, and besides, they are needed here to finish the tablecloth I will give to Jane upon her engagement. Yes, I know he has not yet offered, but he will. Now, run along, and do hurry." She swept from the room like a duchess, leaving Mary with little choice but to don her boots and riding jacket and call for the groom to ready Dapple for the ride.

The news of Elizabeth's predicament must have travelled faster than any horse could carry it, for Mary received an icy welcome when she arrived at Netherfield. The housekeeper opened the door and seemed about to close it again when Mary slipped a foot across the threshold, preventing this most severe cut. "Miss

Bingley is unavailable for company at the moment," the housekeeper intoned. "She does not consort with the family of murderers. She plans to depart for London in the morning and her absence may be of some duration. I will inform her that you called." She stepped forward to attempt once more to shoo Mary outside and close the door upon her.

"I have not come to call," Mary stood as straight as she could. She would not be sent off by a mere servant. "I am on an errand from my mother, to ask after and retrieve her white and green shawl, which she left here last night. I can wait." She stepped into the foyer against Mrs. Harwick's obvious disapproval.

"We are still cleaning the house after the entertainments; some guests have only recently departed. There is nowhere to wait. We will send the shawl to Longbourn should we find it." The housekeeper's eyes narrowed and her jaw grew firm.

"Never mind," Mary smiled. "I can happily wait in the kitchens, where I shall be in nobody's way and where it is warm. I can see myself there." She hoped she did not sound as smug as she felt. It was no secret that Caroline Bingley disliked the three youngest Bennet sisters, and held a particular disdain for Mary, whose skills at the fortepiano came as close as anyone's in Meryton to rivalling Caroline's. Mrs. Harwick was Caroline's choice for the position of housekeeper, having come down from London to fill the role, and seemed to harbour as little amity for the Miss Bennets as did her mistress. If Mary did not threaten the household with her permanent presence, she was certain her mother's shawl would never be found. But whilst she sat in the kitchens, she was fairly certain that all efforts would be made to locate the garment, if only to send it back to Longbourn, and Mary with it.

"Indeed," Mrs. Harwick scowled. "Follow me, Miss Mary."

As she had imagined, Mary was not conducted to the large wooden table in the middle of the main kitchen, where a cup of tea and a plate of leftover biscuits might appear before her. She was led, instead, to a hard bench in the dark hallway that led to the small servants' sitting area, where they might rest for a few moments when not at their required duties. *I am invisible once again*, she thought. *In my dark riding coat, with my dark hair, in a dark corridor! I shall be forgotten and my ghost shall haunt these halls until my mother's shawl is finally returned to her.* This time she did allow herself the smallest of chuckles and made herself comfortable against the wall, whilst she engaged in one of her favourite activities: Listening to the world around her.

Her reward came quickly, for it was the end of the day, and contrary to Mrs. Harwick's exhortations, much of the work had been completed, save the final preparations for dinner. Mr. Bingley had already departed for London, and the rest of the party would be preparing for departure the following day and would not require a large meal. Consequently, there were several maids and footmen at leisure in their sitting room, talking and complaining about their days, unaware of being overheard by the ears of the gentry.

"My feet," one maid moaned, "I never should'a taken the mistress's old shoes, for they pinch me toes somethin' awful. Standin' on that ladder all day, cleaning the chandeliers! Thousands of tapers, all dripping wax that need cleanin'! Where is Polly? She rubs me feet so well when they ache. I have not seen her since we cleared up from breakfast. She has such a way with feet."

"Here, let me rub 'em," a man's voice replied. There was a moment of silence, then a low moan of pleasure, and a third voice spoke, relieving Mary greatly lest some impropriety occur between the first maid and the footman.

"Aye," came the third voice—that of another maid. "And the stains on the table linens! One would think the folk raised in a barn, for all their airs and graces. Do they wipe their dirty mouths on the table covers and drag their plates across their napkins? Why, me children know better than that!"

"Did you know," came the first voice, "that Bessie found seven bottles of wine in the small salon behind the library? Tell them, Bessie."

"'Tis true," a young-sounding maid replied with a titter. "Seven bottles, all quite empty, and not a glass to be found. But I did find," she lowered her voice to a near whisper, "a single silk stocking!" She tittered again, and the room erupted into laughter and lascivious noises.

"At least you have an extra stocking," another footman replied. "I still cannot find those cursed boots! And Robinson is running mad because another set of silver candlesticks has gone missing. That makes three in two weeks, and these are the large ones with the fruit decorations and the gemstones. They'll not be easy to replace."

Mary sat up straight in the dim hallway. Missing candlesticks? Even a simple pair of silver candlesticks would be worth a year's wages for these servants. Three pairs would be worth a small fortune, and if the large ones were the set she was thinking of, Mary estimated their value at nearly one hundred pounds alone.

This was most alarming! And how very unusual for two alarming events to occur so very close together. Thefts and a murder! What strange events these were to be happening in as quiet a town as Meryton. They could not possibly be related. That would be even more strange still. Nevertheless, Mary found herself determined to learn whatever she could about the candlesticks, and also whatever she could about Mr. Collins to help save her sister from a terrible fate.

Chapter Three

Alexander Lyons, Investigator

The sun had disappeared behind the building across the alleyway some time ago, and the world outside was dimming by the moment. In the most elegant parts of London the gas lights would have been lit to illuminate the streets for the wealthy passersby, but here, on the edges of Covent Garden, such marvels had yet to arrive, and this particular evening the lamplighters would not be by for some time. Around the corner, by the theatres where the elite would gather for their evening's entertainment, the streets would glow nearly as bright as daytime; here, in the shadows, however, the streetwalkers offered a different sort of entertainment that was best conducted outside of the glow of lamplight.

Alexander Lyons wrinkled his nose in a grudging fondness for the area he claimed for both home and business. His small office, above a respectable chandler's shop, sat in good company, with a solicitor to one side and a young bookbinder in the brightly lit rooms to the other. His living quarters were on the storey above, directly atop his office; and the bakery at the corner where the alley met the street provided inexpensive and tasty victuals. He smiled at the thought of Mr. Jacob's leek and cheese pies. More importantly, the area provided its own amusements when there were limited funds for a night at the theatre, and he was conveniently situated for any gentlemen requiring his particular set of skills.

Deciding there was to be no more business conducted this day, he set about tidying his office before retiring up to his rooms. He swept the floors, straightened the two chairs that sat across the desk from his own, and ensured an adequate supply of tapers and firewood for the following day, and at last, perused his supply of pens and ink. Satisfied, he left one new quill lying across the pad of paper on his desk, right by the short stack of cards bearing his name and occupation: *Alexander Lyons, Investigator.*

He was about to draw the curtains and snuff the oil lamp when the sound of heavy feet resounded in the stairwell outside his office. It was too late for business, surely, but he stood motionless for a moment, waiting to hear where the steps would ultimately go. To some surprise, he heard the footsteps stop right at his door, and then with a knock and a tentative rattle, the visitor pushed open the door and stepped inside.

"Mr. Darcy!" This was a surprise indeed! "I am honoured by your presence, but what can I do for you?" He took a good look at his visitor, an automatic action borne of the necessities of his trade. What he saw alarmed him. The man looked upset, more rattled even than when he had first employed Alexander the previous summer to find his lost sister. Whatever could have happened?

"Lyons," the visitor greeted him politely. Not even the most dire of circumstances could remove the deeply entrenched manners that every gentleman carried before him as his calling card in society. "How have you kept? You are well, I hope. You look well. Your mother? Your sisters? Please pass along my regards the next time you write. And please, no need for titles. We are friends, I hope. 'Darcy' will do well."

Alexander regarded the tall man before him. What had begun as a business relationship had deepened into something that approached friendship during their weeks working together, first to find Miss Darcy after those rumours originated about some affair, and afterwards to determine the habitual haunts of her erstwhile lover, George Wickham. Their mutual regard, born of similar tastes and a deep respect for the other's understanding and character, had never quite blossomed into a true friendship, for the chasm of societal and economic differences was too great between them: Alexander was a working man from a middle class family in the valleys near Glasgow, whilst Darcy was a gentleman of the highest ranks, almost aristocracy, with an income to match his status. Nevertheless, Alexander was most pleased to see Darcy once more and welcomed the chance to work for him again, should that be the man's intention.

"Do sit, Darcy. Thank you, we are all well, and I shall pass along your regards. What news of Miss Darcy? Is she recovered from her adventures? She was a brave young lady to write to you as she did, in opposition to Wickham's expressed commands. I wish her only the best. But sir, you did not come here to discuss my sisters, nor yours. I see on your face that you have received news that alarms you. How may I help?" He took his own chair and turned up the flame in his lamp once more, so the room was filled with enough light by which to conduct business.

Darcy took his seat and leaned forward, elbows on the desk, then straightened his back and ran weary fingers through his hair, before returning to his initial pose, chin resting on one fist. He expelled a heavy sigh and then spoke. "I need you to solve a murder," he stated.

"Murder?" Alexander's head jerked up in interest. "I find missing wives and misplaced documents. I know nothing about murder! The Runners—" Surely the Bow Street Runners were the suitable men for such a task! But Darcy interrupted.

"Sadly the Runners do not, as a rule, operate this far from London, and I require more discretion than I can demand from them. Lyons... Alexander, I have come to trust you, and you are one of the most intelligent men of my acquaintance. Will you help me?" Darcy took a deep breath and released it in a shudder. "Please?"

"I believe, sir, that you had best tell me the entire story."

"It is a tale best told over port. Do me the honour of joining me for dinner at my house, and I shall tell all I know. Better, bring a small trunk, for if you agree to take this assignment, we will need to leave for Hertfordshire before the sun is fully risen. Have you other business to attend to that cannot wait?"

Alexander shook his head. "I have a report to complete for one client, and a bill to prepare for another, but in all other respects I am at liberty."

"Then bring your documents along; you may conclude your business there."

This was most intriguing! Bidding Darcy to wait a few moments whilst he prepared for the journey, Alexander ran up to his rooms and set aside some clothing and personal supplies, which he quickly packed into a compact trunk that he could carry with one hand. He left a note for his landlord and some coins for the following week's rent, should he not return in time to pay in person. Finally, he took a look at himself in his small mirror, wishing to present a suitable appearance for a fine residence such as Darcy's house.

His reflection was satisfactory, for he looked perfectly forgettable—exactly as an investigator ought to look. Taller than most, he was still not tall enough to command the attention of those who saw him, and certainly not tall enough to remember for his height. He was of average build, with a face that was handsome enough to draw the ladies' eyes, but not handsome enough to keep their regard once he opened his mouth and spoke in tones that denied any pretence to wealth or society. His eyes were an unremarkable brown, and only his hair—a most unfortunate shade of copper—was at all memorable. Fortunately, dark hair powder or a large hat were both easy choices to conceal this most striking of his features, allowing him to ply his trade.

Upon this copper hair, he now placed a new and fashionable beaver hat—purchased with his payment from Darcy's last assignment for him—and folded his greatcoat over his arm, ready for a long journey in chilly weather. At last, ensuring all was in order, he returned to his client and the quest that awaited.

Dinner at Darcy's house was a quiet and elegant affair. Only the two men dined; there was no company expected, and Miss Darcy and her new companion had departed for the family estate in Derbyshire the previous week. Conversation during the meal was light and varied, each man enjoying the other's company, but Darcy steered the discussion well clear of his concerns. *Damn it all,* Alexander thought on several occasions during the admittedly delightful meal, *are these toffs so wedded to their fine manners that they cannot speak of the matters that are destroying them, even to the people they have sought out for the very purpose of resolving such concerns?* Darcy's conversation was light and well-bred, but his eyes could not relinquish some great distress that must be associated with the trouble at hand. *I shall never understand them, no matter how much I associate with them. And better that way, for they are—with notable exceptions—a useless group.*

It was not until the men lingered over the port that concluded the meal that Darcy turned the discussion to his concerns. "I spent several weeks in Hertfordshire with my friend Bingley, helping him learn the ropes of estate management. Whilst there, I was thrown into company with a family with five daughters, the second of which has just now been accused of murdering her cousin."

"That is alarming!" Alexander interjected. "When did this occur?"

"Earlier today—this afternoon," came the reply. "Quite early, probably no later than one o'clock." Alexander's eyebrows shot up, and noticing his surprise, Darcy continued. "I departed the area this morning before dawn and arrived in Town by about ten o'clock this morning. I had an appointment at my club. Bingley had planned to spend some days in London on matters of business and was taking leave of one of the local leaders of society—a rather self-important man with little taste or wealth, but with a knighthood upon his name, and the local magistrate, by virtue of his title if not his intellect." Ah yes, Darcy was a good man and a worthy companion, but he could be most arrogant. Alexander said nothing of his thoughts and Darcy continued. "Before Bingley departed, the magistrate was summoned by two locals who had discovered the body of a man in a nearby stream. The man was a churchman, quite coincidentally the parsonage attached to my own aunt's estate. He was also the cousin of the family I mentioned, and heir to their estate. Alongside his body was found a knife bearing this lady's initials, and a satchel known to be hers, and Sir William immediately set out to arrest her for the parson's death." He stopped and contemplated his port for a long moment before taking another sip.

"Upon hearing this alarming news, Bingley made at once for London, riding in himself and leaving his carriage to follow, so he might inform me as soon as he possibly could. He arrived exhausted just before sundown. His poor horse will never forgive him. I am most troubled by this."

Lyons nodded, careful to keep his expression neutral. "You wish me to avenge your aunt's parson? Find evidence to convict the lady?"

Darcy paled. "Oh, Lord, no! I wish you to prove her innocent. She cannot have done it! I could never believe that. It is absolutely foreign to her character to have done such a thing!" The words fell from his mouth in such a tumble that Alexander could scarcely distinguish one from another.

"You admire the lady?" His lips curled into a smile and he let his brows rise once, quickly, upon his forehead. So this was the crux of the matter!

His companion sputtered. "I do not take your meaning. That is... She is..." He drew a deep breath. "During my time in her presence, I came to respect her greatly for her quickness of mind and witty conversation. Her character is without blemish and..." he drifted off. "And yes, I grew to admire her more than I dared admit even to myself. I believe that had I not heard such alarming news of her, I might have convinced myself she was of no importance to me, but now, with her name, her freedom—nay, her life!—at risk, my heart will not be silenced. I cannot allow her to be destroyed by this. I must save her."

Alexander regarded his host. Darcy in love! He would never have imagined such a thing, for even with his own sister's wellbeing at risk, the gentleman had displayed such sangfroid that Alexander had considered him for a while to be quite heartless and cold. For Darcy now to be so visibly upset, the emotions roiling in his aristocratic breast must be tremendous. Watching the man carefully, Alexander asked, "And what if, after all of my investigations, I discover that the lady is guilty indeed, that she was the true killer of the parson?"

Squeezing his eyes closed, Darcy replied, "Then I should be heartbroken. But I should be satisfied as well that justice was done. Will you take the assignment, Lyons? I am begging you!"

"I accept. I now see why you wish to leave so early. You said your friend, the one with whom you were staying, is in London. Was anybody else part of the party in Hertfordshire?"

"We were a small group. Bingley's sister Caroline was keeping house for him, and his other sister and her husband made up the rest of the party. Caroline was keen to quit the country for London even before now, and with this scandal in the air…"

"Yes, I see. Regardless, we must make certain that they remain there until this crime is solved. Tell me about them all, about everyone you met there. I may wish to engage some of my colleagues in the initial investigations before we leave London. Er… they will need to be paid." He left the sentence hanging.

"Money is of no matter. All expenses will be taken care of, as will whatever you choose to bill me for your services. Do I assume the rates from last summer? I care not what you choose to charge me. I need to know the truth."

"Then talk. Tell me what you know about the inhabitants of the area, and I shall start working immediately."

Darcy rose to pour more port into each glass and Alexander settled himself at a desk in the study, his pad of paper before him, a pencil at the ready. Staring into the fire, Darcy began his recitations.

"Charles Bingley is the grandson of a wealthy industrialist and wishes to establish himself in society with the purchase of some estate. He has about a hundred thousand pounds, which will allow him to live very well, but he is not so removed from trade as to make his wealth seem pure." Alexander snorted; no matter how genteel, the prejudices of class showed through even the finest manners. Darcy seemed not to notice and continued speaking. "He is four years my junior—a year or two younger than you, I believe—and of a most amiable nature. We met at our club. His character is unassailable."

"Might he be involved?" The question had to be asked.

"I would be most surprised. He was at Netherfield supervising the preparations for his journey to London all morning and then visiting Sir William and flying across fields towards London all afternoon. He cannot have had time. And his manner—he is far too determined to like everybody to ever resort to murder."

Alexander jotted down on his notepad, *Investigate Bingley. Too good to be true*, but said nothing and gestured for Darcy to continue.

"Caroline is his sister, one year younger than him. She is a social upstart and is happy enough to forget the origins of the money that keeps her in such luxury. She has little patience for the country, but lives at her brother's expense and so does as he bids her. Murder would involve damaging her fingernails and soiling her gowns. I cannot see her being involved in this sordid matter."

"Has she independent access to some funds? Might she have employed another to carry out this deed for her?"

Darcy scratched his chin. "I would put little past Caroline Bingley." Alexander made another note as Darcy continued speaking.

"Louisa is Bingley's older sister, married to Hubert Hurst. Louisa shares many of Caroline's affectations, and had the fortune to marry a gentleman, thereby ensuring her position in the ranks of the gentry." He paused. "Her greatest pleasures seem to involve spending money she does not have and informing everybody of her purchases and what they cost." The reason behind Darcy's sneer was evident. This was hardly the behaviour expected of a genteel lady who was deemed to be above such déclassé topics of conversation as price.

"What of Hurst himself?" Alexander asked. His hand guided the pencil to form the next section of his notes: *HURST*. He looked up expectantly.

"Hurst has little personality but a large capacity for consuming food and drink. He seems somehow to draw all of the energy out of a room. He has a small estate in Oxfordshire, but contrives to spend as little time there as possible. He is generally happier as a guest in someone else's house, eating someone else's food, and hunting someone else's birds. I suspect his income does not quite support his preferred lifestyle. He is indolent and lazy and dreadful at cards. Those are the residents at Netherfield." Ah. Darcy had little liking for Hurst. Alexander would assess the man himself.

Starting a new page of notes, Alexander asked, "And the rest of the society there?"

"There are the Bennets, of course. The family with the daughter I... admire. Father is an odd chap, more interested in his books than his daughters or his estate. The estate is entailed... was entailed, that is, to the deceased. He was a cousin. I do not know where the estate passes now." Alexander's eyebrows rose again, and he chewed his lip as he noted this interesting tidbit.

"Mrs. Bennet married up in the world. Her family are of the middle class—merchants and village attorneys and the like—and she is no better than others of her race, always seeking to marry off her daughters to the closest available man of suitable fortune or position.

"Jane is the eldest daughter. Truly beautiful to look upon, like a piece of art, really, but as cool as a statue as well, I imagine. She smiles most prettily, but it is the same smile for everybody. I suspect her heart is not easily touched. The younger girls include

Mary, a spinster in the making with her nose in a book of sermons and her penchant for exhibiting mediocre talents, Catherine who is silly and trails behind whoever will lead her, and Lydia, the youngest, who seems determined to flirt with anything in a red coat. She is fifteen…"

Darcy did not need to complete that thought. His sister was fifteen and had almost allowed herself to be ruined by a man nearly twice her years and with a gift for flattery. Alexander kept his thoughts to himself and instead asked, "Anyone else? What of the magistrate?"

"Sir William Lucas. Knighted for some fancy speech before the king, a former tradesman now with a small plot of land and a rather too-grand house upon it. Harmless enough fellow, but no great weight in matters of intellect. John Lucas is his eldest son, itching for some useful employment I think. Charlotte, the elder daughter, is Miss Elizabeth's close friend. There is a younger girl, not yet out in society."

"Which is the lady accused of the crime? I would hear of her."

Darcy's eyes softened and his face relaxed into a faint but blissful smile. *Oh, the man is smitten beyond all hope*, Alexander grinned to himself. He waited for his companion to recall himself and speak further.

"Her name is Elizabeth. Miss Elizabeth's most striking characteristic is her personality. She is firm in her opinions, but I suspect she would not be averse to changing them if presented with sufficient evidence. She argues for the joy of it, and it is my belief that in her home, she derives much joy in this manner. She is witty and determined, and will go to great lengths for those she loves. Whilst I was staying at Netherfield with Bingley, she once walked three miles in the mud to visit her sister who had fallen ill and whom she thought might want a sister's care. She is very pretty; her eyes are particularly fine…"

"If I may interrupt, Darcy, if she is so fierce and determined in her opinions, might she not have the mettle to kill a man if suitably provoked? Women have done so for lesser reasons. You would be cautioned against believing them the weaker sex." He had to ask the question, as much to gauge Darcy's reaction as for the answer. The response did not disappoint.

"No! I cannot fathom it at all. If you had seen her, when her sister became ill at Netherfield, how she attended her selflessly and ceaselessly, you would understand. She voices her thoughts, but there is no malice in her. She would not hesitate to insult a man from his hair to the soles of his feet, but one cannot show such compassion to a sister and then turn around and act with such violence that a man would die." He folded his arms across his chest and challenged Alexander with his glare.

"I must maintain my impartiality, sir, but your fervour does the lady credit. I will hear more about the other denizens of the area another time, perhaps whilst we travel tomorrow. But for now," he started a new page in the notebook, "what of the victim? I would begin to learn as much as I can about the man who inspired somebody to commit murder."

Chapter Four

First Impressions

On a fresh page in his notebook, Alexander jotted down the most pertinent information about the deceased. William Collins, aged five and twenty years, cousin of some sort to the Bennet family (he must determine the exact degree of kinship), lately ordained into the church and most recently serving as parson to none other than Mr. Darcy's own aunt, Lady Catherine de Bourgh. This proved most interesting, and if Darcy had not been in London at the time of the murder—as attested to by all his staff, fifteen or twenty men at his club, including a duke, an earl and three Members of Parliament, and his cousin, a colonel in the army who stopped by for a quick visit at eleven o'clock in the morning—Darcy too might have been a man to suspect. Even so, Alexander placed a quick note and a question mark by Darcy's name. The man might well have paid another to conduct his evil business for him. No matter that Darcy was—

dare he even think it? —a friend, nobody must escape investigation in such a case.

He resolved to learn more about Collins and his connection to the Darcy and de Bourgh families in the morning as they travelled to Meryton, where the crime occurred.

Another most interesting person who happened to be in the vicinity was none other than George Wickham, who had been the instigator of Miss Darcy's disappearance the previous summer. Through his work on the case, Alexander knew more about Wickham than Darcy did, but the news of the scoundrel's current employ in the militia was of some interest.

"He claimed to have been compelled into taking a commission by financial necessity," Darcy sneered, "although why the man believes himself to be exempt from seeing to his own needs, I cannot fathom. His father was my father's steward; he was not born to the ranks of leisure. Even I, with my estates and holdings, put in many an hour managing my lands so they and my tenants prosper."

Alexander made more notes. He knew the bitter history between the two men well. If Wickham had been the victim instead of Collins, he would have considered Darcy a serious prospect for the killer. Darcy was fortunate in the choice of victim.

Before bidding his host good night in preparation of the following morning's travels, Alexander spent some time at Darcy's great desk, penning notes and requests to several agents with whom he worked in Town, requesting them to find information he might need. These being sent off with promissory notes for whatever fees these tasks might require, he retired to a very comfortable room, knowing that his slumber would be short.

By the time the first arc of the glowing sun appeared above the horizon the following morning, the two men were in Darcy's carriage, the wakening city behind them. With them was a large basket of breads and cheese and pastries, complete with two flasks of hot coffee. Darcy clearly intended to travel as quickly as possible, with as few breaks as possible in the journey, so as to achieve Meryton as early as might be managed. A groom had been sent ahead to arrange for a change of horses at the ten-mile mark, for the carriage was moving more quickly than one team could maintain for the entire length of the journey.

As they travelled, Mr. Darcy spoke further about Mr. Collins. "The man is... was a fool," he admitted between bites of a rather delicate French pastry. "I ought not speak ill of the dead, but you had better know the worst of it. He was an upstart with great aspirations but no class or manners. He dwelt upon the minutiae of civilised behaviour such as punctuality and deference to rank, but then presumed to introduce himself to me—to me! I, who rank so far above him!" Darcy snorted.

Alexander suppressed a grin. As much as Darcy was one of the few members of the *ton* whom Alexander not only tolerated, but actually liked, the man was still a model of upper-class arrogance. Nevertheless, this was not the time to expound upon his distaste for the elite, whom, Alexander considered, were as useless as men could be, whilst still at least having the funds to employ such men as himself. Better a good, honest merchant or farmer than a debauched viscount or earl! Maintaining his neutral expression, Alexander merely said, "Indeed. Carry on."

"What else is there to be said about Collins? The man was a mixture of pride and obsequiousness, self-importance and humility. He fawned and condescended and yet held himself above all company. Whilst his death is regrettable, he shall not be missed."

"What of his dealings with Miss Elizabeth Bennet? What cause might she have had to dislike him?"

"Collins and Miss Elizabeth?" The notion seemed to truly confound the man. "I cannot see that there were any dealings, other than he was a guest in her house. And the heir to the estate." He paused and screwed his forehead. "Oh, I see. And he had claimed the first dance at the ball..." Darcy looked up in alarm. "You don't believe he intended to marry her? How could I have missed those signs?" He shook his head. "I was so consumed in denying my own attraction to her that I ignored those so obviously exhibited by another. I am chastened." The look on Darcy's face would have been laughable had it not been so tragic. The gentleman seemed genuinely distressed at the notion that the woman he so admired had been courted by another, and without his awareness of the fact. The shock was so evident on Darcy's face, the anguish so plainly writ, that Alexander realised he could cross Darcy's name from the list he had begun. This was a man who, until a moment ago, had held so little thought for Collins that the idea of murdering the man would be ludicrous. Nevertheless, there were questions to be asked, questions which might not be pleasant for Darcy to answer.

"Did Miss Elizabeth seem to return his regard?"

"I can hardly be relied upon for my clear skills of observation, so it seems," Darcy pondered with a deep sigh, "but I would not think so. The expression on her face as she danced with him last night was not one of growing attachment. Rather, though she tried to hide it, I would say it was an expression of disgust." He turned to stare out of the window at the passing fields and villages and lapsed into silence.

Alexander took advantage of the silence to consider what little he knew. He had the barest outline, a mere sketch of the situation, whose details he would fill in as he conducted his investigations. He was somewhat uneasy still about inquiring into a murder, something as yet new to him. And yet he was experienced in matters of investigation and of prosecuting crimes. He knew what to seek and how to elicit information from reluctant witnesses. At least some of his education—no matter how disparaged and useless here in the environs of the Capital—would be put to use.

Seeing that there would be little more in the way of conversation, and anticipating a long and tiring day once the carriage achieved its destination, he lay his head back upon the well-padded squabs and closed his eyes, willing himself to sleep.

Darcy's plans were good and the two men arrived at Netherfield long before Caroline Bingley and the Hursts had begun to prepare for their departure. They were, in fact, sitting down to their morning tea and toast when the newcomers strode into the breakfast room.

Caroline saw Darcy first, and Alexander realised that his companion had left out a rather important matter in his description of the lady: that she was set on having him for a husband. Perhaps the man himself did not realise her intentions, although from the cringe that flickered across Darcy's face at Caroline's welcome, Alexander rather thought he was aware. "Who is come?" she asked when the door opened, followed by a fluttering of lashes and a low coo of "Mr. Darcy!" The eyelashes fluttered up and down anew. "Whatever brings you back to Hertfordshire? It must be my company! Come and sit and I shall call for more... Oh, you have a friend." In this, her voice was cooler, but she nonetheless allowed her eyes to assess Alexander quite thoroughly, starting at his face, moving down to his feet (*thank heavens I polished my boots last night*, he thought), and back up to his face, where they lingered for a moment before flitting up to his too-long copper hair. Returning to his face, she blinked several times and with a coy smile said to Darcy, "Will you do me the honour of introducing me?"

More information, thought Alexander. *She wants Darcy, but she will happily entertain herself with other men whilst she waits for him to offer for her. She is a social climber with little room for genuine emotion in her heart.* He offered his most charming smile as he waited for Darcy to perform the social necessities. He had no interest in any woman as obvious as Miss Bingley, but if a mild flirtation would gain her cooperation and confidence, he was not above such games.

In short order Alexander had been introduced to Caroline as well as Louisa and Hubert Hurst. Caroline, for all that she was proud and most blatant in her desires, was a lovely young woman. With a more suitable personality, she would have been the season's prize. Louisa Hurst was less pretty but still very attractive, and quiet enough upon first meeting that any shortcomings of character were not as obvious as in her sister. Louisa's husband, Mr. Hurst, did not rise from his table, but merely grunted something that might have been "Mornin'," before returning to his eggs.

Right, Alexander took in the three as keenly as they observed him, *let us see how well I am accepted once I speak. I am certain to betray every one of my most ungentlemanly roots with the first word.* "A pleasure to meet you," he offered in his strongest Glaswegian accent, keeping the closest regard on his company.

"Darcy, why did you bring a tradesman into my breakfast room?" Caroline's beckoning regard became a glare. "And a Scottish one at that?"

"Mr. Lyons is my guest, Caroline, and I dare say my friend, and you will listen to him for he has something to tell you."

"But Mr. Darcy, really..."

"You will listen to him, and offer him every courtesy you would offer me. Mr. Lyons, if you please."

He was invited, with great reluctance, to join the three denizens of the house at their table, whereupon he accepted a cup of tea. "Miss Bingley, Mr. and Mrs. Hurst, I believe you had plans to depart for London this morning. I am afraid I must insist that you remain for several days until I have completed my business."

"Mr. Darcy, how can this… tradesman give us such orders? And from whom did he steal that suit of clothing? He is dressing far above his station." Mrs. Hurst was no more genteel than her sister after all, it seemed. "He cannot command us like a flock of geese or whatever it is he does."

"He can and he will, Louisa," came Darcy's response. "He is here at my request, and he has the weight of the law behind him. I have engaged Mr. Lyons to ascertain the truth behind the death of Mr. Collins and the accusation of Miss Elizabeth Bennet as the culprit. He will require everybody's fullest cooperation, and I shall insist that it be offered to him."

"Really, Darcy?" Mr. Hurst spoke his first intelligible words. "Can you believe we had anything to do with that awful man's death? Or anything to do with him at all, really?" His wife tittered. "We would rather just be getting along back to town."

"And surely you cannot truly believe Miss Eliza innocent?" Caroline sneered. "She is such a lowly creature after all, so unrefined and rustic, covered in mud, with no real elegance or gentility about her. She is exactly the sort who would stick a man with a knife as if he were a pig. She must be the guilty party. I can hardly believe that you would have any care what happened to her."

"Nevertheless, Caroline, I am here, as is Mr. Lyons, and you will remain. Charles is returning this evening as well, and he will echo my words. And he is one you must obey."

Caroline and Louisa turned to each other and wrinkled similar noses before commiserating about such ill treatment and such uncaring relations, thereby ignoring Alexander completely as he finished his tea. Darcy attempted to make polite conversation but soon abandoned his efforts, whilst Hurst helped himself to more eggs and wondered aloud if there were more tea, for the pot was suddenly quite empty.

The first visit, after the two had found their rooms and washed the worst of the journey's dust from their faces, was Longbourn. Alexander had expressed a desire to meet the woman presumed guilty of this crime, and Darcy seemed most eager to see her once more. The distance between the houses was a short three miles, and it was not long before Mrs. Hill, the housekeeper, showed the two into the room Mr. Bennet, the young lady's father, claimed as his study.

Alexander took one step inside and stopped, stunned and in awe. Every inch of space along the walls was covered with shelves, all filled to capacity with books of varying sizes, colours, and shapes. Some were bound in rich red leather, others in dull brown paper; some were fat and tall, others narrow, or squat, or short. All called out to Alexander, speaking in a language he understood intimately—the language of the printed word.

"You admire my collection, do you?" The words from an armchair near the window brought Alexander back to his senses. "No, do not let me interrupt you. I have the same reaction each and every time I enter this room, and it has been my safe haven for more years than you have been alive, I wager." The voice was friendly, if tinged with traces of mockery, and Alexander allowed his gaze to rove across the vast sea of literature before finally, reluctantly, turning it to the man who had spoken.

He sat in a large and comfortable-looking chair that must surely be slightly worn from excessive use, the upholstery fraying just enough to bring a man to his ease, yet not enough to warrant being repaired. The gentleman had a book in one hand, a small glass of sherry or some similar amber liquid in the other, and a half smirk upon his lips. Alexander imagined the gentleman to be around fifty or fifty-five years of age, his greying hair sparse upon the top of his head, his eyes bright behind the spectacles he clearly used for reading. So this, thought Alexander, was Mr. Bennet, Miss Elizabeth's father. His careless attitude hardly spoke of a man who had just now lost a close relation to murder, nor one dreading the direst outcome concerning his beloved daughter. Still, Alexander knew well that people reacted in so many ways to worry and distress, and resolved not to judge Mr. Bennet without more evidence.

Bennet spoke again. "Mr. Darcy, we had not expected to see you in these parts so soon. Welcome. Would you care for a drink? What of your friend?"

Darcy quickly made the introductions and explained his mission in Meryton. "Mr. Lyons is a skilled investigator, and I have engaged him to seek the truth about Mr. Collins. To be blunt, I have engaged him to exonerate Miss Elizabeth from all guilt. May I have your permission to speak with her?" Unlike Bennet's almost lackadaisical demeanour, Darcy's was agitated. His hands were restless and his leg twitched, and judging by the determined expression upon his face, it was only with great effort that he resisted the urge to pace. This was something Alexander knew well about his friend, for during the search for Georgiana, the man had walked the length and breadth of his small office enough times to wear a rut in the floors.

"You wish to speak with Lizzy, eh?" Mr. Bennet pushed his reading glasses up upon his high forehead. He peered long at

Alexander, then sighed a long and sad sigh, as if the investigator's appearance were insufficient to his purpose. "I appreciate the effort, Mr. Darcy, but what can be done that William Lucas will not do? He is the law in these parts, but I imagine that his daughter informs him as to what that law should be. If Sir William will not find the truth, who can?"

Alexander caught Darcy's eye and raised an eyebrow in question. Darcy responded with a blink and a terse nod, and Alexander took over the plea. "If you don't mind, Mr. Bennet, I am skilled in matters of investigation far beyond what a gentleman such as Sir William—capable as he may be—could aspire to. This has been my occupation since I have been in Town—"

"From the north, are you?" Mr. Bennet interrupted. "What brings a man down from Scotland to the alleyways and stews of London? Were your skills not needed there? What can you know of English law? And what interest has one of your caste in my rows of books? Well, I suppose even farmers are taught to read these days. The church has, at least, done that much. Observe away." He waved an indolent hand at his teeming shelves.

Another arrogant toff! Even the lowest of country squires regarded him as so much dross, all for the sake of his low-bred Scottish accent. This was but one reason more why Alexander had little truck for the gentry. Suppressing a grimace, he replied, "My choice of residence has little to do with my abilities, sir. And my knowledge of English law and customs might surprise you. At some later date I would be pleased to explain my decisions to you, or to discuss Aristotle's *Politics* or Descartes' *Principles of Philosophy*, and in Latin if you will, but at the moment time is short. The longer we delay, the more evidence will be lost. May I please speak to Miss Elizabeth? I promise to do my best not to upset her."

Mr. Bennet's face suddenly lost all animation, and he sagged against the back of his chair as if he were a doll with the stuffing removed, falling in on itself. He sat silent for a moment before waving a listless hand in dismissal. "Aye, do as you must. I am of little enough use to her. Do what you can to save my precious Lizzy." He closed his eyes and remained thus, motionless and pale, until the two visitors saw themselves out of the study.

Chapter Five

Elizabeth Bennet, Murderess

The housekeeper was waiting and led them down the passageway and into a bright and rather elegant drawing room at the front of the house. Daylight streamed in through grand windows, illuminating the five ladies who sat at various occupations in the space. No... there were six ladies. There, tucked into the corner of a window seat, almost obscured by the pale yellow draperies, sat another. Alexander would take her account in a moment. For now he returned to the five in the centre of the cheerful room. Enthroned upon a large armchair—a match for the one Mr. Bennet used in his study, but done in a lighter and delicately floral upholstery—sat a lady who could only be Mrs. Bennet. Her handsome face must once have been very, very pretty, and she carried her years well. Blond hair shone beneath the smallest of lace mobcaps, and not one line marred her features. Her mien was imposing, but the flutter of her elegant hands and the expression of unimaginable woe upon that handsome face also bespoke a woman who refused to allow a moment of high drama pass her by unacted upon.

To one side of her, upon a small sofa, sat two very young women—girls, really, not more than sixteen and seventeen years—fussing over what looked like a disembowelled bonnet. Alexander was as keen on fashion as was the next man looking to better himself in the world, but the intricacies and vagaries of women's headwear left him bemused and a bit befuddled. One girl, a very pretty thing with a woman's shape and a fresh and rosy complexion, was holding a pair of scissors and some sort of flower, whilst the other, slightly plainer and with a vexed look upon her face, had just snatched away a length of ribbon, protesting that "No, that is mine, given to me for my birthday! You shan't have it!"

Across the low tea table that occupied the centre of the space around which these three sat, two older daughters huddled together on a second low sofa that matched the first in shape but the armchair in upholstery. At a guess, Alexander imagined them to be in their very early twenties. One of them had him catching his breath in astonishment, for she was one of the most beautiful women he had ever seen. Her face was perfection, every feature without rival, the whole put together in such a way as to be beyond reproach. Her hair was the perfect shade to flatter her flawless skin, her eyes the ideal complement, and her figure, from what Alexander could determine from her position, huddled with her sister on the sofa, lithe and elegant. He whispered to Darcy, "Jane?" Darcy nodded.

The other woman could only be Elizabeth, as much from the despair inscribed upon her countenance as for the lack of any other possibility. She sat absolutely still, wrapped in a large floral shawl that covered her shoulders and arms completely. She would be, in most circumstances, very pretty herself, with eyes much like her father's in brightness and expression and a face that almost approached that of her older sister. But despair and worry had dragged her down even in a single day, and when she turned, Alexander could see a large and ugly purple bruise spread across the side of her head and around her eye. He knew the instant that Darcy saw the bruise, for the man gasped audibly and took a step forward before catching himself and coughing to cover his lapse.

"Mr. Darcy!" the lady of the house exclaimed. "What on earth are *you* doing here?" By her tone of voice, Alexander perceived that his friend's presence was not necessarily welcome.

"What have you done to these people," he whispered, "that they scorn you so?"

"Later," Darcy hissed back before addressing the room. "I heard tell of Miss Elizabeth's unfortunate circumstances and I wished to speak with her."

"My daughter is not accepting guests at the moment, Mr. Darcy." The lady's voice was cold and Alexander could feel Darcy stiffen beside him.

"Mrs. Bennet, please accept my kindest wishes and condolences for what must be a very trying time, but please understand—"

"I believe I said no, Mr. Darcy." Her glare was formidable.

"Fanny," came a tired voice from the doorway, "I have given my permission." Mr. Bennet stood like a rag doll come to life, his voice empty of animation. "Lizzy, will you speak to Mr. Darcy and his friend?"

The sad young lady lifted her eyes and seemed about to refuse, but a glance at her father seemed to change her mind and she nodded.

"Come in, then, sir," Mrs. Bennet's voice was no friendlier than it had been. "Kitty, bring over another chair."

Darcy shook his head. "I would speak with Miss Bennet with as few people in attendance as possible. My friend, Mr. Lyons, might have some words that would best be uttered in confidence."

"Fanny…"

Mr. Bennet's warning seemed sufficient for the lady to shift to her feet and summon her daughters from the room. "Mary," she said as she moved towards the doorway, "you shall remain. In this I will not be gainsaid."

The sixth lady, the one sitting by the window, shifted, catching Alexander's attention. He blinked in surprise. He had observed her, but after the briefest of glances, he had quite forgotten her existence. She was not flushed and florid, nor silly or vexatious, nor perfection or abject misery. In contradiction to the others in the room, each so vivid in her own way, this sixth lady quite blended into the background. He allowed himself to take her measure now. His initial instinct was that she was rather plain, younger than Miss Elizabeth but older than the two girls attacking the bonnet. He looked more closely to assess her age and decided she must be about eighteen. He also decided that she was, when one looked at her properly, really rather pretty, as were all the sisters. Her beauty was quiet, though, not drawing attention to itself, but sitting there silently until one might take the time to discover it for oneself. Her hair was a dark and unremarkable brown, and it curled delicately over a wide and intelligent forehead, and her eyes, while ordinary in their shade, were delicate in shape and sweet to behold, and their expression was one of deep reflection.

Mrs. Bennet cleared her throat, awaiting a response from the men, and Darcy nodded. "Very well. Miss Mary, may we count on your complete discretion?"

The quiet lady replied in a soft voice, "I will swear it upon my Bible." She held up a small volume of that book.

"Then I thank you." Darcy bowed and waited for the others to depart the room. Elizabeth now sat alone on the sofa, eyes downcast, hands twisting a linen handkerchief this way and that, body otherwise perfectly still. Whereas before she had been surrounded by the other women of her family, she now seemed very small and forsaken. Even Mary, who alone remained with her sister, had stayed in her nook by the window, all but concealed, her presence providing the merest pretence at propriety. Darcy took a deep breath, then moved with measured steps across the room until he stood before the sofa. "How do you fare? Are you well?" His voice was soft, his regard intent.

Elizabeth looked up at him with anything but pleasure in her anguished eyes. Her voice was raw, but her tone was not weak. "Why do you come here?" she taunted. "Do you come to revel in my misery, to congratulate yourself on having avoided my fate within your own exalted family? To watch as my mother and sisters suffer for my supposed sins? Go back to Miss Bingley and to your high and mighty friends in London and tell them of the pathetic girl you so despised, who ended up so low. You have never looked at me except to find fault. Well, Mr. Darcy, here is your prize. Please leave me."

Darcy blinked and shook his head slowly, mouth slightly agape. "No... No, you quite misunderstand me," he said at last. "I never meant... I had no notion..." he began one sentence after another with no success at completion. At last he approached the lady. "May I sit, please? May I explain?"

"I cannot see what purpose that would serve, other than to prolong my misery and your exposure to ignominy." Alexander had never seen Darcy so stunned by a retort as the man was now.

"Miss Bennet, you mistake me completely!"

"Do I? I hardly know how. You made it clear to me on every occasion of our meeting that my every word and my every gesture was beneath you. Why do you come now to vex me further? Surely you can revel in my doom from afar." She stood and turned her back on him as she walked to the window. Her motions were uneasy, her stride stiff. She must have been injured beyond the bloom of bruise upon her face. As she walked the shawl slipped off her shoulders, revealing her arms to be covered in a myriad of cuts and scratches. She had been injured indeed!

Darcy looked as though she had stabbed him through the heart with her words. When he spoke there was a catch in his voice. "Please, Miss Bennet, may I sit and explain myself to you? If you hear me speak once and still feel this way, I shall promise to trouble you with my presence no more. But please, allow me to explain myself."

She nodded, though her eyes remained accusing, and returned to her seat. Alexander tried to feign interest in some curios upon the mantelpiece, but he could not help but overhear his friend's address and he found his attention drawn to Darcy's confession.

He watched through the corner of his eye as Darcy lowered himself onto the sofa, a respectable distance away from the young lady, and in a low voice addressed her. "Miss Bennet, please believe me. I had no notion of finding you wanting; at no time did I look upon you to find fault." He took a deep breath before avowing, "Quite the opposite. You drew me like no other lady ever has, and I was too alarmed at my own response to know how to behave. I have not Bingley's gift of conversation or of bringing others to like me so immediately. I thought... I thought you were enjoying our verbal jousts as much as I was. I find you quite entrancing. Oh, how can I explain?" He dropped his head into his hands, which he ran through his hair until it stood on end.

"You do not hate me?" Miss Elizabeth asked at last. "You admire me?"

"How can you doubt it?"

"But your disdain, your superior pride... You did not always find me pretty."

Darcy wrinkled his brow. "I cannot recall such a time at all!"

From the window, Mary spoke up. Alexander had been so caught up in watching Darcy abase himself that he had quite forgotten her presence. Again. "If I may interrupt, Mr. Darcy, I observed the exchange. It occurred at the Meryton Assembly upon your first introduction to our local society. You were not dancing, and Lizzy was seated nearby when Mr. Bingley admonished you to join the activity and suggested Lizzy as a partner for the next set. You said to him these exact words: 'She is tolerable, I suppose, but not handsome enough to tempt me.' Do you not recall them? For I can hear them as clearly as if you had spoken just a moment ago."

Darcy looked stunned, and Alexander ceased his feigned examination of each ornament and decoration. He turned to face the couple on the sofa as Darcy found his voice.

"I most certainly never meant it! I wished only to be left alone, to be rid of Bingley's cajoling. He means well, but does not understand my reserve, the dreadful summer I had survived. I can only apologise most abjectly, Miss Elizabeth—and Miss Mary—for words that were clearly hurtful, but were not intended to be so."

Alexander had to speak now. "You recalled his exact words, Miss Mary? How remarkable."

She glared at him. No, there was nothing bland about those eyes after all. "I do not believe we have been properly introduced." She returned to the book she was holding.

"How rude I have been! I can only excuse my lapse on my distress at Miss Elizabeth's plight." Darcy collected himself with a sign. "Please, ladies, may I present to you Mr. Lyons, my... friend from London. Lyons, Miss Elizabeth and Miss Mary Bennet." All the appropriate words of greeting were exchanged, whereupon Mary addressed the unanswered question.

"I observe, Mr. Lyons. I am seldom noticed myself, and so in compensation, I notice enough for two people. I make a game of it, for otherwise I should often find myself quite without occupation." She trained her remarkable eyes upon him until he blinked and looked away.

"Miss Elizabeth, believe me when I say that you are so much more than tolerable! But this is not why I have come. As soon as I heard the news, as soon as Bingley told me upon his return to London, I knew I must do everything in my power to protect you from accusations I know in my heart to be false. Lyons here is a most accomplished investigator. He will find the truth of the matter and remove all stain of blame from you and your family. Will you trust me? Please?"

Never had Alexander seen such emotion written across Darcy's stony face, and Elizabeth must have recognised his true intention. "I have yet to find reason to amend my impression of your character, for you have yet to prove yourself other than the arrogant and cold man you displayed to our village, but I believe I can trust you, Mr. Darcy. Until now, all people have done is wring their hands in distress, but you are the first to act. I do not return your regard, but I trust you."

An emotion that Alexander identified as anguish flickered across Darcy's face, before being replaced by something more in keeping with the man's stony hauteur. *He adopts that expression when he is in great discomfort, Alexander realised. When he lowers his guard and allows his emotions to be seen, it is a sign of trust and comfort in his surroundings. I must not forget the compliment he pays me when he admits his true feelings in my hearing.* This hauteur was also, of course, the expression that Miss Elizabeth had most likely deciphered as disdain. Of course she would think the man had little regard for her. He would speak to his friend later.

For now, Darcy merely bowed his head. "I will accept what you will offer me. I thank you for your trust." He dropped his voice almost to a whisper and Alexander only just heard him add, "I can only hope to gain your respect and admiration in time, if you will be so generous as to allow me the chance to ameliorate my character in your eyes."

Mary watched this remarkable display from her seat by the window. She had been as surprised as Lizzy at Mr. Darcy's heartfelt apology and unaccountable display of affection, although unlike her sister, she had always presumed that the proud man looked upon Lizzy with more ardour than anger. Other than that very first encounter at the Meryton Assembly, he had regarded her sister with an interested eye and had taken pains to be in her presence, where he might listen to whatever words of wit and profundity might pass through her rosy lips. The man was admittedly a failure in the art of flirtation, but to one whose feelings had not been injured by his offhand insult and whose pride would not allow her to soften her dislike, his intentions had been clear.

Now he had returned from London at the first suggestion of danger, bringing a professional investigator with him. How he even had time to engage the man, less than a day after the terrible event had occurred, Mary could not fathom, but she was pleased for it. Perhaps once she disclosed what little she had learned to him, he would be able to conclude his business even more readily. She must find some time to meet with him and tell him what she had discovered. He must surely be interested in the missing silver.

For now, however, she remained in her spot, watching and listening. Mr. Lyons seemed an interesting sort. He was handsome enough in a forgettable way—very pleasant to look upon, but with no one feature that would live in the mind's eye, to be recalled at any moment. A lady might take in his fine appearance at one moment and not recall his face at all the next. By his dress he was of the upper ranks of the middle class, fashionable enough to mingle with the *ton* for brief periods, but eschewing the ostentation so favoured by the grandest of the elite. His coat, while well cut and of good material, was plain, the buttons fabric and not brass, and his cravat was tied with the utilitarian simplicity of a man who had no valet. His trousers, tucked into tall hessian boots, were likewise neat and clean without the extravagance of volume or pattern favoured by the fops of London, and not a thread of lace could be seen on his person.

If his appearance bespoke a well-to-do merchant, his voice belied this. He sounded nothing like Mary's uncle, the London-based merchant who was every bit as elegant as any gentleman might be. He spoke, rather, with the unabashed tones of a Scottish peasant, his brogue heavy and thick as oatmeal. The red in his hair reinforced this image, and for a moment of Romantic fantasy, Mary pictured the investigator running wild across the Highlands (which she had read about but never seen), kilt whipping around his naked knees, face covered in woad, bagpipes in one hand, a broadsword in the other. She flushed at the image and cast her eyes and her thoughts to the Bible that still lay in her lap. Such fancies were most unbecoming to a young lady of sober thought and religious inclination!

And yet his deportment and vocabulary told another story again. He seemed cultured and educated, refined even, despite his origins, and if Mr. Darcy trusted him—called him a friend!—

there must surely be more to the man than pipes and woad. She watched with all attention as he approached her sister and asked permission to sit.

"Miss Elizabeth," he began in a gentle voice, "I know this might cause you pain, but I need you to tell me of yesterday's events. I must have as much knowledge as possible so as to find the true perpetrator of this crime."

Lizzy swallowed hard at the question and made several false starts before falling silent, her bottom lip caught between her teeth. Mr. Darcy, seeming to be equally uncomfortable, crossed his legs one way and then another, and then found the bell to call for tea, which he insisted be brought and poured before Elizabeth should begin her recitation. Lizzy seemed comforted by the familiar actions of stirring the sugar and holding the delicate china cup, and at last, tea in hand, she started her tale. She began with an account of her walk before breakfast, the inevitable chatter about the previous night's ball, and of Mr. Collins' unwelcome proposal.

Mr. Darcy's face blanched at the account. "I have only now begun to realise that he had some such inclination, but I had no notion he would speak! I never saw you give him any encouragement!"

"Mr. Darcy," Lizzy gave a wry smile, "neither did you have any notion that I believed you to despise me, or that I had very little liking of you."

"You dislike me? It is not a mere lack of regard?" If anything, Mary thought his face grew even paler.

"Your behaviour towards me, your adversarial manner, were hardly calculated to please. I am willing to reconsider my opinions, as you requested earlier, but you cannot be surprised at how your actions were perceived, not only by me but by all of Meryton. And after the tales of your dreadful treatment of poor

Mr. Wickham," she levelled her eyes upon him, "it should be amazing that anybody here will speak to you at all. Perhaps our country manners allow us to behave more civilly than the gentlemen from the city." Mr. Darcy's face went from white to red, but Lizzy ignored him. "Shall I continue, Mr. Lyons?"

Closing her eyes, Lizzy resumed her story. "Mr. Collins offered, I refused, and he chided me for playing the games he believes ladies play wherein they at first refuse the men they mean to accept. Even when I disabused him of this notion in the severest terms, he insisted on talking to Mama so that I might ultimately see sense.

"Did he now?" Mr. Lyons scribbled something into a small notebook he had retrieved from a pocket. "What exactly did he say, do you recall?"

"No, I'm afraid I was too angry to heed—"

Mary cleared her throat. "I recall," she offered. "His words were, 'I am persuaded that when sanctioned by the express authority of both your excellent parents, my proposals will not fail of being acceptable.' Shall I repeat them, Mr. Lyons?"

His head snapped up and he gaped at Mary. "Er, if you please, Miss Mary." She repeated the sentence slowly, and his pencil scratched over the paper as she spoke.

"So Collins," Mr. Lyons said at last, "was convinced of the justness and ultimate success of his cause. He had no reason to abuse you in any way."

"I had not the slightest intention of accepting him, Mr. Lyons," Lizzy replied to the investigator, although Mary could see her eyes flick towards Mr. Darcy as she spoke. "Even when Mama threatened me with never seeing her again, should I refuse my cousin, my father insisted I should never see *him* again should I *accept*. With my parents so at edge with each other, and with Mr. Collins sulking in the background, I resolved to remove myself from the house at once, and so I went out to walk again, to clear my thoughts."

Mr. Lyons nodded and wrote, and eventually asked, "And did you see Mr. Collins again?"

A look of the greatest distress crossed Lizzy's face, reminiscent of the look of horror Mary had observed when her sister had returned so shaken the previous afternoon. She shook and twisted her hands in her skirts, and Mary could see Mr. Darcy move towards her before checking himself. *He wishes to hold her and comfort her!* Mary realised, *but he knows he cannot. Yet.*

Lizzy took a deep breath and released it with a shudder before she spoke again. "I did see him. He must have followed me towards Oakham Mount, where he knew I liked to walk and think. He approached me in the fields where the stream leaves the woods and began hurling cruel words at me for refusing him, shouting again and again that his was the last offer I was likely to receive. He told me this was my last opportunity to accept, and when I refused him again..." she broke off and to Mary's horror, began sobbing. This was so unlike her stalwart and assured sister. What had shaken Lizzy so?

"Miss Elizabeth?" Mr. Darcy was at her side in an instant, his handkerchief at the ready. She accepted it and mopped at her eyes.

"Thank you, sir." She sniffled. Then, with a mighty display of strength, she announced with finality, "We argued and I ran. He shouted at me as I headed for the woods, but I did not turn back. And I never saw him again."

Once more, Mary was certain Lizzy had not told the entirety of what had occurred, but would not speak now, not with these two strangers present, no matter how much they purported to wish to help. But she knew she must learn what had happened that had reduced her strong and determined sister to such agony of spirit.

Chapter Six

The First Evidence

Alexander knew that he would get no more information out of Miss Elizabeth at this moment. She was distraught and seemed to be holding on to the veneer of civilised discourse with the greatest of effort. She needed privacy and the comfort of a sister where she might weep and scream and gradually come to terms with whatever had really happened by the stream, for it was clear that it had been more than a mere argument. He would have the truth eventually, but there was no use in trying to extract it now.

Thanking Miss Elizabeth and her sister Mary, he rose and beckoned to Darcy to accompany him on his visit to Sir William Lucas. Darcy agreed with clear reluctance, but he bade the ladies farewell for the time being and offered Miss Elizabeth one of the most elegant bows Alexander had ever seen. The lady, for her part, rose and curtseyed politely before returning to her sofa. It did not pass Alexander's notice that Darcy left his monogrammed handkerchief in the lady's hands, or that she clenched it as her eyes remained on the gentleman she professed to dislike.

Lucas Lodge was a far more modest residence than Alexander had expected from Darcy's description of the magistrate as a social-climber. The house was small and old with few modern improvements, and it commanded just enough land for Sir William to qualify as local magistrate. It was his status as a knight of the realm, rather than his social or financial pre-eminence in the region, that had led to him being named to his position, or so Alexander surmised.

They were led into the house by a maid-of-all-work rather than a housekeeper or a butler, and were led down a series of narrow hallways before being shown into Sir William's study. Darcy surveyed the dark and cramped chamber in which they waited with a sneer and upturned nose, but Alexander felt quite comfortable in the space and found himself predisposed to like the man who claimed this room as his own.

Sir William, when he appeared, was precisely as Alexander had expected him to be from his friend's description. Perhaps Darcy's skills at observation were clouded only where the lovely Miss Elizabeth was concerned. For his part, the local magistrate was a large barrel-chested man with a deep voice and a hearty laugh. He seemed inclined to good humour, and was somewhat old-fashioned both in his address and presentation, for he still wore a powdered wig and a frock coat that had been the height of elegance some fifteen years before.

He greeted his visitors with a hearty handshake and made not the first comment about Alexander's Scottish origins before sitting down across his desk to deal with the matter at hand. "So, Miss Lizzy. I could hardly account for it, she being my daughter Charlotte's dearest friend for so many years and a lovely lass if ever there was one. But all signs seemed to point to her, and in a case like this, I must bring forth a suspect to the Assizes. A parson—a rector even—and one under the patronage of a grand lady such as Catherine de Bourgh... Well, this must be pursued and the evil-doer found and punished! I'm pleased for your assistance, gentlemen. How can I help?"

Quite satisfied with this introduction, Alexander suggested, "You might tell us of the evidence you did find, and if possible, show us anything you have gathered in. Is the body yet unburied? I would like a look at it."

"Aye, poor Mr. Collins. Silly man, but a sad case, nonetheless."

"Before we begin, Sir William," Alexander tossed out, "Can you think of any reason someone might wish the parson dead?"

Sir William cocked his head and scratched at his chin. Long he pondered, then replied, "No. No indeed. If vanity and foolishness were crimes, perhaps, but the man was no more than annoying. If one wished to be rid of him, one need only leave the room. He was a sycophant, to be sure, but quite harmless. Unless one were forced to sit through his sermons, that is!" He began to laugh but stopped very quickly, recalling the severity of the situation. "Oh, yes. Terribly sorry. Now, the evidence?"

Alexander took out his notebook and pencil.

"Duggins and Ott—for those are the men who found him— were called to the site by one of Ott's dogs, who had come across the body and was barking at it."

"Why were they in the field?"

"A routine survey of the land," Sir William replied. "Checking fences and gates and bridges over the stream and all."

Alexander scratched a note in his book and gestured for Sir William to continue.

"They found Collins when the dog barked at them. He was clearly dead, lying in the stream but with his face out of the water.

He had been stabbed in the neck, and a knife bearing Miss Lizzy's initials was by the body."

"Could it have been a knife owned by somebody with the same initials?" Alexander asked.

"It could be, but for the fact that this knife had been a gift and so proud of it was she that everybody in Meryton had seen it and knew it to be hers. 'Tis not a large thing, sharp enough to slice apples and cut away splinters of wood. And," he cleared his throat, "sharp enough to make a hole enough in a man's neck for him to bleed to his death. I now know that a man's neck is no more challenging to a blade than is a wooden twig. That is a sobering thought."

As he spoke, he reached into a drawer in his desk and pulled out a small object which he placed upon a square of white linen. Alexander reached for the object and drew it towards him. It was a small folding pocket knife, perhaps six inches in length in its folded state—it would likely be a four-inch blade when open—its handle a beautifully carved piece of ivory or whalebone with a stylised trellis of flowers up one side and the initials ERB on the other.

"A lovely object," Darcy commented. "Pity for it to have been put to such ill use."

Alexander flicked the blade and examined it in the light of the window to his side. The knife was wider than he had expected from its length, and would cause rather severe damage when applied with sufficient force. It was mostly clean of blood, which was to be expected since it had lain several hours in the stream, but with slight dark patches at the hinge and along the creases where one material met another. There would be little to learn from the blade itself, but for the confirmation that it was the weapon used.

"We also found Miss Lizzy's satchel nearby in the field." Sir William reached into another cavity in his desk as he spoke. "Here, it contains everything as we found it. A book—definitely Lizzy's for her name is inside it—a small pack of bread and cold meat, an apple, and two linen napkins. It did seem odd that she would kill the man and not remove all traces of her presence at the scene."

"Unless she left before there was a scene to clear of evidence," Alexander concluded. "As of yet, nothing contradicts her story of arguing and running away. If she were in enough distress, she might well have fled without stopping to pick up her bag." Darcy agreed with a firm nod.

"What else have you collected, Sir William?"

"There was an empty sack found some fair distance downstream from the body, with evidence of having held some food. My men reckon it was Collins' snack, and he discarded the sack when he had consumed its contents, long before he had his final confrontation.

"Good. And what else?"

"Her dress, the one she wore when she returned home. Come, it is in this room." The magistrate led them to what was little more than a closet off his study, where a simple walking dress and dark cape lay folded upon a narrow table. Alexander unfolded the dress. "Come now, Darcy, are you blushing? Investigators have no use for such fine feelings; you would be shocked at the things we see every day. I shan't think ill of you if you wish to sit in the study."

Darcy glowered. "I shall stay. It is only a dress, something seen by all. My 'fine feelings,' as you so put it, shall survive unharmed."

The dress, too, was as Alexander had expected. It was covered in mud, not just at the hem, but up one side almost to the high waist, and spattered everywhere with dried muck. The sturdy fabric was rent throughout with small rips and tears, and more noticeably, one sleeve was torn away from the bodice. "Indeed!" Alexander murmured to himself but other than making a quick note in his book, said nothing else. "No blood on the outside of the dress…" he turned it to the inside, "and only enough to account for scratches on the body of the wearer on the inside. Good."

Next he turned his eyes to the cape. This, too, was well covered in mud, both inside and out, and the front was definitely covered in blood. There was a large patch, about the size of an apricot, just above the left breast, and smears and trickles leading down from that patch for several inches. Along the right side there was another large patch of dried blood just below where the wearer's waist would be, and a light coating of blood trailed across much of the front of the garment. "Notice anything?" He asked his companions.

"Lots of things," Darcy replied. "Why not tell us what you see that interests you?"

"What is the game in that?" Alexander teased, but turned immediately to his point. "There is a lot of superficial blood on this garment, enough to point to a nosebleed, or a fairly deep cut. I shall need to examine Miss Elizabeth's right arm," he pointed to the second patch of blood he had discovered. "But the blood is all on the surface; almost none has seeped very deeply into the fabric, and there is certainly not enough to account for the amount of blood a man would spurt when stabbed in the neck to the point that he died from his injuries. Is it possible to see the body, Sir William?"

The magistrate led the men out of the house and to a small structure by the stables. There, he showed them down a flight of stairs into a cool room that might once have been an ice house. "Better this way," he mumbled as he turned up the flame on his lamp.

The lamp illuminated a grisly scene. The remains of the reverend William Collins lay naked on a wooden table, covered with a thin linen cloth. "The doctor from Hertford only finished his examination an hour ago. He is at the inn should you wish to speak with him. I have his report." Alexander listened with half of his attention whilst he walked around the body, taking in every detail. Collins, he saw, was mostly uninjured but for a large bruise on his side and a gaping slit in his neck. Alexander crouched down with the lantern better to examine the wound. "Sliced through the... what-do-you-call-it?" Sir William mumbled. "The something artery?"

"Carotid."

"Aye. You professional men must have a great deal of knowledge of these matters. There's one more thing the doctor mentioned." His voice dropped, and he began to look most uneasy. "The bruise on his ribs was not the only place he was hit. His er... he was felled in the way that will bring any strong man to his knees." Even in the weak light of the ice house, Alexander could see the man's face turn bright red.

"Ah yes, a kick to that most sensitive area," he commented, "can be an effective means of felling an attacker." Alexander pulled the cloth away from the body's groin and grimaced at what he saw. He replaced the cloth at once. A picture was beginning to form in his mind, but not necessarily one that would exonerate Miss Elizabeth. Not without more evidence.

After a few more formalities, Alexander concluded his investigations and with the name of the doctor in his pocket, bid thanks and goodbye to Sir William. "You have some thoughts," Darcy commented as the men returned to the stables to retrieve their horses.

"Aye, I do. Collins' injuries suggest something far more physical than a mere argument. How this bodes for Miss

Elizabeth, I would rather not say until I have more information and time to ponder it all. But I would dearly love to know more about Sir William. You have given me the outline, which I have filled in somewhat upon meeting the man, but pray, tell me more. What of his family? In my quest to find alternatives to Miss Elizabeth's presumed guilt, I must suspect everybody. Even the magistrate."

The men achieved the stables and were soon mounted and riding towards the inn in Meryton, there to speak to the doctor who had examined the body. Not until they had passed through the gates to Lucas Lodge did Darcy speak again. "Sir William, as you see, has great pretensions but little wealth. Oh, he is certainly well set by most men's standards, but despite his success in his previous life as a merchant, he will never attain the standard of living he desires. Unless he somehow inherits it... or has one of his children do so."

"Tell me more."

"Recall that I am almost as much a stranger here as are you, and for some reason, the townsfolk seem not to like me very much." Alexander rolled his eyes heavenward. How could his friend be so blind to his icy demeanour? "What I tell is gleaned from second-hand rumour, which we all know often carries very little truth. But it seems that the eldest son, John, once had a *tendre* for Jane Bennet. With Collins no longer in line to inherit, the entail might be broken, in which case Jane's eldest son might be the future heir. If so..."

"If so," Alexander concluded, "it would behove John Lucas to remove Mr. Collins from the world and press his case with Jane Bennet." He squinted into the distance, looking at nothing. "It would, however, depend upon the entail being broken, upon Jane being able to inherit, upon Jane accepting John Lucas... Did you not say she was being courted by your friend Bingley?"

"Bingley has been paying a great deal of attention to her," Darcy admitted.

"Then Lucas would need to remove your friend from the scene as well as the parson. This hardly seems a likely motive for murder, for there are too many ways in which the plan would almost certainly go awry, but it is still an avenue to pursue. With luck, I shall receive notes from my London colleagues in the morning, and with them, more news on the exact nature and extent of the entail upon Longbourn."

Doctor Hewitt had very little information to add, which Alexander had not already guessed. Collins did not drown, but rather died from severe blood loss when the main artery in his neck had been severed by the knife found nearby. In his opinion, the blade matched the wound exactly, and was almost certainly the weapon used. The injuries to the deceased's body were inflicted through normal clothing and were received sufficiently before the man died for the discolouration to achieve the degree he had seen. "At a guess, I would say half an hour between being kicked in the... bollocks, and being sliced up like tomorrow's ham sandwich."

This time Alexander did not bother stifling a burst of laughter at the image, although Darcy's glare was icy. When he had brought his mirth under control, Alexander asked his next question. "How much blood would you say this particular stuck pig would have lost upon receiving the final injury, the stab wound?"

"Oh, the carotid artery will spurt wildly. Everything close by would be covered, and the attacker's clothing would be quite soaked through, if that is what you want to know. From the angle of the wound, the attacker must have been in front of the man, or slightly to the side. I cannot fathom anyone standing in such a way as not to become quite drenched with the man's life blood.

That would involve a stab from behind, but to do that, the attacker would need the most strangely shaped and sized arms. No, he stood in front."

"Would not the man's cravat have absorbed much of the blood?" Alexander now asked.

"Did I not tell you?" replied the doctor with a frown. "I know it is in the written report I gave Sir William. The deceased wore no stock or cravat; at least there was no sign of it on his person or at the scene. His neck was quite bare; there was nothing to shield the attacker from a rather monumental spray of blood. He would have been quite drenched in it."

"You said 'he.' Do you assert that the attacker was a man?" Darcy was quick to interrupt with his question.

"No, 'twas most likely a man, for women tend not to kill with knives. Still, a woman suitably angered or motivated could screw her courage to the sticking plate and act. Lady Macbeth, recall, dispatched two sleeping sentries with a blade, never mind the blood. I would not discount the possibility." Darcy looked grim.

They thanked the doctor, who had left his report at Lucas Lodge, and ventured outside once again to discuss where to proceed from here in their inquiries. As they departed the inn, Alexander mused, "I have a suspicion of why he wore no cravat, but I do wonder what happened to it!"

Chapter Seven

Missing Objects

After Mr. Darcy and Mr. Lyons had departed, Mary helped Lizzy to her room. She called for Jane to come to her sister's aid. Jane and Lizzy had always been most particularly close to each other, and Jane's calm demeanour and caring manner were exactly what her sister needed. Satisfied that Lizzy was in good hands, Mary found her riding coat and boots and crept from the house without alerting her mother. She did not need any more distractions, for she had a question that she needed answered.

The sporadic rain had finally given way to weak sunlight, and after the intensity of the morning's goings-on, the fresh air was welcome. Mary breathed deeply of it as she made her ride over to Netherfield, hoping that the crisp air would stimulate her mind to seek the solutions she needed. She could not get the fact of the lost candlesticks from her mind, and had resolved to speak to Robinson, the head footman whom Mr. Bingley had chosen to serve as butler when guests were present. It was he who had responsibility for the silver.

Arriving at Netherfield by the tradesmen's path, rather than up the main drive, Mary made directly for the back entrance. She had no wish to confront Mrs. Harwich or Miss Bingley, and hoped to prevail upon the cook, whom she had known since infancy, to assist her. It was not the cook, however, who opened the door to her knock, or even a kitchen maid, but Mr. Bingley himself.

"Oh, I'm terribly sorry, Mr. Bingley!" Mary cried out, embarrassed to be seen attempting to gain entry to his house without his knowledge. "I was hoping... that is..." she sought madly for some reasonable excuse for being at his kitchen door.

"I understand, Miss Mary. You wish to avoid my sister and her beast of a housekeeper. I am doing exactly the same thing. I arrived back from London only minutes ago, and already I need to escape my own house! I was hoping to pay a call on Ja... Miss Bennet and Miss Elizabeth." He dropped his voice to a whisper. "Caroline forbids me to associate with a family brought so low, but I know something about her grandfather that she does not, and I shan't let her dictate whether or not I may go out." He looked about and confided afresh, "However, I still wish to avoid her sharp eye and sharper tongue." He paused for a moment, then reddened and asked, "Is your eldest sister at home? Is she accepting callers?" The hopeful look upon his face cheered Mary more than she would have imagined. "I do wish to speak with Miss Elizabeth too, to let her know that she has many champions in this world, who would see her relieved of this weight."

With a wide grin, Mary satisfied his curiosity. "Yes, she is indeed at home. I believe both of my sisters would be most glad to see you. Some fresh company might do both of them good."

"Did Darcy come? I thought it best he know right away, and he dashed off the very moment I paused to draw breath. Did he bring the investigator he spoke about?"

"Yes, indeed, he did both. He has taken much trouble to help my sister."

"He needed only to learn his own heart." Bingley smiled and gave Mary a quick bow, reassured himself that Caroline was not after him, and dashed from the house towards the stables, leaving the door open. Mary let herself in and made for the kitchens.

"Oh, Mr. Bingley, are you back already?" The cook's back was to the door, but she had heard the sound of Mary entering.

"No, Mrs. Slougham, 'tis only I, Mary Bennet."

"Miss Mary! Now what are you doing here, and at the kitchen entrance? Oh, that nasty Mrs. Harwich will not let you in the front, will she? Well, you are welcome in my kitchen. She has no dominion here! I have some rolls, fresh from the oven, and some fresh butter. And some lemonade? Or would you prefer tea? What can I do for you, my dear?"

This was the reception Mary had hoped to receive, and she gladly partook of Mrs. Slougham's excellent pastry, praising the cook with every tender bite, before asking after her purpose.

"I wondered if Robinson is available. I had a question about some silverware and hoped he might have an answer for me."

Mrs. Slougham's eyes narrowed. "Silverware, you say? Strange thing, that. Have pieces been disappearing from your house as well? Mighty strange business! And not only silverware, but even maids! Polly, who was always so quiet and trustworthy, has not been seen since yesterday! Can you believe that! She vanished right along with the candlesticks, I tell you. That's not something natural! Another roll? Perhaps with jam?"

"Oh, no thank you. I should quite ruin my dinner. But is it true?" She leaned forward and placed her elbows upon the large wooden table, exactly the way she had always been admonished not to do, then rested her chin upon her fists. "Which is Polly? The tall girl with the black hair?"

"No, Polly is the short, pretty one with the large... with the golden ringlets and the round shape that the men admire so much. She's a quiet one, she is, always sweet and happy to go about her duties. She's the last one I'd have figured for such a thing as this, but she and the candlesticks, both gone on the same day!"

"Are you certain she took them?" Something was bothering Mary, and she needed to discover what it was.

"If you're asking if I saw her steal them and run, well no, can't say as I did. But it really is too much of a coincidence, is it not, two such strange things happening at once?"

A prickling sensation ran up Mary's spine as a realisation struck her. "Three."

"Pardon me, Miss?"

"Three strange things. Could the disappearance of Polly and the candlesticks be connected somehow with the awful murder of Mr. Collins? For two unusual occurrences to transpire within a short time, one can say, 'strange things happen.' But three, all at once? That seems almost too much to believe unless one has to do with another."

Robinson, when he was found, was reluctant to talk to Mary about the missing silverware. He was a thin and worried man approaching middle age, and the last few weeks had only aged him. He had a tic under his eye and he continually looked towards the door to the still room as if worried he might be overheard. At first, he denied any knowledge of the loss, and when pressed, admitted that one or two small items might have gone missing, but that he was certain they would be found with no inconvenience whatsoever to the master or—with a sneer and an uncontrolled shiver—the mistress. "Master Bingley would like as not be understanding, for things do grow legs," he said at last, "but Miss Bingley would see me out of the house at the instant!"

It took some time for Mary to convince the man that she was not seeking to betray him to his employer, but rather that she suspected the disappearance of the silver might be somehow connected to the murder. "I am doing all of this for my sister," she pled at last, unable to control the tears that were beginning to form in her eyes. "If we cannot learn who really killed Mr. Collins, she will be charged and hanged, for all that she is certainly innocent. Will you not help me, for Lizzy?"

Robinson sighed and hung his worried head. "Aye. Very well. Miss Lizzy has always been kind. When my son broke his leg, she came over every day with a story to tell him, and no matter that Mrs. Slougham always found nourishing food to give him, Miss Lizzy would send over treats." He stared at the closed door with anxious eyes. "For her, I will speak to you. But please, Miss Mary," he begged, "if this can avoid the ear of Miss Bingley, 'twould be much appreciated!"

The first pieces of silver to disappear had been negligible. A salt dish, or a butter knife. Robinson had not even mentioned these losses, since such small items are so easily misplaced and will often reappear when least expected, in the back of the pantry or at the bottom of a sack of flour. The candlesticks were a more serious matter, for these were larger pieces, as valuable for the artistry in their design as for the silver that made up their weight. It is less easy to knock a large candlestick off the edge of a table than a tiny teaspoon, after all. It was at this point when he began to harbour suspicions of theft.

"When were these candlesticks last seen?" This must be the question Robinson had asked himself every moment since they were noticed to be missing.

"They were most certainly present before the ball," Robinson peered into the distance as he spoke. Was he hoping the candlesticks would appear to him there, in a vision? "After the dancing had concluded, and the guests had departed, the staff brought all of the silver to the breakfast room. We use it as a servery for the dining room, for it leads directly to the kitchens. It was too late to polish every piece and return them to the butler's pantry, but all the doors to the breakfast room lock and the silver ought to have been as secure there as in the pantry."

"And in the morning? Where were the candlesticks?"

Robinson narrowed his eyes further. His perusal into the distance past the walls seemed not to have brought him any answers. "I cannot say for certain. Nothing in the room seemed to be disturbed, and I did not conduct an immediate inventory, for Miss Bingley had provided me with a rather daunting list of tasks she required completed before she rose for the day. The smaller pieces were taken to the pantry at that time, for those are the ones that are more likely to be... misappropriated. The larger pieces were left in the breakfast room, for only the family enter that room. It was not until after we cleared the breakfast dishes that the loss was noted." The man looked exceedingly anxious, and Mary thought that if he worried his hands any further, he would pick his fingernails from his fingers.

Robinson explained what steps had been taken next. All the staff were questioned, of course, and without the knowledge of the Bingleys or Mrs. Harwick. Maids, kitchen assistants and footmen all, they were searched bodily and had their belongings combed through, but not so much as an errant earring was discovered. When questioned individually, not one betrayed any signs of guilt, although two of the kitchen maids were unaccountably nervous, due—so Mrs. Slougham insisted—to worry over being blamed for the loss, for they were charged with collecting the silverware from the dining table and removing it to the butler's pantry after use.

"Who were these two maids?" This was getting most curious! "I would speak to them."

"I shall have Bessie summoned at once, but the other, I'm afraid…"

"Is the missing Polly."

Robinson's head shot up and his eyes opened wide in alarm.

"I had the tale from Mrs. Slougham," Mary confessed. "What dealings have you had with Polly? I do not know her at all."

"Aye, she's a pretty one," Robinson gave a small and nervous smile. "My wife was not pleased when she was taken into employment here at Netherfield. But Polly was not one to make trouble. For all her lovely looks and tempting figure—sorry to alarm you, Miss Mary!—she never made a come-on to the staff, neither to the guests. She always just seemed happy to work and take home her coin."

Mary felt her face flush red as she formulated her next question. Ladies were not supposed to know of such matters, and certainly not sober-minded young women such as herself, although one or two mentions in the Bible did come to mind. Tamar and Rahab, for example, and Judith all fought for her attention. Willing herself to be stoic, she asked, "Did any of the, er, gentlemen pay undue attention to her?" Her attempts were futile; her face flushed even more furiously than a moment before.

Robinson paid her embarrassment no mind. "That is hard for me to say rightly. She was not under my command, and I often had duties that brought me elsewhere. There might have been any sort of seductions being attempted when my eyes were on my own work. But most of the other girls complained of such undesired attention from time to time; Polly did not. I think she kept clear away from the men. Except..." he trailed off and pursed his lips. "Hmmm."

Mary was curious now. "Yes?"

"I did hear her ask Bessie about one fellow. It didn't sound as if he had pressed his attentions upon her, but now I wonder if there was something odd happening." The tic under his eye spasmed as he leaned forward. "He's in the militia, this fellow. Lieutenant, I reckon, by the name of Wickham. Does that mean anything to you?"

Robinson had little else to say about Polly or about the missing silver, other than that the most recent pair of candlesticks to go missing, each three feet from top to bottom and decorated with elaborate designs, and more importantly, encrusted with gemstones, were likely worth upwards of eighty pounds! That was a tremendous amount of money; indeed, a family could survive on that for a year if they lived simply. Robinson surmised that the total value of the missing silver approached two hundred pounds, and then abruptly left the room, calling for Bessie as he disappeared down the narrow passageway.

As she waited for Bessie, Mary mulled over this unexpected revelation. Lieutenant Wickham! Was he somehow involved in this affair? It hardly seemed credible. He had always been so friendly and open, so much the paragon of the dutiful soldier. His attentions to Polly must have been innocent, for he seemed to favour Lizzy, did he not? Surely an honourable gentleman such as he would never... But then she recalled the terrible tales he had told of Mr. Darcy, accusing him of denying Wickham his inheritance and generally besmirching the man's name throughout the area. Admittedly, Mr. Darcy had done little to enamour himself to the local community, but the alacrity with which everybody accepted Mr. Wickham's tales bespoke a long acquaintance with flattery and deception.

Deception was foremost in Mary's thoughts, for Mr. Darcy had proven himself a friend where everybody else had deserted the family. Could he really be so proud and uncaring when he had returned with such haste to comfort Lizzy, and in the company of an investigator he must certainly be paying well to prove her sister innocent of this crime? Perhaps Mr. Wickham's tales of abuse at the hands of Mr. Darcy were not quite accurate; perhaps his history was not quite so pitiable after all! She must learn more about him, for it seemed he might be ensnared in this murder in one way or another.

Her thoughts were interrupted by the timid knock at the door that heralded Bessie's arrival. This was the tall, dark haired maid Mary had seen about, but had not known by name. She crept around the open door to the still room like a timid mouse, and seemed alarmed to find Mary waiting for her, despite having been made aware of the situation. "You... you wished to speak with me, Miss Bennet?"

"I shall not eat you alive, Bessie. Take a chair. I only wish to talk to you."

"I'm sure I've nothing to say that would help you, Miss Bennet. I'm only a maid here, and not even upstairs. I only do the kitchens and help with the servin' and cleanin' of meals. If I've done ought wrong, I beg you not to tell Mrs. Harwick!"

Mary sniffed. "Be easy, Bessie. I am not going to report your imagined wrong-doings to Mrs. Harwick. I only want you to tell me of what you might have seen or heard. Do you know about the candlesticks that have gone missing?"

The girl's eyes widened to discs, and she seemed to shrink back into herself. "I never touched them, I swear it, no matter what that man said! They was there when I left the room, clear as day, and I did not touch them nor see them afterwards! I'll swear it on the Bible, or on my grandmother's grave, I will!"

"No one thinks you took the candlesticks. Your bible and grandmother are quite safe." Mary was growing frustrated at the girl's insistence, but schooled herself to remain patient. "But I believe," she coaxed, "that you can help me find them, so nobody will ever think for a moment that you had anything to do with it! Can you do that? Will you talk to me?"

The girl nodded, her eyes still wide and unblinking.

"Good. Now, when, exactly, did you see the candlesticks?"

"They was there, on the floor beside the table where we lays out the breakfast, when the family was eating, and they was gone when we went to clean up afterwards.

"Who was in the room between breakfast and when you went to clear the dishes?"

"None that I can think. Mrs. Slougham was in the kitchen with her helpers, and everyone was fussing about the house to clean after the ball. But that man what said we took the other silver will blame us for these ones too!" Bessie seemed about to cry and Mary passed her a linen handkerchief, which the maid used to wipe her nose.

"Tell me about the man, the one who said you took the silver."

"He's a handsome one, he is. He was really talking to Polly, all pretty that she is, but he looked at me as well when he spoke, as a warning, like. He said that he knew all about the missing silverware and that if Polly didn't want anyone to know, she would meet him to talk about it."

"Is that so! What did Polly say?"

"Well, she said, of course, that she knew nothing, but the man would not be put off, and she agreed at last. I think he meant to... to take liberties with her." This was said in a voice so soft Mary could barely hear the girl.

"Do you know this man's name?"

"No, I never heard it. But I have done seen him about the town, when Mrs. Slougham sends me. But I can tell you what he looks like. He's young, no more than thirty, and lovely to look upon, with his smart red coat and blue eyes and yellow curls. And when he smiles, it almost makes a girl want to let him take his liberties. Not that I would know such things!" she ended in alarm.

With a grim smile, Mary knew this must be Wickham, for no other officers matched his faultless description.

"I have one more question," she spoke gently, "and then I shall let you go. When was this discussion, when he threatened you and Polly? And when did he wish to meet Polly?"

"Oh," Bessie smiled more easily. "That was the day of the ball, just before mid-day! The master and his guests had finished with breakfast and we was cleaning up when he came in through the kitchen door. He said he had to go to London and would not be able to dance, but that he would get word to Polly when she must meet him." She paused for a moment. "Something odd, though." She was silent for long enough that Mary had to prompt her to resume her thought. "He said he was in London, but I would almost swear it was him I heard arguing with the dead parson in the breakfast room when we was setting up for dinner that afternoon."

"An argument? Here at Netherfield?" Mary took a sharp breath. "How do you know it was Mr. Collins—the dead parson—who was arguing?"

"Oh," Bessie smiled again. "That is easy. I done seen him walk out through the dining room where we was working."

"And the other man? Surely he left the same way." Mary had taken meals in the fine dining room, but had not seen the breakfast room and was unclear as to how the rooms opened into the rest of the house. This was something to explore, assuming she might avoid Caroline and Mrs. Harwick.

"No, miss. He never came through that way at all. When we finished setting the table and went to the breakfast room to see, it was empty, with not a soul there. Certainly no other man left through our way, so he must have gone out through the kitchens."

Two strange happenings had become three, and now four. Mary added the overheard argument to her list of unusual events, to be pondered over deeply when she had the solitude she required. An argument was certainly nothing strange in a home, and especially one presided over by the unpleasant Miss Bingley, but what in the world had her cousin, Mr. Collins, been doing at Netherfield that afternoon? And if Bessie was correct, what had Mr. Wickham been doing there, when he had no cause to be in the house, and when by her accounts he ought to be most of the way to London? It was all quite perplexing. There must be more pieces to this puzzle, she decided, for at the moment it was like a charade with half of the words missing. There was simply no way to piece it together without more information.

As she sat in the stillroom after Bessy scuttled out, she considered what she did know. Silverware had been disappearing, first in small amounts, now in large. On the day before the disappearance of the largest items, Polly and Bessie had been accosted and accused by Mr. Wickham, who attempted to blackmail Polly into a tryst (Mary was proud of herself for thinking of that word). When the largest piece went missing after the ball, the maids would surely be afraid of being blamed for that theft as well.

Recalling the conversation she had overheard between the maids and footman of the very day of the murder, she began to arrange events into some order in her mind. The morning before the ball, Wickham had been in the house and had threatened the maids, demanding that Polly meet him at some time and place to be decided, in exchange for his silence on the thefts. Wickham was then, by his own accounting, to be off to London. Later that day, Mr. Collins had been heard arguing with somebody in that same breakfast room—somebody who sounded much like Mr. Wickham, who ought to be twenty and more miles away.

The next morning, after the ball, the largest and most expensive of the silver candlesticks were taken. Further, Polly had not been seen after the breakfast dishes were cleared. Had she taken the silver, despite all protestations otherwise? Or had she somehow received word from Wickham about his plans for their *rendezvous*? And was the messenger the real thief? What she did know was that by early that afternoon, Mr. Collins lay dead.

A dead clergyman, stolen silverware, and a missing maid. Nothing seemed to make sense and her head started to ache. It was no use trying to match the pieces now. She would simply allow them to drift in her mind like leaves on a calm pond until such time that enough other leaves might appear as to cover the surface. Then, perhaps, she might divine a pattern.

One thing was clear: Mr. Darcy's investigator friend might well have his own leaves to strew upon the pond of reason. She must find him and talk to him. She retrieved her outerwear and her riding bonnet and thanked Mrs. Slougham for her assistance before setting off to seek Mr. Lyons.

As luck would have it, the two men were just returning their horses to the stables as Mary wandered thither to retrieve hers. They were covered in mud and dust, and both looked exhausted. *No wonder*, it occurred to her, *for they must have left London before dawn!* She wondered how little sleep they had managed the previous night, and how long their day would be today.

Chapter Eight

Confessions

Alexander grimaced as he levered himself from his horse. Groaning with every movement, he brushed the grime from his coat and wiped dusty hands on his trousers, no longer caring what colour they might be beneath the layers of filth that now coated them. His joints protested every movement and his head had begun to throb, distracting him from the ache of the large bruise that must surely now be blooming on his hip. He wished for all the world that he might enter the house with little fanfare and be greeted with a warm bath and a cool tankard of ale.

His wishes were for nought, for instead of the bath and ale, he was greeted instead by Miss Mary Bennet on the path between the stables and the kitchen door. She peered at him from beneath the riding bonnet she had shoved onto her head, her eyes tight and her lips a thin line on her face. This morning he had thought her face quietly pretty. With her determined expression and outthrust jaw, he decided he had been wrong. She was plain and looked to be vexing as well. He was in no mood for civilities at this moment.

"Mr. Darcy, Mr. Lyons," she greeted them without warmth, heedless of Alexander's dishevelled appearance. "I wonder if I may confer with you, Mr. Lyons. I have some thoughts on this matter you might wish to hear."

No, he most certainly did not wish to hear her thoughts. Not at this moment, anyway. The ride out to the stream where Collins had been discovered had been difficult and ponderous, the pastures little more than fields of mud. The stile that would normally present no trouble to a man on foot or a horse with solid ground beneath its hooves may as well have been a barrier twenty feet high, for his mount would not attempt the jump. He could not blame the animal, for there was no traction for the beast to grab in the muck, but the stile needed surmounting. On his second such endeavour, the horse had stopped so suddenly before the low wooden fence that Alexander slid right off his back and into the wet and spongy mire that covered the land.

Darcy had laughed, then dismounted to ensure his companion had suffered no serious injury, and then laughed again, before leading the recalcitrant horse and pride-wounded rider a half mile yonder to where they might cross more easily. In the end, the miserable visit had been futile. Whatever marks might have been left in the soft riverbanks had long been washed clean by the flow of the current and the rain that had fallen the previous night, and if not for the large stick with a red ribbon tied to its top, the men would never have located the site at all. There were no incriminating footprints, no mysterious note folded amongst the reeds and twigs confessing, "I, Nemo, killed the parson," no traces of blood remaining in the water.

And so, bruised, filthy, and frustrated, the very last thing Alexander wished to do at this moment was to listen to Miss Mary's thoughts. "There might be a better time, Miss Bennet," he fairly growled at her.

"Sir, this is important."

He knew he was being most uncivil, but with each limping step, he felt he might trip and fall once more. Whatever could this pampered chit possibly have to say to him at this moment? She had remarkable recall, to be sure, but she was a child of privilege, born to wealth and comfort, with little education and less experience of life. How she could possibly have anything to discuss that he would wish to hear, he could not imagine. "Miss Mary, later. Please." His eyes narrowed and his nostrils flared, and still she did not stand back.

"Mr. Lyons, I have some thoughts that will necessarily have import in your own inquiries. We must talk. Mr. Darcy, will you not make him hear me?"

Darcy stared at the girl; he was quite unaccustomed, Alexander well knew, to being ordered about by any man his equal, and certainly not by an eighteen-year-old girl of so little consequence. Darcy's nostrils flared and Alexander believed that were his friend a horse, he would snort in derision.

But before Darcy could open his mouth to countermand the girl, the last restraints Alexander held on his temper broke. "No, Miss Mary," he fairly shouted at her. "He is my employer, but not my master. I conduct my investigations according to my own schedule, not his. Your memory might be prodigious, but I have little time or patience right now for the self-satisfying notions of an uneducated and unimportant piece of upper-class skirt as yourself. You would be best to remember your place and to stay out of the affairs of skilled and professional men. Your interference can only be troublesome. Now if you please, goodbye." He winced with pain as he took another step forward in the hopes of getting around her and finally achieving the house.

But Mary blocked his way, a small and fiery foe, staring down two large men. With her hands planted firmly on her hips, she sneered back, "Self-satisfying notions? This is no mere diversion, sir! This is not simply an assignment bought and paid for by some client. What sort of arrogance do you have in that filthy breast of yours? And we thought Mr. Darcy proud and too far above us! My 'self-satisfying notions' are all for saving my sister from a most terrible fate, not to mention the rest of the family! I may not have gone to school, but I am as well-read as any common gentleman, and I would wager my knowledge of the Lord's teachings surpasses that of most clergymen, my esteemed and deceased cousin among them. As for the remainder of your insults, *sir*, I shall not deign to address them. You are the most ungentlemanly person I have had the misfortune to meet. This is not how a decent Christian man speaks to a lady."

Through the pounding in his skull, Alexander spat back, "I would have thought it clear that I am no gentleman, *Mary*," he stressed the familiar use of her unadorned name, "and far be it for me to claim to be a decent Christian, for none here would consider me such. Good day." Whereupon he stepped around her and stormed off towards the house as quickly as his injuries would allow him, ignoring the gasps and mumbled apologies behind him.

It was only after sitting for far too long in a large tub of hot water and taking the bitter contents of a pot of willow bark tea that Alexander felt adequate to returning Darcy's inquiries into his health. The gentleman had knocked at the door some four or five times whilst Alexander was attempting to remove the better part of Farmer Ott's turnip plot from his hair, only to be shooed away by the man's own valet, whom he had kindly lent to Alexander for the nonce.

Now, clean and cosy in a borrowed banyan, his water-wrinkled feet warm in borrowed slippers, he finally informed Thorne that he was available, should Mr. Darcy still wish to converse. He owed the man a tremendous apology, he knew, and a greater one was owed to Mary Bennet, but he would swallow his pride in the latter respect on the morrow, assuming he could raise his beaten body from his bed.

Darcy arrived some minutes later with a footman who bore a tray of bread and cheese and two tankards of ale. "Drink," Darcy ordered. "The alcohol will take away some of the sting of what I am about to unleash upon you."

"I deserve it all. Berate me until I am flayed to the bone. If you send me back to London, it is no more than I deserve. But the chit would not leave me be."

"She was merely wishing to help. She is a sheltered creature, for all her country ways. They all are. They know so little of the horrors of the greater world."

"Which is why I cannot believe that she would have the first piece of information or conjecture that would help my inquiries. What does she know of the darkness that brings men to wreak such evil? She is a girl, born into luxury, a useless creature from a long line of useless creatures. I have no time for her nonsense."

"This useless creature is the sister of the woman I have come to… grow rather fond of. If she is useless, then so is Miss Elizabeth, and that I will never allow." Alexander had heard this tone of voice before, imperious and judgmental and ice cold, brooking no argument. He had heard it when Darcy had first come to him for help in locating his missing sister last summer; he had heard it when they had found the miscreant who convinced her into an elopement; he had heard it when Darcy discharged the perfidious Mrs. Younge, the companion who had led the young Georgiana into Wickham's greedy clutches. He had hoped to never to hear the tone directed at himself. And yet, he had to admit, it was deserved. Moreover, it was being offered with a plate of victuals and a tall beer, which did dampen the edge of the verbal blade.

"I am chastened," Alexander sighed at last. "Miss Elizabeth is everything lovely, I agree, and I am certain her accomplishments are admirable and varied. But still, what possible use can Miss Mary's thoughts be to my inquiries?"

"You will never know until you hear them. Even unworldly ladies with their attention lost in their devotionals might have an intelligent thought or two in their heads; likewise, their ears are no less capable than yours for hearing information that might have a bearing on the situation."

"I doubt she will speak to me now."

Darcy took another drink from his tankard and pondered the rinds of cheese that decorated the now-empty plate. "It is approaching time for dinner. I intend to ride over to Longbourn, where I hope to be invited for the meal. Charles is still there, and I am certain he will be dining with the Bennets. I hope to convince Miss Elizabeth to offer me the chance at some conversation, to begin to convince her of my better qualities. I still do not quite know why the village is all so set against me, but perhaps if I exert myself to be friendly at dinner, I shall make some improvements in my reputation. Bennet is really not such a bad sort, and his conversation will certainly be amusing if nothing else."

Alexander allowed his eyes to roll. Did Darcy truly not understand how his character was seen in the area? Ought he to speak and elucidate the man, or allow him to find his own way with the family he seemed determined to win over? Darcy had not finished his pronouncements, however.

"I made an initial apology to Miss Mary after you departed earlier; I shall attempt a second, which she may accept in her desperation to help her sister. Regardless, my apologies are meaningless if not followed by one of your own. I shall tell her to expect you in the morning." This was uttered as a commandment from on high. Darcy certainly deserved his reputation for hauteur, even if he was a better man than most beneath his veil of arrogance.

This was no more than Alexander had decided to do himself. "Yes, I will accept my lumps. You may tell the lady I shall present myself for her flogging. I will listen to everything she has to tell me, no matter how it might waste precious time."

"Lyons..."

Alexander snorted.

"I also suggest you tell the lady something of yourself. That, too, might assuage her ire a bit. Just as you misjudge her, you have given her cause to misjudge you. I shall summon Thorne to attend to your injuries with whatever liniment he might find in the stillroom, and then I recommend an early night for you. Shall I give your regrets for dinner?"

A half-second was all that was required for Alexander to agree. The thought of a meal with the cold and haughty Bingley sisters and the indolent Hurst was enough to put a hale man off his food. "That will be fine. Perhaps Thorne can have a tray sent up later instead, and a book?"

"I shall tell him he is at your disposal. Rest well, Lyons, for tomorrow might be a very busy day."

Mary was not happy when Mr. Darcy arrived to pay a call on the family shortly before dinner. It would have been the height of rudeness not to invite the man to stay and dine, and Mary knew that for all her mother's faults, the lady would not let her manners slip, not even at times of great trouble, not even towards a man who had insulted her daughter so coldly only weeks before. Why, all of Meryton had been snickering over "not handsome enough to tempt me," for there was not a soul in the village, not man, woman or child, who did not hold that the second Miss Bennet was by any accounting a very pretty young woman.

Further, Mr. Bingley had made good on his intention to call on Jane whilst Mary was interviewing the servants at Netherfield, and he had not yet taken his departure, having already been invited to remain. There could be no excuse, therefore, for Mrs. Bennet not to extend the offer to his friend.

She did not disappoint. She greeted Mr. Darcy with cool enough civility, but when the moment came when she must invite him to stay or not, the offer was issued with admirable grace, and accepted likewise. Mary was rather taken by surprise; Mr. Darcy could be pleasant company when he exerted himself, and there seemed nothing feigned about the pleasure with which he accepted the invitation.

After sitting in the drawing room for a suitable amount of time, talking meaninglessly about subjects that interested nobody, Mr. Darcy asked, "Do the restrictions upon Miss Elizabeth preclude her from taking the air in your garden, or further afield towards the gates? I know you enjoy your walks, Miss Elizabeth," he directed his attention to the young woman on the sofa at his side, "and I should be honoured to accompany you should you desire some exercise. The sky is clear and the air warm for this time of year, and we need not leave the immediate boundaries of the grounds."

Papa recalled Sir William's orders, and decided that it was permissible to venture from the house, but no further than the gate and the stone wall that encircled the house and its most proximate of lands.

Lizzy did not seem particularly pleased by this prospect. "I am content to remain in the house, Papa," she demurred, but her father flicked his wrist at her.

"Nonsense, Lizzy. You are as pale as a piece of linen. The air will do you good, and Mr. Darcy will ensure your safety and comfort. The man is only here to help, after all." He nodded at Mr. Darcy, and Mr. Darcy returned the gesture.

"Perhaps Miss Bennet and Bingley will join us," he suggested, "and Miss Mary." She tried to avoid his eye, but her mother clapped her hands and said that was a very fine idea indeed, since it would be an hour before they would go in to dine. "Run along and get your bonnet, Mary, for although the sun is weak, your face tends to freckle. Don't forget Lizzy's woollen wrap, for she only has her pelisse now that her walking cape is damaged and in Sir William's hands." She wrinkled her nose at the thought.

Mr. Darcy had been correct. The late afternoon weather was lovely, too much so to waste inside, and especially after the recent rains. After only a few short minutes in the gardens, Lizzy was already regaining her accustomed bloom and good humour. Mary grudgingly agreed that Mr. Darcy's idea had been a good one.

Jane and Bingley made a creditable attempt, at first, to remain with the other three, although they continually drifted ahead or behind as the party walked, and then had to hurry or linger to rejoin the group. Eventually, as they rounded some shrubbery that shielded the rest of the gardens from view of the house, their attempts became less and less sincere.

"Do you think," Jane ventured to suggest, "that I might see if any of the roses remain at the other end of the garden, where it is warm and protected by the courtyard near the kitchens? Perhaps..."

"I would be pleased to escort you, Miss Bennet," Bingley leapt to the suggestion, reminding Mary of a puppy dog eager to please its master.

"Lizzy?" Jane asked her sister. "Would you mind?"

"Go, Jane, and bring me a rose if any remain. I shall be quite well here with my present company."

Jane gave a sweet and pleasant smile, and Mr. Bingley's face took on the appearance of a boy presented with his own sweet pudding after dinner. They walked off in the appropriate direction, deep in conversation, leaving Mary alone with Lizzy and the proud man from Derbyshire.

They walked for some short distance, continuing the pleasant but meaningless conversation from the drawing room. Mr. Darcy paid particular attention to Lizzy, displaying to her all of his charm, but without ignoring Mary's presence or allowing his elegant and friendly façade to slip at all. Perhaps, Mary mused, it is not a façade at all, but the man himself, freed from the pressures forced upon him by a greater society. Lizzy seemed to grow easier in his presence as well, and Mary was well pleased to hear her sister laugh at a small joke or smile easily at a comment he made.

She briefly wondered if he, too, had courting on his mind and began to think of an excuse to wander a slight distance off— although not too far, for propriety must be observed!—but then recalled that Mr. Darcy had specifically requested her presence.

He broached the subject before she could ask after his purpose.

"Miss Mary, you must please allow me once more to apologise most abjectly for the behaviour of my friend this afternoon. Have you recounted the incident to Miss Elizabeth? Yes, I see you have. Then allow me to apologise to you both." He stopped in his path and gazed out over the low shrubs and beds of soil that would, in spring, erupt into a riot of flowers but that now sat brown and bare. Mary thought he might begin to scuff his elegant shoes through the dry dirt, but he remained still. Then he breathed deeply with his eyes closed, before turning to face and address his audience.

"When I call Mr. Lyons my friend, I am not overstating matters." He gestured forward, and the three began moving once more. As they walked, he continued speaking. "Although our first acquaintance was made through affairs of business, I quickly learned to trust his skills and grew to admire his character. He was the soul of discretion in a situation that required the utmost delicacy and..." Mr. Darcy paused again and ran a hand through his hair, disarranging it and making him, somehow, more appealing in his imperfection.

"Ladies," he sighed after a moment, "I feel I need to bring you into my confidence, for the matter might have some slight implication in recent affairs in Meryton. Is it too cold to sit? Yes, it is. The stone bench will soon become uncomfortable. Let us walk that way, through the small wilderness area, for what I have to say must remain between us." He offered an elbow to each lady, and led them along the autumn-brown pathway, speaking slowly and choosing each word with care.

"My sister, Georgiana, is very much my junior, not quite sixteen—very much of an age with Miss Lydia, I believe." Lizzy nodded and Mr. Darcy continued. "This past summer she convinced us to take her out of school and place her in the care of a companion, a lady who seemed most respectable, but in whose character we were greatly deceived. Instead of travelling to Pemberley, as had been the intention of all, Georgiana and Mrs. Younge disappeared."

Another disappearance! This certainly could not have any connection with the missing silverware and housemaid, but Mary looked at Mr. Darcy with a start. There were far too many coincidences in this whole affair. But his attention was on Elizabeth, and he seemed not to notice her reaction.

"We were frantic. I share guardianship of her with my cousin, a colonel in the regulars, and even with his remarkable resources throughout England, we could find no trace of her. At last, after three weeks of the greatest hell I can imagine," Mary gasped at the strength of his language, "I decided to find an investigator, someone who was skilled at discovering what my cousin and I could not. We needed a man not only adept at inquiry but also remarkable for his discretion and trustworthiness. Eventually I was given the direction of Mr. Lyons."

They had now reached the hedge that formed part of the enclosure about this section of the grounds, and Mr. Darcy chose a direction that led along a small pond, now brown and murky and covered with fallen leaves.

"My first impression, upon meeting Mr. Lyons, was not positive. He was dressed neatly enough, but in the garb of the working classes, with no taste or fashion, and he sounded like he had just been dragged across the length of Britain from a hovel in the wilds of Scotland. I was about to depart without ever stating my business, but I decided that if I were about to pay the man for his time in taking the appointment, I ought at least to sound him out about one or two smaller matters. Over the course of the conversation, I began to reassess my initial opinion of him."

"Mr. Darcy!" Lizzy chided, sounding almost like her impertinent self once more, "I cannot believe my ears! Did I not hear you confess, when Jane was ill at Netherfield, that your good opinion, once lost, was lost forever."

"Yes, well..." Mr. Darcy coughed and turned a rather becoming shade of red, before uttering a sound Mary had never heard from him before. Was that proud and aloof man chuckling? Now this was something for her diary! "What I ought to have said," he corrected, "was that in matters of character, I am hard pressed to forgive a serious lapse. I will own, with some embarrassment, to having been mistaken on one or two occasions about the nature of that character before having had a chance to truly appreciate it." He gazed at Lizzy, and to Mary's astonishment, Lizzy gazed back. Perhaps Lizzy's dislike of the man was not so vehement after all! It seemed Mr. Darcy might have reason to hope.

Mr. Darcy cleared his throat and led the ladies around the back of the pond, now heading towards the wilderness once more. "What I discovered was that I must not place such importance upon appearances. Mr. Lyons proved himself to be intelligent and observant, and remarkably well educated. By the end of our initial conversation I was no longer surprised to learn he had taken a degree at Glasgow, or to see him possessing the manners of a man of class and breeding. He has the makings of a real gentleman, never mind his Scotch speech and occasional rough ways.

"Not to belabour the point, he found my sister. He found her within four days, where we had toiled in futility for three weeks. She was discovered in Ramsgate, where her companion had taken her under a false name, and where she was all but ready to elope with a man in whose character I was not at all deceived. He cared not at all for her, but only for her dowry of thirty thousand pounds. This man you know: He is George Wickham of the militia now stationed in Meryton!"

"Mr. Wickham!" Lizzy gasped. "But he is so open and gentlemanly! It is you who have wronged him, by his accounts."

"I?" Mr. Darcy cocked his head. "I ought not to be surprised, although I cannot imagine what stories he has told of me this time. Was it something about a living I refused him? Or an inheritance that I denied him?" Lizzy nodded.

Mr. Darcy sighed. "I shall reveal the whole truth at some later date, when we have the luxury of time and when I can supply the people and documents to reinforce my claims. But suffice it to say, the man seldom utters a word of truth and strives to discredit me wherever he may, in revenge for my having foiled his plot with my dear sister." At this, he ended his speech and stared across the barren lands, defying the sisters to question his statements.

Lizzy seemed quite ready to believe the man, protesting Wickham's behaviour instead. "But he is such a gentleman, so gracious and gentlemanly in aspect, so..."

"So unlike myself?" Mr. Darcy's voice was gentle.

Lizzy paled and closed her eyes as she shook her head. "You must admit, Mr. Darcy, that you did not make a great effort to recommend yourself to our society."

"I did not, I'm afraid. I was still most heart-sore over the affair with Georgiana, which had only recently been concluded. Whilst she came to understand that Wickham never loved her and was content to use her to revenge himself upon me for sins I did not commit, she nonetheless wanted little of my company. She and her new companion—whom I investigated thoroughly through Mr. Lyons' services and who has proven herself as trustworthy as Mrs. Younge was not—did at last go to our country estate. Georgiana wished for time alone, far from the people who love her, but whose chastising glances and expressions of disappointment might interfere with her desire for a period of self-reflection. In short, I was cast from my own home and was in little mood for new company."

"Mr. Wickham is not the paragon of goodness he appears, then!" Mary spoke at last. "May I ask, what have been his other sins?"

Mr. Darcy's eyes widened in surprise at the question, then narrowed under furrowed brows as he grew thoughtful. "What have not been his sins?" he asked at last. "I shall not dive into particulars at the moment, but he is lustful, overly ambitious, lazy, indolent, and has a tendency to gamble away and lose any funds he happens to acquire. Is that enough for you, Miss Mary?"

"It certainly gives me a place to begin," she replied. "I asked because I believe Mr. Wickham might somehow be involved with Mr. Collins' murder."

Chapter Nine

Reconsidering Miss Mary

After Darcy left to pay his call upon the Bennets, Alexander summoned Thorne and asked if he might find some liniment to help soothe his aching hip, now darkening into a rather alarming shade of purple. Thorne returned a few minutes later with a jar full of some reeking herbs and oils and commanded Alexander to lie upon the bed so that the valet might apply the potion to his bruises and aching spine. The combination of the hot bath, cool beer, and tasty cheese, along with the masterful strokes of Thorne's skilled hands as they massaged the liniment into the bruised muscles of Alexander's back and side, soon sent him into a deep slumber. He knew not when Thorne completed his ministrations and left, or when he returned with another tray of biscuits and a small decanter of wine, but it was full dark when Alexander opened his eyes once more.

He was, at first, disoriented. Where was this fine and comfortable bed upon which he lay, half undressed? What was that awful smell, and why did he ache so very much? Within moments he recalled the very long and tiring day, and with it, his mission. He tentatively began moving, one muscle at a time, testing each for its degree of pain, until he was seated on the side of the bed. His hip, whilst still tender to the extreme, did not present him with quite the level of agony he had expected, and despite the pain, it moved well and supported his weight with no additional complaints. The low fire in the grate offered enough light for him to locate an oil lamp, which he soon lit, then checked his pocket watch. Nine o'clock; too late for the dinner he had no intention of joining, too early for Darcy to have returned, and too early to return to the bed to complete his night's slumber. He was also, he realised as he spotted the tray with the biscuits, hungry.

He dressed with only a few expletives and brushed his hair into some semblance of respectability. His appearance would only confirm the Bingleys' impression of him as a heathen from the wilds, but he was not improperly dressed in any way, and he sought few favours from the haughty sisters or the lacklustre Hurst. Whether Bingley himself had returned, Alexander knew not, but understood enough from Darcy that the man would be unlikely to condemn him on this basis of his dishevelled appearance.

The hallway outside his room was empty, but the house was not so very large that he could not find the kitchens without a guide. He descended the grand stairs with only mild discomfort and made his way to where he knew the dining room lay, adjoining the breakfast room where he had first encountered the ladies of the house only that morning.

Although the primary means of access to the breakfast room was through the grand dining room, it might also be entered from a short hallway that bent around what must be the butler's pantry. A man might stand there, beyond the small L of the hallway, and not be seen or heard. What this could mean for his investigations, Alexander knew not, but it was an interesting item to store away in his memory. If he had located the dining room and breakfast room, the kitchens must be very close. And indeed, it seemed that the breakfast room also served as a servery for larger parties, for a back door, disguised as yet another moulded wall panel, opened almost directly into the kitchens.

It was through this door that Alexander passed, greeting maids and off-duty footmen as he traversed into the main kitchen at the very back of the house. A rotund woman of indeterminate age and a cheerful face greeted him askance until he explained his situation and mission.

"Slept all afternoon after a spill and now wantin' warm food for your bones, is that it?" she teased. "Well, I reckon I might be able to help. Sit yourself down at the table and I'll see what's still in the pot." She strode across to the large contraption beside the dying fire. Of course Netherfield would have a modern piece of equipment like this cooking range! Three large pots still sat atop the iron plate, although the coal fire that provided the heat had long since died out. The woman lifted one lid, and the kitchen was immediately filled with the aroma of a hot stew.

"No stew, thank you, but a pot of warm tea if you don't mind. And are those green beans in sauce that I see in that bowl?".

"Will that do you?" she asked as she served some of the beans onto a delicate plate. "I've some onion tart as well, and a piece of the herb pie, and oh, there is some cod in lemon butter that the master enjoys." Alexander's wide eyes and great smile answered her question. She filled the plate, and handed it to him along with more bread and cheese, and then sat herself down at the table across from him. "You must be Mr. Darcy's friend," she began. "You can't be anyone else, for none other is expected here, and the mistress's sort would never venture into the kitchens as long as there's a maid or footman to do her running for her. I do not believe Miss Bingley even knows where the kitchens are, for all that she's been in the house since Michaelmas! Only one who ever lowers himself to enter the kitchens is Mr. Hurst, and only then because he doesn't like to wait." She leaned over towards Alexander and whispered loudly, "That's why I've still got the stew on the heat, for he comes and goes from here at all strange times. Trying to avoid Mrs. Hurst, no doubt." She grinned at her joke.

She helped herself to a piece of dinner roll from a basket that sat atop the table and continued. "We're chatting like old friends." Alexander agreed with a firm nod, although he had been eating rather than talking. "Mrs. Slougham's the name. I've been cook at Netherfield through for nigh thirty years, for all the families who've lived here. They seem to appreciate my cooking, for whilst I am a modest woman in many ways, I know I'm one of the best!"

Alexander could not help but agree, for the food was excellent. With his mouth still full, he gestured his agreement with a generous series of nods.

"I know what you're doing for Miss Lizzy," the cook said, "and it's appreciated. Why, I was talkin' to Miss Mary only this very afternoon. They're good girls, for all that the younger ones can be very silly. They're not proud or uppity like..." she stopped short. "I ought not to speak of the mistress like that. I can trust a good fellow like you to be discrete, I'm sure!"

Miss Mary again. Would he never be rid of her? An uncomfortable prickling in his conscience reminded him that he would not be so vexed by the mention of her name had he not been so unaccountably rude to her that afternoon. It was true that she had returned his entreaties with a forthrightness that was quite unseemly in a lady, but perhaps he might have behaved with a bit more decorum. He might have been more gentlemanlike. His head throbbed anew thinking about their confrontation. And what on earth had he been thinking when he denied being a Christian? Such a blasphemy would see him sent immediately out of the village. Miss Mary, with her pontificating and her omnipresent bible or book of sermons, would surely have the news all over Meryton by morning.

Mrs. Slougham interrupted his thoughts by asking if he wished for more food, or perhaps a cup of tea or some sweets left over from dinner. These all sounded quite the thing, and as they waited for the pot on the fire to come to a boil, the cook inquired after his injuries. They fell into an easy conversation, and were indeed conversing like old friends, the tea and cakes long since consumed, when the back door to the kitchen opened and Mr. Darcy and Mr. Bingley tumbled through. Their voices were at first unaccountably loud, and then suddenly very quiet as they saw the kitchen not quite as abandoned as they might have supposed. Alexander did not require his detecting skills to determine that the men had been enjoying a drink or two before departing Longbourn.

"What ho, Lyons!" Darcy beamed. The effect, so unexpected on his normally dour and reserved face, was somewhat jarring. "Lyons, you have not met Bingley. Bingley stayed for dinner as well," he added unnecessarily. "Charles, allow me the pleasure," and he completed the introductions with an aplomb that bespoke the elegance of completely ingrained manners.

Now Alexander had the opportunity to observe Charles Bingley first-hand. He had heard much of the young man, but until now had not met him. He was pleased with what he saw. The man was handsome enough, if one were inclined to be interested in such details, and effusive in his friendliness. Although many men increase in affability when in their cups, he suspected that for Bingley, sociability was as much a part of his being as were his light brown hair and blue eyes. He welcomed Alexander like a long-lost friend and inquired after health, happiness, and various relations of whom he had never heard. Being from the North of England himself, Bingley made no comment about Alexander's Scotch speech, other than to say how it reminded him somewhat of home, thereby serving to draw the men together rather than emphasise their differences. How Bingley would treat him once sober morning came, Alexander could not predict, but for the nonce he was happy to engage in pleasant camaraderie and forget his aches and bruises.

It was near midnight before Bingley announced he was to bed, leaving Darcy and Alexander in the kitchen alone. Mrs. Slougham had bid the men goodnight a long while before, trusting that they would not burn down the house in her absence.

"We ought to get our sleep as well, Lyons," Darcy said as they watched Bingley's back disappear through the door that led to the breakfast room. "It was an early start and a busy day, although you appear to have had some rest. Tomorrow will be long again, but I have hopes of progress." He stood and stretched, his long arms nearly touching the high ceiling. "But before we part ways, I must tell you this. As we discussed, I spoke to Miss Mary," Alexander stifled a groan, "and I offered a first apology on your behalf. I assured her you would do likewise in the flesh come morning, but Alexander, I really do think you ought to hear the girl out. She is wiser than she seems, and more liberal of thought that you would imagine. She offered me one or two of her thoughts and observations on the affair, and she has information that might be of real value."

"And Miss Elizabeth?" Alexander had to ask this delicate question. "Has she improved her opinion of you?"

Darcy stretched once more. "She was not well pleased to see me when first I entered, but we were able to talk. Miss Mary accompanied us, and she was party to the conversation. I told them—I felt I had no choice if I wished to gain their complete trust—about the affair with my sister this past summer. Much of Miss Elizabeth's disdain of me seemed to have sprung from tales told her by Wickham."

Alexander's eyes flicked open. "Wickham? So that is why the village dislikes you so! 'Twas not only your own miserable behaviour towards them, but a good set of derogatory tales spread by that bounder."

Darcy gave a wry smile. "I was relieved to set the story right on that account, at least. Miss Elizabeth and Miss Mary know all now. When I completed the accounting, Miss Elizabeth seemed less inclined to dislike me. I hope..." He ran a hand through his unruly hair. "I hope that after a night's pondering on my tale, she will reconsider more of her initial impressions. May this be so."

"Did the lady give any indication of this?"

With a glint in his eye, Darcy nodded. "Perhaps she did. She talked easily with me after I confessed the sorry tale, and even Mrs. Bennet smiled at me as the evening progressed. As I took my leave, I suggested a visit in the morning, to which Miss Elizabeth readily agreed. Come with me; we may talk further about the situation, and whilst I attempt to woo the lady, you may press Miss Mary for what information she may choose to give you. Unless," he quipped as he followed Bingley's path out of the kitchen, "she has changed her mind."

The next time Alexander opened his eyes, he was less disoriented but much more sore than the previous evening. His bed was just as comfortable as he had first determined, but he could hardly find a position that did not trouble him, and so eventually he gave up all attempts at further sleep and rose for the day. The sun was still very low in the eastern sky, and the rosy fingers of dawn were still caressing the dried leaves and empty fields. His watch told him it was not quite seven o'clock. Although he suspected the hallways would be empty, the other residents of Netherfield still lost to slumber, he cracked the door nevertheless to seek signs of life. To his surprise, Thorne was waiting for him in the corridor.

"Good morning, Mr. Lyons," the valet greeted him. "Mr. Darcy requested that I see to your needs this morning. May I assist you with a shave, or another treatment of liniment for your injuries? Would you prefer tea or coffee?"

Alexander had never before envied the very wealthy or the upper classes, but at this moment he understood completely the luxury of being so pampered. He loathed the notion that some men were born to serve and others to be served, and yet he found he had no difficulties in submitting to Thorne's exceptional care. Further, he realised, to someone who had been raised with such indulgences as a natural part of life, his own tendencies towards a more pluralistic society must seem quite unnatural. If only the upper classes were not such a useless lot!

And so it was with only a small amount of guilt that he submitted most willingly as he was shaven with expert precision, treated once more to the stink of the soothing balm that calmed his aches, dressed in a suit of clothing that certainly had not come from his own small travel trunk, and was offered a selection of hot drinks and sweet pastries as he prepared for his day.

Being so elegantly engaged is a time-consuming endeavour, and it was nearly eight o'clock when he finally hobbled down the last of the stairs and across the house to the breakfast room. He was amazed to see Darcy already there, a cup of tea in one hand and a newspaper in the other. How in the world had Darcy managed his *habille* without his valet? Thorne had been attending

Alexander until mere minutes before. Could it be that the man could actually dress himself? Upon close regard, Alexander thought that Darcy's cravat was, perhaps, slightly less perfect than was his wont, and the knot more simple. His estimation of his haughty friend rose a degree or two.

"I had expected you earlier," Darcy offered by way of a greeting. "I suppose Thorne took his time with your shave and with your injuries. How do you fare today? You certainly seem to be walking easily."

"I must swallow my words and my pride," Alexander agreed. "I took far too much pleasure in the luxuries of my toilette this morning. Thank you for sending him to me. When he began massaging the liniment into my hip, I thought I might scream from the pain, but now it is much easier. I shall have to apologise for any rough words that might have escaped my lips."

"I am glad to see you improved. Have you eaten in your chamber? Good, for we have a long day. It is far too early for a social call, but I believe it is not too early to request an interview with Miss Mary concerning her sister's fate. Can you ride or shall we take a gig?"

After a brief battle with his pride, Alexander opted for the gig. He did not repent this decision, for the discomfort he experienced in alighting the small vehicle was only a taste of what hoisting himself onto a horse would likely have brought. Even after a good sleep and the benefits of Thorne's therapy that morning, every bump, and rut under the gig's wheels jarred his joints and sent small spasms through aching muscles. The pain would ease as he moved about through the day, but this short ride on horseback would have left him unfit for company, and even now he knew he would have to fight with his nature to offer Miss Mary the apology she was owed.

Their arrival at Longbourn was not met with delight from the housekeeper, who responded to their knock at the main door. "Mr. Darcy, Mr. Lyons," she greeted them through tight lips. "The family is not yet receiving company. Shall I tell Mr. Bennet you called?"

"This is not a social call, but one of business—the very serious matter of Mr. Collins' death," Darcy began. The housekeeper narrowed her eyes at him but did not slam the door closed.

"I will see them, Hill," a woman's voice came from inside the house. Miss Elizabeth walked into view behind the gatekeeper. She had done her hair so as to cover some of the bruise about her eye, and a heavy shawl was draped over her scratched arms. "Mary is awake as well. I am accustomed to walking in the mornings, and although my habits of wandering have been curtailed, my habit of rising early has not."

Hill's expression eased somewhat, and she opened the door wider to allow the men entrance. At a quiet request from Elizabeth, she disappeared toward the back of the house, and Elizabeth herself led the men into the same bright parlour where they had met the previous day. In the sunny room, Alexander could see the bruises were starting to fade; he still wished to make a closer examination of the lady's arms, to compare any cuts with the blood stains he had seen on her walking cape. He would make his improper request when Miss Elizabeth was more at ease in his company.

Mary was seated on one of the sofas. Her expression upon seeing Alexander was icy and disdainful, but she greeted Darcy with a friendly smile and a pleasant word. Alexander cleared his throat. This was something he need best get done, and done quickly. As soon as the ladies turned their attention to him, he began to grovel.

"Miss Mary," he entreated, "I owe you the most profound of apologies. My behaviour towards you yesterday was absolutely unkind and unprovoked, and I am heartily ashamed of myself. I was wrong in my every thought and every word. I cannot expect your forgiveness, but I would be most grateful were you to grant it. And I would also very much like to hear what you wished to tell me." He looked down at his hands. "I am your servant."

How those last words grated, and yet how true they were. The trite expression, uttered so unthinkingly by gentleman and dandies across the realm, meant nothing to them apart from a phrase of salutation or desire to be of use. But to Alexander, sitting across from these ladies of the gentry, they were more correct than polite. He was, to them and to all their landholding race, a servant, a tool through which to achieve a desired end. He was a plaything to him, to be dallied with and tolerated for as long as he was entertaining or of use, as a spoiled child would treat a toy, then to be discarded and forgotten as soon as his usefulness was over. He could be bought with their unearned wealth—indeed, his livelihood depended on as much—and then tossed into the gutters without a thought. He depended on them, and he despised them for their uselessness. As much as his work brought him into the presence of the upper classes, the distinction of rank never failed to eat at him, and he resented both himself and his audience for it.

Whether Miss Mary read any of his thoughts on his face, he knew not. By the time he raised his eyes again, hers were elsewhere. In a voice as cold as her expression she replied to his grovel, "Your words were harsh and cruel, but Mr. Darcy explained your situation and your injuries. Whether I shall forgive you, I cannot say, for you wounded me sorely and my anger is not yet abated. But," she added as Alexander sought a suitable response, "I shall tell you of my thoughts."

She put down the book she had been holding—a book of sermons, Alexander noted—and gestured to the chair upon which her mother had been seated the previous day. With a bow, Alexander accepted, and they all sat in awkward silence for a moment until Hill brought in a tray of tea and breakfast buns and then disappeared back into her demesne. Whilst Mary served the tea with a sure hand, Alexander watched in amusement as Darcy seated himself upon the same sofa as Miss Elizabeth. This lady, at least, seemed not unpleased with her company. Miss Elizabeth had experienced something of a change of heart since he last observed her with his friend. He waited for the couple to tacitly negotiate a suitable distance between them before he took out his notepad and bade Miss Mary offer her observations.

"You may think my ideas of little value, Mr. Lyons," she began, "but I believe otherwise. It is for Elizabeth alone that I offer them to you." She stared at him, and he was struck by the cold fire in her eyes. For all that she might play the part of the forgotten sibling in the family, she could be a forceful young woman when the need arose.

"The first matter that drew my attention was the disappearing candlesticks."

Alexander kept his groan internal. A useless skirt who had read too many Gothic romances, he determined. Nonetheless, he dutifully wrote down *missing candlesticks* upon his notepad.

"Robinson, who acts as butler when the need arises, told me of a series of pieces of silver going astray. They were small items at first, but the most recent was a set of elaborate candlesticks that stood on the floor, and were over three feet in height, of silver and encrusted with gemstones and decorated with the finest artwork. He believes they are worth around eighty pounds."

Alexander's head snapped up. This was not idle fantasy. He wrote *speak to Robinson,* and stared at Mary with raised brows and his mouth agape. She gave a smug grimace and related all that had heard from the butler, whilst Alexander scribbled in his book.

"But it was not only candlesticks that had gone missing," she continued. "One of the maids has also disappeared."

"Surely housemaids are known to wander off on some whim or to meet a lover, and then return when their situations require it," he blurted.

"Polly did not seem that sort of girl." Her eyes defied him to object again.

Now Alexander's internal groan was for his own lack of civility. He would never ingratiate himself to Miss Mary at this rate, and he wondered why the thought bothered him. But he turned a civil face to her nonetheless and asked, "In what way, Miss Mary?"

She spoke of the maid's reputation for avoiding trouble and for working hard and suggested that Mrs. Slougham might relate any particulars the gentlemen—she narrowed her eyes at the word— wished to examine. "What I found most strange, however, was the coincidence of the two unusual events. And then, I realised that there were three such odd happenings, for nobody in Meryton can recall the last time a clergyman - or anybody - was slain in the vicinity. And when I thought further, I realised there were not only three, but rather four strange events at play." She recounted the suggestion that Lieutenant Wickham had been heard threatening the missing maid, and that later on he may have been involved in an argument at Netherfield with none other than the slain parson.

By the time she had completed her accounting of yesterday's queries, Alexander was feeling mightily ashamed of himself, a sentiment which he shared with the ladies. "I can only plead self-pity in the face of my recent injuries, Miss Mary. You have learned more to further this inquiry than did all of my investigations yesterday." He turned to a new page. "Tell me more about Mr. Wickham. What have been your reflections on him?"

Mary's eyes lost a layer of ice. "My thoughts on the lieutenant have changed rather considerably over the course of the past day, Mr. Lyons. What I discovered through Mrs. Slougham and the staff at Netherfield shook my initial impressions, and the confidence Mr. Darcy shared about his sister last evening completely destroyed them."

"I had to tell them, Lyons," Darcy interjected. "I wished them to understand the man better, and to understand my complete faith in you, as an investigator and as a man of good character."

This was a compliment beyond measure, for Darcy did not grant his respect or admiration easily. "So I see. Did you tell them all? Or only about his attentions to your sister?"

"Is there more to know?" Miss Elizabeth's voice was urgent. Alexander wondered what her relationship with the disgraced officer had been? Surely there had been no manner of attachment, had there?

Darcy coughed and requested more tea, which he held stationary in his hands and explained, "Wickham seems to have made a career in trying to extract funds from me. He was a favourite of my father, but upon each gift of money he merely gambled it away and then came back for more, pressing some claim that not even he believed was legitimate. The most recent plea involved the request for the living near Pemberley, although he had previously professed a distaste for joining the clergy and had wished to study the law instead." Darcy shook his head and sighed. "It was after this that he attempted his elopement with my sister."

"But why," Miss Elizabeth asked again, "was he not taken to task for his involvement in Miss Darcy's elopement? Were his crimes not actionable?"

Darcy shook his head. "Alas, no. For all that he is the worst sort of man, there is no law at the moment against visiting Ramsgate or wooing an heiress. Even Mrs. Younge escaped with nothing more than a dismissal, for her actions were reprehensible but within the law."

"And this is why Wickham now graces our town with his presence," Mary spoke again. "He is in need of funds, and a commission in the militia will pay his way and preserve some sort of standing in society."

"So it seems." Darcy gave a great frown and stared into the empty fireplace. His word on the matter was final.

"I cannot see the connections right now," Alexander scratched at his chin, "but I must make inquiries into Wickham's whereabouts on the day of the murder."

Mary gave a great smile that changed her face. For a moment, Alexander thought her lovelier than Jane. "There I can help you. After Mr. Darcy and Mr. Bingley departed last night, I sent a note to Mrs. Forster, lately wed to the colonel who commands the regiment. Through her, I discovered that Mr. Wickham had been sent to London on matters of military business, and he was to remain there until some meetings were concluded, after which he would have a response to return to Colonel Forster. That meeting only took place last night, if Mrs. Forster's note is to be believed."

"Then our scoundrel was away in London on the day that Collins died, and cannot be guilty for that crime, no matter his others." Darcy's voice was rueful.

Whatever Mary might have been about to add was cut short as Mrs. Hill appeared at the door to the drawing room. "Excuse me, Mr. Lyons, but there is an urgent message for you come from London. Mr. Bingley sent a boy. Will you see him in my office?"

"Indeed, Mrs. Hill," Alexander leapt up from his chair. "Darcy, will you join me? It may be the information I requested before we departed Town."

Chapter Ten

Messages From London

Mrs. Hill's office was small but sufficient for three men to sit in some comfort. Alexander and Darcy sat across from each other at the sturdy oak desk and pored over the stack of notes that lay between them. As Alexander had surmised, his scribbled requests on the eve of their departure had borne fruit, and the express rider from Town had handed them over to one of Bingley's own men upon his hurried arrival at Netherfield only a half hour before.

"I see your plan is to empty my purse into the pockets of every inquiry agent and messenger in London," Darcy joked. "Am I to gain profit from my expenditures?"

Alexander did not smile, but nodded with a serious expression. "Aye. Look at this." He handed a folded note across to his companion.

Darcy gave a low whistle. "Bennet has made some poor investments. How much money did he lose on that venture?

Surely that's the entirety of his daughters' dowries." He let the note lie on the table between them. "And yet, I cannot see how it relates to Collins' death. Surely it would now have been to the man's benefit for Miss Elizabeth to accept her cousin, for it would secure the other girls' futures to some small degree, at least."

Darcy scanned the documents on the table. "Anything here about the entail on Longbourn? That might have some bearing on the situation." He ran a hand through them, but there was nothing on the outside of each small note indicating what might be inside.

"Nothing yet," Alexander replied, following suit and picking up notes at random to scan.

Alexander unfolded another note and perused the contents. "Wickham is known in all manner of gambling establishments in Town, it seems, and has debts at more than one of them."

"That is not so surprising. Many men of my acquaintance do." Darcy picked up a second note with the same seal as Alexander's and pointed to it, explaining, "Even amongst the few men you specified, several have such a record to their names." He glanced down at the paper he held and read out, "Sir William Lucas, Mr. Philips, Colonel Forster himself, Mr. Durham from Bowridge—that's about five miles yonder—even Hurst. It seems only Bingley and I are free from such vices, and that only because I admonished Charles never to enter into the gaming halls." He scanned the note and looked up at Alexander. "I see you strewed your seeds wide, for I have hardly heard of some of these men." He perused the paper more carefully. "Ah, these are men who have been known to visit the establishments. Not all have debts. I should be most disappointed to learn so much about Sir William or the local colonel. But the point remains. As much as I wish the man to the devil, Wickham's name on such a sheet is no indication of guilt. Would that it were so."

"Ah, but hear this, Darcy." Alexander's eyes traced over the note he was holding. "Wickham's debts had been increasing steadily for some time, until he was in danger of being refused from the establishments and sought for debtor's prison, but..." he held in his hand the second sheet of the document, "of late he has been repaying what he owes in large and regular remittances. He is getting money from somewhere, and judging from the amount, not from his income from the militia."

"Is that so?" Darcy stared and chewed his lip.

"That is, indeed, so."

Mary listened to the accounting of the notes from London with rapt attention. For all that she might bend the ear of a serving maid or sit quietly and hear sordid secrets whispered by matrons, she could never elicit the sorts of details that Mr. Lyons did. She had neither the acquaintances who might seek out such information nor the weight of consequence to command them. For the first time in her life she wished she were a man who might come and go and meet the people he pleased and make the arrangements he pleased. Perhaps through her Uncle Gardiner in London, she might have access to the people who could learn such details for her, but how long that might take, she dared not think. By the time she received even one response to an inquiry, Lizzy might be tried and found guilty and hanged!

"Let me be certain I understand this," she said, her gaze directly on the two men seated across the low tea table from her. "Mr. Wickham had been in debt to the amount of several thousand pounds, and suddenly and unaccountably is paying them off, fifty pounds at a time. That is a lot of money for a man of no fortune." She watched as both men nodded. "When did this turn of luck begin for him?"

She watched as the investigator examined the notes once more. "Since the first week of September."

Mr. Darcy hemmed and mused, "That is a month after the… incident at Ramsgate. Georgiana was still in a dreadful state and begged me to leave her in peace for a time. That is almost exactly when Bingley announced he had let Netherfield and invited me to stay for a time to help him learn something of managing an estate. I recall how relieved I was at the time to have some useful employment, so I should not chew up London with my shoes in worry about my sister up at Pemberley with no one but her new companion for company. We spent three weeks in London arranging matters from there, before removing to Netherfield at the end of the month. How strange the coincidence of timing."

"Strange indeed." Mary hardly heard the words as they escaped her breath. "But what has any of this to do with Mr. Collins?" She spoke more loudly and Alexander responded with a sigh.

"That is an excellent question, and one to which I hope we soon have an answer."

Any further conversation between the four was cut off as Mrs. Bennet and Jane entered the drawing room. Mrs. Bennet seemed much more pleased to see Mr. Darcy than she had the previous day; Jane's eyes scoured the room and the assembled group and then settled on Lizzy as her beautiful face fell into a slight moue of disappointment.

Mr. Darcy took in her unstated question immediately. "Good morning, Mrs. Bennet, Miss Bennet," he greeted the two ladies. "Forgive us for imposing upon your hospitality at so early an hour, but our inquiries cannot be delayed. Mr. Bingley," he glanced toward Jane, "expressed an interest in joining our small party, but he elected to wait until a more fashionable hour. He asked me to convey his compliments, and his wishes to offer them himself at a convenient time." Jane's face relaxed into its accustomed serene repose.

Soon the other girls joined the gathering in the drawing room, and even Mr. Bennet poked his head in to investigate the sound of so many people talking. "Oh, Mr. Darcy, Mr. Lyons!" He seemed surprised to see them, although Mary knew he had been expecting an early visit. "What news? Any forwarder in your inquiries?"

"We are, perhaps, making some progress." Mr. Lyons rose to shake the gentleman's hand. "A few moments of your time, perhaps?" Mr. Darcy began to stand, but his friend stayed him with a gesture, suggesting that the gentleman from Derbyshire ought rather to stay with the ladies.

Mary watched as her father's face blanched at the request. "Er… Yes, yes, of course. In my office." He indicated the direction with an open hand but a worried face. She leapt up and asked, "May I join you?"

Her father scowled. "No, Mary, this is most irregular. I am certain that whatever Mr. Lyons wishes to discuss need not involve you."

"In a way it does, sir." He murmured something into Mr. Bennet's ear, and her father at once grew even paler, but also less tense. This was a surprise! Mary had not expected Mr. Lyons to take her part in any of this affair, for all that she had refused to accept his apology. He had, she admitted to herself, been making a concerted effort to act the gentleman this morning, and she was relieved that he had disclosed the contents of his messages from London to her. They might never enjoy each other's company, but he seemed to have accepted her role in this task they had in common, and for that she was appreciative.

Her father stared at Mr. Lyons after his quiet invocation and seemed uncertain how to respond. At length, however, he conceded. "Very well. This is not news for a lady's ears, but neither is it detrimental to her moral fibre. And of that, Mary has more than most. Very well, child, but you will not like what you hear."

More curious than troubled, Mary quickly took her leave of her sisters and scurried after the men towards her father's study.

She always felt like a child in this room. While hardly a sacred space where none but the initiate may enter, the study was nevertheless her father's own and private space. Where the rest of the house was a boisterous and busy place, adorned with the trappings of feminine affectation and ringing with the sounds of women's voices and girl-like squabbles and arguments, her father's study was dark and sombre and masculine and very quiet. The books that lined the walls provided as much respite from the noise as solace to the mind, and a faint smell of pipe tobacco and heavy port hung in the air, even on the clearest days when the windows were open to the sky.

Papa took his accustomed chair and indicated to Mr. Lyons to take the one across from him. Mary took a small seat off to the side of the desk and sat as still as she was able, hoping that her powers of invisibility might wash over her, allowing the men to talk as if she were not there.

Her father sat very still for some moments, eying his foe and sizing him up, and Mary began to wonder if either man would speak. At last her father broke the silence. "You have learned about my investments."

Mr. Lyons nodded, his face devoid of emotion. "Did you undertake them on your own initiative, or on the advice of another?"

The older man stared out the window as he spoke. "I thought I had done my research. I've always considered myself a bit of a scholar, and felt that I knew everything, but in truth I ought to have listened to my brother Gardiner when he suggested staying away from the steam horses until the technology is better developed. But they sounded so interesting, and I do believe they will be the way of the future. Perhaps a private investment with an inventor would have been a better choice, or something in the sugar islands... But what's done is done. I'm sorry, Mary. Do not tell your sisters yet, but I lost your dowry. I lost everyone's dowries. I ought to have insisted that Lizzy marry her cousin, for whatever good that would have done us. He's dead now, although he may not have been had she accepted." He hung his head, but whether in shame or helplessness she could not determine.

Mr. Lyons cocked his head and creased his brows at this strange statement, and Mary found herself staring at her father. What on earth had he meant by that? Mr. Lyons asked the very question, to which Mary's father merely replied, "That is, he might not have been in that field at that particular time." She had to accept the answer for what it was, but something seemed not quite right about it. It brought her to mind of Lizzy's slightly evasive responses to any questioning as to her encounter with Mr. Collins in the field. The odd prickling sensation ran up Mary's spine once more. Were these two more pieces to the unknown charade? As much as it might cause her sister grief, she must press for the truth of what occurred that afternoon.

Mr. Lyons had a further question. "Tell me about the entail on Longbourn, sir. Specifically, who is the next heir presumptive? I can request this information from my agents in London easily enough, but if you have the answer, it will save us both time and resources."

Her papa rose from his chair and walked to one of the bookshelves, from which he drew a large and slim book. Bringing it to his desk, he then opened it to the page he sought. It was, Mary could see, a list of names and dates. She had never seen this volume before, and it intrigued her.

"Sons seem to be a scarce commodity in my line," he grimaced. "This is an accounting of all the relations from my father's side of the family, to the best of our knowledge." He pointed to a name part way up one page. "This was my grandfather, John, for whom Jane was named. I knew him, for I was almost a man when he died. He had two siblings, both sisters. My father was the second son, but his older brother drowned, leaving him master of Longbourn. And as you know, Mary, I have but one sibling, your aunt Rose. And so we must retreat a generation. Let me see..." He scanned up the page until he found another name.

"Here, this is my great-grandfather, and here, this is my grandfather's brother from a second marriage. When my great-grandfather died, the young William was taken in by his wife's brother, who was childless, whereupon he took the uncle's name of Collins." Mary stood with wide eyes as her father drew a finger along one name and then the other. "He had one son, also William. This is where the rift in the family began, for William thought he had a claim on Longbourn, for he could not find the marriage lines for my great-grandmother. It came to nothing until his son—the recently departed parson's father—took up this claim and even pressed it as far as the courts in London. The suit was dismissed, of course, but the damage to the family had been done. More to the point, however, is that there were no other sons but this one line."

And so he went, back one generation and another, finding no cadet branches extant, no hitherto unremembered cousins. "Unless there is some part of the family of whom I know nothing and have no records, it would appear that I am the last male of my line. With me, the Bennets shall cease." He fell into a chair and drew a hand across his eyes.

"Do you have the original deed of Longbourn, or any documentation concerning the entail?" Mr. Lyons' voice sounded strange in the sudden silence of the room.

"No. Perhaps Philips has them. I've searched my papers for long enough in hopes of breaking that wretched entail." He opened his eyes and glared at Mr. Lyons, softening his gaze when his eyes alit on Mary. "The Bennets' tenure at Longbourn shall cease... Leave me. This is something I have known, but hearing it from my own lips gives me pause and I would ponder in silence. Close the door, Mary." And so summarily, they were dismissed.

"What happens to the entail, then?" Mary asked as they walked back towards the drawing room.

"That is something we shall need to learn," replied her companion, "for there is no one solution in the law. The outcome depends entirely upon the specifics of the deed and the nature of the entail. We shall require the documents or good records of them to find this solution."

The man was vexing, but he had a remarkably thorough knowledge of legal matters. He must, Mary deemed, have come across such things in his career as an investigator. How strange that the entail should be so uncertain in its conclusion.

"Indeed, we must find the records," she agreed, "for the answer will have import far beyond Lizzy's predicament." She stopped and let out a large sigh. "This is my future, and that of my mother and each of my sisters. But we shall find it together," she brightened, forgetting for a moment that they disliked each other immensely and were only tolerating each other's presence.

The drawing room was now abuzz with the sounds of voices. Mr. Bingley had arrived whilst Mary and Mr. Lyons were discussing the disastrous investments and Bennet family tree, and Mama was doing everything in her power to force the newcomer into closer and closer proximity to Jane. From what Mary could see, her efforts were scarcely needed, for Bingley was in the process of making some excuse to move from his seat by the fire to the empty space on the sofa beside the eldest daughter of the house. Mr. Darcy was still seated beside Elizabeth, and they were talking quietly with Jane and the newcomer.

"Oh, Mary, you're back. And Mr. Lyons. What a merry party we are! We should have such a fine gathering on more occasions," she offered. Mary was mortified. Had her mother completely forgotten the very reason for so many men to be within the walls of Longbourn? It was only due to the murder of Mr. Collins and the danger to Elizabeth that there were visitors at all, for as a rule, young men almost never came by to call unless by invitation from her father to hunt or play at cards or chess.

Mary stopped her companion with a touch to his arm. "Mr. Lyons," she murmured quietly, so as not to be heard by her mother, "I believe we need to speak further with my sister. Shall we attempt to do so now? Perhaps the excuse of a walk in the sunshine will provide an innocent enough explanation to Mama for an absence of some time. If what I believe is indeed true, Mama's nerves would far outshine Lizzy's confession."

The investigator nodded. "These were my very thoughts." Aloud, he greeted Bingley and asked after the man's health ("Well enough, thank you,") and suggested a stroll in the gardens. The sun was indeed bright and the pleasant weather still holding over the area. It was late November; there would be rains and cold aplenty soon enough, and one must enjoy the outdoors whilst one may.

"A capital idea!" cooed Mrs. Bennet. "Run along and find your bonnet, Jane. The warm one, so you do not catch cold, for Mr. Bingley would not like you with a red nose!" ("Indeed, Madam, I would find Miss Bennet lovely with a red nose for every day of the year!") "And Lizzy, you must take Lydia's cape, for yours was covered with blood and Sir William has it now. No, Lydia, I shall not have you crying, for you were to stay inside and help Kitty with the sewing. Oh, and Mary." Her mother blinked as if she had quite forgotten the existence of her middle daughter. "Yes, you had better go as well, to keep Mr. Lyons company. Don't forget your boots. And take a shawl."

With greater alacrity than decorum, the six were soon wrapped in their warm outerclothes and strolling through the gardens close to the house. Mary could see her father through the window to his study, but whether he noticed the small party of walkers, she knew not, for he stood still and did not respond to her small wave. As they had done the previous day, they strolled past the wall of shrubbery, and then separated into two groups once more, Jane and Bingley heading in one direction, the other four towards the pond again.

"There is a small gardener's shed yonder past the wilderness," Mary suggested as they wandered down the brown path, past autumn-bare twigs and the skeletal remains of the summer's foliage. "We may sit in there in warmth, if not the greatest comfort. For Lizzy," she reached for her sister's hand, "I believe you still have something to tell us."

Lizzy did not speak, but her eyes grew shiny with tears, and Mary knew she had been correct in her suppositions.

The shed, as Mary had predicted, was soon warm. There was a small coal stove in the centre of the cosy space, which filled the room with its heat only minutes after being lit. "In the spring, the gardener starts his seeds here, and needs to keep the space warm through late spring frosts," she explained to Mr. Lyons, who rolled his eyes at her in response. He was infuriating, this London investigator, with his uncultured habits and his crude speech. He could be interesting company at times, she admitted, but did he have to be so rough in his manners? A gentleman would never deign to roll his eyes at a lady! He would never dare express such contempt for a comment that was only intended to elucidate!

Then a horrid realisation visited her. She had, in her own way, been behaving as poorly as had Mr. Lyons, for he must certainly have known this before. She, of all people, ought not to presume to judge people on their appearance. The man had already surpassed her expectations with his knowledge of the laws of entail. Why should he not also know about potting sheds? She blushed. "Forgive me. I assumed you to have all the poor knowledge of agriculture as my city-born cousins. I should have known better." For some reason, this brought a genuine grin to the man's face.

The four sorted through the various objects in the shed and soon fashioned seats of some sort out of crates and bags of mulch, atop of which they tossed old tarpaulins and blankets. They were soon seated in some degree of comfort, and Mr. Lyons began his probing.

"Miss Elizabeth," his eyes met and held hers, "both your sister and I believe that something occurred in the field with Mr. Collins that you have chosen not to relate to us. I can only beg you to reveal the entirety of the matter to me. I am your friend; I am here expressly to help you and prove your innocence of a terrible crime. If I know this truth, I will better be able to find other truths; but if you withhold your story and others learn of it, I will not be able to counter it with better evidence." Mary heard the words, but was more alarmed at the sight of her sister's face, which grew paler and paler with each syllable Mr. Lyons uttered, until she was almost as white as the woollen shawl wrapped about her shoulders.

"Miss Elizabeth, will you tell me what really happened? Let me help you, please!"

"Please," Mr. Darcy echoed, his voice rough and unsteady.

Lizzy's face grew tight with distress and she screwed closed her eyes as she shuddered. Then she released a ragged breath and looked directly at the men, first at Mr. Lyons and then at Mr. Darcy. She opened her mouth to speak, but no words emerged. A veil seemed to descend over her features, and her eyes went dull. "I cannot," she whispered at last. "I cannot speak of it. I promise I did not kill the man, but I am afraid I cannot speak further. The shame is too great; I should die of mortification as readily as with the noose. Forgive me, Mary." She let her head hang in despair, but would speak no more on the subject.

Mr. Lyons looked to Mary, who shrugged in confusion, and then to Mr. Darcy, whose face bore an expression of such exquisite agony that Mary was quite taken aback. Where was the cold and arrogant man from that first assembly? He seemed to have melted into this passionate and heart-sore creature who sat with her sister now.

After long moments of silence, Mr. Darcy cleared his throat. "May I... that is, may I presume to have a moment alone with you, Miss Elizabeth? I have something to say that might ease your mind."

Lizzy did not speak, but gave a slight movement that approximated a nod of agreement, and Mr. Lyons stood, offering his arm to Mary as he gestured towards the door. She accepted and in a moment stood outside in the cool sunshine with him, leaving her sister and the enigmatic Mr. Darcy alone in the shed.

Chapter Eleven

Unwelcome Words

The walls of the shed were not so thick that voices could not penetrate them; neither did Alexander wish to wander far enough from the area that he could not be present when needed. He tried to begin a conversation with Mary, but she seemed quite disinclined to talk of trivialities, and thus it was with some embarrassment that they overheard every word spoken by the two people inside.

Darcy spoke first. "Miss Bennet... Elizabeth..." he seemed at a loss, this proud and assured man. "Please, do not fear to speak to Mr. Lyons. He is of excellent character, and his discretion is assured. Further, I cannot believe you to have done any wrong, and society will soon forgive any minor lapses when your name becomes mine."

Alexander heard a noise that sounded like a squeak from Miss Elizabeth. Had Darcy just proposed marriage to her? That was a surprise indeed! He had expected his friend to declare himself after the situation was resolved, but not now, not whilst matters were still so unsettled. For although Alexander quite believed in Miss Elizabeth's innocence, he could not quite prove it yet.

Darcy must have been emboldened, or perhaps he was nervous, for he gave the lady little time to respond, but instead began to speak further. "You cannot be in doubt now about the sincerity of my affections, and when you take the name Darcy, none will dare disparage you for your unfortunate involvement in this dreadful murder, nor will they speak ill of you for your origins and your family, unless they wish to be forever omitted from my society. I am not a vain man," Alexander coughed at that absurd comment, "but my wealth and connexions are such that many members of the *ton* aspire to claim an acquaintance. It shall more than atone for your sad history, for if I am willing to ally myself with such poor relations, far be it for society to snub you!"

Miss Elizabeth now made another noise, but it was no squeak of surprise. If Miss Mary's furious face was anything to go by, the lady in the shed was as little impressed by Darcy's words as was the lady by Alexander's side. And, indeed, the squeak of annoyance was followed by a speech that left Alexander in little doubt as to the lady's strong character.

"How dare you, Mr. Darcy, come here under the pretence of offering your assistance and declaring your affections—nay, demanding my agreement to them—all the while doing so in such a way as to prohibit my acceptance of them!"

Now Darcy sputtered, but recovered himself within an instant. His speech began in quiet, measured tones, but grew more agitated with every sentence. "Do you refuse me, then? I, who have examined my heart and found enough love and admiration for you to allow me to deny my own standing and the expectations of my family? I, who have struggled with my feelings and who have concluded that status must take second place to affection? I, who have chosen to ignore the shortcomings of your family in my determination to raise to my own level? Why, I even recanted my warning to Bingley to remove himself from your sister Jane! I have gone so far as to encourage his suit now, for all that the alliance might not be a wise one for him. I have done all of this, and you would not accept me?"

Miss Elizabeth's voice was no less agitated. "Had you spoken of love alone, I might have considered you. You forget that until only yesterday, the only impression you had left upon me was that of a cold and arrogant man. I had begun to change my opinion of you and to see another facet to your character—one that I might have learned to love and respect—but now I see that my first impression was, indeed, correct. You are all that is proud and haughty, and I should manage quite well without your assistance and without your name!"

There ensued a silence so thick it might be impenetrable to the eye. Mary, who had been standing by Alexander's side as the voices resounded from the shed, now stepped away to face the other direction. Was she struck by anger or shame? Alexander wished he might see her face so as to better judge her response to this strange unfolding of emotions in that gardening shed. He, himself, felt only the greatest mortification at his friend's confession of sentiments so beneath him. What had Darcy been thinking, to have more concern for his own standing in society than for the feelings of the woman he professed to love?

At length Darcy spoke again, his voice tight and very quiet. "And this is all the reply I am to have the honour of expecting! I might, perhaps, wish to be informed why I am thus rejected." Did the man truly not know what he had said? Was he truly so blind to his own faults?

But Miss Bennet had not fallen into silence. "I might as well inquire," replied she, "why with so evident a design on offending me, you chose to tell me that you liked me against your will, against your reason, and even against your character. And further, do you think any consideration would tempt me to accept the man who had striven to ruin the happiness of a most beloved sister? For it now seems that you had taken great steps to separate Jane and Mr. Bingley forever!"

"It would have been for the best," Mr. Darcy spat out, "for I can see little affection in your sister's eyes for the man himself, rather than for his fortune. I heard your mother crowing of her success at the ball. I know how she has worked to throw Jane and my friend together. I would separate him from one who did not love him as he loves her. Towards him, I had been kinder than towards myself, but even that is now overthrown." There was a clatter from the shed that sounded like a pile of boxes being shifted, and then Darcy appeared at the door. "I shall not call off Mr. Lyons from your assistance, but you have said quite enough to me, madam. I perfectly comprehend your feelings and am only ashamed of what mine have been. Forgive me for importuning you. I shall return to Netherfield at once."

He exited the shed, and with a scant glance towards Miss Mary and Alexander as they stood, horrified at the exchange and feigning ignorance of it, stormed off in the direction of the stables, leaving Alexander mortally embarrassed and quite uncertain as to how to act next.

Miss Mary broke the awkward silence. "Mr. Darcy has not changed so much," she opined, "from his first appearance before Meryton's society when he insulted my sister for the first time." She turned to face Alexander and he could now see the anger and hurt etched upon her face. "This time, however, he seemed not to be satisfied by insulting her alone, but must include the entire family in his admonitions." She snorted, a most unladylike sound that made him smile. "If he were truly as grand as he makes himself to be, he would know better than to judge a family based on nothing but their place of origin—for as the family of a gentleman, we are his equals, no matter that we live in Hertfordshire and not in London—or to make such harsh determinations of our characters based on so short and exceptional an acquaintance."

She snorted again and strode toward the shed with determined steps. Alexander did not know if his chosen response would be laughter or rage. Every time he began to find some characteristics to admire in Mary Bennet, she would say or do something to quite upset his thoughts. Now, when he was starting to wonder if she had some sense to her after all, she accused his friend Darcy of behaving exactly the way she herself was behaving towards Alexander.

She accused Darcy of judging her family based on their small country estate and meagre means, rather than on their characters, but she had looked askance upon him for his Scottish home and his middle-class birth. It was true that he had spoken more harshly to her than a gentleman ought, but had Darcy or another of his race been the one to ask her to cease her demands, she almost certainly would have heeded him. Had Darcy been the one limping and bruised and covered in mud, she would not have dared importune him at that moment with her demands, and certainly would have ceded to his need to tend to his own exigencies.

She condemned Darcy for his pride, but she, this useless creature of luxury and frivolity, who had the privilege of spending her time in contemplation of those damned books she carried about rather than working at some useful occupation, had as much pride in her right foot as Darcy had in his large body. She had deemed Alexander a servant, no matter that he was there to save her sister, and she had treated him thus, putting her wishes above his needs.

And it was true; he was her servant. This he understood and resented with every fibre of his being. By birth he was beneath her, there to be bidden by her, to bend himself to her over-bred and useless will. Never mind that by education and experience he was by far her superior. To her, his university degrees and his position as one of the most sought-after investigators in London clearly meant nothing. She surely saw only his strange Scottish speech and his rough country manners. She had taken no time to seek the man beneath the appearance she seemed to disdain so much. No, she was far worse than anything she accused Darcy of being.

And what of Darcy? What had the man been thinking, to offer for Miss Elizabeth in such a way? Alexander had thought Darcy to be the exception that proved the rule, the one man of sense and worth in a society of fribbles. Had the man forgotten his senses?

There was no more time to stew on the matter, for Mary now emerged from the gardener's shed, Miss Elizabeth at her side. Mary's visage was cold, her entire body tense and forbidding. Her sister's character was more easily determined. Miss Elizabeth's eyes were swollen with the evidence of tears, but her demeanour was determined and strong, and she betrayed no hint of her inevitable emotions as she accompanied Miss Mary and Alexander back towards the house.

"We shall talk more later." Mary's voice was as icy as her eyes as she whispered harsh words to Alexander. "Your friend has prevented our knowing what happened to poor Lizzy and has quite distressed her at a time when she has enough troubles. Our task now is to see Lizzy into the house where Jane may comfort her, for I am certain she is heavy of heart at the moment." She turned from him with these words, leaving him an unwanted and disgruntled escort on the path back to Longbourn.

As fortune would have it, they encountered Jane and Bingley in the gardens by the wall of shrubbery. Miss Elizabeth had called on her formidable resources to affect a cheerful expression and a smile for Jane, and Alexander felt his admiration for the lady increase. To so put her own unhappy situation into abeyance for the sake of her sister required compassion and strength of character far beyond what he had expected from a spoiled girl of the gentry. This gave him pause. Were his own prejudices as strong as Darcy's and Miss Mary's, to assume that all the upper classes shared a common selfishness and greed?

He abandoned this line of thought, however, for no sooner had they approached the great doors to the manor house when a call behind them alerted the group to the arrival of Charlotte Lucas.

"Lizzy!" She rushed over and kissed her friend on the cheek. "My father forbade me to visit you, for it would be inappropriate for the daughter of the local magistrate to be seen in the company of a suspect in a violent death, and therefore I am not here, neither have you seen me at all. And," she reached into the large bag she carried, "I have not brought the lavender sweets you enjoy, and I have no book of charades to keep us entertained for an afternoon." She turned her sensible face to the others. "I shall not bid you all good day, for I am not here at all! We must hurry inside before my lack of presence is noted!" Whereupon she bestowed the group with a brilliant smile and dragged her friend into the house.

This seemed a fine time for Alexander to take his leave. Darcy would, he was certain, be waiting at the stables. No matter how angry or arrogant, his companion would not leave him with no way to return to Netherfield. After a quick goodbye to Jane, Bingley hurried after him and across the wide gravel drive that led around to where the gig would be waiting. "My sisters have no idea that I am here either," the younger man grinned. "They suppose me to be at some lecture at the assembly rooms with John Lucas. I did promise to meet him there so as not to make my outing a complete lie. Will you join me?"

"Yes, indeed," Alexander nodded. "I would speak with the man, and also with the local attorney, Phillips. His rooms are adjacent to the assembly hall, are they not?"

"Aye," Bingley grinned. "Here is young Dick with my horse. Let me meet you there." He mounted his steed and rode off towards the village.

As Alexander had expected, Darcy was waiting with the gig by the stables. His face was dark and resolute. "I shall not be set off my course," he replied to Alexander's raised brows. "I shall see her vindicated, and then I shall leave, for she does not return my affections."

The resolve on Darcy's face melted into misery. The expression would not last for more than a few moments, but once more Alexander felt a perverse honour at being privilege to his friend's deepest emotions. "Take heart," he consoled. "You have been wrong about the lady several times before." Darcy's dark eyes looked up at him. "Your words were as cruel to her as mine were to Miss Mary the day before, but that lady and I seemed to have reached some sort of tentative accord, at least enough to exchange information concerning this investigation." He did not mention Mary's recent condemnation of the man, nor his own misgivings about Mary. "Miss Elizabeth's response bespoke a great deal of emotion. She must feel very strongly towards you in one way or another, else your words would not have eaten at her so. Allow her time to calm herself, as I required time after my horrible words to Mary yesterday, and then present her with the greatest and most selfless gift you can manage: a humble and abject apology, completely devoid of the wrappings of pride or conceit. Then you may step back and allow her to learn her own mind—and heart—where you are concerned."

The smallest sliver of hope began to gleam in Darcy's eye. "Then you do not believe she hates me?"

"I do not believe the lady herself quite knows how she feels towards you. Until yesterday she scorned you, then came to trust you, and was by way of starting to like you, until you shocked her with a proposal—yes, I heard it all through the walls—and insulted her low origins and her family. And do not forget that she is under the darkest suspicion for a most serious crime. She is worried and upset and confused. Allow her to come to a reckoning with her own feelings before demanding them for yourself. Right now she needs a friend. Offer to be that to her and let whatever may follow do so naturally."

He stopped his oration as the groom came around with the gig. Darcy did not meet his eyes, but nodded quietly to himself.

"Where is Bingley?" the man asked at last.

"He is to meet us at the assembly rooms, after which I shall pay a visit to Phillips. Will you join me?"

"The better to occupy my thoughts," Darcy acknowledged. "Here's the gig. I shall drive."

The short ride into Meryton was much easier than had been the early morning trip to Longbourn. With every stride and motion, Alexander's hip had eased, and although he knew the following morning would bring fresh pain, he was pleased enough to survive the motion of the cart with little more than a grimace.

He eased himself out of the gig with nary a twinge and prepared to make the acquaintance of the magistrate's son.

John Lucas was a large man of around his own years. He bore a remarkable resemblance to Charlotte, but on him the features were almost handsome, whereas Charlotte was quite plain. He greeted Bingley with pleasure, Darcy with cool civility, and Alexander with caution.

"The investigator from London, eh? Father mentioned you. He was pleased enough not to have to take responsibility for this affair. Dreadful business." His voice was deep and resonant with a lilt at the ends of his sentences. Alexander wondered if he was a singer.

"I have business with Mr. Phillips at the present, Mr. Lucas," he bowed politely, "but if you please, I would take a moment of your time later on. I am seeking as much knowledge of the deceased parson as I can find, and where better to begin than with the people who knew him and talked to him. Where might I find you?"

Lucas's mouth twitched and his entire body stiffened in momentary alarm, but he responded easily enough, giving his most likely locations, depending on the time of day. *What was that about?* Alexander wondered. Were there more secrets in Meryton than he had ever imagined, or was it merely his presence—a stranger from the north here on unpleasant business—that had people uneasy? He would tackle that thought later. Now he needed to meet with the attorney.

Darcy accompanied him up to Mr. Phillips' rooms. "What will you ask him?" the tall man asked as they waited for the attorney to complete his current meeting. "Will you tip your hand?"

"No, not yet."

"But surely you have enough knowledge of this sort of matter that you do not need a country attorney's advice!"

"You forget, Darcy, that my expertise is in Scots law. Of course we learned of English legal matters as well, but the details are not identical, and in each situation, it is the details that matter. Every entail is its own entity, depending on the terms of the original deed. Ah, here is our man."

Mr. Phillips was Mrs. Bennet's brother-in-law. He was polite and serious and ready to sit down to business and took no delay in addressing the issue at hand.

"How much do you need to know," he asked. "And in order that I not be redundant, what may I assume you already know?"

"Assume we know as much, but no more, than the average man of some education," Alexander replied. Phillips nodded once, a sharp and definitive gesture, and reached for a package of yellowing papers.

"I have expected your visit since this mess began. I took the liberty of finding all the documents I have that might relate to matters. I shall begin with the business of entail." He raised his brows and Alexander nodded. They understood each other perfectly.

"Entail," Phillips began, "is the practice of ensuring the continuance of a property within a family, without alienating any part of it. What that means is that it may not be sold, in part or in whole, and cannot be willed away, but must pass to a predetermined heir, almost always from the male line. Where there are no direct heirs, one looks to uncles, then cousins, of further and further kinship. In the case of Longbourn, the recently deceased Mr. Collins was the son of Bennet's own second cousin. As far as anybody knows, there is no other heir."

"What happens to Longbourn now that the heir presumptive is no more?" Darcy asked.

"You are not the first person wishing to know this," Phillips gave an unexpected smirk. "Fanny—that is, Mrs. Bennet—of all people asked me this some two or three weeks past, when Mr. Collins first arrived. She seldom cares for such matters, although the threat of losing her home has long played upon her mind. She believes she will become homeless should her husband die, forgetting that she has family who will gladly take her in. But I digress. Back to your question," he patted the papers before him.

"What happens in such a situation depends on a great many details. Entails can be broken by act of Parliament where there is sufficient incentive on both sides, although this can be very costly. Other particulars include whether the original holder of the property in fee simple—that is, before the entail was created—is still alive, and what the nature of the deed of entail is. All manner of different details can be entered here, and the outcome depends upon them. In some cases, the property reverts to the crown. In others, the property can be divided equally amongst living daughters, or pass through a daughter to the oldest daughter's first son or the oldest grandson, regardless of which daughter bears him."

"And in the case of Longbourn?"

"To be held in trust and available for residence by the widow and any unmarried daughters until the birth of the first grandson who was not heir to another estate. Longbourn would immediately become his, even if he were at some later point to inherit some other property."

This was interesting, to be sure. Collins' death ensured that Mrs. Bennet and her daughters would not be removed from their home by some upstart cousin. One of her daughters would surely provide such a child. "Did you tell this to Mrs. Bennet?" Alexander asked.

Mr. Phillips spat out a burst of laughter. "What? Tell this to Fanny? Are you mad? She likely would have stuck a knife in the man himself! No, I merely informed her that there is no one answer to such a question, and that she had better become accustomed to accepting Mr. Collins, for at the time it seemed certain that he—or his son—would eventually inherit. I saw no purpose in telling her of the particulars. She is not always the quickest at comprehending such matters. Still… I wonder if she somehow learned of it."

After a few other questions that provided no new knowledge, the interview was concluded, and Darcy and Alexander made their way back to the street by the assembly rooms. "What do you make of that, Lyons?" Darcy scratched his chin and ran a hand through his hair before replacing his hat. "That bodes rather ill for Bennet, does it not?"

"Indeed, assuming the man knew the terms of the entail. He feigned suitable ignorance, but he seems rather too academic a man not to have pursued this line of inquiry himself." Alexander tried to picture the situation as he described his thoughts. "He adores Miss Elizabeth and cannot imagine her bound to a man such as you have described Collins to be. Knowing that Collins' death will not only rid his favourite daughter of a useless sort of man, but will also ensure his family's security in their home, he takes steps to dispose of him."

The words did not quite ring true, and Darcy voiced Alexander's own concerns. "Do you really see Bennet rousing himself to such a degree as to abandon his den and ride out across muddy fields to fight a man into submission and plunge his own daughter's knife into the neck, thereupon to return home without any one being the wiser and pretend such shock upon hearing the news?"

Alexander could scarcely imagine Bennet rousing himself to walk to the stables unless it was to greet a messenger with a bag of new reading material.

"No," Alexander concurred, "but it does open the door to the notion that Mr. Collins might have had more than one enemy."

Chapter Twelve

Miss Margaret of Bowridge

Mary was positive. She had been thinking of matters all the previous night whilst unable to sleep, and again this morning before the men from Netherfield arrived, and again after Charlotte had come and sequestered herself with Jane and Lizzy in the latter's bedchamber with her book of charades. Now Mary had come to a determination. She was positive she knew the whereabouts of the missing maid, Polly, and was going to find her!

Getting permission to go out on her quest was easy. A quick request to Mama "to call upon an acquaintance" was met with, "Oh, it's you, Mary. Yes, be back by dinner." The request to Papa to take the phaeton was also granted with hardly a glance at the asker. The hour was still early and the weather holding fair, and Mary was soon on the road, certain she would be back in time to speak once more with the rude and condescending Mr. Lyons and relate her news.

Perhaps she ought to reconsider her opinion of Mr. Lyons. He could be polite when he wished, but she still chafed at his insults of the previous afternoon. Why could not such intelligence and a passion for the truth be matched with a gentlemanly disposition? And what on earth had he meant by that statement about not being considered a Christian? Insufferable man! Still, he was a worthy opponent and a more worthy ally, and Mary determined to put aside her antipathy for the man until the cloud above Lizzy's head had been removed.

It was a five-mile drive to Oakville, the next village on the road to London. It was slightly smaller than Meryton and had no assembly rooms, and consequently when the people of both towns wished to socialise and dance, it was in Meryton that they did so. The Bennets were on a friendly basis with several genteel families from the immediate vicinity of Oakville, and the road between the towns was well and often travelled. Mary knew the route intimately and hardly needed to guide the small horse that drew her cart, so well did the creature know where he was going. And when she pointed him down the lane to Bowridge, where her friend Margaret Durham dwelt, the beast turned almost before her tug at the reins.

To her relief, Margaret was indeed at home. A sickly young woman with weak eyes and a pronounced limp stemming from a childhood illness, Margaret Durham was quiet and intelligent, with a serious nature to match Mary's own, but with moments of outrageous humour that would ensure that she would never be forgotten in a room or turned invisible to her family. "Mary Bennet!" she announced to the room as Mary was shown in, "I had not expected you today. What brings you here? It is not our planned visiting day! Is all well?"

Mary greeted her friend warmly and explained, "We are all well, but matters are not all well. You must have heard of the dreadful affair of my cousin Collins. He was," she lowered her voice, "murdered in the fields!"

"Oh! I had heard of it indeed! Is it true that Sir William suspects dear Elizabeth? That cannot be so! What dreadful news. But should you not be in mourning for your cousin, rather than running about Hertfordshire paying visits?"

The prim and proper lady who formed Mary's backbone sat up rather straight at this accusation. "He was not so close a relative that we *must* mourn him, and not so beloved that we *wish* to." She raised her chin and peered at her friend through half-closed lids.

"Besides, I believe most firmly that helping my sister must take precedence over a mere custom. For as John says in the Bible, '*But whoso hath this world's good, and seeth his brother have need, and shutteth up his bowels of compassion from him, how dwelleth the love of God in him?* My sister hath need, and so I shall do what I can to help her."

"And very proper it is too!" Margaret concurred. "Is that why you have come? May I be of any help?" Her eyes grew bright at the idea and the smile that so often betokened some mischievous comment spread across her thin face.

Mary shifted closer to her friend and dropped her voice. "I was hoping you would ask!"

Unlike Longbourn and Netherfield, where the kitchens and staff areas lay to the back of the house, at Bowridge the realm of the servants was literally below stairs, for the house sat atop a rise of land, and what was the main storey at the front rose to the level of the first storey at the back as the hillside dipped back into a valley. Thus, the kitchens still opened upon the back fields and kitchen garden from their low doorways, but were reached from the main part of the house by several staircases seldom travelled by the feet of those who dwelt above.

It was down one of these, leading from the servery just off the main dining room, that Margaret led Mary with her slow and careful steps. Margaret wished for no pity due to her limp, and Mary offered her none. The young woman was every bit as capable as a more able-bodied lady, even if her efforts took more time. Upon achieving the lower floors, Margaret found the main kitchen and introduced Mary to the head cook, named—quite amazingly—Mrs. Cooke.

"I do believe she made up the name for the express purposes of gaining such employment!" Margaret teased in a whisper. "I have never heard a breath of Mr. Cooke, but I suppose he must have existed at some point." She leaned closer. "Although, every cook is a Mrs, regardless of whether there was ever a Mr." Mary giggled, seeming for that moment the girl of eighteen summers that she was.

Introductions were made, although Mrs. Cooke retained a leery eye, and Mary set about her task.

"I was hoping," she began, "that a woman of your great reputation and influence amongst your peers will have heard something that may be of value to me." She attempted a friendly and innocent expression, which the cook returned with a trace of a scowl and a suspicious eye. "This is nothing at all untoward, nor is anybody in any danger. I merely wish to inquire if a certain young maid has been seeking employment about these parts." Mrs. Cooke's eyes narrowed and Mary hastened to explain, "I believe she has done nothing wrong! Nothing at all! But she may know something that will help to save an innocent woman from a terrible accusation, and may help to find a man whom we suspect does carry some guilt." She searched her repertoire of facial expressions and found what she hoped was a friendly and encouraging smile.

"And why would you think this young girl is in these parts, Miss? If I may ask?" Mrs. Cooke's voice was no friendlier than her glower.

"'Tis simple, really, a matter of logical deduction. The girl is local to Meryton, this I know, and has never travelled from the village further than Oakville. She wishes to run from some threat, the nature of which I do not know exactly but wish to find out, and she has not been at her position since the morning that Mr. Collins was murdered. Her first thought would be to travel to London, where she might find employment and disappear into the huge hordes of people there, but being so poorly travelled, I suspect she made it as far as Oakville and quite gave up on her plans, seeking to remain here if she could find a suitable position. It is not a bad choice, for the man she fears is very well travelled and would never think to seek her almost on her own doorstep. He will certainly look to London or further, never imagining that to Polly, Oakville may as well be China."

Mary glanced up at her friend. Margaret stared at her with mouth agape, and Mrs Cooke's forbidding expression had softened by the smallest degree.

"That sounds a good argument," said the cook, "but if we do find this girl, what will become of her? I'll not be the cause of a good soul being dragged into some sort of hell."

"Oh, nothing will become of her unless she wishes it," Mary's smile was genuine. "I desire only to talk to her. I have no authority to force her to do anything. I can only ask."

"Well," the cook allowed her head to bob up and down upon her neck. "Well. I may have a notion." She shuffled back on her chair. "Wait here, if you don't mind," and she rose and lumbered out of the room.

She returned a few minutes later with a very young footman. The lad must just have moved out of the stables, for he was tall and handsome, but with the lankiness and spotted face of adolescence. "John lives in the village; his father is the smith. He was telling me of a young lass that was coming around asking for work." She offered the chair to the boy and at Margaret's invitation he sat, his posture perfect but his hands pulling this way and that at each other.

"I shan't cause trouble, John." Mary sought her most soothing voice. "What can you tell me about this girl?"

His voice was surprisingly deep for so young a man, and despite the restless motion of his hands, he spoke with calm assurance. Mary understood why he was elevated to footman at so young an age. He would be an asset to the household, and might rise to butler one day. "I saw her yesterday, for I had business in the village escorting Mrs. Durham and her sister. While the ladies were at tea with the mayor's wife, I went to say greetings to my Pa, and there she was, this girl, sitting in the corner taking some food that Ma had left for her. She's a very fine thing to look upon—nigh on the prettiest girl I've seen in a long time... present company excepted," he prevaricated. "But she didn't look like she was the sort to come on to men." His face flushed a deep red and he flickered his eyes away from the three women around him. "We talked a bit—friendly, like—and I thought she might find a position here. Mrs. Durham is a very kind employer and Mr. Durham well respected, and the girl seemed like she wished only to work hard for her keep. That's why I mentioned it to Mrs. Cooke, here."

"This girl's name?" Mary prompted.

"At first she said it was Polly, but right away changed it and said she mis-spoke, and it's Molly. Whichever it is, I don't rightly know."

"That's just fine. Where is she now? Do you know that?"

"Not that, I don't. She was sleeping in a barn she found, but was planning to come by here today to talk to Mrs. Cooke and beg for a position. She might be here soon, from what I recall."

Mary allowed another genuine smile to form on her lips. "That's fine information. Thank you John." The young footman rose, bowed, and hurried from the room in what he must have imagined was a sedate and footman-like manner.

It was not a half an hour later that a tentative knock came at the kitchen door and Mrs. Cooke ushered in a very nervous looking young woman. Mary took one look and nodded. It was the girl she had been seeking and was quite proud of herself for having divined where the maid would be.

The girl was, as everyone commented, extremely pretty, with a figure that matched her lovely face. She curved in the right ways at all the right places and made her simple working dress look like a ball gown. And yet, for all of that, Mary could see that this was no temptress. The girl seemed to wish to hide her beauty behind a simple linen kerchief used to hold back her hair and a choice of clothing that covered but could not disguise that which another might flaunt. Her beseeching manner and modest address gave Mary the deepest impression of a girl who wished only to work an honest day and live a simple life.

Mrs. Cooke allowed the girl to introduce herself and state her business—namely the search for a position—before ushering her to the large table where Mary and Margaret sat. She caught herself short upon seeing Mary and faltered in her step. "Miss... Miss Bennet!"

"Hello, Polly."

The girl's eyes filled with tears. "Oh, please don't make me go back. If he finds me, he'll blame me for certain, although I'm sure I haven't done anything wrong! Please, I beg of you, Miss Bennet!"

"Be easy, Polly," Mary interrupted. "I am not here to take you anywhere, or to betray your whereabouts to anybody. But I would dearly like to talk to you. Perhaps together we can stop him, so that he will bother you no longer. Will you talk to me? Will you do that?"

The young maid looked from Mary to Mrs. Cooke to Margaret and back again, eyes wide and terrified like a rabbit caught in a trap. "I promise I mean you no harm, only help," Mary tried once more, and was rewarded by a slight relaxing of the girl's shoulders and a flicker of her eyelids.

"Sit, please. Mrs. Cooke, would it be too much trouble to ask for some tea and biscuits, if Margaret does not object? Thank you." She turned to the maid and reassured her, "We only wish to find out more of what you know. I believe you have done nothing wrong, and together, perhaps, we can ensure that you are never blamed for something you did not do."

Polly nodded with slow deliberation. "Very well, Miss Bennet. I shall try."

"Thank you. My first question, so that we may all be certain of whom we spoke, is this: Who is 'he?' Who is this man who terrifies you so?

"Why, I thought you knowed that! It's Mr. Wickham, from the officers with the militia."

"I did know, but I needed to hear you say it. I would not be found suggesting answers to you. Miss Durham here will be our witness, should we need her. Now, what, exactly, did he say? Again, I believe I know what has transpired, but your words must be your own and not mine." She gave the girl a reassuring pat on the arm, and Polly seemed to draw strength from it.

"I never done nothing wrong, but Mr. Wickham—I do not like the way he looks at me! I'm grown used to men staring at me, but he makes me scared, how he does so. He told me that some precious items have been going missin' from Netherfield, and that if I didn't do what he told me, he would tell Miss Bingley that I was the one what took 'em! But I never did, I swear it, Miss Bennet! I never did!" The young maid had grown quite agitated as she spoke.

Mary needed to calm the girl's nerves. "Nobody believes you took them, Polly. You have been accused of nothing. But please tell me everything. What did Mr. Wickham ask you to do?"

"I think... I think he wanted to have his way with me." Her voices dropped to a whisper. "He scares me, that one, with his lustful eye. He told me to meet him in the patch of woods out by Oakham Mount the following day, the day after the ball. I was so scared to lose my position, I was ready to agree to him, but I changed my mind. I had decided to tell him no, and face whatever lies he threw up against me."

Now here was something Mary had not considered. The insight into Wickham's character was no of little surprise to her, although Margaret had uttered a shocked gasp at the maid's accusation. Rather, something else had bothered Mary. "I had thought Mr. Wickham was sent to London the previous day, not to return until his affairs there on the part of the militia were concluded. He should have been in London for two nights, not only one."

"I know nothing of that, Miss Bennet. Only of where he told me to meet him."

Mary rested her arms upon the table and leaned forward. "And did you? Did you meet him? I need to know what happened."

The girl paled but did not look away. "I was there, when he said. I left the house after clearing up from breakfast and went straight to the woods. I waited there for a long time, and I thought he would not come after all. But then I heard somebody, and when I looked out into the fields, I saw Miss Elizabeth walking, and after her, the parson Mr. Collins. They had a right row they did, and he was yellin' and screamin' all manner of horrid things at her, and then he knocked her to the ground and I thought I might have to run out of my hiding spot to save her. But she's a brave one, and strong too, and she showed him a thing or two! My brothers always told me to kick a man like that if I don't like what he's doin', and it seems a good trick to know. She kicked him and ran, and then I heard him."

So there had been more to Lizzy's encounter with their cousin than a mere argument! In the aftermath of Darcy's ill-conceived proposal, Mary had neglected to press her sister to confess the whole story. The maid's evidence accorded with what Mary had imagined, and she steeled herself to confront her sister once and for all on the matter. But for now, she had the remainder of Polly's story to extract. The girl had said that she heard 'him.'

"Him? Mr. Collins?" Mary needed to clarify Polly's tale.

To her wonder, the girl blinked in surprise. "Oh, him too, yellin' and cursin' her like the devil himself." She spoke these words as if they had little relevance to her accounting. "No," she added more gravely, "I meant Mr. Wickham. He came after all, but he must have seen the fight and he turned his horse and galloped straight towards the parson, lyin' in the mud as he was. Knowing Miss Elizabeth was safe and seeing Mr. Wickham like that, it shook me so that I turned and ran through the woods, and then kept goin' till I found myself in Oakville. And so scared I was, bein' so far from home, I could not go any farther."

"I see." This was promising news indeed! "You saw my sister leave Mr. Collins alive, and you saw Mr. Wickham ride towards him. And nothing else?"

"No, nothin' at all." Her eyes were still wide, but there was less fear in them.

"Will you tell that to a magistrate? I promise to do everything I can to keep anyone from blaming you for the lost silver. It could mean my sister's life."

Polly seemed to shrink back in her chair at this request. Mary could almost see the battle waging in the girl's thoughts, and Margaret shifted in her chair, so uncomfortable was the air in the kitchen. At last the maid took a deep shuddering breath and looked at the table in front of her, bowing her head. "Yes, I will. I could not live with myself if my silence cost Miss Elizabeth her freedom or worse. I will speak."

Chapter Thirteen

Interviews and Letters

Alexander's next planned visit was to Colonel Forster. Whilst it seemed that Wickham could not be involved in this affair, he knew enough about the lieutenant that he could not discount him without very good evidence. There was also the matter of inquiring into the colonel's experience at the gambling tables in London, for every possibility must be examined in the case of murder.

Colonel Forster was pleased to welcome the two men into his office. He was in his middle thirties and short and squat, but with a commanding presence. Alexander had no doubts that he was a formidable leader and that he had good control of his soldiers. He seemed to know of both visitors, presumably from correspondence with colleagues in London. Alexander supposed that information was this man's stock in trade as much as it was his own.

The colonel greeted both men with a hearty handshake. "Mr. Darcy, of course! I know your cousin, Fitzwilliam, from the regulars. Good man. Fine officer. Well respected by all."

"Mr. Lyons, always a pleasure to meet an acquaintance of my colleague. He mentioned you when he was searching for that girl in the summer. Find her? Excellent! How can I help you?"

In a few brief words, Alexander outlined the situation and stated his desire to know the whereabouts of George Wickham on the evening before and day of the murder.

"Strange one, that Wickham," the colonel harrumphed. "Diligent enough when on duty. Knows he needs to earn his keep. But I don't like the stories I hear of him. Drinking to excess, whoring, always at cards. Still, reliable for when I need him."

"Had you known him before he joined your regiment?" Alexander had his notebook and pencil at the ready.

"Ran into him once or twice in London. Spent time at some of the same clubs. I'm not afraid to say I've enjoyed a game or two of cards in my day, but I keep my bets low and losses lower. I'll be in debt to no man." Alexander scratched in his notepad. So that seemed to deal with the good colonel's involvement in the gambling clubs. He would, of course, have to confirm what he had heard, but from the colonel's voluntary and unconcerned mention, Alexander doubted the soldier had told anything by the unvarnished truth.

"And what of Wickham?" he asked. "Have you heard any talk of how he fared?"

"Don't know much about Wickham's success at the tables, but I imagine he is more free with his blunt. Had the notion he joined the militia to help pay some debts. Still, not my business as long as he does his duties."

"Where, may I ask, was he around the time of the murder? That is, on the afternoon of Wednesday last."

"Can't help you much there, boys. I sent him to London the previous day with some paperwork that needed tending. Sent him around mid-day. He was to report to my command office that evening and join the officers for their dinner, then stay until the matter was dealt with. Likely take three days. Don't expect him till this afternoon or evening. Whilst in London, he had some light duties. Nothing too taxing, but enough to keep him in town, mainly ceremonial at the dinners, representing our regiment, that sort of thing. For all that his character is dubious, he looks good in a uniform and represents us well. I've sent him on these missions before, and he executes them to everybody's satisfaction."

Darcy leaned forward and asked in his most formal voice, "Would it be a matter of indiscretion to ask what, exactly, his business in London was about?"

The colonel roared. "Undergarments! We have been asked to test a new design for undergarments, and Wickham was taking the list of our men's measurements for the uniform committee to examine and make up some samples for my men to try out." He dropped his voice and looked behind him for any eavesdroppers. "See if they chafe, if you understand me rightly."

With a guffaw, Alexander scratched out the word *mission* on his notepad, then confirmed, "So he was to present himself and his list in London the evening before the murder, stay for dinner, and generally be available until the er, garments were completed, and then return today at some time with his package of military supplies."

"Yes." The man was brief and to the point. Alexander sighed, and the colonel elaborated, "If he had not been present when expected, I would have been informed by express. For all that we are a militia regiment and not regular, our superiors do not take well to slackards."

"Then it looks, Darcy, like our man cannot have been in Meryton at all when Collins was lying in that field. Thank you, Colonel. If we have further questions, may we return?"

"Absolutely! Always glad to help in the cause of justice."

Alexander stood to leave, and Darcy followed suit, each man retrieving his hat from the small table at the door to the colonel's office. "No joy," Alexander breathed as they exited the building. "He could not have done it, nor can I imagine the first reason right now that Wickham would have to slay the parson."

"We seem to be at an impasse, then," Darcy shook his head. "The evidence against Elizabeth seems less than conclusive, and we have some irregularities that might cause one to look elsewhere, but until we can propose an alternative, Sir William will likely carry through on his intention to lay the charges against Elizabeth. And I cannot allow that to happen." His voice had been more and more tense as he spoke until Alexander felt the man might expire of an apoplexy before him. Darcy had a rough road ahead, desperate to save the woman he thought he could never have.

"Relax, friend," Alexander sought to calm his companion. "The game is not lost, neither the threat of the accusation nor the irrevocable loss of your lady's favour. We need merely to attempt a different approach to the matters. As for the former, we have been concentrating our efforts on the other denizens of the village, and to little effect. Perhaps we ought, rather, to draw our focus in on the victim himself."

To Alexander's amusement and Darcy's consternation, it was Darcy himself who provided the next item of information that helped to forward the case. It was presented to the gentleman upon a silver platter, sealed with a familiar crest, the direction inscribed in a precise and very particular hand.

"A letter from my Aunt Catherine," he sighed, seeing the envelope sitting atop a pile of similar correspondence for the various residents of Netherfield. "How in blazes did she learn my whereabouts?" He frowned at the letter as if it might leap up and bite him, then tentatively reached for it and held it a fair distance from his body.

Alexander had not had the pleasure of meeting Lady Catherine, but from what he had heard of her from his friend and Colonel Fitzwilliam, Darcy's treatment of her letter was not undeserved. She had been a thorn in Darcy's side during the summer when Georgiana had been missing, and had threatened on several occasions to remove the girl from the guardianship of her brother and cousin, who had been named such in the late Mr. Darcy's will. The lady would not have been successful in a court of law, but from what Alexander understood of her, she would not have been above sending trusted servants to physically remove the girl to her estate at Rosings. Once ensconced there, in that veritable fortress of a house, it would have taken a small army to free her into her brother's care once more. Lady Catherine, from all accounts, was not a woman to be gainsaid; she would go to any lengths, within and without the law of the land, to achieve her ends.

And thus, Alexander mused with a grin, if Darcy were anxious about the contents of the letter, he was likely in his rights to be so.

The two men had returned to Netherfield for a late tea in lieu of dinner and in order to sit in privacy to discuss the fruits of their investigation; it was thus that Darcy eyed the letter, sitting at the far edge of the table, all the while the men ate their bread, cheese, and leek pies. At last he seemed unable to resist the morbid urge to find out what was inside, and begging Alexander's indulgence, broke the seal.

Within moments, his face flushed red, then turned pale, and then flushed red once more.

"How on earth…" he began, then "What gives her the right? Who does she think…"

"Darcy?" Alexander was torn between mirth and concern as his friend sputtered and expostulated to the half-read missive. At last Darcy took a deep drink of his ale, straightened the pages of the letter, and began to read.

Nephew,

At last I have discovered your direction. How dare you travel from London and not inform me, your closest of relatives? ("How conveniently she forgets my sister and my uncle!" he complained.) *It is my due, and your duty, to keep me informed as to where I might find you. You are fortunate that others have taken more care of their responsibilities and obligations, and have kept me informed as to where you might be located, should I have need of you.* ("Damn Richard! He must have told her I was out of town and staying with Bingley. I shall have to retaliate for this most unwelcomed treason!")

It has, consequently, come to my attention that you are now residing in the county of Hertfordshire, at the estate of a young man of your acquaintance. I shall not deign to opine of the worth of this friend, for surely one with bloodline such as yours need not associate with the son of a merchant! ("The nerve! Lyons, I am mortified!") *But we may discuss your choice of friends at a later time. What is of greater import at the moment is that you are residing in close proximity to my parson, the most reverend Mr. William Collins, who holds the living at the rectory at Hunsford.* ("What? Is he the one who told her where I was? I ought to have killed the man myself. No, Lyons, I did not mean that. Put away your notebook.")

You will, of course, treat the man with all the condescension and respect due to my own station, for he holds the living at my leisure and thus he is my representative whilst travelling. ("Can you imagine, Lyons?

She wishes me to treat that uncouth and foolish man with the civility and deference due to a duke—for my aunt would accept no less! The very nerve of her! How pleased I am that I did not receive this missive whilst he was alive. But listen, there is more.")

My servant Collins has informed me not only of your own presence in the area of Hertfordshire in which you now visit, but also that of a young man whose presence ought not to be welcome to you. Mr. Collins has not yet divulged this man's name, but he has intimated quite clearly that you yourself know the person. I do hope, Nephew, that you have not been consorting with people whose stations are so far below your own. Rank must be preserved and a Fitzwilliam, by name or descent, must never associate with those of such low breeding as this person Mr. Collins did mention. I should advise you that... ("Oh, never mind this. She has very definite opinions as to how I ought to have Thorne launder my stockings. Let me see... here, she picks up her thread.")

Mr. Collins has spoken with this unsavoury person and has attempted to convince him of the error of his ways. In his most recent correspondence—for he takes seriously his obligation to inform me of the affairs and local concerns of every place which might benefit from my advice—he has related the outcome of one such attempt, in which the unsavoury person did not agree to a reformation of character. Therefore, be you aware, Nephew, of the likely necessity of my own arrival in your current vicinity should this person be named, with my most trustworthy men, to deal rightfully with this man, whom Mr. Collins assures me has done our family a great wrong.

Your affectionate aunt, to whom your devotion is due,
Catherine de Bourgh

"The man was insane!" Darcy exploded when he had finished the letter. "What on earth was he thinking?"

"Am I to understand," Alexander's voice was a calm contrast to his friend's, "that Collins somehow learned of Mr. Wickham's involvement in the, er, incident this past summer, and sought to convince Wickham to give himself up to her ministrations? And that he threatened Wickham with full exposure to your aunt if Wickham did not agree?"

"Indeed. I cannot read it any other way."

"Was Collins so self-assured that he would truly have approached Wickham and insisted that he 'mend his ways' and give himself up to justice? I know that Wickham's arrogance knows no bounds, but surely Collins…"

"Collins was a puffed-up mushroom, whose own sense of self-importance was augmented by the weight of that of my aunt. She views herself as so much greater than she is, and a man of obsequious vanity and little intelligence such as Collins would subsume this glamour of power into his own sense of self-worth. In contemplation, it comes as little surprise that he would assume the authority of the Prince himself in accosting someone he deemed as lowly as Wickham."

"But Wickham has not transgressed the law. His actions are outside of the realm of civilised behaviour, to be sure, but your aunt would have no legal recourse against him. English law does not differ from Scots in this respect. Convincing a lady to an elopement for her dowry is reprehensible, but quite legal. What could your aunt do?"

Darcy ran a hand through his hair and shook his head. "Aunt Catherine believes herself quite above the law, for such is reserved for lesser mortals. She would have no difficulty in apprehending the rat and subjecting him to her own brand of justice, herself as judge, jury, and executioner. Wickham would be in his rights to be fearful. My aunt knows little mercy."

This shed new light on what they had previously learned. Before, Wickham had been a mere distraction in the case of Collins' death. With no motive and no opportunity to commit the crime, it had been a matter of desire rather than evidence that had the men seeking hints to his guilt. But now, the story had changed. Alexander levelled his eyes upon his friend and asked, "Would her retributions be severe enough that Wickham might kill to avoid them?"

"Yes," Darcy leaned forward with an intensity seldom seen even on his serious face, "Yes, I believe he might. The man is lucky to have been elsewhere at the time of the murder."

Mary arrived home at an early enough hour that neither parent expressed any interest in her whereabouts over the past several hours. There had been damage to neither horse nor phaeton, and there were no stains of mud or any other substance upon her frock that required explanation, and thus she felt no need to explain her actions. She had promised Polly that she would keep her tale in as much confidence as possible, and this she determined to do.

Part of a story was now beginning to coalesce out of the scraps and tatters she had assembled, but as of yet, she could think of little reason for Mr. Wickham to wish harm upon Mr. Collins. The parson had been silly and endlessly annoying, to be certain, but one does not kill a man for that! No, if anybody had reason to kill her cousin, it could only be her father! For what man of virtue could stand by and watch his daughter attacked by the man who would one day usurp his own family's position in their own home? But this could not be! Papa was a thinker, a scholar and a debater, but never had been a man of action. Could he even have summoned the strength to prevail in a struggle against a much younger and larger man such as Collins had been? It was too strange and too unsettling even to contemplate. For if Papa had killed their cousin, what indeed would become of the Bennet daughters now? Nobody seemed to know what would become of

Longbourn without its present master and without its heir. Did Mr. Lyons know? The thought of him and his insult left an unpleasant taste in Mary's mouth, but perhaps she must seek him out. She had information he might desire as well.

With these thoughts tumbling through her mind, she entered the house through the back door and made her way up to her bedchamber to wash and prepare for dinner. Passing Lizzy's room, she heard the sound of voices and animated chatter. Charlotte must not yet have departed, and she and the two older sisters must be at charades.

Better let Lizzy have what diversions she could! There would be time enough for worry later. Mary was about to enter her own room, next along the corridor to Lizzy's, when Mrs. Hill came bustling up the back stairs. Mary moved to the side to allow the housekeeper to pass, but did not enter her bedroom, for the look on Mrs. Hill's face was far too interesting to ignore. Her forehead was furrowed and her lips pressed into a thin line, but her eyes were curious and intent. Something unusual was transpiring. Mary stood still as Mrs Hill brushed past her and stopped by Lizzy's door, upon which she proceeded to rap soundly.

Jane opened the door. "Mrs. Hill!" It was an uncommon event for the housekeeper herself to interrupt the ladies in their private rooms.

"If you pardon, Miss Bennet, a letter for Miss Elizabeth." Her voice suggested that she was as curious as Mary as to the contents of the letter.

From inside the room, Lizzy's voice sounded. "For me? But the mail arrived at breakfast time, as it does every day. How is this letter arriving only now?"

"It was sent special delivery, Miss. Not an express, but a private rider just came past. He said he had other business in London, delaying the letter by a day since it was not urgent, but it was still faster than the regular mail. He was insistent that I pass it on to you at once and not let another have her hands on it." Mary knew, as did everybody, that person in question was Mrs. Bennet.

"Thank you, Mrs. Hill. I shall read it at once. Is the rider awaiting a response?"

"No, Miss. He's gone to the inn and then home tomorrow. He repeated that the letter is important, but not urgent." The housekeeper gave a curtsey and scurried back to her regular duties.

"How fascinating." Lizzy's voice sounded clearly from inside her room. She had not shut the door fast, nor seemed to be making any effort to do so, and Mary had little difficulty in hearing each word she uttered.

"What does it say, Lizzy?" Jane asked.

"Who is it from?" That was Charlotte's voice, calm and sensible. "Who could have written something that needs your personal attention, but that is not a matter of urgency? I have never heard of a private rider, except in instances of the extremely wealthy with matters of dire importance."

Jane spoke again, a tinge of excitement colouring her normally placid tones. "What is it about?"

"Let us sit," Mary heard Lizzy reply, "and I shall read it to you."

Chapter Fourteen

A Letter for Elizabeth

Mary listened to the sounds of the three young women settling themselves down upon various surfaces in preparation for Lizzy's recital of the letter. She heard the soft rustle of skirts being arranged and rearranged, the scrape of a chair being moved across the floor, and the distinctive plop-plop of two shoes falling a short distance to the ground. At last, Lizzy began to speak.

"The salutation is from Lady Catherine de Bourgh! That was our cousin's benefactress. Whatever can she want from me? Surely she, too, is not blaming me for his death! I cannot even account for how the news reached her in time to write this letter and send it to me with such haste, for the rider asserted it was not urgent. I am quite at a loss."

Charlotte's voice sighed, "Read it, dear Lizzy, and perhaps she will explain her meaning."

And so Lizzy began to read.

Miss Bennet,

You can be at no loss to understand the reason of my letter today. Your situation might otherwise have recommended some note of gratitude to myself, but as I have been led to believe that you are a well-bred sort of girl, I shall excuse the lack thereof on your rightful reluctance to introduce yourself to one so far above your own station.

"What on earth can she be on about?" Charlotte exclaimed. Jane expelled a sort of laugh and asked, "Lizzy?"

"I cannot account for it, Jane! But here, let me continue."

It was I who suggested to my parson, Mr. Collins, that he take a wife from amongst his fair cousins, and upon receiving his frequent correspondence, it soon became apparent that you were the one fortunate enough to become his choice.

"Fortunate! Oh, far from it!"

"Please, Lizzy, what else does she say? Can she yet know that he is dead?"

"Here, Jane, let me read further."

As her sisters and their friend talked, Mary settled herself upon the floor in the hallway and listened with only the faintest sense of guilt at overhearing the contents of a private letter. Lizzy was, after all, reading it aloud to Jane and Charlotte.

As the future Mrs. Collins, there will be much expected from you, and I shall endeavour to offer every assistance as you accustom yourself to your role as a leader of society in our community. If you heed my advice...

"Oh, Jane, she is explaining all about the best cuts of meat from the butcher, and where to place my bread in the pantry so it should not be eaten by mice. Is the whole letter like this?"

"Let me read it, Lizzy." That was Charlotte speaking. There was a momentary silence, then the rustle of paper being transferred from hand to hand, and Charlotte let out a most ungenteel exclamation. "Does she really imagine to order you to fold your linens in this manner and not in that? I believe she already has chosen your curtains and the fabric to cover the sofa, and even the dress you shall wear on the second Sunday of each month! I cannot imagine any lady of sense wishing to spend her life bowing and scraping to such a woman! But now she writes more of Mr. Collins. Here, I shan't read what might be private." The paper rustled again, presumably as it was passed back to Lizzy.

"She writes on and on about what will be expected of me as Mr. Collins' wife! Oh, Jane, Charlotte... what she writes of my supposed 'wifely duties' cannot be read aloud! What can she have been thinking? I cannot believe the man was so arrogant as to assume my acceptance with so little encouragement by myself. I would never have agreed to him, but now I am even more satisfied with my choice." She paused, then added the expected words, "Although I do sorely regret the man's death. But listen:"

Mr. Collins has written much about the unsavoury goings-on in your village, and I must inform you that this sort of affair will not be condoned at Hunsford. I do not tolerate any manner of gaming whatsoever, and shall be most displeased should your presence presage such unacceptable activities.

"Does she believe you to be the master of the gaming dens? I wonder what else she might mean." Charlotte sounded incensed. "The woman must be mad!"

If ever the militia arrives in Hunsford to do their little exercises, you will ensure that the colonel calls upon me so I may instruct him as to the proper conduct of his officers.

Further, when your sister marries the gentleman who resides at the neighbouring estate, I will not tolerate visits from his sister, for that manner of vice has no place in my village. I am most fortunate that Mr. Collins is wise enough to inform me as to all these illicit goings-on, so we may be prepared to take action and prevent their incursion into our happy part of Kent.

"And I thought Mr. Darcy to be officious and arrogant! And so on she goes, detailing all those matters of which she does not approve. I cannot imagine there is a single public house or gaming den in all of Kent, for all that she seems to command authority over such matters!"

"I had not thought," said Charlotte, "that there was much gaming occurring here in Meryton, for we never see evidence of it."

"And yet," Lizzy's voice filtered through the cracked doorway, "such there must be, for I cannot imagine our cousin Collins having had the imagination to create it from the air. I had not thought him wise or perceptive enough to have discovered such dens of iniquity, but perhaps his overt piety gave him cause to search them out."

Now Jane spoke. "Why should she assume that I am to marry Mr. Bingley?" Her voice was innocent of guile. "He is pleasant and has given me hopes, but no more than that. Did Mr. Collins have knowledge of which I was unaware? And why should Lady Catherine refuse visits from Caroline?"

"That," replied Charlotte, "is a most strange question indeed."

The three women now began discussing Caroline Bingley's assets and faults and seemed to have little more to say about the letter. Mary scrambled up from her undignified position on the floor with as little noise as possible and crept down the hallway to her own room. As she changed out of her day dress and into something more suitable for dinner, she pondered the words she had heard.

Mr. Collins, it seemed, had not been averse to searching for vice even where it was not apparent, and then relating his discoveries to his patroness. Had he, perhaps, discovered something that an unknown person did not wish him—or Lady Catherine—to know? Could that person have had something to do with his death? This, she decided, must be discussed with the odious Mr. Lyons as soon as might be possible.

Dinner was a dreary affair. Charlotte had departed shortly after Lizzy had finished reading her most unexpected letter, and the gentlemen did not come to call and therefore were not invited to remain to dine. None of the ladies had expected their visit, for both Mr. Bingley and Mr. Darcy had dined with them the previous day; two evenings in a row would be tantamount to announcing an engagement! Lizzy did not mention the strange letter from Lady Catherine and now seemed quite low in spirits after her afternoon's respite with her friend and sister. Mary could see Mr. Darcy's strange and insulting proposal and the reality of the situation begin to wear at Lizzy's normally cheerful disposition, and she wondered again how soon she might be able to arrange an interview with Lyons.

She could, of course, write him a note. It would be appropriate and expeditious, and not out of keeping with the most generous interpretations of propriety, for they were colleagues of a sort. It would be a simple matter to explain that she was simply passing along information he might need for his inquiries. And yet, for some reason, she felt compelled to offer the information in person, to watch his face as he heard what she had to say, and to hear his responses and meet them with replies of her own.

His intellect was admirable, even if his manners were not, and whilst she could never call such a rude and heathen sort of man as himself a friend, there was something satisfying about encountering a man who would listen to her as he would another man, who would not scoff at her suggestions or laugh at her proposals in spite of his initial reluctance to hear her at all.

Recalling their easy conversation after the interview with her Papa, she recollected that he could be rather pleasant company as well when she forgot her antipathy to him and he forgot to be rude. Ought she to give him a second chance? He was a smart man, with a thirst for fairness and a sense of right and wrong that rivalled her own and a face (not that a lady of pious sense and discretion noticed such things) that did not repel the eyes. If only she did not dislike him so much! Nevertheless, there was nothing to be done for the moment. Lyons and Darcy must surely be out elsewhere, inquiring into whatever aspects of the situation men such as they were investigating, and she… she must remain at home, as was expected of ladies such as herself. It seemed somehow unfair, and she could think of no remedy for it.

Thus, she sat quietly through the meal, eating only enough so as not to draw her mother's attention and questions, and saying almost nothing. Since she was little heeded at the best of times, her listless spirits seemed not to be noticed. Jane answered every question with calm equanimity; Lizzy's lack of humour was easily explained, and Lydia could only talk of the officers who had walked past the hat shop that day, and what cunning plans she had for the bonnet in the window, if only Papa would give her the coin to purchase it. Kitty, living as always in Lydia's shadow, merely opined that she would have far better results with the bonnet than would her younger sister, thereby sparking an argument that lasted well into the final course of the meal.

It was only after the tea dishes had been cleared away that Lizzy approached her next sister in age. She settled herself on the sofa next to where Mary was attempting to read by the poor lamplight and reached across the space to close Mary's book and set it on the low table before them.

"You are out of sorts," she stated. Mary nodded. Lizzy, of all the family, would be the one to take note of Mary's spirits. "What has brought you to such doldrums? I am the one who ought to be moping, and perhaps I am. But I hardly need assistance in that endeavour, for I am more than capable of enough moping for us both."

Mary emitted a sad sort of laugh. "I cannot rightly say. Perhaps I had set myself up to find all the truth of this horrid matter with Mr. Collins, and yet all I can do is talk to servants, whilst the investigator Mr. Darcy has engaged is able to travel hither and yon and ask all manner of questions of all manner of people. And when I do have some small iota of knowledge he might wish to consider, I cannot even traverse the distance to Netherfield to tell it to him. Nor do I know why I wish to talk to him, for I am still quite angry at his insult." For a moment, Mary was quite aware that she was sounding exactly like the eighteen-year-old girl she was, and not at all like the smart and well-considered lady she wished Lyons to consider her. And that thought vexed her even more greatly than had her previous quarrel.

Lizzy reached an arm about her shoulder and pulled Mary into a quick embrace. "I was more than slightly angry at Mr. Darcy's affront as well. You surely recall it, for you were able to reproduce his vile slander word for word. And how much more angry I was this very morning, when in his attempt to convince me of his merits, he reiterated his faults and insulted not only me, but the entire family I love. And yet..." she pressed her lips together, "I find myself thinking about him more than I ought, and even recognising some merit in his speech."

Mary sniffed. "Merit in his slander?"

"No, dearest. He had no cause to disparage any of us, for unless his family is without blame, he has no basis for his cruel accusations. And knowing as we do that his own sister was ready to elope with the son of a steward, it is hard to imagine all his relatives completely exemplary models of their station. No, the more I ponder it, the more I am inclined to consider not his words but the force of character behind them.

"Mr. Darcy has most certainly spent his whole life with the expectation of associating only with the first circles of society. With his wealth and status, he could well have married the daughter of a noble—indeed, I have heard rumours that his very uncle is an earl. Do you understand my meaning, Mary?"

Mary shook her head. "But how does this excuse his words of censure of our family? We are not earls, but we are gentry."

"It does not excuse his words. But it does excuse his thoughts. He offered me marriage. For him to do that, he had to discard nearly thirty years of preconceptions as to his future relations. His words were his attempt to assure himself of the propriety of his offer; by voicing them to me, he sought to convince me that he had taken account of our different stations and would offer me his support and his affections, nonetheless. It was badly done, but perhaps it is understandable. And of greater import, he wasted no time in coming to my aid at the very first moment that he heard of my trouble. It seems he is sparing little expense in the process as well, for which I must be grateful."

"And do you forgive him?" This Mary had to know. "Even after his confession about trying to separate Jane from Mr. Bingley?"

"That, I own, brought me greater grief than his insult to me. But he reconsidered his actions, and he changed his mind. I find I can respect a man who is not so set in one course that he cannot reconsider when confronted with new information."

Mary allowed her eyes to drift from Lizzy's face as a thousand thoughts rushed through her head. "Then I ought to consider Mr. Lyons' willingness to hear me, rather than his insults?"

"Perhaps," Lizzy offered with a gentle squeeze of her sister's hand. "He did, after all, apologise most profoundly for his offence, and he sought out your opinions. If he has injured you with his words, think not on them so much as on his actions. Those reveal the true measure of a man. Words can deceive, but actions seldom do.”

“Then do you think to forgive Mr. Darcy for his words? Will you accept him?”

Now Lizzy’s smile was sad. “I cannot imagine he will ask me again, for I was not gentle in my refusal. If I am fortunate enough to be permitted once more into his company, I should be pleased for the opportunity to attempt a distant sort of friendship.”

Mary gave her sister a warm embrace. “You talk of Jane being too good, but it is you who are the good one, Lizzy. Few women would think kindly of a man who had so recently offered her such words of abuse. I shall take your words under the most serious of consideration. I pretend to be so intellectual and serious, but you have the true intelligence of understanding the human heart.”

She released Lizzy from the hug and rose to take her book into the day room at the back of the house where she might have better light by which to read. The small salon was by the entrance to the kitchens, and she thought she might beg a cup of hot water to sip whilst she pondered her pages. She pushed open the kitchen doors, so silent on their well-oiled hinges, when she heard Mrs. Hill talking to her husband, who managed the male servants of the estate and acted as butler when the need arose. Her entrance must have gone unnoticed, for the couple did not cease their conversation.

“’Tis an un-Christian thing for me to say,” Mary heard Mr. Hill sigh over the sound of the fire, “but I cannot say I am sorry to see the man departed for good. I was getting near on ready to tell the master, and that would not have gone well for either of them.”

“We can thank heaven that he never bothered the Misses. Poor Nan had enough of a time stilling his wandering hands. ’Twas only last week that I came upon her screaming at him to leave her be, and him...” the housekeeper’s voice dropped almost to a whisper, "with his trousers around his knees, trying to force himself upon her!" Mary stifled a gasp at Mrs. Hill's comment. Had Wickham been in her own home, trying to interfere with the servants? Had the man no limits to his depravity? Nan was barely past childhood—she certainly could be no older than Lydia. The Hills were quite correct that they were well served to have Mr. Wickham no longer paying visits to the house!

But then Mr. Hill spoke again. "I heard of it! How I struggled to keep my temper! That girl is but a child, my own sister's whelp. I was near on ready to strike him myself." At his next words, Mary felt her knees buckle beneath her. "I cannot imagine he learned that in his fancy school; surely most parsons know better than he did to keep their distance from girls and ladies that aren't their wives. For certain, Old Mr. Ainsworth was the most respectable gentleman ever to stand before a congregation. He would have no truck with a man like Collins."

The ground swayed beneath Mary's feet. Mr. Collins! It could not be! Her cousin had been a clergyman, a devout reverend, a rector of the church, who had enjoyed the condescension of Lady Catherine de Bourgh of Rosings! A Christian! A man of faith! As much as Mary had disdained the man for his foolishness and obsequiously patronising ways, she had not once thought him so brazen a hypocrite as to preach modesty and then assault the servants. And Nan, barely past childhood, had been forced to fight off and evade his wandering and unwelcome hands and worse... she had scarcely avoided a fate worse than death. How, under God's heaven, could a man of the church behave in such a foul manner? Could he...? Lizzy's words came rushing back to her. *Words can deceive, but actions seldom do.* Oh, how much Mr. Collins' words had deceived them all; how his actions had shown the true measure of the man!

Holding herself up against the door jamb, Mary experienced, for the first time in her eighteen years, the sort of crisis of belief that could shake a stronger man's soul. Until now she had believed in the inviolate goodness and rightness of the Church and those who were ordained to lead it; suddenly she saw it as a body led by men subject to the weaknesses and sins to which all flesh is vulnerable. Some would fight to maintain the purity of their souls, to lead their congregations by the glowing examples of their own moral lives. Others - clearly! - would gladly sully their hands at the first temptation, and hope that the Church would stand by and watch. The ground that quavered beneath Mary's feet was not the solid floor of Longbourn, but the foundation upon which her carefully constructed persona of piety had been built.

But through this horrible experience of doubt, another question made itself known to her: could somebody have learned of Collins' reprehensible behaviour and taken action? Nan's father was long dead, but Mr. Hill doted on his niece. Could he have sought revenge upon her attacker? What of her other family? If both Mr. and Mrs. Hill knew of Collins' dreadful proclivities, others might as well! There might have been more than one man who wished him dead.

Not for the first time that night, Mary wished fervently for a few minutes with Mr. Lyons, whose actions recently had been nothing but laudable, to talk over all the many, confusing, and dreadful things she had learned that day.

Chapter Fifteen

Things Done at Dinner

Dinner at Netherfield was no more pleasant an affair than had been dinner at Longbourn. Miss Bingley insisted upon Alexander and Darcy both being present at dinner, and had rather insinuated that if the two could not spare her their time for the course of a meal, they might be more comfortable at the inn in Meryton. She had delivered her ultimatum by means of a visit from Mrs. Harwick to Darcy's guest chamber. The housekeeper had conveyed Miss Bingley's sentiments in the most civil of tones, but Alexander, who was reclining on a chair in Darcy's room, heard the threat behind the words and prepared himself to rise and organise his few items of clothing for removal to the inn. He stood and groaned as his hip throbbed, drawing his friend's notice.

As for Darcy, the man had seemed ready to request his belongings be packed up and moved, but the sight of Alexander favouring his injuries had stopped whatever action he had been ready to take. "The beds at the Red Lion, as comfortable as they might be, cannot be good for your leg, Lyons," he had explained with a huff and a shake of his formidable head. "Thorne can tend to you better here." Consequently, he had informed Mrs. Harwick that they would be pleased to join the family for dinner and asked what time ought they to present themselves?

Miss Bingley had been confident in the acceptance of her command, for dinner was an elaborate and drawn-out affair. After the late tea he and Darcy had shared during their discussion of the case, Alexander had little interest in the elegant soups and delicately roasted vegetables and pies that graced the table. Mrs. Slougham's divine creations were wasted upon him this particular evening. Platter upon platter of fried sole and potatoes in a delicate creamy dressing and French pie and broccoli in sauce swam before him, one heavy course replacing the next, all the while Darcy picked at his own plate of roast capon and Hurst consumed serving after serving of whatever was before him.

As intricate and well-crafted as the food was (he must disappear into the kitchens to compliment Mrs. Slougham), the conversation was insipid. Caroline prattled on about how tedious she found the country, with no entertainment, company of any quality, and no good help to be found anywhere.

"I always insist that Charles hire the best of cooks, and our chef in London is one of the finest in the city, for we entertain guests from the highest echelons of society. It is hard in the country, but we had heard that the cook here at Netherfield was acceptable..." (*Acceptable?* Alexander thought. *The woman is a wizard in the kitchen*), "but it really is so difficult..."

Alexander wondered if she heard herself speak, for he and Darcy were suddenly relegated to "company of no quality", and this sumptuous meal hardly supported her assertions of the lack of good help. For all that he had no appetite, Alexander was well aware that the food was superb.

Mrs. Hurst was somewhat less critical than was her sister, taking the conversation instead to great meals she had enjoyed over the years, both within and without London. She talked of the meal she had taken once at the country estate of some baronet of whom Lyons had never heard. Alexander fought to keep his attention on the monologue in case his opinion was wanted. "And when Hurst praised the chef, Miss Elliot—such a beautiful woman, but I wonder why she is not married; could it be she has no dowry? Fortunately my own dowry will be enough to do very well by any daughters we have—well, Miss Elliot told us all about the new chef her father—that is Sir Walter—had recently hired from France! Well of course dear Hurst was pleased with the meal, for a French chef..." and on she had spoken, although her words seemed to drown in the glass of wine Alexander held in his hand.

"Oh, Louisa dear, you must tell us how you know the Elliots," Caroline cooed. Was she trying to impress him, Alexander wondered, in this strange attempt to situate herself with the upper ranks of society? If a passing acquaintance with a baronet of no importance was a mark of such éclat for Miss Bingley, how she would swoon to her of his invitation to dine (only once, mind you, but it did occur) with the very son of an earl! Nevermind that the earl was Darcy's uncle and that the son was Darcy's cousin Richard; if she wished to impress with her connections, she was sadly outclassed.

Mrs. Hurst was still talking. She made some comment about her husband and the baronet's heir presumptive having been at Oxford together, and something about an unfortunate marriage that had caused a rift in the family. "... he ought never to have married the girl, but her father was the sponsor of the wrestling team where he met Hurst, and so wealthy and influential, and it had seemed such a fine match at first, but who was to know that the cousin had expected an offer! So it was through the means of this younger Elliot that we came to the notice of Sir Walter, whose own taste in fine clothing and excellent cuisine quite approaches our own…" On she talked; Alexander returned to his wine.

Louisa then passed the conversation to Caroline, who began praising and abusing other meals they had experienced over the years. Charles' club was deemed to have an excellent chef, even if women were not permitted to partake of meals there, and the hotel in Bath where they had once stayed was allowed to have provided reasonable pastries and pies.

"Not Bath! Miserable place," Hurst groaned. "Smells dreadful, too many people wandering about day in and day out, all very fancy but with no real class. You might have enjoyed the fare, but I could not find a good ragout in the whole town." He patted his ample stomach and settled back into the meal on his plate. "Some amusing entertainment, though, whilst the women were at tea."

Darcy swallowed a yawn, causing Alexander to snicker, which he hid behind a cough and a request for more wine, which was brought to him as the present course was removed and the second brought to the table.

As the meal progressed, Alexander found himself slipping further and further into a wine-dulled fog. His ears caught snippets of conversation—"the coaching inn on the road to Scarborough had terrible bread…," "…seventeen feathers in her headdress, can you imagine it!…," "…haven't been back to the estate in months, or is it already two years?…"—but he could not bring himself to focus on any one thread. He allowed his eyes to wander across the table, transfixed in some strange way by the arrangement of dishes and platters on the white embroidered cloth.

Forcing himself out of the mist of wine and exhaustion, he brought his full attention to the beautiful tableware. The platters themselves were of exceptional quality—exquisite china and polished silver fought for pre-eminence at the table, and Alexander wondered if any of these valuable pieces would be the next to disappear from the household's storage rooms. A sudden inspiration, fueled by boredom and the effects of too much wine— struck him, and he decided he was willing to incur the wrath of his hostess. He was thought to be a lout; let him prove it with his actions.

In the most unrefined manner he could muster, he picked up a large silver platter, now nearly devoid of its burden of sliced ham, and raising it above his head to peer at the hallmark, asked, "I say, Bingley, this must be worth a pretty penny. Any idea what it would set a man back?" Whereupon he replaced the platter atop the crisp linen cloth and sat back to observe his audience. As far as he knew from the servants, the master and his guests were quite unaware of the missing candlesticks. Perhaps, however, someone did have some knowledge! He leaned back to watch through half-closed eyes.

The first thing he noticed was Darcy giving his head a quick shake as if to wonder if he had heard correctly, and then blinking furiously before settling back in his own chair to enjoy the show. Bingley sputtered, "I don't... that is, I really couldn't... I hardly recall...," whilst Louisa Hurst turned quite unaccountably pale and Caroline intoned, "This is hardly suitable conversation for the dinner table," although her face could not hide her great discomfort at the question. The only person who showed no reaction was Hurst, who hardly deigned to look up from his plate. "Decent ragout," he mumbled between mouthfuls.

The little display had been instructive to Alexander. He had learned, foremost, how best to disconcert his hostess, for Miss

Bingley's wide and horrified eyes, though she schooled them within moments—had set him almost to laughter. The woman so obviously doted on her brother's fortune and yet was quite put out by the mention of cost and value. This could not be due to good breeding, for the lady had shown few other such influences in the time of Alexander's sojourn at Netherfield. Many ladies of greater social consequence and less wealth would gladly have spent hours enumerating the exact cost of the silver, the workmanship, the provenance and the import duties on such a fine piece of tableware, and Alexander had not imagined Miss Bingley to shy away from expounding upon her prosperity. Was she, perhaps, so ignorant of the details of the platter's value that she could not speak of it, or was there some other reason behind her display and discomfort? Mrs. Hurst's response, too, had been interesting. What cause could she have to react so visibly to his déclassé comment? He resolved to solve these small mysteries over the interminable coffee service that would undoubtedly follow the meal.

But this was not to be. Caroline seemed quite out of sorts for the rest of dinner, and upon rising to leave the gentlemen to their cigars and port, she caught the corner of the tablecloth and tripped, sending the glasses of wine that remained on the table over onto their sides and spilling the deep red liquid all across the formerly pristine tablecloth and onto Darcy's white waistcoat.

The ensuing fuss and bother merely resulted in more spilled liquid and the abrupt end to an unsatisfying meal, leaving Alexander feeling at odds with the world and in much more discomfort from his injuries than he had been before he sat down to dine. A second moment of inspiration struck him, and he waved Darcy upstairs to be tended to by his valet. "I shall join you when you are ready; send Thorne and I shall attend. But I have one quick errand to run first."

Ignoring the others, he slipped through into the breakfast room-*cum*-servery and thence into the kitchens, where the dishes from the elaborate dinner were sitting piled upon the large wooden table. He found his object and reached for it, winking at the kitchen maids who were staring at him with wide eyes. It was but the work of a moment to discover what he needed. He winked again and slipped back through into the breakfast room, through the short crooked passage that led directly to the main hall of the house, and then up the stairs to his rooms.

He did not wait for long. A discreet knock upon his door informed him that Darcy was respectable and desirous of conversation, and within moments Alexander was seated once more upon that large chair. "Did you enjoy my little display?" he asked, eyes drowsy and a smirk upon his lips.

"It was unexpected," Darcy replied. "May I ask the purpose?"

"I wished to gauge their reactions. Miss Bingley and Mrs. Hurst did not respond as I had imagined. Your friend, however, seemed more alarmed by my hoisting the platter than by my question, and in truth seemed about ready to burst into laughter. But what of Caroline? She seemed more than unsettled by the question. And Louisa Hurst went so white I thought she might fade into the linens."

"I cannot account for it at all. I would have thought Caroline to be one to crow about her belongings of great value. But I see by your smile that you have a theory." Darcy let his head fall back upon his neck and shrugged his shoulders.

"Indeed I do! I returned to the kitchen right now and examined that platter again. There is a mark on the bottom, not a craftsman's hallmark, but the mark of ownership. It is not Bingley's, nor does it belong to Netherfield itself. No, that platter belongs—or belonged—to an estate called Elm Ridge. Do you happen to know whose that might be? For I have a thought."

"I do know, but tell me what you surmise."

"Hurst. Am I correct that Elm Ridge is his familial estate? Aha! And I also surmise that the estate is entailed and he cannot sell it or any part of it, but that it brings in very little income and has left him in rather straightened circumstances. He sold his brother Bingley his family's silverware in order to raise some blunt, and for some reason the fact of this embarrasses Caroline beyond her tolerance."

"You have earned your reputation once more, I see," Darcy bowed his head toward his companion and offered a mock flourish with his hand. "Caroline only sees herself through the lens of wealth and prestige. To her thinking, if the *ton* should discover the extent of Hursts' penury, it would destroy her own standing in society. It is a matter of conceit, nothing more, and nothing less."

"Both sisters are equally concerned with these appearances?"

"As they have been ever since first I made their acquaintance. To tell the truth, Lyons, I have no idea how Bingley himself became the man he is, as unconcerned with ostentation and image as his sisters dote upon it." Darcy stretched and yawned. "I believe you look as tired as I feel. Let me send Thorne your way once more to tend to your side, and perhaps we will have a clearer view of matters come morning. Shall we meet at breakfast? Whatever plans you wish to pursue, I am your servant."

Alexander sighed at the comment, once more so thoughtlessly tossed off. This meaningless expression of social convention, so commonly uttered, so frequently heard, vexed him with each utterance. Darcy could not begin to comprehend Alexander's loathing, and thus Alexander said nothing. Darcy was no man's servant. If any man was the servant, it was Alexander himself, here in this gilded cage because he was paid to be so, dining with people he despised because it suited his employer. Still, he would not abuse Darcy with his thoughts, for the man spoke with good intentions, even if the deeper meaning of his words stung. Thus seemed Darcy's lot in life: to insult with the best of intentions. Perhaps Miss Elizabeth would soon be in a position to take him in hand and educate him as to a better use for his words.

"Goodnight, then," he replied. "Hopefully the morning will bring the pieces we need to complete this puzzle."

After a restless night, Alexander was eager to cast his frustrations to the wind in the hopes that the fresh air of morning would stimulate some productive thoughts. He had risen early and dressed in his roughest clothing before wandering off to the stables in search of a placid mount. His hip was now a riotous shade of purple that would rival anything the dressmakers and textile merchants of London could concoct, but it was less painful to move and not as stiff as he had imagined. Thorne had, once again, treated it with the odorous liniment and a rather excruciating massage, but the therapy had done wonders; indeed, it had been the only experience of any value from the previous evening.

"Yer awake before the nobs," the young groom greeted him. "Even Mr. Darcy does not rise this early, and 'e's a big one for a ride before 'is breakfast. Them's not fancy riding clothes neither," the lad surveyed the simple buckskins and worker's coat he wore. "I thought for a moment them was the ones what we lost last week and wondered who put them in yer room!" He laughed at his silly notion and scurried off to find a suitable mount to saddle up for a ride. Before long Alexander was in the saddle and moving across the open and empty fields.

The world that he saw was a dull affair in shades of greys and browns; the blue skies that had graced the region the previous two days had retreated into the gloominess of November, with no trace of colour remaining above the horizon. The clouds did not seem to portend rain, but neither did they promise sunshine.

Likewise, the fields had long since given up their verdant crops and sat void and wan, barren against the bleak sky, skeletal trees pointing mockingly at the pale firmament, mirroring the emptiness that had somehow settled upon his spirits. He had thought, the previous day, to be making headway against what had become a troublesome case, but now he felt bereft. Perhaps it was the aftereffects of the large quantity of wine he had consumed, or the soul-numbing conversation at dinner; perhaps it was the monotony of the landscape in a place where everybody and nobody seemed to hold the answers he needed. He allowed the horse to take its own pace and set its own direction, and he rode for a long time, letting his mind grow blank in the hopes of some clear picture taking form within.

How long, exactly, he had been riding he could not say, for he had left his watch fob with his better clothing back at Netherfield; nevertheless the sun was much higher in the sky when, at last, he returned and eased himself off his horse. His hip ached, but he welcomed the sensation. It was a burst of intensity in a faded watercolour world, reminding him that he was alive and vital. He stretched this way and that as he sought to ease the cramp that had taken hold in his bruised joint, and began his slow limp towards the house, feeling better for his efforts despite the pain.

"Mr. Lyons." Mrs. Slougham's voice greeted him as he made his careful way through the kitchen door. "Mr. Darcy was inquiring after you. He has a visitor. Shall I send up some more tea in a few minutes? Or coffee? I believe you might wish to change before greeting them. They are in the library." The cook then bustled out of the main kitchen and into the smaller scullery, leaving Alexander to his own devices. He took the servants' stairs up to his room and quickly washed in the hot water he found waiting and changed his clothing. He was uncertain whom, exactly, he was to meet, but from Mrs. Slougham's tone, it was somebody who would not appreciate his horse-scented working clothes.

The muted sound of voices greeted him as he approached the library. Pushing open the door, he could see Darcy seated on one of the large armchairs, talking to a second person who was hidden behind the wall where it shaped the room into an L. The smell of coffee, hot and fragrant, drew him into the space, and before he glanced up at the second person, his eyes alit on the tray on the side table, covered with an assortment of breads and pastries and cheese and jam. He had not realised until this moment that he was hungry, and he fought the impulse to take his breakfast before acknowledging his company.

His more civilised sense prevailed, however, and he took one more step into the room, where he could see the entirety of the space behind that small partition of a wall. There, in a chair similar to Darcy's, but rather dwarfed by it, sat Miss Mary Bennet, a cup of tea in her hands, a scone with jam on a plate on the table before her. Alexander was unaccountably pleased to see her.

Why, exactly, that was, he could not say. She was smart enough, and certainly observant, with a keen memory that allowed her to consider what she had seen and to relate it to others. But since his thoughtless insult, she had been cool to him and he could not blame her at all. There was little else he could say to her that had not been said and he had thought not to have anything more to do with her, other than as the sister to the woman he was here to aid, and yet the sight of her dark eyes and cautious gaze gave him a momentary flush of pleasure.

More unaccountably, for all of her guardedness and the reserve behind which she held herself, he somehow felt she was pleased to see him as well. Resolving to do whatever he might to improve their rapport, he bowed low and greeted the lady with every ounce of civility and warmth he could summon.

"Miss Mary, what a delight! It is most pleasant to see you once more. Are you here to relate news of Miss Elizabeth? Has Sir William, perhaps, suggested he will not be seeking to charge her? Ah, you surely would like more tea. Please, allow me."

He helped her to a fresh cup of tea before assembling his own food, and then with bread and cheese before him and hot coffee in hand, he settled on the third chair by the table to hear what had brought her across the damp fields so early in the day.

"Sir William, alas, has not given any suggestion of abandoning his plans, although neither has he made any immediate moves to officially lay charges against her," Mary explained. "However, I have come upon some items of news that might prove valuable to your own efforts on my sister's behalf." She took a sip of tea and wrapped her shawl around her shoulders. Alexander was strangely affected by the sight.

"Are you chilled, Miss Mary? Is the fire not warm enough? Some more tea?"

"Thank you, no, Mr. Lyons. I am somewhat chilled from my ride, but the room is not cold. I was pressed by necessity to ride around the back of the estate to come to the kitchen door through the fields rather than along the main drive, for Miss Bingley has given express orders that I not be allowed in her house." Alexander's eyes shot up. "My association with a presumed murderess has rendered me unfit for her association. I do not feel the loss, never fear. Fortunately Mr. Darcy met me in the kitchens, where I was in conversation with Mrs. Slougham—"

"I came to inquire after your own whereabouts, Lyons."

"And thence he spirited me up the servants' stairs to this very room. Miss Bingley never deigns to enter, so I have heard, and if Mrs. Harwick hears voices, she will assume it is you two gentlemen speaking and will not interrupt."

Alexander chortled his approval. "You have everything worked out perfectly. And you are certain I cannot stir the fire? Now, what news, Miss Mary? For you are certainly come with news!"

Chapter Sixteen

A Valuable Exchange

Mary surveyed her audience. It was a rare event for a young lady such as herself to have two men so eager to hear what she had to tell them, and she savoured the experience. Seeing two sets of eyes fixed upon her and Mr. Lyons' notebook and pencil at the ready, she began to speak.

"When we parted ways yesterday," she explained, "I took it upon myself to explore a notion I had. I took the phaeton and went to Oakville to visit my friend Margaret Durham." With a minimum of ado, she sketched the nature of her friendship with the young lady at the Bowridge estate. "I thought that perhaps the missing maid from Netherfield might have achieved Oakville, there to seek a position. It turned out that I was correct.

"Polly—for that is the girl's name—has lived in Meryton all her life. I do not believe she has travelled more than ten miles in any direction, and whilst she might have had London in mind for her eventual destination, I believed the shock of the distance would have quite overcome her. Oakville is the next town over on the road to London; Oakville is where I sought her. And," she paused for effect, "where I found her!"

"Smart girl!" The look of pride on Alexander's face set her heart racing. "That is exactly the logic I so admire. Why did the girl flee? Did she tell you as much?" he asked. Mary was rather certain he knew the answer, but he wished to hear her say it, much as he had wished to hear Lizzy recount her meeting with Mr. Collins in her own words.

"I promised her I would not tell her story if it were not quite necessary; but her tale, if true, frees Lizzy completely from blame. She had been threatened by Mr. Wickham," she explained. "He threatened to blame her for the loss of the silverware unless she agreed to meet him in the field. His intentions, she fears, were not honourable." Mary felt her face flush. This must surely be a topic all too familiar to Mr. Lyons at least, if not to both men. Why could she not even broach the subject without succumbing to these feminine fits of embarrassment?

She was relieved that Mr. Lyons did not appear to note her discomfort. Instead, he wrinkled his nose and sighed, "Alas, whilst Wickham sounds the perfect candidate for this, being aware of the theft, involved in gaming both in town and in London, and responsible for Polly's flight, he was known to be in London on military business at the time of the murder." Darcy's dark head nodded its agreement.

Now Mary felt a triumphant smile form upon her face as she protested, "But no! Listen! This is not all I have heard, for Polly kept her agreement the following day and waited to meet Mr. Wickham in the woods by Oakham Mount. Oh, I have so much to tell you!"

She took another sip of her tea and recounted Polly's tale of the confrontation between Lizzy and Mr. Collins. "She said she most clearly heard Mr. Collins shouting at Lizzy as Lizzy ran off into the woods. Lizzy left him alive! We must tell Sir William, and he will surely release her from all suspicion!"

The look on Mr. Lyons' face was not encouraging, however. "Did she remain until your sister had gone home?"

"No," Mary was tentative. "She herself left almost immediately, because—"

"Then she did not see Miss Elizabeth depart the area."

Mary shook her head.

"Alas," Mr. Lyons sighed. "This is certainly helpful, but it proves little. Miss Elizabeth might well have recovered enough to allow her anger to replace her fear, and she could have returned to Mr. Collins as he lay in the mud and dispatched him with her knife."

"Lyons, you don't seriously believe—" Mr. Darcy expostulated.

"No, not for a moment. But whilst this is certainly encouraging evidence, it is not conclusive and will not deter someone hoping to secure a quick arrest. Think for a moment: we now know that Miss Elizabeth did not tell all the truth when she was first questioned. Taken in that light, somebody might conclude that this evidence points further towards her guilt and not her innocence. We must continue our investigations until we have discovered the true killer."

"Gentlemen," Mary's voice was determined, "there is more. Please hear me out."

The men stopped and stared at her.

"You did not ask why Polly departed so quickly, without ensuring that Lizzy was well. She ran away because somebody else was riding up, and that somebody was none other than Mr. Wickham himself!"

Without waiting for their stunned expressions to settle she added, "After Lizzy escaped into the woods, Polly told me, Mr. Wickham galloped up on his horse and, hearing Mr. Collins' abuses, rode out to him rather than towards the spot he had mentioned for the assignation. He was there! Lizzy left Mr. Collins alive, before Mr. Wickham found him!"

With some satisfaction, she let her glance flit from one man to the other and then back again. As they gaped at her, each with eyes wide and heads shaking, she thrilled at the shock of power she felt tingle at the base of her spine. Pride, she told herself, is a mortal sin, and yet she could not rue the pride she felt at that moment, having discovered something neither man had even contemplated. She bit back a smile and waited.

"Here? In Meryton?" Mr. Darcy exploded. "How can that be? He was assuredly in London!"

"Was Polly quite certain?" Mr. Lyons' voice was more steady, but his tone betrayed his alarm at this news. "Could it have been another man whom she mistook for Wickham? She must have been some distance away."

Mary shook her head. "She was quite positive. She both saw and heard him, and had not the first doubt that it was, indeed, he who rode up."

Mr. Lyons scratched at his chin, then asked, "Say, Darcy, how far is it from here to London? About twenty miles?"

"Twenty-four, I believe, from Longbourn to St. Paul's. Perhaps twenty-two from the field by Oakham Mount."

"Indeed!" Alexander was silent for a moment. "Miss Mary, did Polly observe the encounter between Wickham and Collins? Did she tell you anything?"

"No. After witnessing the attack on my poor sister, as soon as Mr. Wickham diverted his path from the woods to where Mr. Collins lay by the stream, she fled. She found the road near the back of the woods and kept walking until Oakville, where she found a warm barn for the night. 'Tis only some four miles further along from the Mount."

"Just so," Mr. Lyons' eyes seemed focused on some point far beyond the walls of the library. "Twenty-two miles—that would take a fit man two hours on a fast horse, although he would have to change at—"

"At Southgate. That's ten miles from the centre of London, and almost exactly half way here, with a coaching inn and a stable to hire a horse. That is where we stopped on our journey here. Quick! I need one of Bingley's fastest riders and some paper to write a note!" Mr. Darcy leapt up from his chair and charged from the room, shouting his orders to anyone who might be near enough to heed them.

It was some minutes before Mr. Darcy returned, leaving Mary and Mr. Lyons together in the library. Mary was distinctly uncomfortable, although she was not quite certain why. Only yesterday she had talked with the man after her father's confession about losing her dowry, and then later on walked with him whilst Mr. Darcy made his terrible proposal, and she had not been bothered by his presence then. Nor did she fear the man in any way. Despite his rude insult on the first afternoon of their acquaintance, he had not once uttered a threatening syllable to her. And yet now, all she could sense was his presence, more overwhelming than could be attributed to a man of his size, impinging more heavily upon her senses. A glance at his face revealed only a mild expression and a slight smile, and yet when she closed her eyes, Mary could feel him everywhere in the room, looming and pervasive.

It was, she realised with a start, his very proximity that gave her pause, and she knew not what to make of that alarming idea. Instead, she sought some topic of conversation. There was one question which she needed to ask, although it would not enamour her to the man. Nevertheless it had played upon her, and after the shocking revelation overheard between Mr. and Mrs. Hill the previous night, it was one that she knew she must soon ask of herself.

"Mr. Lyons," her voice sounded weak in the sudden silence of the room, "I would ask something impertinent. The afternoon when we… crossed paths here at Netherfield, you suggested that none would consider you a decent Christian man. What did you mean by that? Do you not consider yourself as such?"

He stared at her, unblinking. "I ought not to have said anything. Pray, forgive me for that lapse."

"And yet I find I cannot shake the idea from my mind. I have had my own faith in the Church disarranged of late, and I find I am struggling to define my devotion to God and to the men who are in authority in the established church. Having lived my entire life secure in philosophies I now dare to question, I would dearly like to know what you meant by your statement."

Mr. Lyons stared at her a while longer. "Please, forgive me if I do not answer your question completely. Suffice it to say that whilst I endeavour—despite my deplorable behaviour to you that afternoon—to comport myself as a good Christian gentleman ought, I am not in communion with the Church of England. Do not fear, although a Scotsman, I am neither a Presbyterian nor a Papist, either!"

This was most confusing! "And yet you have such a determined notion of justice!" Mary cried out. "I cannot fathom so deeply seated a sense of right and wrong devoid of the foundations of religious morality!" To her own ears, her voice was shocked and indignant.

To her surprise, Mr. Lyons laughed. "I find that I do not require the saints upon one shoulder and the devil upon the other to whisper into my ears of right and wrong. These are notions so well-established in my own breast that not all the saints in heaven, nor demons from the depths, could shake them loose."

Mary expected to be outraged by such notions. Surely goodness came from God and evil from the devil! And yet she could not scorn the sincerity with which the man spoke, and she found herself contemplating his words. Indeed, her own recent internal struggle with the flaws of the church had not weakened her own concepts of right and wrong, but rather, had been inflamed by them. If she had not such a definite sense of morality deep within herself, would she have been so struck by the news of Mr. Collins' shameful deeds?

Could this strange man, so enigmatic with his rough country speech and cultured thoughts, so low-brow and erudite all at once, possibly have some insight into the canker that gnawed at her spirits? The same instinct that guided her to Oakville to seek after Polly now whispered to her to trust him. She was staring at him, and he returned her regard with guileless eyes.

"May I ask you another question, Sir?" she began. "Or, rather, may I tell you of something that disconcerts me greatly? I would value your thoughts on it."

He raised his eyebrows. Had she noticed how kind his eyes were before? How open his features? Pursing her lips, she breathed out very slowly, then began her tale. She recounted the conversation between the Hills and her horrific realisation that her cousin, an ordained clergyman, an official of the Church, had been discovered assaulting a young girl, barely even a woman. That such terrible actions might be undertaken by an unholy man such as Mr. Wickham was terrible enough to contemplate; that a parson, a man supposedly committed to God, had done likewise had shaken her to her core. She talked of her shock at the man's actions and of the dawning of doubt in the goodness of the Church, and of her dreadful feelings within that arose from this gnawing suspicion, and as she spoke, she hardly noticed Alexander moving closer and closer to her, till he was at her side, handkerchief at the ready, until she found herself taking it into her own hand and dabbing at her eyes.

"This has upset you greatly." He had no need of being a skilled investigator to discern her mind, and yet hearing the words was comforting.

"I cannot expect you to understand..."

"And yet, I assure you, Miss Mary, I do. To a point, at least. You have always found your comfort in the immutable and unassailable foundation of your Church, and now you have discovered that so much of what you believed is built on the fallibility of ordinary men. Fear not; where true morality lies is far beyond the foibles of human flesh." She nodded. He did understand.

"I must not doubt." She needed to refute the words he had spoken, that seemed to find resonance within her soul. "'*But let him ask in faith, nothing wavering. For he that wavereth is like a wave of the sea driven with the wind and tossed.*' I cannot allow myself to be tossed in the waves of suspicion and disbelief."

"Ah, but do not forget that only when you trust yourself to the tide and you leave the safety of secluded shores, that is when you experience the greater world, in all its glory. Do not be afraid to be that wind-tossed wave that reaches new and wonderful shores."

She could find nothing to reply to that most unsettling and intriguing thought and allowed herself to stare at the remains of the tea and cakes upon the table.

Mr. Lyons broke the silence after a moment. "Your account intrigues me greatly, but it does raise a point far beyond that of the nature of the Church and the weaknesses of men. All theological implications aside, Mr. Collins is reported to have imposed himself upon a very young niece of your family's butler, a girl whom he loves as his own daughter."

Mary nodded, her eyes still on the crumbs of bread and rinds of cheese.

"This sets Mr. Hill as yet another man who would be Mr. Collins' enemy. The question is whether he hated the man enough to wish him dead, and whether he would take action to ensure that result."

"That sounds rather improbable." Mr. Darcy's voice sounded from the doorway. He strode in with his accustomed confidence, his task having been completed. "It would give the man incentive enough to see Collins dead, but the parson was twenty years younger than Hill, and likely double his size and weight. I cannot see it. Nor was there any report of Hill's clothing being tainted by blood, and after the ado at Longbourn, if such had occurred, we would have heard news of it. Still, it does increase the very real possibility of there being more men in Meryton who might have reason to wish ill upon Collins."

Mary took a sip of her now-cold tea and whispered, "I have more information."

"You do?" Lyons' eyes were wide and his smile wider. "You amaze me, Miss Mary. Speak on!"

"I overheard… that is, I had not intended to listen in, but I could not help but hear a part, and then I felt I must know more… that is…"

"Never mind the excuse, girl, what did you hear?" His eyes no longer seemed kind, but rather cross; his voice rough and impatient.

Mary flushed red from anger now. At the very moment when Mr. Lyons began to improve in her eyes, he said something to vex her once again. "I am not a 'girl,' nor am I a maid to be called so. I have a name and you are invited to use it." Her eyes narrowed at him.

"My apologies again, Miss Mary. I am merely anxious to hear what was said that might help your sister.

With a glance towards Mr. Darcy, who smiled encouragingly, she sighed. "Lizzy received a very strange letter today from Lady Catherine de Bourgh—"

"My aunt?" Darcy burst out. "Writing to Miss Elizabeth? What on earth could have occasioned that?"

"Lady Catherine seemed intent upon giving Lizzy the advice she would require upon marrying my cousin. It seemed that Mr. Collins had been encouraged by Lady Catherine to choose a wife from amongst our family, and that he had written to your aunt to inform her as to his choice. More importantly, he seemed to have written to her about a great many things he had noticed in Meryton. If I recall, she wrote, '*Mr. Collins has written much about the unsavoury goings-on in your village, and I must inform you that this sort of affair will not be condoned at Hunsford. I do not tolerate any manner of gaming whatsoever, and shall be most displeased should your presence presage such unacceptable activities.*' I cannot imagine what unsavoury goings-on he had discovered, but he was not a man to keep his secrets."

"And," Mr. Lyons continued, "if somebody had discovered what Collins knew and was prepared to tell, we might have yet another motive for murder!"

Chapter Seventeen

George Wickham, Lieutenant

Alexander watched as Darcy returned to the door to the library, which he pulled closed with an audible click. "We shan't be disturbed now. I would appreciate a few moments to sort through what we have learned." He settled himself into the chair opposite Alexander and leaned forward, elbows on his knees. His face was serious but calm, his lips tight and his jaw tense. "Let me think aloud, Lyons, and tell me where I have erred."

Alexander regarded his friend, imposing in his massive chair, his large head bobbing upon his cravat-encrusted neck. Even for a morning spent doing nothing but musing, he was impeccably dressed. Alexander did not have such fine clothing for his most elaborate evening wear. But he could not—would not—fault Darcy for having been born to riches and living appropriately. Heavens knew the man did as much good with his wealth as he could, and his lands sustained thousands of people in comparative comfort. He met the probing eyes with his own and nodded. "Speak, and we will listen."

"The tale as we have it is thus," Darcy intoned. "Wickham is known in the gambling dens of London and owes a small fortune; of late he has been repaying his creditors with unaccustomed regularity. Coincidentally, this began at the same time that the silver from Netherfield began to disappear."

"Go on," Alexander prompted, as Miss Mary's lips twisted into a small smile.

"I believe that he was somehow procuring this missing silver to pay some of his debts, although how he was obtaining it, I cannot yet say. If I recall, Colonel Forster mentioned that Wickham was frequently sent to London on military matters. This would be a perfect place to conduct the business of disposing of the silverware and paying his creditors, with no questions asked about his whereabouts and no tales of the silver being sold or being seen in the vicinity of Meryton." Alexander blinked his approval and gestured for the man to continue.

"Under the guise of a threat, he had an assignation planned with the maid Polly in the woods near Oakham Mount, although we know that he was supposed to be in London. The distance is not so terribly great as to make this impossible; indeed, he may have had other reasons for returning to Meryton as well as his tryst with the maid.

"As we have heard from various sources, including my own Aunt Catherine's letter, Mr. Collins was known to have discovered some of the less respectable affairs in the village and was also known to have reported them and challenged men about them. If he had learned of Wickham's theft of the silver it is entirely within what we know of the man that he would have threatened Wickham to bring him to justice. Whether Collins might have told

Lady Catherine or Colonel Forster makes little difference; the truth would be out and the man's career ended. He would be captured and imprisoned or transported. His life would, to all intents and purposes, be over. This could well be incentive to murder.

"We also know that Wickham was in the field the day Collins died. He is a young and fit man, tall and strong and trained in combat. Collins would have had little chance against a determined enemy such as the lieutenant. I surmise he might have heard the man's cries, found him injured and prone in the mud with a knife at the ready, and with no witnesses. Within a moment, all of his problems would be over. It all makes a very neat picture."

Alexander listened to this recital with great interest. All of this he had considered himself, and hearing it spoken aloud by another gave the narrative greater and greater credibility. Miss Mary's head was nodding its gentle agreement as well, and she chewed on her bottom lip as she listened, her eyes almost closed in contemplation.

It sounded so sensible; every detail fit. He could not be quite certain why something still bothered him. And when Miss Mary finally turned her dark eyes to meet his, he could see that glimmer of uncertainty reflected therein as well.

He mentally chastised himself; he was seeking trouble where there was none to be found. Here was a solution that perfectly fit the problem. At the very least of it, Miss Elizabeth seemed to be quite cleared of all wrongdoing, and he and Darcy need only visit Sir William and explain their conclusions for the lady to be freed from her burden.

And yet... Miss Mary felt it as well. She, too, was unhappy somehow. Was it, perhaps, their strained relationship that bothered her? He had not been successful in his attempts to apologise for his initial lapse of social grace and his dire insult, and at every moment when he felt that perhaps they might forge some semblance of a friendship, he said something wrong, thereby returning matters to their previous unhappy state. She was a smart creature of unusual understanding; she might become a trusted confidante indeed if she could rid herself of the rigidity of the manner that seemed to prevent her from understanding her own mind. Was the quiet dissatisfaction that marred this happy solution rooted in her antipathy for him? Perhaps it was so. He must wipe that from his mind, for after this investigation was complete, when Sir William would assuredly relinquish all claims to Miss Elizabeth's guilt, he would never see Miss Mary again.

And again, he was not certain why that notion vexed him so.

"What is our next step?" Darcy stood up and began pacing. Now that a solution seemed at hand, he looked impatient and eager for action.

"I believe a return visit to Colonel Forster might be the place to begin. I would speak to him once more before speaking to Sir William. And then we must seek out the lieutenant himself: George Wickham."

They descended to the kitchens through the servants' stairs up which Mary had initially arrived. She had avoided the notice of both Caroline Bingley and Mrs. Harwick thus far, and she expressed little interest in having that pleasant situation change. Mrs. Slougham was rolling out pastry for the afternoon's pies as the three emerged from the alcove where the staircase emptied out. Alexander breathed deeply of the rich stews that would fill some of those pies and wondered how long he would remain at Netherfield once his duties to Darcy had been completed.

"Are those for tea?" he asked the cook, giving her a broad smile and a wink.

"Aye, laddie," the woman returned. "If you think you'll be missing out whilst you are on your business in the village, I'll put one or two aside for you."

"Bless you, Mrs. Slougham!" he graced her with another smile. "By the way," he stopped his two companions with his question, "have any more pieces of silver gone missing? I don't suppose any pieces have been discovered, have they?"

The cook shook her head. "No, none have returned, but neither have any more vanished on us. We are being most particularly careful about counting the pieces and locking the room where they are stored, and whilst I am afraid to tempt the fates, we seem to have all that we should."

"That is excellent news! I do believe your troubles with the silver are at an end." Alexander bowed to her and received a sweet biscuit for his trouble, and one for each of his companions.

"To the stables?" Darcy asked as he chewed upon his biscuit.

"Indeed," Miss Mary replied. "And I shall accompany you. This is all in aid of Lizzy and she is my sister. I will not be gainsaid." Her steely eyes defied either man to object. Alexander wondered if she had a verse from her bible ready to defend her pronouncement. Something about a woman of valour, perhaps? Certainly not the bit about Eve. He wisely chose not to ask, leaving Darcy to debate the decision.

"Are you quite certain, Miss Mary? The barracks, where the colonel's office is located, is not a pleasant place for a young lady such as yourself. I would be pleased to ride to Longbourn immediately upon the completion of our tasks to inform you as to the outcome."

But Mary would not be denied, insisting that she had accompanied her sisters on more than one occasion through the encampment, and that her sister's fate was of far greater importance than her own comfort. Alexander was strangely moved by this assertion. In truth, he was uncertain whether to be pleased or upset that Miss Mary insisted upon joining the men. Her singularity of purpose was hardly ladylike, being, rather, a quality deemed undesirable by so many members of the ton, and yet he found it attractive. He could not but admire the determination with which she had set out to help her sister, and allowed his thoughts to wander, for a short moment, to a future in which some lady held his own wellbeing in such a steady place in her heart.

The girl—no, the lady, he corrected himself—rode well, keeping up with Darcy and himself with ease. She mounted her horse without assistance and took the hedges smoothly and with confidence. Riding behind her as she urged her mount across the meadow towards the lane towards the militia's encampment, he could not help but admire her form and grace on horseback. Despite her prickly manner and the well of doubt in which she now found herself, it was a pity he would soon leave these parts, leaving her here never to meet again.

Colonel Forster seemed surprised to see Miss Mary but welcomed her as generously as he did Alexander and Darcy. He showed her to a seat and offered to call for tea, which she refused with the grace of her fine upbringing. When she decided to act the lady, Alexander realised, she could do so with remarkable assurance. She did sit quietly whilst the men spoke, but Alexander was constantly aware of her attention on every word he or the colonel uttered.

After the preliminary social niceties, Alexander posed his first question. "You mentioned to us yesterday that Lieutenant Wickham was often sent on these missions to London." The colonel nodded. "How frequent would these be? How many times, since you have been in Meryton, has he travelled thither?"

"Only twice before; he has been with our unit for a short time, but he did bring some letters of reference from previous superiors remarking on his diligence in such affairs."

Darcy raised a single eyebrow. "Did you confirm the veracity of these accounts? Were the letters authentic?"

The colonel reddened. "I did not. He had a valid commission and I needed men. But he did seem to know enough about the running of a regiment and the duties of an officer that I had no cause to question his letters. He also seemed conversant with the area around Meryton. He seemed to know of places and landmarks, but needed directions to locate them exactly."

"As if," Darcy asked, "he had heard of them through another?"

"Exactly." The colonel's voice was conclusive.

"When did Wickham first arrive at your doorstep?" Alexander needed to know more precisely the chronology of events. The colonel began shuffling through some papers on his desk, murmuring something about looking up the exact date.

"I can answer that," Mary's light voice sounded strange in this very masculine space. Three sets of eyes turned to her. "It was Tuesday, the 19th of November, some eleven days ago. It seems so very much longer, for all that Mr. Wickham set about insinuating himself in all of our lives."

"Indeed, Miss Mary," Alexander was intrigued once more by her accurate accounting of events. "What can you tell us about your meeting?"

Mary closed her eyes and thought for a moment. "It was a fair day, and Mr. Collins had arrived only the afternoon before..."

"Is that so?" Darcy interjected. "How... coincidental."

"Indeed!" Alexander echoed.

Mary continued as if she had not been interrupted. "Lydia had expressed an interest in walking into Meryton to hear more of some gossip, and my sisters and Mr. Collins chose to join her. In truth," she lowered her voice, "Papa encouraged this decision, for I believe he was already at the end of his patience with our cousin. I had opted to remain at home and complete the embroidery I had begun, but after the others departed, the sun seemed so welcoming that I abandoned my work and went after them.

"They did not see me, but I had nearly caught up with them by the time they had achieved the village. There they met with Mr. Denny, whom Lydia thought very handsome in his red coat, and with Mr. Denny was another gentleman, whom I heard him introduce as Mr. Wickham."

She stopped her recitation and let her eyes travel from one man to the next, alighting upon Darcy. His face went white. "Yes, I recall." His voice was terse, his tone icy. "That was the first time I had seen him since the... incident the previous summer. I was most distressed to see him, furious that he had disturbed the time I had hoped would help me to recover my equilibrium after the turmoil of that experience. Maintaining my temper took every ounce of energy I had, and I believe my manner did not go unnoticed by Eliz... by the ladies in the party."

"That is true, Mr. Darcy," Mary concurred, "but I saw something nobody else seemed to notice. Whilst everyone else's attention was on you and Mr. Wickham, I was able to watch Mr. Collins. I was nearly upon you, close enough to hear the loudest voices, although nobody saw me. Nobody ever seems to." Her voice dropped and Alexander felt his heart break at this confession. She blinked once, then said, "When Mr. Collins heard Mr. Wickham's name pronounced, I could see him startle, almost as if he had heard the name before, and something of the man, but had not before made his acquaintance. All the while my sisters were talking, and when Mr. Bingley and Mr. Darcy rode up, Mr. Collins was staring hard at Mr. Wickham as if trying to make up his mind about something. I would be prepared to say that it was not the first my cousin knew of Wickham."

Alexander screwed up his eyes and thought hard. This was most interesting, although he was not certain what to make of the information. "Do you think," he said at last, "that Collins knew of the business from the previous summer?" Colonel Forster looked rather confused, but Alexander ignored his quizzical expression. "How much did Lady Catherine know of the affair with Georgiana, Darcy?"

"We had to tell her that my sister was missing; we thought, for a time, that Georgiana had gone to Rosings, and it was one of the first places we inquired after her. It would not have taken too much work to learn some more of the details once the affair had concluded. Georgiana herself might have answered her aunt's insistent and probing questions; Collins might well have learned the name through her."

As Darcy spoke, Alexander kept his eye on the colonel, watching as realisation dawned on the older man's face. "I cannot believe I took this man on as an officer," he said at last. "The gaming I could excuse, but this is... not what I want in a leader of men." He sighed and frowned. "Might Collins have threatened him?"

"We believe so," Alexander replied. "May I ask, sir, when Wickham returned from London?"

Colonel Forster furrowed his brows. "I cannot rightly say. I have not seen him since his return. He did not report this morning, but if he had returned late last night from London, it would not be unexpected for him to sleep past morning manoeuvres."

"But he did return?" Mary asked.

Once more the colonel screwed up his nose. "His horse was in the stables when I went to inspect the beasts for the exercises. I had assumed the animal returned with his rider upon his back. Shall we ask the grooms?"

The lads on duty the previous night were soon found. Lieutenant Wickham—known best as the officer riding Peredur—had indeed returned the previous evening, just as the last rays of the sun were fading into darkness.

"He ought then to have reported first thing this morning," the colonel grumbled. Alexander nodded but turned to Darcy and grimaced.

"Whilst we were sitting down at Caroline's interminable dinner," he murmured. Darcy's eyes did not waver from the young grooms.

"Did you see the officer who rode in upon Peredur?" Alexander began his litany of questions.

"Yes indeed, sir," the older of the two lads bobbed his fair head up and down.

"You knew him? You recognised his face?"

"Yes, I did, sir. It was the same one what sneaks out for 'is meeting plans at night, sir."

Now Darcy's eyes flickered over to meet Alexander's. The man's habits had not changed since the events of the summer.

"And it was certainly Lieutenant Wickham?"

"Yes, sir. That is the name I was told when first 'e arrived. It was most certainly 'im. He gave me a sweet for taking extra care of Peredur for 'e had ridden long yesterday."

Darcy took over the questions. "Did Peredur seem particularly hard-ridden when he arrived at the stables?"

The boys looked at each other and shrugged. "No more 'n usual, sir. It's a long ride from London, but if a man takes it careful, it's not hard on a strong 'orse like Per. His shoes was worn more than I'd have thought, though, for 'e was reshod the day afore the lieutenant took him out to London. When I went to check 'is hooves for stones, the markings on the new shoes was flattened like 'he'd been running full out for twenty miles or so. No so much as to be worn thin or need redoin', not at all, but enough for someone what sees shoes every day to notice."

Darcy's eyes found Alexander's once more, and Mary gave a little cough.

"Then I eagerly await the results from the message I sent this morning," Darcy pursed his lips. "I believe I know exactly what they will tell us."

"One more question, lads." Alexander had not quite found all the information he needed. "When next did you see Lieutenant Wickham?"

The lads shrugged again. "I've not seen 'im since 'e come in last night," said the older.

"Nor me," the younger concurred. "He often comes for a morning ride, but not every day, so it's not strange for 'im not to be here, though."

Alexander inquired after who else might have seen Wickham and thanked the grooms with a coin each. Darcy chuckled, "More from my coffers? Nevermind; 'tis money well spent."

Further inquiries revealed little else. Wickham had been seen entering his small room at about five o'clock the previous evening, but had not been seen since. An examination of his rooms proved them to be quite devoid of all signs of the man.

"See here," Mary pointed to the bed. "It is neatly made, but not pristine. Had he slept in it and then made it, it would be tidier here at the corners. But it was made yesterday morning and then sat upon several times." She pointed to where the blankets were slightly askew and to where the sheets had pulled marginally from the corners of the pallet. Alexander silently applauded her perspicacity. He had observed the same things, but was proud of his unwitting protégée for having discovered this herself.

"His dress uniform is in his wardrobe," Darcy commented. "Colonel, what would he have worn for his mission to London?"

"Standard issue uniform," the colonel's response was curt. "Clothes are cut for riding. Still waiting on the undergarments, though. See if they chafe."

"This uniform?" Mary pointed to a hook on the back of the door, upon which hung a dusty red coat and white riding trousers. An odoriferous linen shirt and stockings lay in a small basket in the corner; a yellowing cravat lay crumpled on the floor beside the basket.

Colonel Forster shuffled over to the uniform; the room was most compact and the four people now invading its space reduced it to little more than a closet. "This is almost certainly from yesterday," the colonel gave a sharp nod. "He has only the one uniform, and this still soiled from the journey. He did not beat out the dust, nor did he take his underclothes to the launderers for cleaning. His second coat—this blue one for business around the encampment—is in his closet by the dress suit. He is not in uniform today, unless he has taken the clothing of another."

Alexander was amused to see Miss Mary's face grow a deeper and deeper shade of red until he thought she might faint. Instead, she asked in a very low voice, "Then what is he wearing?" Did she imagine the man running about England wearing nothing at all? He swallowed a laugh.

"He arrived in his own suit of clothing," the colonel assured her. "I cannot see them amongst his few belongings; he must be wearing them."

"So he did a runner, did he?" Darcy sounded disgusted. "Trust the man to run up a tremendous gaming debt, kill the person who found him out, and then bolt. I shall write to Richard immediately to have him set up a search..."

That frisson of uncertainty threaded its way up Alexander's spine once more. "I am not so certain, Darcy—" he began.

"No, indeed," Miss Mary spoke again. "For if he were to abscond from here, why return at all? It would have been quite as easy to take his horse one direction, then steal another and flee to somewhere completely different, thereby confounding anybody who tried to find him. And if he did return here for some good purpose, why leave behind the few belongings he had?" She picked up a rather fine wooden box, carved with great care and skill, and filled—once she had it open—with a small fortune in bank notes and items of personal value.

The colonel seized the box and rifled through the contents. "Nearly a hundred pounds in here! Letters, a silver watch on a fob, a lock of somebody's hair. He would never have let this go."

"And more to the point," Mary stated, "is that he brought his horse back, but none is missing. If he did, indeed, 'do a runner,' as Mr. Darcy so quaintly put it, how did he leave?"

The colonel paced the few short steps up and down the small room. "What in the name of the devil is going on?"

"That," Alexander stated, "is what I am here to discover."

Chapter Eighteen

Elizabeth's Confession

Colonel Forster, in his clipped manner, announced that he would mobilise his men to search for Wickham in and around the encampment, and he strode out of the small room, barking orders to that effect. "I shall send a note immediately upon any discovery," he informed Alexander as he disappeared down the long corridor.

"Where to now?" Darcy asked as the three found the closest exit from the barracks towards the gate where they had left their own horses. "Sir William?"

"Yes, exactly what I had thought." Alexander smiled with satisfaction. He could become accustomed to working with such a team as this: Darcy, level-headed and eager for action, and with the financial and social means to ease his way; He, with his years of legal training and experience and his assortments of associates in London who knew where to get the information he needed; and Miss Mary Bennet, smart, insightful, and with her phenomenal memory. He must appreciate what he had now, whilst it lasted, for the case would soon be over.

The three completed the short trip to Lucas Lodge in very little time and soon were sitting in the magistrate's office, waiting for him to appear. He had been busy on some business related to his own property, but Lady Lucas insisted he would be summoned immediately. She had looked askance at Miss Mary and seemed about to say something, but Charlotte had descended the stairs at that very moment and Lady Lucas had refrained from her comment, almost certainly something against the sister of a murderess being entertained at Lucas Lodge.

Charlotte had shown them into the magistrate's office, frowned at Darcy, grinned at Alexander and Miss Mary, and then departed, calling out to her mother about needing to run some errands in the village. Alexander was positive that when they arrived at Longbourn—their next planned stop—they would find Charlotte there.

Sir William arrived some few minutes later. His expression, upon seeing Miss Mary, mirrored very closely that of his wife, but he said nothing and greeted her with civility. He turned to Alexander and asked, "How can I help you?"

"We have news," Alexander kept his words brief and to the point, "that will exonerate Miss Elizabeth Bennet and that point to another perpetrator of this wicked crime." Carefully, with as little elaboration as he could manage, he explained the circumstances of Polly's evidence. "The maid was waiting in the woods, saw Mr. Collins attack Miss Elizabeth and saw Miss Elizabeth repel him, and then she witnessed Miss Elizabeth escape into the woods whilst Mr. Collins shouted curses at her. The parson was most certainly alive, for no man could sustain such a string of abuse with his neck spewing his life's blood into the stream." He stopped to take note of Sir William's reaction. The man seemed to bend a little, no longer under the weight of something he felt most distasteful, and a quiet smile of relief flickered on his corpulent face. Alexander would not offer the possibility of Miss Lizzy returning to finish Collins off. If the magistrate ignored that possibility and pronounced the lady free from suspicion, he certainly would not announce it.

"Further," Alexander added in a rush, hoping to forestall any such ideas from encroaching on the magistrate's thoughts, "there is substantial evidence that Lieutenant George Wickham of the militia was involved in some substantial manner and might very well be the culprit you seek." Once more, with carefully chosen words, he set out the evidence they had amassed, from the tremendous weight of debt, to the missing silverware, to the threat against Polly and the assignation in the woods, and finally to the trip to London, stealthy return, and the man's subsequent disappearance.

"You are certain he returned to Meryton at the time of the parson's death?"

"Almost certain," Alexander would not create evidence that did not exist, nor would he prevaricate on anybody's behalf. "We have one witness and require only one note of corroboration before I would assert this with complete confidence."

"That note would be…?"

"A reply from an inquiry at the coaching inn at Southgate," Darcy stated, "as to whether a man matching Wickham's description rode there on the morning of the murder, hired a fast horse, and returned later that day to collect his own before hastening back to London for his evening engagements. His own horse had more wear on its shoes than it ought; the race to and from Southgate would account for this."

"Well, well, well." Sir William reclined in his chair and crossed his arms across his chest. "Well done, lads. Capital. If this maid,

Polly, is prepared to repeat her claims to me and in the presence of witnesses, I believe we can allow that Miss Elizabeth is indeed free of all guilt in this dreadful matter. Where can I find the girl?"

Mary offered the information, which, by the look on his face, surprised the magistrate. "She is at Bowridge, in Oakville. She is afraid of Wickham and the accusations of theft with which he threatened her, but she assured me she would speak."

"Then let me summon my man and coach and go forth directly! Capital! I shall assure her she has nothing to worry about concerning the silver, and hope to have good news for you this evening. Miss Mary, Gentleman, I thank you. Until later." He pulled himself up from his chair and departed the room with as little ceremony as with which he had arrived.

Charlotte Lucas was sitting with Miss Elizabeth in the morning room when Alexander and his companions arrived back at Longbourn. He had expected this to be so; from the smug look on Mary's face, she had surmised likewise. The ladies rose to greet the newcomers, and Alexander watched Miss Elizabeth's expression transform from glum resignation to cautious optimism as her eyes fell upon Darcy. *She has had a change of heart towards Darcy,* he thought, *and knows not how to let him know. She has learned to look beyond first impressions and has discovered that good can lie hidden, if one takes the time to seek it.*

Then he wondered if Miss Mary, perhaps, would dare to follow her sister's lead and search out the good in himself. He had no thoughts of a real friendship between them, but he would welcome the opportunity to converse with her in ease, free from the distraction of their strained relationship. She was an interesting girl, if very young, and he wished to understand her better.

It had been decided on the ride over that Darcy would make the announcement of their morning's work. He had, in a private moment, expressed some concern about being in Miss Elizabeth's company once more and hoped that his words would soften the lady's rancour. Miss Mary agreed to the request and Darcy executed his duties with aplomb, presenting the ladies with a most elegant bow and proclaiming, "We bear good news." His face was a study in stoicism, his accustomed mien when uncomfortable, but soon he relaxed and offered a heartfelt grin as Miss Elizabeth met and held his eyes.

"What news, sir?" Miss Lucas asked at length, when it seemed that neither her friend nor Darcy was inclined to anything but gaze at each other.

Darcy blinked and inclined his head towards her. "News that all but completely frees Miss Elizabeth from all blame in this affair."

"You have spoken to my father?"

"We have just done so, Miss Lucas, and he is off to confirm some information we had for him."

Charlotte grabbed Elizabeth's hands and squeezed them. "This is excellent news indeed!" she beamed. "Will you tell more, sirs?"

Darcy looked to Alexander, who shook his head. "Not at the moment, I'm afraid," he replied. "I would tell the family all at once, but I do need to speak with Miss Elizabeth again. She has something to tell us that will settle some questions I have in my own mind, even if they do not affect the outcome of the inquiry. Miss Elizabeth? Will you agree to tell us the entire tale?"

Lizzy paled but sat straight. "Yes. I suppose I must. But..." she peered towards the doorway. She was afraid, Alexander thought, that her mother or sisters would come upon her as she related her tale.

"Shall we return to the garden paths?" Mary suggested. "It might be easier to talk outside of the house." Alexander nodded in approval. Once again the lass had seen the heart of a problem and swept it away with a word.

Lizzy's face melted in relief. "Yes," she breathed, "that would suit me well."

Charlotte stood and pulled her friend up to standing and then into a warm embrace. "You will tell me what you must later, Lizzy. I will not intrude upon what must be a difficult matter to discuss, but will walk into town and start spreading the rumours of your complete innocence." She kissed her friend upon the cheek, curtseyed to the others, and bustled from the room.

It was not long before the small party was once more walking the paths that led into the further gardens and towards the wilderness. By tacit consent, their aim was the same gardener's shed where Darcy had made his disastrous proposal only the day before; it seemed to Alexander that both he and Lizzy felt that they must repair their friendship in the same place it had been rent, and thus they led Mary and himself to that spot.

With a flick of his tinder Alexander lit the coals in the stove, and soon the shed was suffused with warmth. The boxes were still arranged around the centre of the space for their chairs, and Mary indicated to her sister to sit. "Lizzy," she began, reaching across the narrow space for her sister's hands, "you can delay no longer. We have heard enough to have an idea of what happened, but we must know exactly what transpired. Would you be easier talking to Mr. Lyons alone? I should be satisfied to wait outside for you."

Miss Elizabeth's eyes were shining with unshed tears, but she was a young woman made of stern stuff and instead of accepting her sister's offer, she squared her shoulders and took a resolute breath. "No, I thank you, Mary. This is a horrid tale, for what happened is to my great shame, but it is bothering me day and night and I cannot sleep well for the memory of it. Perhaps it will weaken its hold of me in the telling; at the least, I shall know that I can come to you for succour, for you shall know the worst."

She took one more deep breath and stared at her audience, gathering her inner strength and preparing to tell her tale.

Alexander sat perfectly still as he waited for Miss Elizabeth to speak, hoping not to distress her further. Although she had agreed, the words seemed unwilling to come. He glanced at Darcy and gestured with his eyes for his friend to move closer to the lady's side. The gaze that Darcy returned spoke of great unease and—so Alexander imagined—fear of yet another rejection. But he glanced once more at the terrified young lady and edged towards her, watching for gestures that would betray her distaste for his actions. When none seemed forthcoming, he moved closer again until he could take Miss Elizabeth's hand in his own. To Alexander's pleasure, if not his surprise, the lady seemed to gain strength from Darcy's proximity and she turned her head to offer his friend a tentative smile. At last, she opened her mouth and began her confession.

"The day began as I have already told you," she whispered. "Mr. Collins asked me to marry him, I refused, and I had the interview with my parents that you already know of. Needing silence, I took my satchel with a book and some food and set out to where I thought I would find the peace and solitude I would never know in the house. I was almost at my destination of Oakham Mount when I discovered that I had been followed." She shuddered again, and Darcy shifted an inch closer to her.

"It was Mr. Collins. I was more surprised than angry at first, for I did not take him to be a great walker, and it is a good distance from the house to where he found me—near on two miles. He called after me and I ignored him at first, for the distance was still enough between us that I might be believed not to have heard him, but he kept coming, and calling louder and louder. Eventually I stopped to ask him to leave me alone, and that was an error, for it allowed him to catch up to me."

Alexander could see her start to shake and almost regretted insisting upon hearing her tale. But no, it must be told, and better here, amongst friends, than in a cold court of law should it come to that, surrounded by uncaring strangers.

"What happened, Miss Elizabeth?" He kept his voice quiet and low. Darcy inched closer to her again and pulled an embroidered handkerchief from his coat pocket. Absently, Alexander wondered what size collection of handkerchiefs she would have by the time they resolved the case.

"I allowed him to reach me, and instead of renewing his suit or pleading with me, he began to shout at me. He abused me with every breath, accusing me of tempting him and being too high and mighty and unwomanly in my manner, and then of having unnatural inclinations myself, and of leading him to sin. At first I tried to counter his aspersions, for I never gave him the first suggestion of returning his regard, and if he saw it, it was all in his imagination."

Darcy squirmed in his place and his face went red, but he remained silent and did not let go of Miss Elizabeth's hand. She did not look at him, but allowed her eyes to drift toward some distant place, far beyond the walls of the small shed.

"It was evident that he had not come for rational discussion, and I began to fear him. I had with me a small folding pocket knife that I use for slicing food, and I drew it from my satchel in hopes of being able to protect myself. But he kept coming closer, all the while shouting curses at me, using language that a lady ought not to hear. My next instinct was to let him rave to the wind as I took my leave, but he would not allow me to go. For a man of his size, he could move with surprising speed when he wished, and he was strong in his rage. He grabbed my hand with the knife and twisted it, and the blade sliced into my arm," she held up her free arm and allowed the shawl to fall to her elbow, revealing a wide bandage. "Then he… he…" she broke off and was wracked with shuddering gasps as tears began to stream down her face. In an instant, Darcy closed the last inches between them and wrapped his proximate arm about her shaking shoulders, pulling her close and letting her weep against his chest. Mary stared in fascinated horror, her mouth moving without sound, her face turning more and more red, until she diverted her eyes to a particularly interesting piece of gardening equipment in the corner.

After a long while, when her sobs eased and her breathing became easier, Alexander asked again in his soft tones, "Can you tell me what happened next? I must know."

She shook her head as the sobs intensified once more.

"Then may I surmise? You need only confirm or deny what I say." She nodded but could not stop weeping.

"I believe he attacked you bodily. I have seen no serious bruising on your arms, but I surmise he pushed you to the ground and threw himself upon you." She nodded again and Darcy's face grew purple, but now in anger and not embarrassment. "You struggled, and he grabbed your dress and tore at the bodice and the sleeve. Did your nose bleed from the attack?"

"It did." She forced out the words between sobs. "He kept pulling at me and trying to rend my dress. He said it was only what I ought to expect, having brought him to the edge of passion and then having denied him so cruelly. He said," she sobbed, "that he was only taking what ought by rights to be his."

Alexander took a deep breath. There was no kind way to ask the following question, but it had to be asked. "Miss Elizabeth, did he… did he impose himself upon your body in any way? What I mean is…"

"I understand your meaning, Mr. Lyons," her voice was momentarily strong. "He exposed my stays," her voice faded at the word, "but he was not able to act further. After he knocked me down, he pressed me into the ground and sat upon me and began removing his cravat. I knew that I had this one chance to save myself, and I did the only thing I recalled. Whilst his hands were busy with his cravat, I twisted sideways and knocked him off balance, and before he could right himself in the mud, I kicked at his ribs, and then…" she chewed her lips and stared at her hands, "I kicked him with every ounce of my strength in that place where a man must never be kicked."

With this statement, Alexander watched her shrink into herself and try to pull away from Darcy in mortification. Darcy's face was still red, but his friend only pulled her closer to offer his strength and comfort, and Alexander heard him whisper to her, "Good girl!" Then, after a moment, "Please promise you will never do that to me!"

When Miss Elizabeth was able, she finished her story. "He was on the ground in some distress, and I struggled to my feet and began to run, as quickly as I could in the mud, to the woods nearby. There is a clearing in the trees surrounded by thick shrubbery and low bushes, where I often go to read. It is hard to find if one does not know of it, and I thought I might be safe there. As I ran, I heard him yelling in pain and cursing me with all his vigour. But I also thought I heard another voice in the distance. I did not stop; I just knew I had to escape to the safety of my space in the woods."

The tears were running freely down her face, but her voice was growing stronger and her attitude was much easier than it had been since she began her recitation. Alexander dared a last question. "Did you recognise the second voice at all?" He was certain he knew the answer, but he needed to hear it from Elizabeth's mouth.

She shook her head. "I cannot say for certain, it was so distant and my thoughts were awhirl."

"Do you have any notion?"

With a great gulp of air, she admitted, "I cannot be certain, for I was thinking only of running, but it was certainly a man's voice. And I was so very scared, and for a moment it sounded to me like…" she stopped and sniffed loudly, "like my father."

"Do you still believe it was he?"

"I cannot say. I do not even know if it was a man's voice or my imagination. I just had to run."

Between sobs and sniffles, Alexander was able to tease out the last details of Miss Elizabeth's story. She had ignored the shouts and cries behind her and had fled into the woods, and thence straight through the shrubbery towards her haven, thus incurring many of the scrapes and cuts upon her arms and body. She had fallen onto the ground in pain and in anguish, and in the midst of her tears and covered in her warm (if blood-covered) cape, had fallen asleep. Upon waking she had returned home not through the field, but sought instead the slightly longer path home that led along the road, where the eyes of farmers and travellers might keep her safe. Thus she did not see Collins' body, nor did she see anyone else who might have been in the vicinity.

Elizabeth was now held securely in the circle of Darcy's arms, and she rested her tear-stained face upon his chest. Miss Mary eyed this improper display with alarm, but Alexander stayed her reprimands. "Come," he said to her quietly. "Let us leave Mr. Darcy to comfort your sister. I believe she has need of his strong arm and soft handkerchief. I dare say he brought his entire collection with him this morning, in the event that your sister might wish to mop her eyes." He watched Mary's eyes grow more leery. "They cannot engage in any sort of improper behaviour in a cramped gardener's shed whilst we are right outside the door, but I believe they would appreciate some privacy. Will you join me?"

Mary reached into her cape's wide pocket and withdrew a small Bible, which she placed on the wooden crate in the centre of the room. "A reminder to them," she added through thin lips and with narrowed eyes, but she rose and allowed Alexander to guide her from the shed.

"Darcy is a gentleman," he spoke quietly as they wandered around the small plot of lawn that surrounded the shed. "Miss Elizabeth has gone through a terrible ordeal. She has remarkable inner strength, but it is never an easy matter to recover from such an attack. Darcy will do everything he can to help her feel safe and will not harm her. He cares too much for her."

Mary said nothing, but gazed into the wall of naked trees that formed one edge to the small lawn. Alexander took her silence as invitation and spoke further. "He has admired her for some time; her danger alerted him to his own. He has experience soothing his sister's wounded soul. I have no doubt he will strive to soothe Miss Elizabeth's as well."

They walked in silence around the shed for several minutes before Mary spoke. "What do you make of her notion that she heard Papa?"

"Yes." Alexander wished to discuss this. 'Twas a pity they were not colleagues, she and he, that they may try their ideas on one another to see which ones had merit. Nevertheless, he added, "I have an unpleasant thought about that."

"If Papa saw Mr. Collins attempt to impose himself upon Lizzy, he might have done violence to the man. That is what you are thinking, is it not?"

"Aye," Alexander admitted. "And—"

"And that would accord with Papa's strange comment that had Lizzy accepted Mr. Collins, he might be alive today."

"Aye."

"This is a pickle."

For a third time, Alexander could only respond, "Aye."

Eventually, at Alexander's gentle prompting, Darcy escorted a pale but calm Elizabeth from the shed. Mary scuttled over to her sister and detached her from Darcy's arm with a scrutinising glare. "You ought not to have allowed that..." Mary began, but Miss Elizabeth rolled her eyes and let out a huff.

"Mary, Mr. Darcy is a gentleman, and you were only feet away."

"Still, it is not becoming, Lizzy. Loss of virtue in a female is irretrievable; I am of a mind to tell Papa, and then he would require Mr. Darcy to marry you, for you were alone with him for some several minutes." Alexander noticed with amusement that Darcy did not seem at all vexed at this statement and actually allowed himself a smug smile. Miss Mary continued, "But I shall not speak, for I do believe your virtue is intact."

"More so than after Mr. Collins attacked me," Elizabeth grimaced.

This seemed quite to change Mary's approach. "Oh, yes, indeed! Are you well now, Lizzy? Are you troubled from your confession?"

Elizabeth rewarded her sister with a sad smile, "I believe I shall be well. It was strangely healing to tell of my ordeal and be believed and not scorned for it. I had expected the censure of all for having caused Mr. Collins to act as he did. I had not imagined I would receive such sympathy or understanding. Mr. Darcy was of far greater comfort than I would have imagined." She dropped her voice and Alexander only just heard her tell her sister, "I misjudged the man badly, and I am pleased for the chance to amend my opinion of him."

This was as he had hoped. Whilst he was heartbroken for the ordeal the young woman had suffered, he was pleased for his friend. He was certain that Darcy would not speak yet, not until he was more assured of a positive reception to his entreaties, and likely not until all was concluded and the immediacy of the events were in the past, but taking the name Darcy would go a long way to erasing any remaining traces of scandal that might attach to the lady and her family because of this accusation. It would, in time, become yet another one of those strange tales one relates to one's children and grandchildren whilst sitting at the fire or rowing across a summery pond.

Chapter Nineteen

Finding Lieutenant Wickham

When Mary and her companions returned to the house, the drawing room was abuzz with activity, so much so that at first their entrance went unnoticed. Mary glanced around to discover the main source of the din. Charlotte had returned with Mrs. Lucas, who now seemed to believe that the Bennets were acceptable acquaintances once more. Mama sat in the arm chair that faced the window and away from the doorway, talking in hushed tones to her guests, while Papa and Sir William stood by the fire, each with a glass of amber liquid in one hand. Jane sat on the window seat—Mary's own favourite spot—with Mr. Bingley upon a chair by her side. The greatest noise seemed to come from the round table in the far corner of the room, where Lydia and Kitty sat, doing unspeakable things to the remains of a bonnet, arguing with every snip and tug and placement of a pin.

Then, as if reacting to a single cue, the entire company seemed to stop and notice the newcomers at once.

"You have returned my daughters, I see," Papa drawled. "Feel free to keep them next time," whilst Mama wailed, "Mr. Bennet! Have a care for my nerves!"

"What news, Darcy?" Bingley sprang up and with a glance to Jane, moved to his friend's side to shake his hand.

"I shall allow Lyons to tell you of it, for it is greatly to his credit that we have discovered this much."

Mr. Lyons, for his part, stood aside and gestured to Mary, who quailed to find herself the centre of attention. "If I have been diligent in my actions and quick in my thought, Miss Mary has been more so. Together, we have discovered clear evidence that Miss Elizabeth is innocent of the death of Mr. Collins. Sir William," he addressed the magistrate, "have you told them? May I assume by your presence that you have confirmed our information?"

"The telling is yours, my lad," came the jovial response. "It seems our Lizzy is quite free from all suspicion. Capital news, is it not?"

"And we are most delighted by this," Papa returned. "Are we then to expect that Mr. Lyons' task here is completed? Will you be returning to London, sir?"

Mary's eyes darted to her father. Was he now concerned that the investigation might turn on himself? What had his comment been about? Was Lizzy correct in her belief that Papa had come across the injured parson and dealt the fatal blow? She watched him carefully for his reaction as she waited for a reply.

But before either Mr. Darcy or Mr. Lyons could speak, Charlotte leapt from her chair, crying, "Oh Lizzy, what wonderful news!" It seemed Papa's question would remain unanswered for the moment.

"Are you pleased now, Miss Lizzy?" Mrs. Bennet's querulous voice emerged from the chair, "Having caused all this fuss and ado for nothing? We had to refuse three dinner invitations because of your trouble. Oh, there you are, Mary. Have you been here all along? I did not notice you."

"They wished only to revel in our strife, Mama!" Jane objected, but her voice was drowned out by her mother lamenting over the hardship that would be incurred in restoring the Bennet family to its former standing in the neighbourhood.

"Well, it is as it should be," the lady sighed at last. "I suppose I ought to ask Hill to arrange for a large table tonight, for we will have three gentlemen to add to our numbers, as well as Sir William and Lady Lucas."

Lady Lucas regretfully refused the invitation, claiming a prior engagement, to which Sir William added, "And I, at least, must be on my way home to consider where to seek next for Collins' killer." He bowed to his hosts, shook Papa's hand, and prepared to depart with his wife scurrying behind him.

If Mama was at all nettled by the refusal, her pique was softened by the thought of three unmarried men gracing her table that evening, and she hoisted herself from her chair and hurried off to the kitchens to confer with Mrs. Jackes, the cook.

"Mr. Lyons, Mr. Darcy, please sit and tell us all!" Papa gestured to the sofa before taking the chair that Mama had just recently abandoned. Mr. Darcy found a seat next to Lizzy and Jane, and Mr. Bingley pulled up some light wooden chairs to join the circle around the tea table, leaving the space beside Mary the only place for Mr. Lyons to sit.

Once again Mary listened as Mr. Lyons recounted much of what they had learned. He said not a word of Lizzy's tearful accounting, save what Polly had told them, and emphasising the likelihood of Mr. Wickham's involvement in the affair, including his disappearance. Mary was relieved to see that her Papa seemed neither particularly elated nor distraught at the news, but accepted it all with his accustomed complacency.

"I still cannot believe it!" Lizzy cried. "Mr. Wickham! He seemed so good, so gentleman-like and such pleasant company. Even after everything I have heard, and which I cannot deny, my mind has trouble accepting him as a killer. I am pleased to be released from this spectre of guilt, but for it to have been Mr. Wickham... I am sorely grieved."

"And where can he have gone? I do hope he is not in any distress!" Jane's sweet nature even now could not be denied. When all of the regiment was seeking the man as a possible killer, she was worried for his wellbeing. Mary could not quite bring herself to think as her sister did, but she also could not help but admire Jane's true Christian spirit.

This again! Jane, for all of her goodness, had never been particularly pious. She attended services as was expected of her, but her devotion was no more than any other. Her sweet and good nature did not grow out of a particular love or study of the words of the Lord. It was, rather, wholly innate and separate from any external teaching. Mary sighed. This presented one more complication to the unsettled nature of her own philosophies, and she must think seriously on it when she had the luxury of time and the strength to pursue these troubling ideas.

From the corner of her eye, Mary could see her younger sisters working at their bonnet. Kitty seemed unaffected by the tale of Wickham's disappearance, but Lydia... Lydia was sitting unnaturally still, her eyes blinking rapidly, her mouth tight. Mary was certain she knew something.

As the others around the small table sat expressing their amazement at the turnout of events, Mary reached across to tap Mr. Lyons' arm. He pulled back with a start, but soon caught the meaning in her eyes. She rose and gestured with her head, and he followed her across the room to where the youngest Bennet sisters played with their headgear.

"Lydia," Mary pulled a chair beside her sister's and sat upon it, "what do you know of Mr. Wickham? Do not try to tell me you know nothing, for I can see in your eyes that you do. Remember Proverbs: *'Lying lips are an abomination to the Lord: but they that deal truly are his delight.'* You must not cast mistruths to the ears of the Lord."

"You are being silly, Mary! Leave us!" Lydia's protestations sounded weak to Mary's ears. They must have sounded weak to her own as well, for she paled. Mr. Lyons then pulled over another chair and sat himself down on Lydia's other side.

"If you know something, Miss Lydia, it would be best to tell of it now, for the truth will out, and you can be branded either a helper or a hinderer; lying will not help Mr. Wickham, nor will it help you."

The girl looked from her one side to her other, surrounded as she was by accusers, and opened her mouth as if to speak but then shut it again quite soundly.

"Lyddie?" Kitty's voice was a whine from across the table. "Did you do something foolish? Oh no, Lyddie… tell me you did not! Is that where you went last night after we were all in our rooms?"

"Tell us what happened, Lydia…"

"I would caution you to speak now, Miss Lydia, for you must know it cannot remain a secret…"

The girl threw her bonnet down onto the table and propped her chin between her fists, a pout etched upon her face. Mary watched Mr. Lyons' face as he realised that this young woman, who looked so grown and mature in her fine gowns and elegant coiffure, was little more than a child better suited for the schoolroom than the drawing room.

"Tell us, Miss Lydia, and perhaps I can arrange for another bonnet for your attentions…" He glanced across to Mr. Darcy, who would assuredly bear the cost of the bonnet. Mary chuckled, and Lydia snorted.

"A bonnet! All you can think of is a bonnet! Ha! He offered me silver hair pins and silk stockings! He—" She stopped, having realised how much she had said, then snorted again and sighed, "I suppose there is no use, for he shan't be bringing me my presents, no matter that I promised I would keep his secret."

She looked again from Mary to Mr. Lyons and back again and finally asked, "Shall I really get a bonnet?"

"I stake my reputation upon it."

"Very well. We were coming in from Meryton just before dinner, and it was growing dark already. Mr. Wickham came riding in along the laneway, and as the others went inside, he whispered to me and I heard him. He was all covered in dust, for he was only now back from London, and he called me over to speak to him. You know he pretended to like Lizzy, but his eyes were always upon me, you see! For I might be the youngest, but I am the prettiest after Jane, and so very much more fun!" She batted her lashes at Mr. Lyons, who had the good grace to look aghast.

"He liked me and told me that I was the only one in Meryton he could trust. He needed me to come with the cart for him at eleven o'clock, for he had a meeting he needed to attend, and that no one must know of it. The arrangements were just as before…"

She stopped with wide eyes. "Oh! I think I ought not to have said that!" She clapped her hands upon her cheeks, looking like some caricature in a broadsheet. Mary was disgusted with her sister and ashamed for what Mr. Lyons would now think of the family. Perhaps Mr. Darcy had not been wrong in saying what he did in his proposal to Lizzy.

Gradually the story emerged. Almost from his first arrival in the village, Wickham had preyed upon Lydia's lusty and gullible nature. When he had told her how he needed her help, she had been only too pleased to subject herself to scorn and scandal in order to please him. She had, she told her sister, long since discovered a way out of her bedchamber, by climbing out of the window and edging along the overhang to where she had piled chairs and ladders by the kitchen garden. From there it was an easy matter to creep through the dark space to the stables, far beyond earshot of the main house.

"Lydia!" Mary gasped. "Surely you did not—"

Lydia giggled. "I might have allowed a kiss or two. Perhaps some more. But do not be jealous, Mary. We cannot all be as fortunate as I!"

How shameful! Whatever had her sister been thinking, allowing a man such liberties? But Lydia had more to relate, as she announced.

On several occasions, she related with pride, she had hitched the light cart to her favourite horse and driven to the next field over from the regiment's encampment, where she would find Mr. Wickham and drive him to a certain location he had identified, there to conduct whatever business—presumably illicit—he had. She would then return home alone, with no one the wiser for her nocturnal adventures. This she had done the previous night as well, leaving him in the same secluded location as he requested of her. Until now, she had no notion that anything was amiss.

So this was how Wickham had managed to escape the area! If whomever he had been meeting had a horse or a carriage to take him to Town or elsewhere, he could be anywhere in England by now!

"Did you see who he had arranged to meet?" Mr. Lyons' question came just as Mary opened her lips to speak.

"No. I did hear a horse once, but it may have been somebody completely unrelated to the business."

"And he said no names?"

Lydia shook her head. "No. Not once."

"Miss Lydia," Mr. Lyons spoke softly, the voice he might use to calm a scared horse, "I need you to describe for me exactly where you drove him. Can you do that?"

Lydia could, and did, relate with as much precision as she seemed capable of the exact place to which she had driven Mr. Wickham. It was about three miles distant to Longbourn, in the opposite direction to the regiment's encampment, rather close to Netherfield. Since the encampment was past Meryton in the other direction, it would have taken a man near on two hours to cover the distance on foot. A light cart and a quick horse could cover the same ground in a fraction of the time, hence Mr. Wickham's need for clandestine transportation.

"I am coming with you," Mary stated as Mr. Lyons stood to depart. "Do not try to convince me otherwise." Mr. Lyons stared at her, then gave a sharp nod and went to inform his friend.

The day was now well into the afternoon and the sun at its zenith, but the air was cold and the lanes hard. The fields were slowly giving up their liquid, the spongy mud ceding to dry earth that would be covered with frost each dawn. Darcy had reluctantly taken leave of Lizzy, who had been advised by all to remain with her parents and Charlotte, and accompanied Mary and Mr. Lyons on their ride across the fields to where Lydia had taken their quarry.

Mary knew the location exactly. Lydia had described a small hunting cabin a short way off the lane leading to the back entrance to Netherfield's park, screened from the sight of travellers by the wall of trees that shielded the laneway, but near the fields where birds took flight and stags and rabbits ran. It was private and secluded, yet easy to find, and it provided shelter and warmth for a man who chose to linger there in waiting, or for men seeking a place for some activity that defied the law.

She led the small party along the roads and paths and laneways, although she knew that Lyons would find the spot easily without her assistance. Without their leaves, the trees stood as naked sentinels along the way, stark and grey against the harsh white sky, which even cloudless, the sun could not quite brighten into blue.

The horses grew skittish as they approached, and each clip of a hoof upon the packed earth of the lane sounded as a pistol shot to Mary's ears. At last they were skirting the far boundaries of Netherfield, past which the woods lay, and then into the woods they plunged, the path just wide enough for a horse to traverse if the rider were careful and the progress slow. On the nights of his *rendez-vous*, Wickham had told Lydia to leave him at the edge of the wood, from where he would cover the remaining short distance on foot. Today Mr. Lyons suggested they may wish for their horses to be closer at hand.

At last she could see the small hut take shape through the bare trees. Made of wood, it seemed to melt into the surrounding trees, but solid and wide where they were sparse and slender, squat and low where they were tall, reaching for the heavens. The low roof hung heavily over the doorway by one corner, two small windows blank eyes to the left of the portal.

They had made no attempt at stealth, but neither did anybody speak as they dismounted and tied up their horses. Mr. Lyons led the way, his one hand reaching into the large pocket of his riding coat. *Did he have a pistol hidden inside?* Mary had not thought to ask, and the notion that there might be danger had not occurred to her at all. *Or was it, rather, a short blade with which to protect the trio? Surely Wickham would not be armed!*

Mr. Lyons crept to the door and nudged it open with his foot, standing to the side so as not to be in direct sight of anybody inside. There was no noise from within, and Mary watched in fascinated horror as he inched his body towards the doorway, and then from around the protection of the door itself, peered within. With a gasp, he staggered backwards, shouting, "Darcy, keep her away!"

He was unhurt and there seemed to be no danger from within. Heedless of Mr. Lyons' words, Mary eluded Mr. Darcy's outstretched arm and stepped towards the hut. The window was dirty, but not too filthy to see through, and sunlight from the opposite window illuminated the space.

There, in the pool of light, lay the very still figure of a man, a dark patch of gummy liquid beneath where the back of his head once was, sightless eyes staring up at the low ceiling.

Mary reeled backwards, the world growing dark and rushing in upon her, and only through the greatest test of strength did she manage to find a tree against which to lean whilst the darkness retreated and her stomach ceased its need to empty itself. With heaving breaths and a voice that sounded quite foreign to her ears, she stammered, "I think we need no longer wonder about what has happened to Mr. Wickham."

Chapter Twenty

A Shocking Discovery

It was a small comfort to Mary that Mr. Lyons looked as shaken by the discovery as she was. He, too, had lurched backwards several paces, and whilst he did not require a tree to support his weight as she did, his face had taken on an unhealthy hue and he looked quite ill. Only Mr. Darcy, who had not seen the body inside the hut, stood strong, and even his face was white with the knowledge of what they had found.

"We'd best go for Sir William," Mr. Lyons said at last. "I must return to the cabin and make a closer examination of the scene, but from what I did notice, it seems very unlikely that Wickham died from anything other than someone else's hand. Stay with Mary, will you?" He spoke to Darcy; Mary realised she did not now mind his use of her Christian name, such was the concern with which he had spoken it.

Darcy walked over to Mary and offered his arm for support should she need it, as well as a hard sweet from within his coat pocket. He spoke little but kept her attention on himself and her horse whilst Mr. Lyons took a deep breath and strode with false confidence back into the hunter's cabin.

He emerged some minutes later, his hands now covered in thick brownish-red sludge, which he wiped off onto a patch of moss that clung to a nearby tree trunk. "I shan't presume to do Sir William's job, but it looks a clear case of murder to me. The injury is to the back of the man's head. Sorry, Miss Mary. Firearm of some sort—the shot went in near the base of his skull and emerged out of the top of his head, just into the hair. The man would need to be a contortionist to manage that by himself; besides which, there is no weapon in there. Whoever killed him took the pistol with him when he left. My guess is that the killer was waiting for Wickham, came up on him from behind, likely by surprise, and shot him before Wickham knew he was in any danger. Despite the horrid mess of the body, it was a much neater slaying than was that of Mr. Collins, with the mud and the spray of the severed artery. Oh, Miss Mary, are you well?"

Mary had felt herself waver as Mr. Lyons spoke, but she pulled herself up and breathed deeply of the crisp autumn air. In her mind's eye, she saw for a moment the image of Lizzy, returning from her walk on that fateful day, arms scratched, dress torn, walking cape covered in mud and blood. Sir William had taken the clothing, but what of the blood? There had been a lot, but not so much as she had seen under Wickham's head in the hunting cabin, and what was it that Mr. Lyons just mentioned of a spray from a severed artery? The blood on Lizzy's cape was in distinct blotches, not a spray at all.

She asked about this in as strong a voice as she could manage.

"This was the first thing," Mr. Lyons said, "that convinced me entirely that Miss Elizabeth was innocent. Upon examining her dress and cape, it was clear that she had been set upon by somebody, but that the blood was all her own—from a bleeding nose and the cut on her arm, I suspect. The blood from Mr. Collins... are you certain this does not distress you unduly? The blood from Mr. Collins' neck would have been a tremendous volume, drenching her cape rather than merely blotching it, and would have sprayed out at a wide angle. Whoever killed him would have been covered from head to foot, and not just a light splatter.

"Then if we are to find his killer, we must find the soiled clothing." Her voice sounded stronger in her ears. She would not show weakness before these men; if Mr. Lyons was going to disdain her, it would be for better reasons than this.

Darcy cleared his throat. "Do we know that the same man killed both men? Or are we now searching for two killers?"

"This is a matter I would prefer to contemplate in some warm location away from the gruesome sight yonder." Mr. Lyons gestures to the hut. "I'm for Sir William, to inform him of our find. I shall meet you back at Longbourn. Miss Mary, please go with Darcy. When he tells this news to your sister, she might have need of your comfort."

And like that, she was dismissed. 'Twas better this way; Mr. Lyons would not linger with Sir William, but would impart the news, show him and his constables the place, and leave them to their business. Still, before he could mount his horse and ride off, she had to ask, "Should we not see if there is anything in the immediate vicinity that might point to the identity of the killer... of Wickham's killer? Could he have left some item, or an impression of a boot, by which we might know him?"

To his credit, Mr. Lyons turned from his purpose and faced her, then executed a short bow. "You are correct. I do not imagine there is anything here for us, but the search is important. I had thought to do it with Sir William, but if you are pleased with the task, I am pleased to pass this duty to you, should Darcy consent to remain with you. Your skills at observation are remarkable, and I am certain I could not do better myself. But for many reasons, do not enter the cabin. That is a realm I would leave as untouched as possible for the constables."

Mr. Darcy agreed, and with his assistance Mary began her search as Mr. Lyons galloped off to find the magistrate. The ground here in the woods was dry and hard, but covered in leaves, and not even their own feet left marks worthy of notice. With her eyes on the ground, Mary made a slow examination of the outside of the hunter's cabin. The front, which faced the small clearing wherein the horses were still tied, had little else to reveal, and as much as Mary wished to examine the inside for evidence, she also knew that she could not enter that space again, certainly not with Wickham's body lying sprawled on the floor in the muck that had once been his head.

Instead, she moved to the back of the cabin. This wall was blank but for the one window which had allowed in the light that had illuminated Wickham's body so clearly. Avoiding too close an examination of that window, she peered at the ground, hoping to find some dropped button or calling card or other such clue. All of these were sadly conspicuous in their absence. She sighed. No killer who had planned such a surprise attack would be careless enough to announce his identity to the world. He would have arrived early and hidden inside, where it was warm and comfortable and where he might hide to better surprise his victim. But if he wished to surprise Wickham, he could not have ridden, for Wickham would surely notice a horse where there ought to be none!

She mentioned all of these thoughts to Darcy, who nodded and appraised her with approving eyes. "You think these matters through very carefully, Miss Mary."

She stopped her examination of the ground and raised her eyes to his. "Yes. I observe things. Because I am so seldom included in everybody else's activities, I amuse myself by watching and trying to discern their purposes. I suppose it has become a habit, or a game, even."

The gentleman coughed and flushed a pale pink and then asked, "May I inquire as to whether you have observed your sister Elizabeth; whether you have insights into her purpose?"

Standing up to her full height, Mary considered the man frankly. This was a strange place for such a discussion, but she knew that he was a man who needed to be certain of his reception. A week ago, she suspected, he would have arrogantly supposed that the world would fall in with his plans and that the thought of refusal would never have crossed his mind. But he had been chastened since then. He had suffered a refusal, had seen men laid low by violence, and he had come to know his heart with respect with Lizzy; more importantly, he had seen her in the aftermath of a terrible attack and a cruel accusation, and had learned something of her strengths and her frailties, and he would not now assume that her thoughts necessarily might accord with his own.

As if sensing the direction of Mary's own musings, he spoke, "She has suffered an ordeal and I would be there to comfort her and lend her my strength; but she also has the right to be wary of men, for Collins did not acquit the rest of our sex well. In your opinion, would she now welcome my suit or spurn it? I would not harm her further by pressing where I am not wanted."

This was not a question Mary had expected from the man. Could he really be that understanding of her sister's needs? How different this glimpse of Mr. Darcy than the one he had shown to Meryton only a few short weeks before! She thought before speaking. "I believe, sir, that this is a question you had best ask of Lizzy herself. I truly think she will appreciate the request, for it shows your desire to do well by her and see her happy, whether or not her happiness involves you." She thought a moment more. "But I also believe she will now welcome your suit, if you do not press her. I feel sure that she has come to examine her heart, and she has quite changed her thoughts about you—this I have seen. I do believe that now she likes you and in time will come to love you. But be gentle and undemanding of her, for she may need to learn to trust you—to trust everybody again."

Mary watched a succession of emotions play across Darcy's face, normally so stoic and stern. Anger, hope, frustration and confusion, and a hundred other sentiments all mixed together fought for supremacy, and of these, outrage won. She had come to think that his accustomed arrogant demeanour was less one of pride than of acute discomfort. When he felt at ease with his company, he allowed his feelings to show upon his face. "She did not like me before? She made me aware that she believed that I did not like her, but I had thought..."

"No, sir, you had it right initially. She did like you, and she did not, and you fascinated her a great deal. Her own feelings were so confused that she did not know how or what to think. She had so many contrasting accounts of you that it was best to pretend to a serious dislike, so as to protect herself from distress. But now, I see how she looks at you. Be gentle and understanding, and I shall soon wish you joy."

As she had been speaking of her sister's heart, Mary had also been eying the ground. With her thoughts so engaged in Lizzy's regard for Mr. Darcy that she almost stepped into a small patch of muddy earth that had been partially covered with leaves. The ground had dried somewhat, preserving what looked like part of an imprint of a foot. "Mr. Darcy! Come, sir, and see what I have found!"

He hurried over and peered at the patch of drying mud. "It is the side of a boot... See, there is the toe, and there the heel." He turned his own foot over as far as he could to inspect the bottom of his own boot. "And yet..." He peered closely at his foot, and then at the imprint in the mud.

"And yet," Mary completed, "this was not a boot. See how your heel is so much higher and more pronounced than this print. The man could never ride in those boots, for there would be nothing to catch the stirrups; his foot would slide right through!"

Mr. Darcy knelt down by the patch, heedless of the damage to his buckskin pantaloons. "You have it exactly, Miss Mary. This is the imprint of a shoe, and not a boot at all. Now why would a man be traipsing through the woods at night in dress shoes, when such are only worn indoors or on dry city streets? Anybody would know to wear boots, for such are made for rougher use such as this."

Mary stared at the imprint. There was something strange, something that played at the corners of her awareness, something that she thought might be very important. If only she could determine what it was!

The sun had long passed its zenith by the time Mary and Mr. Darcy returned to Longbourn. She was colder than the dismal autumn weather could excuse, and would be quite desperate for a cup of tea had the image of Mr. Wickham's body not imprinted itself upon her consciousness. Upon leaving the horses with a groom and entering the house, Mrs. Hill was upon both riders immediately, divesting them of their outerwear and asking if they would like warm bricks for their feet. Mary wondered if her appearance matched her state of mind.

"There is a message for Mr. Darcy," the housekeeper announced once the two had assured her of their wellbeing. "A lad from the inn at Southgate is here, says it is most important he speak to you."

Mr. Darcy thanked her and set off after her to the kitchens, where the lad waited. Mary trudged after him, her interest in the message encouraged by the knowledge of the warm fire that always blazed when meals were being prepared.

The messenger who awaited them was about Mary's own age or a bit younger, a strong and tall youth with an intelligent face and greasy brown hair. Darcy seemed to take more notice of the boy's countenance than of his appearance, for he greeted the messenger politely and with great civility asked after his message. This, too, was something in Mr. Darcy's favour that Mary must convey to her sister. The man seemed to have little concern for the lad's appearance, but rather seemed to sense his essence. Of greater import, he was a man who gave the same polite attention to a filthy lad from the stables as he likely would to a peer. Mary found herself growing more and more pleased with the man she felt would soon become her brother.

"I had your note, sir," the youth spoke in clear tones. Although he was visibly nervous and kept fidgeting with a button he had in his hands, his well-modulated speech was more in keeping with his sensible face than his filthy hair. "I... I was the one to read it, since none of the others at the stables know their letters and Mr. Newman—he be the innkeeper, sir—was busy at the moment and it looked important."

Mary stared at this young man. It was unusual for a stable hand to know his letters, and she wondered what might become of him should he find himself in better circumstances. Mr. Darcy seemed to have the same thoughts.

"What is your name, lad?" Darcy's voice was easy and friendly.

"Evan, sir."

"A Welshman? Yet you sound like you are from these parts."

"Me mum, sir. She works at The Hart—for that's the name of the inn. She's the one what taught me to read and write, sir."

As Darcy kept up an easy conversation, the lad seemed more and more comfortable. Darcy asked after his work at the stables, the nature of his learning, the horses he preferred, and his choice of cheese or meat pie before his return to The Hart Inn at Southgate. Mary watched with amusement at this new facet to Mr. Darcy's character; the cold and haughty man could be most polite and even friendly with a stable hand of low birth and lower prospects. So rapt was she in this scene that she nearly missed the quiet arrival of Elizabeth, who drifted up to the kitchen door and stood just on the threshold, out of Mr. Darcy's line of sight, observing this unexpected interaction. Lizzy's eyes roved over the boy and then settled on the man and grew soft and tender. Mary hoped that her sister would not allow either her fear or her pride to impede what would certainly become a most happy union.

Forcing her attention from her sister and back onto Evan, she searched for what she hoped was an encouraging look to affix to her face as she waited for Mr. Darcy to return him to the matter at hand. At last, the lad continued.

"You asked about this man upon the grey and white. I remember him well. He has come through several times of late, always on that same smart horse called Peredur. Sometimes he would stop for an ale and to give his beast a rest, other times he would race through one day, then come back of a mornin' and change horses, only to return later that same day to switch back to Peredur. This is what he done—did—the day you mentioned in your note, that is the twenty-seventh day of November, that is Wednesday last."

"Do go on," Darcy encouraged. "Please tell us exactly what happened on that particular day."

"It was like this: He had come through at quite a clip the afternoon before, stopping only long enough to let Peredur rest a touch and drink. I think he was late for something important in Town."

"What time would this be, Evan?"

"I recall thinkin' he was later than his custom, and right when I did so, I heard the tower clock chime four in the afternoon. I remember that, wonderin' if he had somewhere to be in Town at five."

"Very good!" Mr. Darcy beamed his approval and Evan beamed back, emboldened.

"The next mornin'," he spoke confidently now, "nigh on ten of the clock, he was back and at a race as well. He did not stop but to change horses for Brown—he asked specifically for Brown because he's a fast one—and he asked us to have Peredur ready for when he returned some few hours later. By three o'clock, he said, havin' business in London at four. That is a good ride for a horse, more than ten miles in an hour, but not more than Peredur or Brown could manage. He arrived as 'e said, changed back horses, and took off for London at a tear."

"Did you notice anything unusual upon his return?" Mary asked. She suspected that this young man would take note of anything strange. She had turned to face Evan, but could feel Lizzy's eyes upon the back of her neck, listening, watching Darcy.

"Not so much his appearance, but 'is temper." The messenger scratched at his greasy head and Mary had to fight her inclination to request Mrs. Hill draw him a bath before allowing him to leave.

"What of his temper, lad?" Darcy asked.

"He seemed mighty upset, angry even. I was afraid 'e might vent his spleen upon his horse, but 'e always treated the beasts kindly, even when pressing 'em to speed."

"Did he give any indication as to the cause for his temper?"

"Not in that way, sir, but he mumbled something about not having the silver and having to use the last of his coin, having made a long ride for no purpose. And then he mumbled sompin' about hoping he would be alive to come by it again."

Chapter Twenty-One

A Happier Proposal

When Evan had finished his recitation and Mr. Darcy had satisfied himself that the lad had nothing more to tell, he was sent off for a warm meal and a pocket full of biscuits for the ride back to Southgate. Mary could see Lizzy still standing at the kitchen door, her bottom lip caught between her teeth. Darcy rose from his chair and as he turned, his eyes met the pair he had confessed to admiring so much and he stopped in his place. Lizzy took a tentative step towards him, with one hand outstretched. In a second, he had caught it in his own and he lowered his head to whisper in her ear. She nodded, a wondering look upon her face.

Unsure whether she ought to stay for the sake of appearances or leave the couple in privacy, Mary coughed. "Do you..." she began, "do you perhaps wish to sit in the salon I so often use?

Nobody will bother you there." Mr. Darcy's eyes smiled at her, and Lizzy bowed her head.

"Stay, Mary," Lizzy begged as Mary turned to leave the two to their discussion. "I would have your support."

Mr. Darcy did not look pleased, but neither did he object. He bowed in a most elegant manner and offered Lizzy his arm to lead her into the salon, like a prince leading his chosen one into the finest ballroom in the country. Mary followed behind like the reluctant lady-in-waiting, knowing she was not really wanted, but was needed regardless. Lizzy was strong and would thrive, but as long as she felt she needed Mary's presence, Mary would offer it.

The salon was small, but not so small that Mary could not remove herself some reasonable distance from her sister and Mr. Darcy. She took her favourite chair to the far corner of the room by the window, which still allowed the weak light of the afternoon to suffuse through the space, whilst the couple sat side by side on the settee by the lit fireplace.

Mr. Darcy spoke in low tones, sure to be unheard by anybody passing through the hallways, but just audible from where Mary had folded herself up with a book. "Miss Elizabeth, before anything else is said, I would gladly answer any questions you have of me. I would withhold nothing from you."

His words were confident enough, but his voice held that note of uncertainty that brought Lizzy's attention to its meaning.

"Is everything well, Mr. Darcy? I am most relieved to be released from this horrid accusation, but I can tell that something bothers you. Oh..." she raised a hand to her lips as her eyes grew wide with a horrible thought. "Was it Papa? Do you now believe it really was Papa I heard approaching? I could not tell who it was, exactly, and perhaps I only wished for it to be my father so he might protect me as he did when I was a child. I cannot believe—"

"Be easy, Elizabeth," he glossed over her name, "for I have no particular thoughts of it being your father. However, I did wish to suggest remaining here to allow Lyons to continue his investigations. I had initially retained him to prove your innocence, but until your cousin's killer is found," his voice caught, "the shadow of suspicion will never be far from anybody involved."

She nodded with slow and considered movements. "Yes. I had thought similarly. Even if it was Papa, we need to know the truth. But if it was, indeed, him...?"

"Then we shall have to decide how to proceed next. But that, my dear, is not what I wished to discuss with you. I have other news to impart as well, which will not be so welcome."

Lizzy had turned her head, so Mary could not see her face, but she did not miss the sharp intake of air and strangled, "What news?"

From the corner of her eye, Mary watched Mr. Darcy reach into a pocket and retrieve yet another piece of embroidered cloth. "Here, Miss Elizabeth, my handkerchief." How many of these must Lizzy now possess? Surely she must marry the man, if only to return to him his linens!

When Lizzy seemed unlikely to succumb to a fit of the vapours or any similar behaviour expected of finely bred ladies, Mr. Darcy presented his news. "We have discovered the location of Mr. Wickham."

"Oh!" Lizzy exclaimed in a thick voice. "Dare I ask... I hope he is not hurt. As much as the man has done ill to us, I would not have him harmed. Has he admitted to killing Mr. Collins?"

Mr. Darcy shook his head sadly. "I am sorry. He has admitted nothing, but I do not believe he is the murderer. For he, too, has been killed." He paused, but when Lizzy did not faint, he continued, "We discovered his body in the hunting cabin just a short time ago. Lyons has gone off to tell Sir William. For all that Wickham was a blackguard and a scoundrel, I do not believe he was a killer. He was…," Mary heard Mr. Darcy's voice break, "he was kind to animals. He did not have a murderer's empty soul."

Mary expected her sister to dissolve into a fresh flood of tears, but it seemed that Lizzy was made of sterner stuff. She sat in complete silence for a full minute—Mary counted the seconds against the clock upon the mantelpiece—and then said in a calm voice, "I see. I am grieved by this news, for I had once considered him a friend. Thank you for reassuring me of his true essence, beneath the layer of his disrepute."

Darcy sent a questioning glance towards Mary, and she returned an answer in a like manner. He took a deep breath and turned his body towards Lizzy, who still sat quite still on the settee at his side. He reached over to take her hands in his own, and Mary suddenly noticed some activity in the garden outside—a gust of wind whipping the fallen leaves into a pocket-sized maelstrom—which demanded her full attention. Her eyes were averted, but she could not, however, block his low voice from her ears.

"Miss Bennet…. Elizabeth… I had promised myself to delay, to give you time, before I dared declare myself, but I am unable to keep these feelings inside. If you feel as you did when first I returned to Meryton, speak now and I shall forever be silent on the matter, but… how my heart will break but I will honour your wishes. But if you have any feelings for me, if I have reason to hope…"

Mary brought all her attention to the pattern the leaves were making in the air, spiralling upwards, now down to the earth, then up again, whipping dust and dried grass into the action as they spun, but Lizzy's reply reached her ears, nonetheless.

"How my heart has changed! I had thought you proud and too fine for the likes of me, with my uncouth family and my country ways. But you have shown yourself to be a very different sort of man. You returned here at the first suggestion of trouble and befriended me and sought to help me when so many of our friends and acquaintances shunned me. Miss Bingley would not even allow my sister into the house!

"You showed such kindness to me, and not only to me. You might have warned Mr. Bingley to follow his sister's lead, but instead you encouraged his visits to Jane; you gave heed to Mary and urged Mr. Lyons to hear her; you spoke generously of a man whom you had every reason to despise, but in whom you could not see the ultimate of evil. And you treated that messenger lad with kindness and respect. It is easy to put on an act of magnanimity for one you are trying to impress, but you did not know I was in the room when you spoke to Evan. You were good to him not to convince me of your merit, but because that is the man you are. I know now that I judged you ill at first and have quite reversed my earlier feelings."

Her voice died away and Mary wondered if she had buried her face in a handkerchief.

Darcy's breath sounded in the silent room. "Then if I ask for a courtship, you will not refuse me? I know you have cause to fear men."

"I do not fear you. You have been nothing but kind. I know you will never hurt me."

"No! Never!" he exclaimed.

"Then I should be most pleased to accept you."

At the rustle of fabric shifting on the upholstery of the settee, Mary shifted noisily in her chair and coughed quietly.

"Oh! Mary!" Lizzy blushed. "I had quite forgotten you were there!"

Mary felt her face flush deep red. "I believe I have something I forgot in the kitchens... Pray excuse me!" She darted from the room as quickly as her manners would allow her. Lizzy and Mr. Darcy were as good as wed. She could afford them some minutes in private, no matter what her books of sermons said about a lady's reputation.

Never had Alexander imagined Longbourn to be such a great distance from the woods by Netherfield. The three miles seemed to stretch on forever as he finally set his horse on the path to the manor house. The day had been exhausting, perhaps more to the spirit than to the body, and he was sore in need of some comfort. A cup of tea, a warm scone, and some pleasant conversation that had nothing to do with death and murder would be an excellent start. Another of Thorne's foetid liniment massages would be welcome as well, for his hip was aching and his entire back painful, each percussive clop of his mount's hooves sending a reverberation of pain up his spine. He would need to make the three-mile ride to Netherfield later on; for now, however, he wished only to sit and be warm.

Sir William had returned from duties in the village moments before his own arrival at Lucas Lodge and had not been pleased to be called out once more. "Never has this position of magistrate been so demanding!" he had complained as he shouted to his grooms to leave the saddle on his horse. "Thomas may have the title as soon as this affair is over, for I have quite worn myself out with it!"

That assumed, Alexander grimaced, that Thomas Bennet did not conclude the affair at the end of a hangman's rope for the murder. He imagined the man quite innocent, but some questions remained that needed answering before he might be certain.

Despite his grumbling, Sir William was a diligent man and sent for his two constables to meet him at the hunter's cabin. All knew where the small hut was located; the men would find it with ease. This transpired, and the four spent a rather unpleasant hour examining the remains of Lieutenant Wickham and the environs in which he was found. The constables had brought a cart with which to transport the body to the cold room at Lucas Lodge and a note had been sent to Doctor Hewitt from Hertford informing him of the news and requesting his presence and expertise once more. Soon Alexander and Sir William were alone in the dreadful hut, examining the floor and sparse furnishings for clues.

The hunting cabin housed a table and two chairs along one short wall, an iron stove with a chimney that vented directly through the roof near the centre of the room (thereby to warm the entire space), and a rough cot along the other wall upon which a man might take a rather uncomfortable rest. From the discovery of a blanket on the floor behind the stove, it seemed that the killer had waited partially hidden in the darkness and then had surprised Wickham with a flintlock pistol or Blunderbuss to the back of his head. The small lead pellet the two men had located on the ceiling by the far wall, where it had embedded itself in the wood after exiting Wickham's head, seemed the right size for either weapon. Had Alexander been a betting man, he would have put his money on the Blunderbuss with its devastating power. Although, he conceded to Sir William, at such close range a flintlock would cause equal damage.

The killer had cleaned up well after himself, leaving little for searchers to find; only a small partial print of what looked like a man's shoe gave any indication of who might have been the one to see Lieutenant George Wickham to his eternal rest.

Thankfully Sir William offered to relate the news to Colonel Forster; this was now an official matter involving both the local magistrate and the dead man's commanding officer. Alexander was no longer needed in any official capacity and it was with this relief that he had set out, at last, for a house that felt like a home and where he might take a rest.

This was a thought that had come to him quite unbidden. He had had a home once, as a lad in the village near Glasgow, with his Mum and Da and sisters. It had not been large or elegant, as were these grand manor houses here in the south, and there had been winters when food had been thin on the table, for all that Da was a skilled physician and in the employ of the baron. But there had always been laughter and noise and love. Then his world had fallen apart. Da had died and the kindly baron had died, leaving his family to the whims of the man's feckless son. Thanks only to his father's benefactor, Alexander's own way had already been paid at the university. His mother and sisters had gone to live with a cousin, and Alexander's home since then had been a small room, or two in his flush years, with nought but his books for company.

Netherfield was not a home. It was a house, and a grand one at that, much finer than anything he had seen in the north, but it was cold and empty of the humanity that endears a place to a man's heart. It was a museum, a temple to wealth and opulence, but Caroline Bingley and her querulous sister and gluttonous brother-in-law did not live there. They existed. Charles might one day make it a home should he stay. His was the generosity of personality that warms a room without a fire, that creates a sense of belonging. But with Caroline as the de facto head of the household, anywhere would be as cold as a tomb.

Lucas Lodge had the spirit of a home for Alexander, a place where people did not just bide their time, but invested their lives.

Sir William would not tolerate anything less, and Charlotte's sensible and irreverent personality certainly ensured that the veneer of social expectations would never drown the familial ambiance that suffused the home, but Alexander had been but a transitory visitor in that house, stepping from entry hall to office and out again, with nary a glance at the rooms in which living occurred.

But Longbourn... here was a house, elegant and pleasing in appearance, large and enduring, but nonetheless a home. Mrs. Bennet, for all her frivolity and nervous afflictions, was a mother who loved her family, and that love showed. The fires burned warmly to keep her children comfortable; laughter and quarrels sounded equally through the rooms, and the small trappings of familial life—a book left on a table here, a scrap of embroidery on a sofa there—lent the otherwise imposing edifice an aura of comfort and modesty. The staff, too, whilst never leaving their stations, seemed more a part of the family than the Hursts did at Netherfield. They cared for the family, genuinely loved the girls and each other, Alexander reckoned. Alexander thought of Mary's account of Mr. Hill—his outrage at Collins' assault of his niece and his thankfulness that the parson had not bothered the young Bennet sisters. This was a household that thrived on care for one another. It was not just a house or an estate's manor, but it was a home. It was a place where a man might take his ease and laze with his feet up before a warm fire, where he might talk comfortably and candidly about absolutely nothing of any relevance with a friend of good understanding and a similar desire merely to be. Not to impress or deduce or astonish, but merely and wonderfully to be. And for the first time since he had departed for school at the age of eighteen, he ached for a home.

More to the point, he ached desperately for a bath. With Longbourn at last in sight, he grew increasingly aware of his own physical condition. Not only exhausted and in pain, but he was also covered in blood and muck and the dust of the road and the stench of decay and horse. He could not possibly enter through the front doors; perhaps Mrs. Hill would be so kind as to find him some warm water so he might wash and improve his appearance before intruding upon the family.

He rode around to the tradesmen's entrance and left his horse to the attention of the groom there. It was a short walk around the corner of the house and through the kitchen garden, where he found the kitchen doors. His knock was answered after only a moment's delay, and there to greet him was none other than Miss Mary.

He had not expected her! One of the maids, perhaps, or the cook, or even Mrs. Hill, but certainly not one of the squire's own daughters! He was, of a sudden, even more aware of his bedraggled appearance and of what a terrible spectacle he must be for this gentlewoman. His body reacting before his mind could consider his actions, he bowed a low and elegant bow, and was astounded when the girl... when the young lady laughed at him. Had he heard her laugh before? He could scarcely recall, and the sound was intriguing.

"I know I am beneath your notice, Miss Mary," the words came out before he could exercise control over his tongue, his tone indignant, "but it is hardly fitting to find humour in the gore which I know covers my body and clothing so completely."

She dropped into a quick curtsy. "I do apologise, Mr. Lyons, but you make such polite obsequies to me, with the manner of a royal prince, whilst you look as if you had just rolled in the sties. Come in and sit a moment. Would you care to bathe? You must be quite fagged."

Alexander could do nothing but nod, his tongue suddenly dumb.

"Then do not linger. Here is a table and chairs." She pointed to a widening in the hallway where a messenger or neighbouring servant on an errand might sit for a spell. "It would not do to have you in the kitchen where the food is prepared all filthy as you are. Sit a moment and I shall summon Mrs. Hill." She ran off, but before Alexander could think about anything other than that his feet were not moving, she hurried back. "It will take some time to heat the water for a bath, but you may use the servants' bathing room, if you do not object. It is here, just around that corner, and it is not needed at this time of day. Mrs. Jackes is preparing tea. You may wash your hands in the room yonder whilst we wait."

This he did with great alacrity and even having his hands free of the stench of death helped buoy his spirits. He took his seat once more, and he and Miss Mary sat in silence for some moments until a young kitchen maid shuffled towards them, carrying a tray of tea and bread. Mary poured and Alexander sat motionless, his eyes taking in every gesture. She carried out her task with a graceful economy of motion, her every action considered and precise. It was only when she placed the cup before him, with a small plate of food at its side, that he stirred himself back to animation.

"Tell me what you saw," she requested as he took his first sip. The tea was hot and sweet and he groaned in the pleasure of it before he could catch himself. "It might not be fit conversation for the drawing room," she added, "but I would like to know."

She pinned him in his place with those fine dark eyes, still so innocent to the ways of the cruelty of men. For all that she vexed him and irritated him, he respected her a great deal, and thought that he might like her as well.

"You do not wish to distress me," she stated. "But I will hear it. I am made of sterner stuff than you imagine. Do not underestimate me."

At that he let out a sharp bark of laughter. "No, Miss Mary, that is not a danger. I shall never underestimate you, for you are a formidable opponent. Very well. But guard your ears, for this tale is not a pretty one."

He finished his tea in two long draws and pushed away the plate of bread. This telling would not go well with food. Then he took one long deep breath, and on the exhale began his accounting of what he had found in the hunting cabin.

"There is no question that this was not an accidental death," he concluded. "Whilst it is possible to believe that Mr. Collins was killed by the happenchance fall of a knife in a struggle, Wickham's death was quite deliberate. It could not have been a self-inflicted wound, caused by some accident with a pistol, but it was planned and executed. We are dealing with a soulless murderer, and somebody in our midst."

Mary, to her credit, had not flinched when Alexander had described the gelatinous mess that had once been Wickham's handsome head, nor the devastating injury that had ripped the back of his skull apart and covered the space in blood and brains and shards of bone. She did, however, glance at his hands and turn a slight shade of green, until he assured her that even before visiting the room where the linens were washed, he had washed them to the best of his ability in the stream that ran through the woods.

She told him about the shoe print she had found in that partially dried puddle, matching the description exactly of what he had found. "You have a good eye. Most men would not have found that."

"I am," she retorted, "no gentleman!" Her smile now was genuine, and it suited her well. But she did not allow it to linger. "Then we are seeking a man with badly worn shoes and a suit of clothing that is drenched with blood and gore, and upon finding him, we shall have our man."

"No, for again, our killer was thoughtful and thorough. The blanket he used for warmth and to conceal himself, he also used as a shield against the blood. His clothing would have emerged quite pristine, although I cannot speak for his shoes. I dread to think what he must have walked across to escape that deadly hut."

"They would be as filthy as would Mr. Collins' killer's boots...." She stopped and raised her eyes to his. A crease appeared between her brows; something was bothering her.

"Miss Mary?"

"I do not know. There is something... but I cannot find the thread." She wrinkled her nose and pursed her lips, and Alexander thought for a moment she looked like the little girl she had been not so many years before. He was not so much older than her—only six or seven years—but where his childhood seemed a lifetime ago, hers was only now behind her.

She was about to speak further when Mrs. Hill came through the doorway to the servants' stairs. "Mr. Lyons, your bath is ready. If you will follow me, sir, and leave your clothing with John to be cleaned. We will find you something suitable to wear."

It was some time later that Alexander emerged from the bathing room, much more satisfied with his place in the world. The water had been hot and soothing to his aches, and the fire bright and warm to ease his rebirth, like a Scottish Aphrodite, into the world. His skin felt raw, for he must have scoured every inch of skin twice over at least to remove the taint of murder from it, but he was pleased enough to don the borrowed clothing—almost his size—that he found waiting. The suit was of good quality and well cut, and only slightly out of date; Mr. Bennet's closets must have given up their trove for his benefit, but he argued not. Even the house slippers, so strange on his feet after the boots he almost always wore, seemed to fit adequately. He brushed his red hair back with raw fingers and surveyed himself in the glass. Yes, he was presentable enough for a family of no pretensions. Sucking in a breath, he opened the door and prepared to find the Bennet family and his friend Darcy.

Chapter Twenty-Two

An Evening at Netherfield

Darcy and Miss Elizabeth were in the front drawing room, where Sir William paced back and forth before the roaring fire. He strode over to greet Alexander and clapped a large hand upon his shoulder, his face tight and his eyes exhausted. "Sad business, this," he murmured as he greeted his young colleague. "Still, this exonerates Miss Elizabeth completely, for she could not possibly have killed Wickham." He sighed and looked much older than he had upon their first meeting. "By the by," he whispered even more quietly, "do we know the cause of the bruising on Collins', er, tender parts? Polly said nothing, for she was too distant to see what transpired, but may I assume that Miss Elizabeth caused that particular damage?"

Alexander hid a smirk. "I believe that might be the case."

The magistrate shook his head in feigned alarm. "I hope Mr. Darcy knows to keep himself under good regulation! It seems the young lady knows how to take care of herself!" Alexander allowed a snicker to escape, but Sir William would not be quieted. "As soon as I'd seen Colonel Forster and washed, I came right over to see if my daughter's suppositions were correct. She is a perceptive one, my Charlotte." He nodded towards the sofa where Miss Elizabeth sat, Darcy on a chair right at her side, and beamed as proudly as if he had made the match himself. "See how well they look together. Capital! Capital!"

Hearing this quiet exchange, Darcy looked up to smile at his friend. For what may have been the first time since Alexander had met him, Darcy looked completely at his ease and very happy. Their first interactions had been over the disappearance of Darcy's sister and every meeting since then had been with the cloud of the girl's low spirits or Miss Elizabeth's indictment haunting the man's spirits. Now there were no further clouds. His sister was safe and recovering from her ordeal, Miss Elizabeth was acquitted of all wrongdoing, and Darcy seemed to have secured the lady's affections. "Come and sit, Lyons, and tell us what news you have." He beckoned to the sofa across from the one upon which Miss Elizabeth and Charlotte Lucas were seated, right next to none other than Miss Mary.

He sat, as ordered, and suffered the inevitable comments about his garb and appearance. It was only when Miss Mary leaned over and whispered, "You must be much more comfortable," that he began to feel more at ease. He congratulated Elizabeth again on her freedom, rejoiced with Charlotte, planned an outing for the following day, should the weather remain fair, wherein Miss Elizabeth might escape the house after her incarceration, and generally conversed about nothing. The fire was bright, the house cheerful, the company most pleasant. This was what he had longed for. He ought to feel completely satisfied, and yet...

"He is still out there." Miss Mary spoke the words that whispered in the corners of his mind.

"Aye."

"What can we do to find him? I have such a notion that I am missing some important thread."

"Aye."

"Do we know that the same man killed Wickham as killed my cousin? Is it possible that it was Wickham, after all, who stabbed Mr. Collins, then to be slain himself by another?"

"Aye, 'tis possible, but unlikely. How many people have been killed in Meryton in your memory?"

"You do not talk about accidents or mishaps, I assume. The answer is none, or at least none that I recall."

"Then it would be strange to have two killers suddenly appear at once."

Mary nodded. "More strange things," she sighed. "There have been altogether too many strange things."

An idea began to stir at the base of Alexander's mind. He rose from his seat and began to pace the one or two steps behind the sofa that were allowed him by the space in the room. At last he said, "Shall we walk? I think better when my feet are moving."

"Are you not tired, Mr. Lyons? It is not becoming of me to say, but you look exhausted."

"I am, Mary, but I think better when my feet are moving. Will you walk with me? I have my notebook; I would like to enumerate these strange things. Perhaps, seen in a new manner, they will form a clearer picture."

The day was growing late, and the weather had turned cold and very windy, and a walk was a pleasant thought to neither Alexander nor Mary; it was decided that they would retire to the back parlour instead, where Alexander might pace at will and sit when necessary to make notes. Charlotte and Sir William were beginning to take their leave once more, and a word in Darcy's ear led to the agreement that all four of the people involved would assemble in the parlour immediately upon the Lucases' departure.

Of Jane there was no sight; Upon Mr. Darcy's report, it was learned that Mr. Bingley had called earlier with a note from Caroline. Once more, Miss Bingley seemed to know of the good news even before Elizabeth. The lady having been cleared of wrongdoing, her family was no longer barred from the halls of Netherfield. Rather, the acquaintance was no longer a social deficit, but rather an asset, for how many dinner parties might Caroline carry on the basis of her intimacy with a wrongly accused lady? In favour of fame by association, Jane's company was now welcome, and she had been invited to take tea and dinner with Caroline and Mrs. Hurst, to which invitation she had readily agreed when Mr. Bingley had echoed the invitation. A further invitation had been issued to Miss Elizabeth, should she wish to join them for cards after dinner.

But that would be later. At the moment the four wished to discuss the mystery at hand, and once Sir William and Charlotte had been seen to the door, they gathered as planned.

Mary began by setting out once again her four strange things. She explained again about the odd coincidence of the missing silver, the missing maid, the unexpected argument between people who ought not to have been in Netherfield's breakfast room, and the death of Mr. Collins.

"We have found the reason behind the maid's disappearance," Alexander stated when Mary concluded her account. "She was afraid of what she had seen and of Wickham and had fled as far as she dared."

"And that is connected to the missing silver," Miss Elizabeth added, "but what of the rest? How does the silver connect to the argument or the murder?"

"Murders," Darcy's voice was grim, "for surely Mr. Wickham's demise is connected to Collins'."

Mary wrinkled her nose again. "I am beginning to wonder," she mused, "whether the key to connecting all of these strange events lies at Netherfield, for so much seems to originate there."

"Then we had best send a note to Bingley," Darcy tossed off, "informing him that Miss Mary will be joining us." Alexander almost laughed at the impish look upon his friend's face.

Mary seemed pleased with this decision, but she was not completely satisfied. "Before we do, gentlemen, I would like very much to know what has been happening at Netherfield. Have you noticed anything unusual or untoward, which might focus our thoughts this evening?"

Darcy shrugged and turned his eyes to Elizabeth, who smiled at him. Alexander pondered this question more deeply. "That is hard to say, for I have hardly been in the house, other than to sleep, and for that one painful dinner."

"What? A dinner presided over by Caroline Bingley painful?" She clucked. "I ought not to speak so, seeing as she is your friend's sister, Mr. Darcy, and likely to be Jane's sister before long."

Alexander answered. "You speak truth, Miss Mary. It was a tedious affair, and I, not hungry at all, forced not only to partake of each of Mrs. Slougham's delectable dishes, but also to hear Miss Bingley and Mrs. Hurst recount every meal they have enjoyed in the company of their betters. Mrs. Hurst seemed even more desirous of overstating her social position than was Miss Bingley; she talked of status and connexions and of the fabulous match any daughter of hers might have thanks to her splendid dowry. Is she always thus, Darcy? At first I had taken her as being less a social climber than her sister, but that monologue nearly gutted me.

"And her husband! I thought Hurst's plate might fill itself again at the mention of the dishes they described. Apparently there is a rather dissolute baronet named Elliot... or was it his nephew whom Hurst met through the sponsor of their wrestling team, or was it a cousin? Miss Bingley plied us with as much description as rich sauce, and I am afraid I had surfeit of all of it. Oh! I have it now. The sponsor's chef produced a fine ragout, as fine as Hurst ever had. And that, I am afraid, is all I can tell you of the goings on at Netherfield. However, should it ever be a matter for your concern, Mrs. Slougham is a most excellent chef, her meals surpassing most everything I have tasted. Your own cook excepted, of course!"

"And nothing of the missing silver?"

"My word, Lyons!" Darcy burst out. "Have we not told her of the silver platter? I do not see how it is relevant, but every detail might have its meaning." He turned from Miss Elizabeth's fine and flashing eyes to meet those of her sister. "Our friend Lyons decided to flaunt his lowly origins and disrupt the decorum at the meal, and he hoisted a platter above his head to examine the mark, so as to observe the reactions of those present. The platter, it transpired, came from Hurst's estate. I suspected the gentleman was somewhat financially embarrassed, but he admitted it readily enough."

Miss Mary sucked in her cheeks and frowned. "Could this be the piece Wickham had hoped to take to London to sell to pay his debts? For surely, that is why he was angry with the outcome of his return to Meryton on the day Mr. Collins died. He raced back with such high hopes and was denied both his silver and the attentions of Polly."

Miss Elizabeth, who had been listening with rapt attention, now dared to speak. "And once again, we are brought back to Netherfield. I shall find some paper for Mr. Darcy to write his note, for I believe Mary will be a most useful addition to our party there this evening.

It was decided that the gentlemen would dine at Longbourn, as per Mrs. Bennet's previous expectations, after which they would accompany the ladies to Netherfield for Caroline's card party. Alexander was pleased to make the return trip in the coach; his horse would be tied to the team drawing the carriage and he need ride no further that day. Whilst the ladies retired to their rooms to change for dinner, he and Darcy were able to talk in privacy for the first time that day.

"Shall I continue?" Alexander asked. There was no need to clarify as to his meaning.

"Yes, I believe you had rather better. This whole affair is far from completed."

"I have accomplished my assigned task. Miss Elizabeth is freed from all suspicion."

"Indeed. But until the killer is apprehended, I shall not rest easy. If you will accept a new commission from me, I would like to extend your assignment here."

"I would have done it without your request and without your purse. I have grown rather fond of the second and third of the Miss Bennets. But I accept."

"I would have paid you regardless, had you taken it on as your own task. We are friends for a reason," Darcy smiled, "for we see eye to eye on so many matters."

This bit of business out of the way, the men sat in companionable silence, Darcy reading some tome he had borrowed from Mr. Bennet's library, Alexander scribbling at his notebook.

Under *Collins*, he noted the parson's propensity to moralise and reprimand people for their supposed lapses, completely and conveniently forgetting his own. He made note of the abuse hurled at Miss Elizabeth as he accosted her, of his accusations of the wicked goings on in Meryton, and of the man's threats to inform his patroness of their deeds. Indeed, the man had written of many such unacceptable activities in his letters to Lady Catherine de Bourgh. Finally he made note of the parson's own and very serious lapses of conduct, having attempted to attack two women in the short time of his stay in the vicinity.

Then he indicated some aspects of the man's appearance and *habille: large, heavy-set, bruise on ribs, injury to...* he took a deep breath and wrote *bollocks, missing cravat, stab wound to neck—carotid artery, much blood loss.*

Cause of death: neck wound, exsanguination.

Reason for death: undetermined.

Next he started a page labelled *Wickham,* wherein he made more notes, indicating the man's questionable character, as evidenced by his experience with the man the previous summer, Wickham's gaming habits, his debt, and his recent attempts at repayment. He also noted Wickham's attempt to have his way with Polly; it was more subtle than Collins' attacks, but no less coercive. Then he indicated Wickham's involvement in the thefts of silverware: *Threatened Polly with blame; none other knew of it; therefore W must be involved.*

But that was not true. Somebody else must have known. If Wickham was the seller of the silver, somebody was liberating it from Netherfield for him, for he could not have such free access to the house as to take whichever pieces he desired. So the real questions were: who is the thief? And why steal to hand it over to Wickham?

What hold did Wickham have on the thief? If Alexander could answer that question, everything would fall into its rightful place.

The notes on Wickham were not quite complete. Alexander wrote: *young, healthy, very fit; excellent physical condition, accomplished horseman. No injuries other than mortal wound—gunshot (blunderbuss?) to back of head; pellet rent skull completely, exited top of head behind hairline.*

What did this tell him? That the killer, assuming only one, felt physically capable of besting the large and lumbering Mr. Collins, but that he needed the element of surprise, and a weapon that would allow no reprieve for Mr. Wickham. Was Collins' murder unplanned, hence the signs of a struggle and the use of a knife which might have missed its mark? This was possible, even probable. But Wickham's death had been meticulously planned. The killer allowed no room for mistake.

This, too, Alexander jotted down in his little book before closing it and staring into the warm fire until it was time for dinner.

Dinner was a pleasant affair, as enjoyable as the one the previous night under Caroline Bingley's watch had been disagreeable. Mrs. Bennet's cook was, perhaps, not quite equal to Mrs. Slougham's capabilities, but she had nevertheless prepared a delicious and satisfying meal. The foods were plentiful and varied, but not so much so as to render the next course unwanted, and conversation flowed lightly. Darcy was offered the seat directly beside Elizabeth's, signalling the family's acceptance of his offered courtship and presumably, his imminent offer of marriage. Mr. Bennet seemed to be taking great pains to make himself agreeable to his future son and spoke loquaciously and intelligently on a great number of interesting topics. Alexander was pleased to see Mary as interested in the efficacy of vaccinations against smallpox and the use of electricity to animate frogs' legs as she was in the latest news from the continent. Having some considerable knowledge of medical science himself gleaned from his father,

Alexander allowed himself the luxury of the conversation and was rather disappointed when the meal was over and it was time to depart for Netherfield.

The ladies had taken great care with their appearance. This was Elizabeth's first excursion from Longbourn since the ordeal had begun, and she announced her determination to put on a strong and confident face. The bruise around her eye was fading, and with the judicious application of cosmetic creams it was so concealed as to be almost unnoticeable. Likewise, her scratched arms were encased in long gloves. She confessed in the carriage that she knew Caroline Bingley would not take well to the announcement that she and Darcy were courting. The mistress of Netherfield seemed not to have abandoned hopes of one day being mistress of Pemberley, and Elizabeth anticipated some small war of wits, in which she would wear her finest gowns and display her finest manners as a suit of armour.

Mary, too, was looking extremely well. She had opted to forego her usual selection of sensible and modest gowns of unflattering style and colour, and wore instead something that was likely taken from one of her sisters' closets. The light green silk turned her fair skin rosy and illuminated flashes of emerald in her dark eyes. A daringly low neckline was made less so by a lace fichu, but this did not obscure a rather alluring figure from Alexander's eyes. Miss Mary Bennet, he realised with a start, was a very attractive young woman!

To nobody's surprise, Caroline kept her politeness to the edges of civility. She had invited Elizabeth in order to benefit from the young woman's notoriety and to please Jane, but had not desired Mary's attendance at all and scarcely deigned to acknowledge her.

Instead, she turned to Alexander's friend. "Mr. Darcy," she purred as the party from Longbourn was shown into the card room, "you must be so pleased to be back at Netherfield. Now that this *dreadful* business with poor Eliza is over, you will no longer need to spend so much time at Longbourn." How she could say these words whilst three of the Bennet sisters were in the room, Alexander knew not. The woman was as cold as ice, and no matter how lovely to the eye, he was certain that Darcy had never felt the first inclination of affection towards her.

Darcy glanced over towards Alexander and rolled his eyes towards the ceiling before turning back to Caroline. "I am afraid, Miss Bingley, that you are mistaken." Was that the hint of a smirk upon his friend's face, a cheeky glint in his eye? Indeed! Darcy was about to put Caroline in her place and was enjoying the experience! "I imagine I will be spending a great deal of my time at Longbourn." Darcy's face was a picture of guileless tranquillity. "I have requested, and been granted permission, to court Elizabeth. I imagine it will only be a matter of time, when this unfortunate affair is over and settled, that we will announce our engagement. If, of course, the charming Miss Elizabeth should honour me with her acceptance."

At that instant, Alexander wished he had the talent of an artist, for Miss Bingley's horrified expression was one so picturesque he wished to preserve it for eternity. She recovered herself right away and, with a voice as sweet as treacle, congratulated Elizabeth and wished Darcy joy. "You will have a lifetime of pleasure at her family's table," she then said, and went to inquire as to Jane's comfort.

Bingley hurried over at the announcement. "Darcy, you old dog, what wonderful news! I am so very pleased for you." His eyes slid over to where Jane was seated near the fire, and he gazed at her with the amazed expression of a child presented with a tray of delectable sweets. *There shall be another announcement within days,* Alexander thought with a smile.

As sometimes occurs, the party now separated into two groups. The women gathered at one end of the large room by the main fireplace where the light was brightest, the men at the other at the elegant chest wherein Bingley stored his fine port. Some soul had set out four crystal glasses and Bingley poured a libation for each. Only Hurst declined a glass, as he was still sipping on the brandy that had been in his hand when the guests had arrived.

"What do you make of this affair?" Bingley's curiosity seemed at last to have defeated his attempts at self-regulation. "Did I hear the news right about poor Mr. Wickham? It is quite dreadful, is it not?" His eyes were wide and despite his sombre words, his face was all excitement at the prospect of the salacious news.

"It was most distressing," Alexander hoped to keep his responses short and terse so as not to encourage rumour. "But it is true that the man is now dead. Most shocking."

"Is it true that he was, himself, suspected of killing Mr. Collins?" Bingley's morbid curiosity would not be denied.

Hurst coughed into his brandy. "Strong stuff, this," he muttered. "Can't get this French brandy so easily these days. Costs a small fortune for those who have it. My pockets are too bare for these luxuries, so I'll enjoy yours, eh, Bingley?" He coughed again and closed his eyes as he half reclined in his chair.

"What are your plans as of now?" Bingley had not ceased his questions. "Are you to London, now that Miss Elizabeth is relieved of her troubles?" His eyes were wide and Alexander was reminded of a dog wishing to please its owner.

Something itched at the corners of Alexander's mind, and with a warning glance to Darcy, prevaricated, "Indeed, my task is accomplished. I was engaged to prove Miss Bennet innocent, and such has been achieved. Colonel Forster has assumed responsibility for the inquiry now, and I have little further cause to remain in Meryton. I shall likely remove to London tomorrow."

Darcy blinked at Alexander in surprise but said nothing. Bingley gave another great grin. "I am pleased your task is completed. I wish you a safe journey back to London."

Hurst, his own eyes still closed, mumbled, "Good job, then," and relapsed into silence.

The evening of cards was much as Alexander had expected. The games themselves were not unpleasant, although of little real interest, and the conversation stiff and uninteresting. Caroline seemed so concerned about asserting her superiority that she quite forgot about displaying it in her actions. Every discussion seemed subject to her arbitration, and no matters of any weight or import were tolerated. Alexander believed that he had heard enough about Lord So-and-So's ball to see him through several lifetimes. After two rounds of Loo, Alexander was fighting to keep the yawns from escaping his lips. Caroline had finally exhausted her repertoire of tales from this lavish ball or that, which pleased Alexander greatly, for he felt that if he were subjected to one more recounting of Mr. Rushton's dinner party or the time they had been rescued from a garden maze by Colonel Brandon, he would be reduced to tears. Hurst seemed to have found the best solution to this tedious recital, for he was snoring on one of the sofas by the fire, a half-empty glass of brandy on the table by his side. Even Caroline herself seemed to be flagging. Her elaborate descriptions had long since lost their lustre and with every side-long glance at Darcy and Elizabeth, so intent upon each other that they were blind to the others in the room, her tongue lost some of its honey sweetness and took on the bitter edge of lime.

It was with the greatest relief that Alexander saw a maid bring in a tray of tea and sweets, with another decanter of port for the men. This, at least, would give him some respite from the boredom of the game and the drone of Mrs. Hurst's lacklustre chatter about the fine circles in which she moved in Town and her celebrity in London due to her impressive dowry. "Why, it was even more than Miss Darcy's," she fluttered her eyelashes. "When it became known amongst the best families, I was seen to be quite the lady to know. I never received so many invitations to tea as the week that news was somehow found out." Released into the air, Alexander imagined, by the lady herself. "Charles was so proud to bestow that amount upon me," she cooed, "for it marked our family's arrival into the circles of the elite. Our grandfather's stain was quite forgotten." Alexander had to fight his inclination to growl at the women. The "stain" of industry of which she spoke was exactly that which had allowed her to aspire to such social éclat, and which marked him as quite below her notice. How he detested the nouveau riche even more than the peerage.

As the maid took her leave, Caroline poured tea for the ladies and then moved to the rich red liquid, which she served to the gentlemen. Bingley took his with scarcely a glance at his sister, and Alexander accepted his cut crystal glass with a smile he did not feel. He would much rather be sitting over a flagon of ale at the pub, or a mug of tepid water with Mary's insightful comments for flavour. He almost did not notice when, distracted as she seemed to be, Miss Bingley tripped over some object on the carpet—or was it her skirts?—and dropped Darcy's brandy glass, which then shattered as it hit a table and landed on the carpet.

She cried out as she stumbled into the pile of shards, one of which could now be seen protruding from her hand where she had fallen. The wound bled freely and Alexander was not certain whether the lady felt more pain from the injury itself or from the irreparable damage the blood would do to her fine and costly gown.

"Oh, Miss Bingley!" Mary called out and rushed over to offer what assistance she might.

"Get away!" Caroline replied, then recovered herself to add, "I would not have you injured as well." She took a deep sniffling breath and whined, "Perhaps one of the men with thicker soles on their shoes might help me."

Seeing no servants about, Alexander began to move towards the doors to summon somebody, but Mary stayed him with a touch to the arm. "I will go. I know where to find Mrs. Slougham. I suspect Mrs. Harwick would be of very little assistance." At which comment, she dashed out of the door into the hallway, calling for help.

Mary breathed a deep sigh of relief. She had thought she would go mad, sitting there staring at cards whilst Miss Bingley and Mrs. Hurst mentioned every illustrious person they had ever met, or seen, or heard mention of. It was perhaps un-Christian of her, but she could not bring herself to care that Caroline had once been at the theatre when the Duke of Somewhere had been present, or that Mrs. Ferrars had been seen riding in the park just when Caroline happened to be there. And once more, she had harped upon that tenuous connection with the baronet Sir Walter Eliot, for he was a mere handbreadth away from the peerage!

She was grieved that Caroline had tripped and injured herself, but not so grieved that she did not relish the few moments away from the stifling card room. She found the breakfast room, which led to the kitchens, and then passed through the doorway, calling out for Mrs. Slougham. The lady appeared in a moment, and upon hearing of the accident dispatched two capable maids to assist Miss Bingley and another to find Mrs. Harwich, "for whatever good she will do."

"Miss Mary, come and sit here a moment," the cook ushered her to the bench in the hallway where she had waited that very first day of the ordeal, when Mama had forgotten her shawl. "I am thinking you are in no hurry to return. We shall go up together in a moment, once I have my basket of bandages and salves ready. Sit yourself there; I shall be but a minute."

The silence was blessed. After Miss Bingley's grating voice, she revelled in the absence of all human noise. The maids had all rushed out to help their mistress or find the housekeeper, and the one young girl tending the fire in the kitchen said not a word. Mary closed her eyes and the memory of her previous rest upon this very bench flooded her mind. She could hear, in the silence, the echo of the maids' and footmen's complaints about the wine bottles and the silk stocking and the missing boots and the missing silver and the missing maid, and in the midst of these silent voices, the *frisson* of a notion threaded its way up her spine.

"The Lord was not in the wind...nor in the earthquake... nor in the fire... but a still small voice."

Was this what she had known all the time? Was this still small voice of memory the key to finding the answers that had so eluded Alexander... Mr. Lyons and herself? She hurried to the girl at the fire. "Excuse me, but where might I find Bessie?"

The girl looked up with frightened eyes. "Bessie, Miss?"

Finding a smile, Mary hoped to reassure the girl. "I mean her no harm; I merely have a question I believe she can answer."

"Oh, very well, miss. She is folding laundry in the room past the stillroom. Shall I show you?"

"Thank you, no. I can find my way."

As luck would have it, Bessie was keeping herself amused with the company of a tall and handsome footman whilst she went about her task of ironing table linens. The footman was thankfully mostly dressed, with only his coat having been removed and placed over the back of a small wooden chair. It transpired that this was the exact man Mary needed to find. After initial inquiries, when she posed her question, he responded, "Yes, Miss, I know exactly of what you speak. We never did find those boots at all. We had thought they were under a pile here or fallen behind a table there, but they might as well have been spirited away by elves."

After one further question, Mary found herself smiling most smugly, and she hurried herself back through the hallways to find Mr. Lyons. He would surely find this information most interesting indeed!

Chapter Twenty-Three

In the Woods

With the fuss and ado in the card room circling around Caroline and her wounded hand, it was a simple matter for Alexander to take a moment with Mary. The look in her eyes told him that she had learned something of great import. Nobody spared them so much as a glance as they talked quietly by the doorway. The word in his own ear quickly led to a word in Darcy's ear, and of course, Miss Elizabeth's, and using the excuse of releasing Caroline from the obligations of hostess, the four departed the room. They would wait for Jane in the small parlour that Mr. Bingley provided for their use until he could rejoin them, which suited them all very well.

In a voice quiet enough not to be overheard, Miss Mary divulged the information she had shared with Alexander some minutes before.

"It cannot be!" Miss Elizabeth gasped, her voice a near silent echo of her sister's. "I cannot believe it—not he, to be sure!"

Darcy was less vocal in his shock, but his slack jaw and stunned eyes betrayed his amazement at the news. "You are quite positive, Lyons? Miss Mary?"

Alexander nodded. "I cannot confirm Miss Mary's report with the footman, but I have no reason to disbelieve her. All the pieces now fit, and they form a perfect picture. If we are mistaken, it will all come to nothing, for our plan," he glanced at Mary, "will only come to fruition if the suspected killer knows some details we shall not provide. If he acts as we believe he will, that in itself will be proof of his guilt."

"But..." Elizabeth had not given up her disbelief, "It is just too shocking to accept. But I have been wrong about men before." Her eyes alit on Darcy and remained there. Then with a gasp she whispered, "Poor Jane! This will quite devastate her. I wish I might be able to warn her, but I know I cannot. Oh, dear Jane, poor Jane!"

In the same whispers, plans were discussed, objected to, refined, and discussed again, and at length were settled upon. "I cannot like this," Elizabeth repeated at every iteration. "It is dangerous; we know the man is armed and is quite evil. He would not hesitate for a second, but would murder you as easily as a butcher slaughters a chicken. I really cannot like it at all."

Nevertheless, when Mary begged her sister to keep the plan from their father, Elizabeth replied, "I said I did not like it, not that I would prevent it. This man must be found out and his guilt must be made apparent. I can think of no better way of achieving these ends." And thus the scheme was settled.

Before long, Jane made her elegant way into the parlour and the carriage was summoned to take the Bennet sisters home. Darcy bid Elizabeth goodbye with a long kiss to the back of her hand, and Bingley did likewise with Jane. Alexander let his eyes linger on Mary. Did he wish to bid a similar farewell to her? He had grown to respect her and like her, but he refused to engage his heart, for even were they to suit, their stations in life were too dissimilar. He would not woo her similarly, for she was not his to woo, but he did extend to her a gesture which he believed would satisfy her more, and offered her a firm handshake, as he would offer to a man worthy of his respect.

At last the three men returned to the card room, where Caroline was lying supine upon a sofa, a lavender-scented cloth upon her forehead, a large white bandage wrapped around her hand. Surely that shard was a wee thing! Alexander recalled seeing only an inch at most of the clear crystal lying on the table where it was placed after removal, and only the tiniest tip of that had been red with blood. The wound had bled profusely, but it could not have been nearly dire enough to warrant that quantity of white wrapping. Further, should she not be resting in her chambers? No, her public exhibition was yet another gambit to gain the men's attention. She ought to be above such childish measures.

Alexander cleared this throat to get everybody's attention and, after asking after Miss Bingley's health, announced his definite plans to return to London the following day.

"Are you really leaving us so soon, Mr. Lyons?" Caroline did not sound as bereft as her words would suggest, nor as weak as her position collapsed on the sofa would suggest.

"Indeed, madam, my task is complete."

Bingley made an approving noise, but said nothing, allowing his rapidly bobbing head to speak for him.

"Is that so? You are really leaving?" It was one of the few times Hurst had spoken unprompted. "You've solved your problem, then, although you have not found the killer?"

"Just so, Hurst," Alexander kept his voice light. "I had considered remaining to assist with the inquiry, but I was not engaged to do Sir William's job for him. Mr. Darcy asked me to exonerate Miss Elizabeth from the crime of the murder of her cousin, and that I have accomplished. Miss Bennet's name is completely free from all stains, and any damage to her reputation will soon be repaired when she takes another name." He turned his head to face Darcy so everyone might take his meaning. "The rest—finding the real killer—was only my onus should we not have found clear evidence to clear Miss Elizabeth. I shall, of course, inform Sir William of everything I have learned, and then shall be off for my own residence and my waiting clients. I shall stay for breakfast, Miss Bingley, and then shall trespass upon your hospitality no more."

"Just like that, eh?" Hurst reached for the scandal sheet at hand and began reading. "Hmmm, listen to this account of the new chef at the club—" he began.

"Indeed, Mr. Hurst. Just like that. Perhaps you will be so good as to tell me about this excellent chef during our morning repast, but for now, I believe I shall retire for the evening. I have to pack and prepare for my journey tomorrow. Good night, everybody." At which he exited the room with about as much pleasure as ever anybody had departed a soiree.

The following morning dawned bright and cold. Alexander had prepared his few belongings the night before and now had them stowed in Darcy's comfortable coach. That gentleman, too, had announced his need to return to London for a day or two to complete some pending business, but had promised to return as soon as he possibly might. The two announced their intentions to depart immediately upon Alexander concluding his interview with Colonel Forster.

Caroline did not come down for breakfast. Through her sister, Louisa Hurst, she sent a message wishing the men well on their trip back to Town and begging their forgiveness for her neglect of her duties, but her hand pained her to excess. Mrs. Hurst did not seem particularly concerned about her sister and, upon delivering her message, set about helping herself to a plate of eggs and dried fruit.

Her husband, Hubert Hurst, hardly glanced up from the newspaper that concealed the large plate of food before him. He murmured something that might have been "morning" to his wife and returned to his meal and whatever article it was that had engrossed him so. He made no further comments about the new chef at the club, rightly assuming, so Alexander imagined, that his audience could not afford membership even were he to be of suitable social standing.

Once more the injustice of class struck Alexander as he scowled at Hurst. He was the picture of indolence, sitting there at his groaning plate, concerning himself with little but his belly, at the expense of his brother-by-marriage. The man did not even need to feed himself, for by his idleness and status, might rely on others to feed and house him in his stead, whilst Alexander had to save and account for every penny that he disbursed for his own sustenance. There sometimes seemed little justice in the world.

Bingley himself was waiting at his friends' pleasure, chatting happily and ensuring that they had everything they needed for their trek. Darcy had to remind the man several times that they were going to London—a distance of only twenty miles—and not to Russia. "Do not forget," Darcy commented, "the inn at Southgate is fine and more than capable of seeing to our needs. It is only two hours or so distant. Between The Hart and the basket of cakes that Mrs. Slougham has given us, I believe we may survive the coming ordeal."

Bingley emitted a most strange sound and said, "Indeed you are right." He seemed rather discomfited. "I have done the ride on horseback in a morning and still arrived in time for breakfast. I stand chastened." But the smile he offered suggested that he would gladly command another basket of treats if his friends so much as thought about it. He stood at the side of the table, handsome and tall and very young, with his sister seated across from him and his round-bellied brother-in-law between them. They made a fascinating tableau. With a last lingering look, Alexander committed the scene to memory and turned to exit the room.

Colonel Forster was pleased to see the man. He had been apprised of everything which Sir William knew and was grateful to Alexander for his part in solving at least part of the strange affair. "I would never have imagined Wickham a killer," he sighed, "and I am relieved he was not. His death is a blow to the men, but it is somehow easier to accept the man as a victim than as a perpetrator. I hope the true killer is found and caught soon."

Begging the colonel's indulgence, Alexander recounted to him everything he himself had learned since departing Sir William's company the previous afternoon. The colonel gaped at him as he spun his tale, uttering oaths and expressions of incredulity at regular intervals. "No, it cannot be! By God! I cannot believe it! Damn it all!" But eventually he conceded that Alexander's conclusions were likely true.

"Well, then, better be getting on that!" he said in parting. "God speed Darcy, God speed Lyons. We shall have our work set for us! I'll be off to Sir William this instant. This will end soon."

And, having taken appropriate leave of everybody of whom it was required, the two men drove out of town in Darcy's large and sumptuous coach.

It was late, long hours past sunset, when a small shape slipped through the shadowed and naked trees near the hunting cabin where George Wickham had breathed his last breath. The sky was clear and the moon full and bright, but in the woods, bare and slumbering, darkness reigned. The figure crept from tree to tree, scouring the forest before each further step, until the cabin was in sight. Only then did it dare to make the slightest noise.

"Mr. Lyons? Are you there?"

From behind the small shape, a hand reached out and wrapped itself firmly around the slight shoulders whilst another covered the whispering mouth. The person tried to scream, but the clamped hand forbade any sound.

"Mary, hush! It is I." The answering voice was barely a whisper, a hiss through the empty trees. "You are lucky he has not yet come. I might have killed you by accident. Now what in blazes are you doing here?"

Ignoring the shocking oath, Mary twisted around in her captor's hands to face him, freeing her mouth as she did so. "Mr. Lyons, I am here to see this to an end. And I knew he would not yet have arrived, for I know the plan as well as do you. He has not even received the summons yet."

"Hush, Mary! You have to leave immediately. This is no place for a lady. It is dangerous and I would not have you hurt. Go home."

"I cannot, and I will not. I did not walk all this distance for nothing. Now let me join you."

He could not see her eyes in the darkness, but the determination he knew must be reflected therein burned into him through the darkness. Short of hoisting her bodily and carrying her back to Longbourn, there was little he could do to remove her from the area. Hopefully if he acquiesced, she would see reason and behave herself.

"You may stay to observe the outcome, but you will stay back, preferably behind a tree, once he arrives. I will not have some dire injury or—God forbid!—your death on my conscience. Promise me that." He hoped his voice conveyed the full weight of his intentions. If he dared, he would have shouted, but silence, even now, when there was no chance of being overheard, was of utmost importance.

"Why did you say that?" He felt her shift beside him in the darkness and he imagined her eyebrows pressing together.

"What? Why did I say what?"

"'God forbid.' Why did you say that?"

"Mary, please! This is hardly the place or the time..."

"I think it the very place and the very time. We are sitting here in the woods at night—in God's own creation rather than our own—waiting to confront a killer who will almost certainly be armed and prepared to do us... you... the greatest injury. Does a man facing death not wish to know his God?"

This was the strangest location to delve into personal theologies, and yet at the same time, the ideal location as well. Alexander felt Mary shiver beside him. "Come, you are correct—it is still too early. Let us sit a while yonder. If you have no objection, I have a blanket for warmth." He found her hand and led her silently through the trees to a small structure of sorts under a low-hanging branch. The structure was more a collection of assembled twigs than anything a man might call a building, and it provided little protection from the wind or precipitation should any happen to fall, but it did offer the safety of a blind. Unless one were looking, one would see nothing but more fallen branches and leaves. "There is not much room, but..."

"I understand you. I have no objection." She shivered again, and he tugged her down to the low seat of wood and moss, upon which a dark blanket lay discarded. Tugging the heavy cloth about his shoulders, he extended an arm to allow her to nestle close and then wrapped her up beside him in the relative warmth.

"We had best not be found like this," he began, and Mary laughed.

"No indeed, although somehow I know I can trust you completely to act the gentleman, even though you declare yourself none."

They were silent for a time, the only sounds the faint rustle of leaves as an errant gust of wind disturbed their slumber, or the brush of an animal—a rabbit or squirrel, or possibly a distant deer—through the scrub. Then Mary whispered again, so low he could scarcely hear her, though she was mere inches away.

"I would return to our recently abandoned topic." Her voice held an edge of confusion. "You know more of the essence of right and wrong, of good and evil, than do many religious men, even those in orders. I have tried to take your measure, and I have failed. You said you were no Christian, and you have not corrected that assertion."

"I said that I was not in communion with the Church of England—and yet that does not imply that I live outside of the morality that lets us build our society and our institutions. Right and wrong, good and evil: these are concepts that are independent of any one doctrine of thought."

"But without the Church, without God, to guide us, how can we know which actions are good and which evil?" He could hear the frustration in her voice, even in the whisper that was little more than articulated breath. She was not asking such questions out of a desire to justify her own beliefs, but out of a real need to understand. Alexander thought he knew the reason.

"Even with the teachings of the bible and the Church, men still do evil. Your cousin, rest his soul, was a relentlessly moral man, with fire and brimstone in every breath when he felt something went against his view of the world. He railed against sin and confronted men he believed were gamers and sinners—and whom he knew were dangerous in some way or another—and he wrote about them to his patroness to inform the world of their shortcomings. But this did not stop him from succumbing to the sin of lechery, from attempting to force himself upon two women in the very short time he was in Meryton. His notions of right and wrong seemed to vanish when applied to himself."

Mary was silent; Alexander could tell she was thinking. "Then how do you find your sense of morality? For you are not a gamer, nor an over-indulger, nor a glutton, and I feel not the first bit of danger sitting here with you in rather compromising circumstances. You exude the qualities of good and just, and yet..."

"And yet I have no longing for Heaven or fear of Hell to set my feet on the right path?" She nodded; he could feel the motion. "Perhaps it is what is within us, as individual men and women, that defines God, rather than converse."

If Mary were about to object to this heretical statement, her words were cut short by a sharp bird call in the distance and Alexander's finger before her lips. "He is coming. Silence."

Mr. Lyons pressed his hands onto Mary's shoulders. He said not a word, but the meaning was clear: *Stay. Do not move.* She had felt so brave earlier, creeping out of the house as she had. Escaping Longbourn had been an easy task. She pled a headache immediately after dinner and retired to her room, informing the maid not to bother her for she would be asleep. It was not difficult to change into the overlarge shirt and workman's trousers she had liberated from the storage rooms behind the barn, and then into the warm coat she found. These were much easier to don without assistance than her dresses. This late in the year the sun dipped early below the horizon, and there was little wait until the sky grew inky. As soon as it was sufficiently dark she had pulled on her heavy walking cape, her walking boots, and the thick woollen hat she had found, and made her escape.

Lydia might have been a fool to play the hackney driver for Mr. Wickham, but the girl had also boasted about how simple it was to creep from the house, even with the servants all up and about. The windows on their side of the house sat above a deep terrace that formed the roof of some of the lower rooms. From an open window, there was only a drop of a foot or eighteen inches—nothing at all for a young and active woman. The roof terrace led around to the side of the house by the kitchen garden, and there one could always find piles of crates or wood or some other object leaning against the house, with which one might climb down to the ground. Indeed, Mary had taken a walk earlier in the day and ensured that a convenient pile of accoutrements were located exactly where she might need them to descend from the roof. Had some servant found a need to remove the pile of ladders and crates, the tree just a few feet along had well-spaced branches to aid in a descent and re-ascent at the end of the adventure. So Lydia had described it, and so it was.

There were no servants in the kitchen garden after dark, and the tree-shielded laneway to the back entrance led directly there, leaving no more than a few dark feet for discovery. And so Mary escaped. It was a long walk to the cabin, but she was strong and her feet knew the way well; even the cold air of the first day of December was little more than a nuisance to her as she travelled in silence. She moved quickly but was in no hurry, for it was not yet nine o'clock and the man would not leave his own abode until after ten. Still, she needed to be early, to convince Alexander—Mr. Lyons—that she should be allowed to remain.

Until now, her plan had gone perfectly. She had felt altogether too comfortable with the man, talking of deep and serious matters as equals, quite forgetting that she did not like him. When this recollection slipped her mind, his company was really most pleasant indeed. He did not tease her or chide her, and he weighed her questions with the same sober consideration as he did Darcy's. He listened to her and paid her attention, and his tone was respectful, not at all condescending as Mr. Collins' had been. It really was a pity the man was so low-bred, for were he a better rank of person she might welcome him as a friend. But the time for such niceties of society were in the past and in the future; now, in the present, with a murderer approaching, she needed to place her full faith in him. She laughed at this, the need to place her faith in a man who had no faith of his own, since there was real danger afoot. And, for the first time since she set out on her adventure, she felt afraid.

His warning to stay still went well heeded. The hunting cabin was not far away—perhaps a hundred yards through the trees— but the thought of that small hut, and what had so recently lain inside it, caused her to shiver far beyond what the cool night air had caused. She was profoundly thankful that Mr. Lyons had chosen another place than the cabin to sit his vigil. He turned back to her once, and she could see the pale orb of his face against the darkness of the woods, and then he was gone.

The speed with which he vanished into the woods astounded her. The bright moon overhead filtered through the naked trees, casting shards of white lights hither and yon among the trunks and limbs, and within moments, he had melded with the chaotic array of light and shadow and become one with the forest. Of his movements, she heard not a trace. Even on the leaf-covered earth, where the most silent of rodents left a brush of sound in their wake, Alexander's steps were silent. For all that she could hear or see of him, he might be a wraith, to disappear so completely and without a trace.

She sat for a minute, counting the seconds with each breath, and then another. It must now be well past ten o'clock, the hour when the message was to be delivered. Would the man truly have risen to the bait and come, or would this entire adventure have been in vain? Still, the signal had sounded; somebody was approaching. It could be a tramp, or a messenger, or some hapless farmer walking through the woods on his way home. But the signal had sounded, and the lookout in the trees knew well for whom he waited. It must be him! Holding her breath as long as she could, Mary counted the seconds for another minute, and then a third, and still there was silence.

The weight of Mr. Lyons' hands had faded from her shoulders, and in the dark and white striped woods, Mary's bravery began to return. She would not interfere, she convinced herself; she would remain safe behind a tree, where she could not be seen, nor hurt. Discarding the heavy blanket on the bed of leaves and branches that formed their bench, she inched forward. Her cape was dark brown, and with the hood pulled low over her eyes, her face would be shadowed. No one would see her. Slowly she crept, one foot after another, feeling the ground for twigs or leaves before shifting her weight, moving this way and that in a crooked path towards the hut.

And then she saw him. He was nothing at first, a dark mass against more darkness, gradually coalescing out of the shadows to take the shape of a man. He was of average height, that she could discern, but every other aspect of his appearance was disguised by the large and voluminous coat he wore, seemingly not his own, or perhaps acquired for just such nefarious doings as this. Had she not known whom to expect, she would not have known him at all. Her heart lurched. It was true, then. It was indeed he. Some part of her had hoped she had been mistaken, but the bait had been taken and her suppositions proven correct. Her thoughts echoed Lizzy's from the night before. *Poor Jane.*

Onward, the killer approached. If they had planned well, he would be expecting the woods to be empty; the *rendezvous* was scheduled for much later, after midnight. The message he had received at ten o'clock suggested that the sender was only at that moment leaving London, that the bright light of the full moon would allow him to travel and return without anybody in town being the wiser of his absence. And so, this heavily cloaked man had arrived early to set his trap. Just as he had done with Lieutenant Wickham.

Mary shivered. Somewhere in the many folds and pockets of that overlarge coat, with its many capes and layers, lay the Blunderbuss that had so reduced the lieutenant's skull to splinters. In her mind's eye she envisaged that same ferocious weapon pointed towards Alexander—she did not bother correcting his name, even in her thoughts—and erupting in an explosion of death. This was something she had known, but the immediacy of the possibility stopped her footsteps as she crept, leaving her gasping for air.

"I told you to stay," a voice breathed in her ear.

He was annoying and vexatious and irritating beyond belief, but she had come to respect him so very much, and as she considered the possibility of his death, she realised how much she would mourn him. Even in the very few days of their acquaintance, whilst she had tried to convince herself of her intense dislike for the odious man, she had grown to like him very much.

"I had to see... I had to know."

"Mary." His whisper was a command equal to the bellowing of a sergeant major. "Here. You will stay here, behind this tree. It is large enough to shield you. Do not move. I do not request this. I insist upon it. Just, for the love of God, stay still." She bristled at his command, but obeyed. For now. She crouched down to steady herself and her hands came upon a large stone, almost the size of her face. She would not need it, but she picked it up, regardless. It would be a poor weapon, but 'twas better than none. She knelt on the cold and hard ground, waiting for what, she knew not. Her heart hammered in her chest and she prayed that the killer could not hear it.

The shape had drawn closer, but she still could not see the man's face. He walked with barely a sound, something surprising for a man of his apparent girth. As he approached the cabin, he reached into a fold of his coat and withdrew something long and slightly curved at one end: the weapon that had killed Wickham. He braced himself at the cabin door, almost invisible in the dappled light of the moonlit woods, and scoured the surrounding area once more, stopping, listening, stopping and listening some more.

Seemingly satisfied that he was, indeed, alone, he turned to the door of the cabin and turned the handle.

"Damn it." The words, though mumbled under his breath, sounded as explosions in the absolute silence of the woods. In what looked like an instinctive move, he transferred the Blunderbuss to his left hand and tried the door handle with his right. He rattled the handle once again and then, with an audible huff, set his shoulder to it to force it open.

And that is when the forest seemed to explode around him.

Chapter Twenty-Four

Facing a Killer

Mary had not realised that Alexander was no longer at her side. She had approached much nearer to the hunting cabin than she had imagined, and in the shards of moonlight that filtered through the trees and into the small clearing before the hut, she could see the action as if it were being unfolded on a stage for her entertainment. The whirl of limbs and weapons and the flares of lights must have been over in seconds, but to her they seemed to be drawn out as if the earth had slowed and time had stopped its relentless march.

As the killer lowered his arm to ram his right shoulder against the barred door, Alexander leapt from around the side of the hut, short feet away, and hurled himself against the man, sending his fist into the man's cheek. The crunch of bone against bone reverberated through the silence of the forest and Mary felt her stomach lurch within her as blood began pouring, dark and thick in the striated light, from the man's nose, now visible from under his hood.

The man grunted at the force of the impact, but before he could react to this unexpected blow, Alexander had darted behind him to grab his left arm—the one still holding the pistol—and wrenched it behind his back. For a moment, Mary could see the muzzle of the dreadful weapon point directly towards her, sheltered behind a tree though she was, but Alexander had not completed his assault. With the offending arm, pistol and all, firmly pressed up against the man's back, Alexander shifted around to his front and sent a powerful blow upwards from his waist to connect with the man's chin, sending him reeling into the building, cracking his head upon the old wood. Alexander now seemed to be holding the man upright with the arm bent behind his back, but with a fluid motion that amazed Mary with its simplicity and elegance, he swept a foot behind the murderer's leg and knocked it from under him, sending his head back into the wooden cabin one last time and knocking him to the ground.

The fight, such that it was, was over in a moment. The hulk of the heavily clad man lay slumped against the hunting cabin, his eyes half closed and all glazed over. From all around came the sounds of flints being struck and torches and lamps being lit, and the woods blazed into life, revealing a veritable army of dark-clothed soldiers from the locally stationed militia. Colonel Forster strode forward from their midst and surveyed the pile on the ground.

"Got him, eh? Good man, Lyons. Wickham was no angel, but he did not deserve to die." The colonel turned to command his men to ready the ropes and horses with which to drag the suspect back to the town's gaol.

What the men did not see, however, was that the fallen hulk had begun to stir. With wide eyes, Mary watched as the hooded eyes blinked once, then twice, and then opened. The arm which had been wrenched behind his back looked quite useless, but that hand still held the Blunderbuss, and that hand was in easy reach of the man's good arm. Horrified, Mary saw him slowly shift to take the pistol into his good hand, and then with a shout, fling that hand forward with the pistol pointing before him, directly at Alexander.

Time seemed to stop. The soldiers froze in their positions as if turned to stone by Medusa herself. Only their eyes moved, flicking from one another to the fallen man with his threatening pistol. Alexander too seemed transfixed, his own eyes directed towards that deadly muzzle, pointing so ominously towards him. Mary felt her knees shake as she slowly, silently, stood up behind her tree, holding onto it for support.

Alexander was a fine man, a good and just and honest man, and he had saved her sister. He did not deserve to die, not here and not now. She began to search her memories for a prayer to offer for his eternal soul, but stopped herself. If God could not accept such a decent man as Alexander into Heaven, then God did not deserve her prayers.

As she grappled with her beliefs, the man seemed to be grappling with his hold on consciousness. The pistol wavered, the hand that held it unsteady, and in the lights of the hundred lamps and torches, the man's eyes could be seen as glazed and unfocused. Once more the hand shook and the pistol danced through the air, threatening every man in the woods, before centering once more on Alexander.

Mary's fists clenched in horror and dread, and she discovered that she still held her stone. She had no particular physical strength, no real skill at all, but she had played baseball with the village children and knew how to throw a ball. She reached back and took aim and let the stone fly, praying to God for it to reach its target.

At once there was a crack, followed by an explosion, a great burst of sound and a flash of light that tore from the muzzle, followed by absolute silence and then the oaths of a hundred men. Mary was dimly aware of somebody screaming, somebody quite close to her. With a start, she realised that the screamer was herself. She could not look, dared not look, to see what had become of the man she had begun to think of as a friend. She pictured him lying crumpled on the leaf-carpeted ground, a pile of rags and gore and bone, his spark seeping into the dry wintery earth with his lifeblood. She pictured him wounded, a hand torn off, a hole through his middle, dooming him to a slow and painful death. She pictured him like Wickham, with half of his head gone, splinters and torn skin where his brain used to be.

She dared not open her eyes, and yet somehow she did, and she stared at what she saw with horror and amazement and wonder. For there, still upright and somehow still whole, stood Alexander, his face a mirage of unidentifiable emotions.

The killer, now without a useful weapon, groaned and cursed, and from above a blur fell through the air, crashing down on the man from the building's roof, pinning him to the ground and sending his head, one last time, into the hard wood of the hut. The man groaned and fell silent as his eyes rolled back into his head and he sagged, unconscious and unarmed.

Two things now occurred at once. The militia descended on the fallen criminal with ropes and bindings to secure him, shouting and calling and ordering each other to various tasks. But Mary saw almost none of this, for she had rushed from behind her tree towards Alexander—miraculously uninjured Alexander—and without a thought for her actions, enfolded him in a fierce embrace.

"There is a God. He saved you. Oh, thank heavens! You are well."

For his part, Alexander gaped blankly ahead, his own eyes as of yet unfocused on the world of living men, so intent had they been on their first view of the world to come. But his arms, of their own volition, wrapped themselves around Mary's shoulders and she felt him sag in her arms, their desperate embrace the only force keeping them from crashing to the ground.

The figure that had toppled the killer hoisted itself from the ground and limped over to where Mary held Alexander upright. "Are you well, Lyons? Miss Mary, allow me to assist you."

"Mr. Darcy!" His presence had not been part of their carefully laid plans.

At the sound of his voice, Alexander seemed to return to himself.

"Darcy, thank God! What happened? How am I not dead? I had thought myself to be meeting Wickham and the saints within moments. What in heaven's name were you doing upon that roof?"

"I will divulge the entire story later when we are warm and dry. For now, let us see how the soldiers have fared with their prey."

The three staggered across the small clearing to where the soldiers had lashed their prey to a plank of wood, which they would drag with its burden through the woods to the laneway at the far end where their horses and carts would soon arrive. The captured killer was still unconscious, his hood now fallen back and revealing his face to the world.

Mary sighed as she stared at the blank face. This was not unexpected, but it pained her nonetheless. This man had stolen, bribed, lied, and killed two men. His conviction and punishment would be no loss to her, but would certainly cause great distress to somebody she loved. "Why did you do it? Was it really so important?" she asked the prone figure, knowing he would not answer.

"Well, there's that." Darcy stared down at the captive. "Bingley will not be pleased. I'm afraid," he announced to the man lashed to the plank, "and this will quite disturb his plans to offer for Jane, for now at least. But this little reign of terror is over. You've had your last ragout, Hubert Hurst."

Alexander stared at the activity around him, the lights from the lanterns, the rush of men hustling this way and that, the shouts and cries and the buzz of energy as they all set about their tasks. It was all very present, all very real, and yet he felt so far removed from the scene that it was almost as if he were viewing pictures in a book. He could look down and see his feet, but they seemed to be somebody else's; his ears reported to him of noise that seemed to echo in another room; even the pain in his hip from his attack on Hurst throbbed through another man's body.

How strange it was to be there, and not be, to feel so keenly and not at all. He had stared down the flared muzzle of the pistol, down into its black and murky depths wherein lay the face of God... or the devil. No, he decided, the devil was the one holding the pistol. No man with a soul worthy of heaven could do what Hurst had done and kill a man in cold blood.

But what had happened next? He had seen Hurst's finger twitch upon the trigger, seen the glazed look in his eyes focus for that one terrible moment upon him, seen the flash as the powder had exploded. He ought to be dead. And he was not. The enormity of this realisation left him stunned and rooted to the ground, unable to move.

For there had been one more event, between the twitch of the finger and the explosion of the powder: he had heard a crack, the thud of some object hitting another, and the pistol's aim had been jarred ever so slightly from true. Something had hit Hurst or the weapon, and the assassin had missed his mark. Could it possibly have been…?

From somewhere in the chaos, Mary had come rushing up to him and had wept words of thanks for his safety, and then had done what no lady ought to do, but which he very much appreciated, and threw her arms about him. At that moment, when she offered him her strength, his own was suddenly sapped away, and he felt his legs weaken beneath him, but Mary held him upright. More than the astonishment with which he had discovered his still-beating heart was the astonishment with which he realised that Mary cared about him—cared enough, at least, to throw propriety to the winds and embrace him and sob against him and whisper, "Thank God, thank God," again and again whilst a small army of Colonel Forster's men looked on.

Somewhere from the fog that surrounded him—them—came a voice that pulled him back through the mists. Darcy. What in blazes was he doing here? He ought to be in London, conferring with Hurst's bankers and man of business, confirming their suppositions. The world swam and shifted and then settled into some sort of focus, and all that he had imagined in that fevered dream at the barrel of the Blunderbuss now seemed to be true.

The soldiers were completing their task and with the greatest of efforts. He pulled himself from Mary's embrace, surprised that his arms were wrapped about her just as surely as hers were about him. Darcy offered Mary one arm, and then took much of Alexander's weight on the other, and the three stumbled their way to the captive.

Hubert Hurst. Whoever would have imagined it? Certainly not he upon first meeting the man. Hurst had been laconic, indolent, passionless even, except when the topic changed to food. Only then did the man seem to rouse himself to some degree of enthusiasm. It was hard to imagine him, rotund and soft as he was, rousing himself only to debate the merits of *The Times* over *The Observer*, or whether Loo was to be preferred over Whist at the card table. To summon the image of him wrestling a man into the soft mud on the banks of that icy stream and then plunging a knife into the tough skin of his victim's neck stretched the mind to incredulity. And yet, so it had happened. That and more. He had also waited in hiding for an officer of His Majesty's militia, held a pistol to the back of the soldier's head and had blown a hole through it.

It was an effort to fight the inclination to spit in the unconscious killer's face; if Mary had not been there, he might have done it, but for some reason he still wished to impress his worth upon her. Instead, he ground his boot heels into the packed earth and turned a sneer towards the trussed man on the plank and said, "Take him. I cannot abide his face any longer."

Later on, Alexander could hardly have said how he returned to Longbourn. He had vague flashes of memory of Darcy dragging him through the woods, Mary at his side, his hip throbbing with every step. There was a carriage, and some horses—two or three, he could not recall—waiting to spare them the three-mile walk in the chilly air. He recalled the rough scratch of an old blanket as it was tossed over his shoulders, and the press of hard and cold metal in his hand as somebody handed him a flask. "Drink," the voice said. He did not need to be coaxed.

All the while, Mary sat at his side in silence. She knew, somehow, that silence was what he needed right now. There would be a need, later, for talking, when everything he had seen and done would need airing, every motion and gesture waiting to be analysed and dissected like a cadaver in an anatomist's laboratory, but that time was not now. Now he needed peace, and like a guardian angel, soundless and protective, Mary was at his side to keep him safe from interruption and chaos.

It was not until they had descended from the carriage and been hustled through the kitchen door and into a cosy room with a warm and blazing fire that Alexander thought to ask why they had come to Longbourn. Netherfield was, of necessity, out of the question. He would be spending enough time there over the coming days as he spoke to Bingley and Caroline about any knowledge they might have as to more of Hurst's less savoury activities. The staff, as well, would need to be questioned, and then there was the business with Mrs. Hurst: had she known about the murders and everything leading up to them? And if so, what had she known?

Still, Alexander had thought they might retire to The Red Lion in Meryton for the night, or possibly to the barracks where Colonel Forster would surely be busy at this business until well into the deepest hours of the night. And so he asked his friend, and his friend answered.

"After I left you at Southgate, I found I could not return to London and leave you in peril. I ordered my driver to turn around. The lad—Evan was his name—set me up with a good team of fresh horses and we were soon set upon the same road back to Meryton." Darcy prodded at the fire as he spoke; sparks flew from the burning wood, glowing their quick bright lives and then dying into embers. Miss Elizabeth hovered by his side, worried eyes widening each time he seemed to favour the leg on which he had landed. "Here, are you comfortable, Lyons? Shall I request another pillow? More salve for your hand?"

Alexander's hand was quite tender and raw. He had not noticed the pain at first, being so overwhelmed by the events of the night and distracted by his aching hip, but the evidence of his first move against Hurst was now writ bold upon his bruised and swollen knuckles.

"I am well. Do sit, Darcy, you are as wounded as I am, having taken your landing on that leg as you did. Will you not sit?"

Elizabeth dragged her suitor to a chair, and all but pressed him into it before moving to a bottle-laden tray and returning with a glass of brandy for each man, then pouring a cup of chocolate for herself and her sister.

"I am sitting, Lyons. Are you satisfied?" Darcy took a long sip of his brandy and closed his eyes in the pleasure of it. Alexander did likewise, feeling every muscle ease as the amber liquid flowed through his veins.

"I am satisfied," he purred. "Continue with your tale."

"I had to return to Longbourn. I had to see Elizabeth and reassure her of the worth of our scheme. She wished to confer once more with Mary as well," he nodded to the young lady where she sat with her feet in a tub of warm water, naked feet scandalously exposed to the eyes of the two gentlemen, "but upon trying her room, we discovered that Mary was not in her bed. It did not require much experience in investigation to determine where she was, and thus, on horseback, I rode out to try to catch her. But I did not leave without ensuring us a warm and comfortable place to stay the night."

"Not to belabour the tale, I passed Miss Mary, but left my horse far enough distant from the cabin so as to keep my presence there quiet, and I managed to hide myself behind some trees near the cabin as Forster's men arrived and took their posts. With the noise they made, I found myself able to climb up on the roof using the two trees at the side. And there I waited until I was needed. I had thought to land upon Hurst before he could fire that accursed pistol, but he rallied more quickly than I'd have thought. My apologies for that, Lyons."

Alexander shifted on the sofa, testing his leg. The bruise from his mishap some days prior was less painful than it had been, but the muscles were very stiff from the hours sitting out in the cold night air and now protested the abuse Alexander had put to them when he had tackled and felled Hurst. "I still do not know how I am alive. He aimed directly at me, and fired... I saw the flash from within the muzzle, and I was too close even for him to miss..." his voice faded.

"Mary saved you," Darcy's words hung in the air. "I could just see her through the line of trees. She hurled something at him—a rock of some sort, I believe. It struck his arm precisely as he pulled on the trigger."

"I promised not to move," Mary spoke for the first time since she had taken her chair and begun to soak her feet. "but how could I not act? Afterwards, I heard the men talking, and I heard that Colonel Forster sent one to examine the scene. The pellet was lodged in a tree some ten feet beyond where you stood. He surmised," she swallowed hard, "based on where Hurst sat and your position, that it missed your head by about six inches."

"Then I have you to thank for saving my life." His eyes met hers and held them, and he felt a jolt in their mutual gaze that might have been electrical, so powerful did it seem to him. He and she, by this fortuitous and brave act, would always be connected in some way. She had disobeyed him not only once, but thrice, and in doing so had disarmed a killer. His killer. Nothing in his experience could destroy a bond so strongly forged at that.

"I prayed as I threw the stone," Mary whispered. "I prayed to God. But how could a benevolent Father put his children in a position of such peril? In that moment, I doubted more than I have doubted in my life."

"And I," Alexander breathed back, "believed more strongly in those moments that I stared down the muzzle, more than I have in my life. Your actions were human in origin, but the inspiration behind them, and the success with which your stone hit its target, seemed to me to be divine."

"Then perhaps," Mary returned with a cheeky grin, "we may find we have more in common than we had initially supposed."

"Indeed, I dare say we do!"

Chapter Twenty-Five

Explanations

Alexander slept late the next morning. It was nearly midday before he opened his eyes to the world, and immediately he regretted his actions. The light stabbed his eyes through the chink between the curtains and the willow bark tea he had taken before retiring had long since ceased to soothe his aches. His head pounded, a polyphonic counterpoint to the throb in his hip, and he bemoaned the third glass of brandy he had accepted from Darcy the previous evening. At the time it had dulled the pain; now it exacerbated it.

Allowing his eyes to become accustomed to the shard of light, he wrenched himself from the bed and shuffled to the window, unsure whether to open the draperies or close them more firmly. Sense reigned over sensibility and he pulled the two curtains apart, allowing the bright daylight to flood the room.

The outside world greeted him with a brilliant glare; it had snowed overnight, and the dusting reflected the sun's valiant efforts a hundred times. The snow was not deep, nor would it last, he believed, but for the moment it was bright and beautiful and pure, a welcome balm after the previous days of sordid death and violence. Overhead the sky was a watery blue, the haze of the unexpected snow not quite departed, diffusing the sun's light across the landscape. It had been clear when he and his friends had returned to Longbourn; the snow must have been an early morning gift from the heavens.

He turned to face the ordeal of dressing and finding something hot and restorative for his breakfast—a cup of coffee would be most welcome right now—when a knock sounded at his door.

"May I enter, Mr. Lyons? I have a tray." Thorne. Of course Darcy would have kept his valet with him. It would be as unthinkable for him to be without the man as it would for Alexander to leave his abode without his left arm.

"Yes, please." He prayed that there would be coffee on that tray, and he was not disappointed.

"I have a small jar of the liniment from Netherfield, if you would like me to apply it to your injuries." The scent of the pungent balm wafted across the room as Thorne uncapped the jar, and Alexander thought he had never smelled anything so welcome in his life.

Sometime later he descended the stairs, moving with greater ease and looking quite smart in the clothing Darcy had sent with the valet. He seemed not to be the only member of the household who had slept past the first blush of morning, for Darcy, Elizabeth and Mary were still sitting at the breakfast table, as were Mr. Bennet and Colonel Forster.

"We thought you would sleep till dinner! Good job, Lyons," the colonel greeted him. "Our prisoner has wakened and is singing a most entertaining song. Sir William is with the blackguard now at the town's gaol and will join us once he has completed his business there."

"Indeed, Lyons," Mr. Bennet echoed, "we have much to thank you for, although keeping two of my daughters awake past midnight is not included. Nevertheless, I trust you slept well? The bed was to your liking?"

"Most comfortable indeed, Mr. Bennet. Please allow me to extend my gratitude for your generous hospitality." He eyed the sideboard with its array of warming dishes and platters and set about the arduous task of filling a plate for himself. The eggs did not suit his drink-weary head, but the still-warm buns and a good serving of cheeses and jams called him and he listened. Already he was feeling more himself; another cup or two of that strong coffee and some good food in his belly might well have him at his best again.

He found a place at the table near Mary and nodded with open appreciation as she reached for the coffee urn and poured a long stream of the steaming and fragrant liquid into a cup.

"Not so generous," Mr. Bennet responded as Alexander settled himself before his meal. "I believe I was on your list of possible suspects for a time. Being removed from that list is adequate compensation for a night or two in one of our guest rooms."

Darcy laughed, a sound still foreign to Alexander's ears. "Indeed, Mr. Bennet, I believe I was on that list as well for a few moments."

"But only a few," Alexander replied around a mouthful of warm bread. "If you had indeed been the culprit, you would not have engaged my services to find the truth, nor would you have allowed Miss Elizabeth to become implicated in the sad affair. You were one of the few whose time on my list was very short."

"And I?" Elizabeth asked with a grin, her eyes sparkling in the bright sunlight that streamed into the room.

"You, I am afraid, were a more serious consideration than was Mr. Darcy, for there was much evidence to implicate you. Your knife was the one that ended Mr. Collins' life; your satchel was found at the scene, and your dress and walking cape were damaged exactly to the extent I would expect from a struggle of the sort that resulted in Collins' death. You also had the greatest reason to wish him dead, for it was apparent that he would not accept your refusal of his offer, and the man could be... coercive if he did not have his way. I had to consider very carefully that you might be the killer after all."

He glanced around at his tablemates. Mr. Bennet and Miss Elizabeth accepted this assessment with mirth and repressed chuckles, but Darcy's eyes looked hurt, as if he could believe that anybody might possibly doubt his beloved Elizabeth. "I offered this as a possibility when you engaged me, Darcy," Alexander offered with all sincerity, "and you accepted it. Do not now accuse me of having come to do this job with veiled intentions."

The tall man shook his head. "No, no, you are correct, Lyons. But whilst you had implied the possibility, I could not imagine you might doubt her at all after meeting her. When did you accept her innocence?"

"I have to admit, the scratches and bruises on her arms and face were troubling, but her dress and cape—the ones Sir William obtained—were the proofs of her innocence. A severed artery will spray pints of blood in all directions, and yet the patches of blood on the cape were concentrated and not nearly large enough to signify the sort of damage that would kill a man. The very blood that convinced Sir William that she might be the culprit was that which convinced me of her innocence."

"And a wise decision that was too," Mr. Bennet added with a chuckle, "or I should have you out in the hedgerows in a moment!"

"Pray tell, Mr. Lyons, of those with whom I had the pleasure of keeping company on that infamous list of yours," Elizabeth's eyes sparkled. Darcy was a very lucky man to have engaged her affections. She was a lovely young woman and she would keep him from descending too far into the serious depths which Alexander knew dragged at him.

"Indeed, my list! This was a rather strange phenomenon, for we started this quest wondering who in the world would have reasons to kill Mr. Collins, and ended up discovering that the better question was who did *not* wish to see him dead!" He leaned back with a smug smile, taking perverse pleasure in the shocked expressions around him. This was the part of a case he enjoyed the most, when it was over and he could revel in the story-telling. He took another drink from his cup and Mary, seeing it was the last, promptly refilled it. He smiled his thanks, and she smiled back.

"Your dear father—if I may, Mr. Bennet?—was a rather serious contender for my attentions. Not only had Collins imposed himself upon his beloved daughter and threatened her, but the man stood to inherit the estate. Having seen a vindictive and highly suggestible streak in Mr. Collins' character, Mr. Bennet might have felt that by ridding the world of his cousin's son, he would thereby save Miss Elizabeth from a most unpleasant future and save the rest of his family from the parson's less-than-compassionate whims. There were two details, however, that suggested that Mr. Bennet was not the killer. The first was the exact nature of the deed of Longbourn, which was unknown to Mr. Bennet. Mr. Collins was the very last possible heir to the estate. With his death, Mr. Bennet did not know what would become of his lands. Would they revert to the crown? Or would they somehow be passed along to his daughters in common, or to a grandson? With that question still unanswered, I cannot see Mr. Bennet possibly dooming his family to homelessness, to rely purely on the goodness of friends and relations for their maintenance. We did not learn until after the parson's death that the oldest grandson who has no other estate, regardless of which daughter bears him, will become the new squire.

"Further, Mr. Bennet did not learn of Collins' most appalling attack on Miss Elizabeth until after the man was dead. If this had occurred prior to Collins setting out that day, any father would well be in his rights to be furious and demand satisfaction, although I would never countenance anything so vile as murder. And if he had seen Collins attack his daughter, I might have given full weight to his consideration as the perpetrator of this crime. But Mr. Bennet was not seen near the stream where Collins was found, nor were any of his clothes or boots covered in mud, as the real killer's must have been. Had your father been the man you believed you heard, Miss Elizabeth, I would have heard of his absence from the house by one of the servants, for he is so accustomed to remaining in his study. Thereby, I moved Mr. Bennet to a much lower position on my list of possibilities." He offered her a bow of his head and she sighed in relief.

"Then there was Mr. Hill, who saved his niece from an attack similar to the one you escaped. He certainly had excellent cause to hate Collins, and the passion to commit the crime, but he could not have been away from his duties for that length of time, nor is he a large enough or young enough man to have bested Mr. Collins in a struggle. I even considered Colonel Forster for a moment—"

"What? Me?"

Alexander chuckled at the man's outrage. "However, I dismissed you almost immediately. I had no real reason to suspect you of wrongdoing, but your habits of visiting the gaming clubs in London opened the door so some possible motives. Never fear, Colonel, your insistence upon your good standing has been confirmed, and I never thought you anything but the best of men. You will forgive me if I investigated where my instincts told me not to bother. A man cannot be too careful in matters such as this."

"Well. Yes, I suppose. Very good." The colonel settled back into his chair with his arms crossed about his chest and did not look entirely pleased with Alexander's confession.

"I had a great many people on my list, from John Lucas, who might have wished to marry Elizabeth and secure Longbourn through a son, to Robinson, the butler at Netherfield who had to account for the missing silverware, to John the footman, who may have seen something at the Netherfield ball. But they, like you, were discarded almost as soon as I considered them."

The colonel gave a brisk nod and allowed his face to settle into something less ferocious.

"Of course, George Wickham seemed the most likely man to have done the vile deed." Another sip of coffee and Alexander's head had almost stopped its dull throb. "He was embroiled in all manner of seamy activities, from gaming to engaging with young women—"

"Not at the breakfast table, Lyons," Mr. Bennet's eyes had lost their indulgent glint.

"—to threats. Do not forget: this is the man whom we spent all summer hunting when Mr. Darcy's sister disappeared, who felt himself so done out of his fortune that he would have destroyed a young gentlewoman's life to capture her dowry. He was hardly a man to be trusted, and I would not have put murder past him. And yet—" he pursed his lips and frowned, "and yet I could not quite see him as Collins' killer. Still, it was only when he himself was found slain that we felt confident eliminating him from consideration."

"But how," Elizabeth frowned, "did you know it was Mr. Hurst?" She had been toying with a piece of roll all through Alexander's analysis of her partners on his list, which was now reduced to a pile of crumbs on her plate. "All the while I have known him—and I did spend several days in his presence whilst Jane was recuperating at Netherfield—I have not once seen any indication of so passionate a nature as to commit murder once, let alone twice."

"Nor I," Darcy added, "and I have known him much longer still. I attended his wedding to Louisa Bingley just a year past. When I think of the times I have dined with the man, played cards with him, hunted with him..." Darcy's eyes flew open in horror. "I hunted with him, out in the wilderness, with a lethal weapon in his hands!"

"He deceived everybody, Darcy." Alexander knew his words would be of little comfort to his friend; how much worse would Bingley feel at the news that his brother-by-marriage was a murderer? Caroline Bingley might have wished to rise in the estimation of the *ton* through her association with a wrongly accused lady, but those hopes were now dashed. No feigned friendship with Elizabeth could atone for her much closer association with a real murderer.

"But I still do not know," Elizabeth repeated herself, "how you discerned his true nature."

Alexander's head had stopped its pounding, and he was thinking clearly. He raised his coffee cup towards Mary as if it were a crystal goblet of the finest wine, and announced, "For that, I shall refer you to the lady who really solved the mystery. Miss Mary Bennet." With which he smiled proudly at the young woman by his side and sat back to allow her to divulge her conclusions.

Five pairs of eyes turned to her, and Mary felt herself quail at the sight. She was the forgotten one, the girl who seemed to fade in the wallpaper, so often ignored or passed over that she had begun to wonder if she were actually invisible. But now she was the star of the production, the one towards whom everybody had turned his focus. It was terrifying, and rather wonderful! For so long, she had wished to be the object of somebody's attention. Now this wish had come true, and the stage was hers.

She began to speak, but before she could emit two words, the door was opened by one of the footmen and Sir William and Charlotte were shown into the breakfast room.

"Awfully sorry to come by so early, but it looks like everything you surmised was true. Masterful piece of work, Lyons.

"Not I," Alexander returned. "It was Miss Mary who deserves the credit, and we are about to hear her tale of how she arrived at this answer."

"Capital, capital! I long to hear it! Is there more tea, Bennet?"

Eventually, after the newcomers were seated and settled with plates of pastry, Mary began her tale.

"I first began to notice something amiss when I went to Netherfield the very day of the first murder, after poor Lizzy had returned home so badly scratched and beaten, all covered in mud and blood. Mama had left her shawl there at the ball the previous night and bade me go and retrieve it. Acting on Caroline's orders, or perhaps just on her own sense of propriety," Mary rolled her eyes and sighed, "I was sent directly down to the kitchens, for I was not permitted to be in the main part of the house." A giggle escaped her. "Whatever will Caroline do now?"

"Whatever indeed? I should like to have been present when Sir William told the news!" Charlotte did not permit her usual sensible and placid face to conceal her glee at the thought.

Mary resumed her tale. "Whilst I was seated in the corridor leading from the kitchen to the staff members' sitting room, I heard some of the maids and footmen discussing the previous night's ball. There are always tales to be told, and having little else to do as somebody was searching the house for Mama's shawl, I listened. I do believe," she grimaced, "I might have been present in the room and they would have told their tales, regardless. Nevertheless, I heard about an excess of empty wine bottles in one room, of a single stocking, of a pair of missing boots, of some missing candlesticks, and of a missing maid!"

"Whose stocking was it?" Charlotte asked, her face a picture of innocence. "Surely not mine—" She stopped short at the gasp from her father and burst out laughing.

"I never did solve the mystery of the stocking, nor that of the seven empty bottles of wine. But the tale of the silver intrigued me, as did the missing maid. I began asking questions, and to my horror I discovered that not only had one very valuable pair of candlesticks gone missing the previous night, but that this was only the most recent and most audacious in a series of disappearances. This seemed very strange, especially coming, as it did, right at the moment of Mr. Collins' murder.

"Now, one strange event, like a murder, is horrifying and alarming, but strange events do happen. A second strange event occurring at the same time might be said to me a quirk of fate, a coincidence. But the missing maid, well, that was a third strange event, and all of a sudden I felt these incidents could not be unrelated. I needed to know more, and I was fortunate enough as to have my questions well received.

"I learned that the missing maid, Polly, had been threatened by Lieutenant Wickham the previous morning, before the ball. He had been in the kitchens at Netherfield for reasons best left private and he had threatened to cast the blame for the thefts of silver upon her if she did not meet him for as assignation the next afternoon.

"As we spoke more, I also learned that there had been an argument in the breakfast room at Netherfield that very afternoon. The maid, Bessie, identified one of the belligerents as Mr. Collins—although what he was doing in Netherfield the afternoon of the ball, she could not imagine. The other, she told me, sounded every bit like Mr. Wickham, although he, too, had no reason to be there. This, I realised, was a fourth strange event that I needed to consider in relation to the other three. They must be connected!"

"Was she certain it was Wickham?" Colonel Forster asked. "He ought to have been off to London that day at noon. He had a mission to discharge and was needed at the London office by sunset, which is mighty early at this time of year. He could not have been at Netherfield in the afternoon, arguing or not."

Mary felt Alexander move at her side and she glanced at him. He raised his eyebrows at her, asking tacit permission, and she answered with a smile. He winked at her and took over the tale for a moment. "Nobody saw him, or nobody who would admit it, but we found a bright young lad at the coaching inn at Southgate who told us of Mr. Wickham racing through at great speed later that day. We know the ride can be done in two hours, rather less if the man is fit and a strong rider and changes horses half way. This is what Wickham did, thus ensuring he was in Town at his appointed hour, whilst still having been arguing at Netherfield that very afternoon."

"It is also," Mary added, "how he contrived to be in the fields near Oakham Mount for his tryst with Polly, whilst still being seen in London for both his morning and evening duties."

"Well, well," the colonel clucked as he scratched his chin. "But surely he did not travel all that distance merely for a chance at a kiss in the woods. Any chance for more tea, Bennet? Shall I go to the kitchens?"

Lizzy rose and summoned a maid to request more tea, then returned to her chair next to Mr. Darcy and turned her eyes back to Mary.

"Not at all," Mary nodded as tea was brought in and Lizzy began to pour. "This was precisely why he seemed to carry so much guilt for the murder. It would seem as though he could not have been in Meryton to kill anybody, and therefore who better to have done the evil deed? The tryst was merely an added inducement for the journey. But we were mistaken. His real purpose was to meet with Hurst to collect the silver that he would use to pay off his debts."

"Slow down, Mary," her father frowned. "If it was Wickham in the field that day, why do you say that Hurst was the real killer?"

"There were a few clues that led me to this conclusion. I realised, far too late, that I had missed something important on my list of strange events. The fifth item on my list of strange things ought to have been the missing boots that the footman had mentioned to the maids whilst I waited for Mama's shawl at Netherfield that day. Hurst had been traipsing through the wet fields and knew that such a quantity of mud on his boots would be noted, for he was such an indolent man and was known never to venture out further than the stables to take a chaise into town to visit the pub. He knew this and prepared by finding some old clothes to wear, so his own would not be muddied, and by leaving a pair of his shoes where he might change into them after his meeting in the fields.

"The grooms in Bingley's stables mentioned such a set of missing clothing," Alexander interjected, confirming this supposition. "Well done, Mary!"

"The boots themselves were left somewhere safe where he could change. My supposition would be that Mr. Hurst selected some shed or barn near a laneway where he could leave his chaise and horse and thereby return to Netherfield pristine, but it might have been in any one of a number of locations. I suspect it was one of Ott's outbuildings, since it was Ott's dog who led the farmers to Collins' body. I imagine the dog had found the boots and had followed the scent of their owner to where the crime had been committed."

She took a deep breath and stated, "When I learned whose boots were missing, I knew we had the killer. This also explains why we could not find my cousin's cravat. I believe Mr. Hurst found it and used to it to clean his hands and face of mud and blood, using the water from the stream. Once he had discarded the soiled clothing and changed into his own again, no one would be any wiser as to his activities. With the sole exception of those boots!"

Sir William wrinkled his nose. "But Hurst, as you said, was a sedentary man, hardly one to be grappling in the mud. Collins was no athlete, but he was large and heavily built. It could not have been an easy task to fell him."

"This is where Mr. Lyons had the next clue. He had learned that Hurst was once a member of a wrestling club at university. His corpulent appearance disguised but did not detract from his strength, or more importantly, his skill. He knew very well how to subdue a man, especially one who was already incapacitated from an extremely painful injury." Mary blushed a deep red at the thought, and Lizzy coughed delicately into her napkin.

"But what about Wickham?" The colonel now asked. "He was seen approaching the injured man in the field that day. Surely it might still have been he who plunged the knife into the man's neck."

"The maid Polly saw Wickham approaching from one direction and was close enough to identify him without any question. But Lizzy heard a man approaching from the other direction, and this was whom she believed might have been Papa, who sometimes rides his lands in rough clothing. Poor Lizzy did not stop her escape to confirm her supposition, but fled into the woods, and so was not able to see that this other man might really have been Hurst. What followed, we can only guess, but I believe this occurred: If Wickham also saw this other man drawing near and saw Collins lying injured and cursing in the mud, he might have taken himself to hide in the woods, thereby being in a position to observe the murder. The other—Hurst—did not see Wickham because he came through the woods and had not yet emerged fully into the field. Only Polly, who was so close, could see him clearly."

"And so," Charlotte supplied, "Wickham saw the murder and attempted to bribe or otherwise coerce Hurst, and Hurst dealt death to him with his pistol."

Darcy shook his head sadly. "A sorry end to a sorry life. For all the grief he caused me, we were friends once, and I find myself mourning him more than I had thought possible." Mary saw Lizzy's hand creep across the edge of the table to Darcy's and grasp it in sympathy.

"Then how," Sir William now pondered, "did this relate to the argument Miss Mary heard about? I do not grasp that at all."

"I believe there was a third party to that heated discussion, besides Mr. Collins and Mr. Wickham, and that was Hurst himself. The breakfast room leads directly into the kitchens, and there is a short passageway that bends just before the doorway to the room from the main part of the house. After my cousin threatened Hurst and Wickham with exposure of their scheme, Mr. Collins left through the adjoining dining room, where the maids saw him, and Wickham exited through the kitchens. Hurst might well have taken the other door to the bent hall and remained there out of sight until the hallways were empty of staff or residents of the house. He was fully aware of the plan and thereby knew where to find Collins."

"Capital, Miss Mary, capital!" Sir William burst into a solo round of applause. "Perhaps having your nose always in a book has taught you a thing or two. Capital!"

Mary's father narrowed his eyes and fussed with a linen serviette that lay across his plate. "But there is one matter you have not explained, my dear, and that is the question of why. Why would a man like Hurst wish to pull this strange ruse and steal silver for another man, and then murder two people? I have hunted with him once and he seemed not at all the sort to exert himself for anybody, let alone two men he disdained."

Mary glanced over to Alexander, who now took the lead once more. He returned her smile with a wink, and she felt inordinately proud to have been the recipient of not one, but two winks that very day. She was grinning like a schoolgirl as he began to speak.

"It was a matter of insolvency. Hurst's estate, like Longbourn, is entailed and therefore cannot be sold in whole or in part, or mortgaged in any way, and it is in a crisis of debt. The man was reduced to pilfering his own silverware in order to raise some funds, and I suspect there is not a stick of furniture remaining in the house. I pity his tenants greatly. We learned this through our inquiries in London, which informed us that he had been gaming and coming up short, as well as through our observances at Netherfield. One of the platters at Caroline's dinner had Elm Ridge's name and crest embossed on the underside. That is Hurst's family estate; it was his own platter that had found its way into Bingley's supplies, presumably sold for some outrageous amount to cover one or another of Hurst's debts. If we were to take a survey of the remaining silver in the butler's pantry, I would imagine we should find several similar pieces. The man was quite embarrassed."

"Have your men in London confirmed this?" Bennet asked.

"Not as of yet, but no man who had the interest derived from thirty-five or forty thousand pounds would resort to selling and stealing his own family's silver. If his wife's dowry were still intact, Hurst would have a respectable income, and more so since he was living on his brother's purse."

"But why, then, was he giving the pieces to Wickham and not selling them himself?" Charlotte's question seemed to be on everybody's mind, for it was echoed by a wave of nods from around the table.

"Hurst was in bad straits, but was not desperate, for he had a home of sorts with Bingley. As long as he was married to Louisa, he knew that Bingley would provide him with a comfortable existence. The man who was desperate was Wickham.

"Wickham was deeply in debt, to the point of fearing for his life, and needed urgently to repay his creditors. When Wickham discovered the extent of Hurst's debts and the loss of Louisa's dowry at the gaming tables, he threatened to reveal the information unless Hurst would abet him in his schemes. The danger to Hurst was not Charles Bingley's discovery of the situation, but Louisa's. She was inordinately proud of her dowry and the status it provided herself and her future daughters. If Hurst's wife had learned of his carelessness and gaming habits, she might have forced him to leave or to agree to a separation. Both Bingley sisters had built their reputations upon their wealth, and Louisa would in all likelihood not abide a husband fit for debtor's prison. Thus, Hurst was an easy target for an experienced Machiavelli like Wickham.

"It was an easy matter for Hurst to pilfer the valuable silverware from Netherfield. He passed it along to Wickham, who then took it to London when sent on military duty, where he sold it. With the income from the stolen silver, Wickham would pay enough of his own debts to remain welcome at the tables, and any money he won with Hurst's silver he would then share.

"Mr. Collins discovered this ruse and threatened to expose the scheme to his patroness, Lady Catherine de Bourgh. I do not know if he genuinely believed this would stop the men, but the danger of being exposed troubled Hurst greatly, for exactly the reasons that Wickham was able to blackmail him so successfully. Wickham, it seemed, could be kept quiet with money—or silver in lieu. Collins was not so easily bought and nothing would detract him from his aim. Our conjecture is that when Hurst found the injured Collins in the mud by the stream, he attempted to convince him, first by words and then by force, and when he found the knife that Miss Elizabeth had attempted to use to defend her own honour, he took it and used it to keep Collins quiet forever.

"For Hurst believed that if Louisa had heard of her husband's terrible losses, she would have Charles banish him from the house, and as Miss Bingley mentioned at dinner, everybody knows that Charles has one of the best chefs in London. When we all commented that Hurst cared for nothing as much as his belly and the food that he put into it, we were quite correct. He killed two men so as not to lose ready access to some excellent ragout!"

Chapter Twenty-Six

Goodbyes

Alexander remained at Longbourn for two more days. Darcy had requested the time to console his friend Charles Bingley and to have more time with Miss Elizabeth before returning to London, and Alexander was pleased for the respite. He had some business to attend in Town, but his letters could just as well be written at Longbourn and there was nothing else so pressing that another day or two would put him out, especially since Darcy insisted on paying his regular fees until the moment Alexander was back in his office. A two-day holiday at another's expense was not an arrangement to refuse, and so Alexander made himself comfortable at Longbourn.

This was not an arduous task. Mrs. Bennet, for all her foibles, was a superb hostess and her table was always generous with excellent food. The room he had been offered was far superior to his plain suite in London, and whilst he knew he would soon desire the tranquillity that accompanies solitude, the cheerful and abundant noises of a house full of engaging young ladies was like returning home. He had had this notion before, and he was quite amazed at how much he missed the home he left as a youth, for until now he had only considered it as a part of his childhood and not as a part of his soul.

Meryton was a pleasant enough village, with enough of interest to entertain a man for a day or two, especially in the company of an interesting companion. As often as not, that companion was Mary, who expressed delight in showing him the village and her favourite places nearby. There was a tailor where Darcy had made an order for a suit to replace the one damaged by mud in the fall from the horse on his first day in the area, and a coat to replace the one fouled by Wickham's gore when Alexander had examined the body.

The fabrics seemed far finer than anything Alexander had imagined, but the tailor insisted that there was no mistake, and proceeded to cluck and fuss over the investigator as he stood as still as he might in the middle of the room whilst he was measured and re-measured and asked to move this way and that to assure a proper fit. "I have your direction in London, there to send the completed coats. You will, of course, take them to a tailor of Mr. Darcy's choosing for a final fitting," the tailor stated. "I have cut them so as to be donned without the assistance of a valet, as Mr. Darcy requested, but they will still require some minor alterations to ensure the best fit." It seemed that Darcy had taken full responsibility for this addition to his wardrobe!

There was also a public house in the front of the inn that served a fine stew and good ale, several shops with items for the ladies, from which he purchased small tokens for his mother and sisters, and a respectable bookshop. Mary showed him the bookshop with delight. For all that everybody took Elizabeth for a bibliophile, it was Mary who possessed her father's real passion for books. She introduced him to Mr. Wells, the proprietor, and then took him through the collection. Her chosen volumes, until now, had been books of a religious bent, of sermons and teachings and treatises. "But perhaps I ought to move to a broader study," she sighed, "for I now wonder if God is found just as much in the universe He created as in the teachings of the Church. If I cannot find God also in a butterfly or in the tides or in the force of steam, perhaps I am seeking Him in the wrong places."

At times, when Darcy was engaged at Netherfield, Miss Elizabeth joined them for walks through the chilly countryside or into the village to take tea with her Aunt Phillips or to Lucas Lodge to summon Charlotte's attention for a time. Alexander found he derived a great deal of pleasure from such simple things and almost regretted the need to return to London.

It was only when Darcy returned with tales from Netherfield that Alexander began to feel the pull to return to his own abode and his occupation. The descriptions his friend offered of the chaos and confusion and total despair in which the Bingleys now found themselves made him realise how much he felt a need to work to help people find solutions to the troubles that vexed them so. Although a very small part of him felt bad that it was he, along with Mary, who had cast Bingley and his sisters into such grief, he could not feel guilt at having rousted a murderer from his nest, for whom might the man have killed next?

"Charles is distraught," Darcy sighed after dinner the night after Sir William had officially charged Hurst with the crimes. "He feels responsible for having permitted his sister to marry such a man as this and to have entrusted him with such a fortune as was Louisa's dowry when he knew that Hurst's estate was bankrupt. He feels he ought to have had the man investigated before granting his permission."

Alexander smiled a sad smile. "That does form a large part of my business. It is never pleasant to tell a father or brother of a prospective lover's sad affairs, but it often saves greater heartache at a later date."

"Charles has taken the full weight of the blame, but if I recall, it was Louisa who insisted so vehemently upon Hubert Hurst. He was the family's first entrée to society. He was landed, his family from some of the best circles. His grandmother was the daughter of a baron, I believe, which for the upstart Bingley sisters was akin to being nobility itself."

Darcy sat in silence for a minute, lost in the flickering flames that leapt and danced in the hearth. "Caroline is quite at sixes and sevens. Her entire life has been spent in the pursuit of social advancement, and now that hope is quite dashed. She has been screaming at the servants and breaking everything she can find, and Charles has had to confine her to her rooms. As for Louisa, nothing can entice her to leave hers. From what Mrs. Slougham says, all the woman does is weep and wail."

"Mrs. Slougham?" Alexander had taken a definite liking to the cook. "Why is she above stairs? Is her realm not her kitchens, wherein she works her magic?"

"So it is, but Mrs. Harwick had her bags packed and left almost before the news of Hurst's arrest came out. All of a sudden, the Bingley household was far beneath her. So Mrs. Slougham is now the *de facto* housekeeper at Netherfield."

"How the mighty have fallen. Alas. What will the three siblings do now?" Alexander stretched himself out of his comfortable chair and strode across the drawing room to a tray which held a decanter and two empty glasses. He filled one for himself and then, at a glance and a nod, one for Darcy as well.

Darcy accepted his glass and swirled the brandy inside it, sniffing the distinctive aroma, but not drinking. "Charles had not quite settled upon a plan when I left him. He says he wishes to remain, for despite his feelings of responsibility, he has done nothing wrong and he believes that Meryton will continue to accept him. He also wishes to offer to Jane—this can be of no surprise to you—and that cannot be done if he removes himself permanently from the area before they are wed. He will have to wait for some time before he will take this step, for the sake of appearances as much as of a real need to come to terms with what has happened. Jane will have to wait several months yet.

"His sisters, however, cannot remain. That much is clear. They have done little to enamour themselves to local society, and with the notoriety now upon them, there seems little chance of their warm welcome. I have recommended sending both to spend the next several months at Scarborough, where they have an elderly aunt. News will travel, of course, but Scarborough is a very long way from London and they have a better chance at surviving the trial and execution of justice at such a remove."

Now Darcy drank of his brandy, and Alexander did likewise. There was still much to be said and asked, but the fire seemed to forbid further conversation for a moment. At last Alexander asked his last question.

"And what of you, Darcy? What are your plans?"

"Why," he raised his eyebrows and tossed his great head, "to marry Elizabeth, of course! Out of respect for her cousin, we shall wait for some weeks before announcing our engagement, and then I hope to be wed as soon as possible and to leave for Derbyshire. Lizzy... Elizabeth might be absolved of all wrong, but people can be fickle in their choices of memory, and she has spoken to me of how favourite places now fill her with dread rather than with pleasure. While I shall never try to keep her from her family, we both believe she will be happier away from Meryton."

"May I be so bold as to expect an invitation to the wedding?"

"Alexander, my friend, you may count on it."

By the end of his second day of leisure, Alexander was quite ready to return to London. His hip, while still shades of blue and green, no longer vexed him and his jolted and aching muscles had recovered fully. Enforced leisure was not the life he desired, no matter how he might enjoy the trappings of such an existence from time to time. He was, therefore, relieved when Darcy announced their return to London the following day after breakfast.

He stowed his small bag on the back of the carriage and watched as the servants secured it for the journey. Next he personally placed his valise of personal effects and books on the cushioned benches inside. Darcy might wish to talk, or he might wish to sleep, or to contemplate the world. The man was prone to be taciturn at times, and it would do a fellow no good to impinge upon his need for solitude; therefore, having a book at hand was a good plan.

Darcy announced he would make one final visit to Netherfield to see how Charles was faring, which gave Alexander some time to ride into Meryton and take his leave of Colonel Forster and Sir William. These gentlemen said everything proper, thanking him for his invaluable assistance and offering to put in a good word anytime he needed it. As he departed Lucan Lodge, Charlotte dashed out of the kitchen to delay him for a moment. "I cannot thank you enough for your efforts to absolve my friend from this crime. If my father had carried through with his plans to charge her that day, I do not know what I would have done. But she is free from all blame, and I believe happy with your friend."

Alexander returned her words with a deep bow. "It was your doing that kept her safe at home until Darcy could engage me to return here so as to prove her innocence. If you must thank anybody, think of yourself first." He bowed once more and turned to his horse for the last final ride to Longbourn.

Darcy had returned from his errands with no great smile upon his face but a look of grim satisfaction, and suitable goodbyes and obsequies were made to the Bennet family. At last, it was time to take his leave of Mary.

She walked with him the long way to the drive where Darcy's fine carriage awaited. Darcy himself was saying his more temporary goodbyes to Elizabeth and would not mind the delay. Mary led him out of the side entrance to the house and through some of the gardens and shrubberies where they had had some of their first conversations, not quite close enough to take his arm, but neither so distant as to prevent intimate conversation.

For a while, Alexander was quite at a loss for what to say. He was unaccustomed to being tongue-tied and hoped that Mary would begin the conversation. It was only when they passed the wall of hedges and shrubbery that Mary finally spoke.

"I am pleased that she accepted him." She did not need to clarify her comment.

Alexander kicked a stone from his path and nodded as he chewed his upper lip. "I believe they will be happy. They are very different, but in ways that complement each other."

Mary's eyes drifted away from him and towards the horizon. "Will you return for the wedding?"

"Darcy has requested my presence. I shall do everything I can to attend."

There was more silence before Mary whispered, "I should be pleased to see you once more."

Equally quietly, he responded, "And I you."

"We did not start off too well," her voice was a bit stronger, more confident after his affirmation, "but we made a fine team in the end."

Alexander stopped walking and reached out a hand to stay Mary's steps. He turned to face her. "I was wrong. When I spat those cruel and untrue words at you that day, I was wrong. I ought to have stopped my descent into self-pity and heard you then. I deemed you nothing but a silly girl with a smattering of useless 'accomplishments' that rendered you fit for little more than decorating a sleeve or making a hash of some Scottish air. I could not have been more mistaken, and for this I will always chastise myself. I have also learned to look beyond appearances and my own predetermined notions. Hah! What an investigator I am, making such a harsh and sudden judgement based purely on my own whims! Even now, my first apology rings false in my ears. This one comes from the heart. Will you accept it?"

"I believe I accepted your first a while ago. You were not wrong. I did little to give you confidence in my skills at observation, for if I truly took note of everything I saw, how could I have failed to notice your sorry state that day? You were covered in mud and looked quite ill-abused by your horse, and I could see that you were walking with some painful injury. I ought to have let you go, or at least waited until you had a moment to wash and rest before demanding you hear my ideas."

"Then we were both wrong, but also both right, for your ideas were fundamental to finding the solution, and for that I cannot thank you enough."

"You saved Lizzy. That is thanks enough for me."

They walked along for a few minutes more. The air was cold, but the ground was dry and the sky azure, and the trees no longer looked like skeletal remains, but like carefully wrought ornaments, just awaiting the first coating of icy frost to turn them into crystalline displays.

As they rounded the last corner of the house before the drive, Mary turned to Alexander with a shy grin. "You offered me something more valuable than your apology," she blushed. Alexander noted again how pretty she could be when she smiled and when her eyes sparkled and danced. "You offered me your friendship, and that is something I can cherish forever."

He was stunned beyond words for that brief moment until he found his tongue. "As I shall cherish yours." He now stepped close enough to offer her his arm, and together they walked the last yards to where Darcy was waiting with the coachman and the team of horses.

"There is one more matter, though," Mary's voice sounded vexed, and Alexander could see her pinch her lips together in displeasure. He was wrong once more, he realised. She could be very pretty at times, even when not smiling.

"Will you elaborate, Miss Bennet?" he teased.

She exhaled sharply, almost in a snort, and turned her narrowed eyes to him. "For all our conversations about religion and faith and the nature of God and good and evil, you never did explain to me your comment about not being considered a Christian. And that troubles me."

He offered her a wide smile that reached far beyond his lips and bowed before taking her hand to shake firmly, as he would a man's. "That, my friend, is something for our next encounter after your sister and my friend wed."

"Then after the wedding, you believe we may meet again?"

"Miss Mary," he stated as he climbed into the carriage, "I am counting on it."

❧

More from Mary and Alexander

You can read about Alexander Lyon's first case with Mr. Darcy in the prequel novella, **The Mystery of the Missing Heiress**.

Here is a taste of Mary and Alexander's next adventure in **Death in Highbury: An Emma Mystery**.

from

Miss Mary Investigates 2: Death in Highbury: An Emma Mystery

Chapter 1 ~ An Unexpected Delay

Monday, May 11, 1812

This was most definitely not how the journey had been planned.

Mary Bennet let out a shattered breath as she stared once more at the letter that had fallen onto her lap. What was written within could not be true! Surely it was false! But she knew the writer. He would not lie. She read the letter again and took a deep breath as she strove to regain her equanimity.

"Miss?" A timid voice sounded from the doorway. "Would you like more tea, Miss? There is hot stew and bread as well, or biscuits whilst you wait."

"Tea and biscuits, thank you." Her voice sounded as ragged as her thoughts, but the young maid paid it no mind. She dropped a quick curtsey and dashed out of Mary's sight, presumably in the direction of the kitchens.

Tea would be good. It was normal, ordinary even, on this day when nothing was ordinary. Mary took another look around the room, as details she had previously missed made themselves known to her. The blue curtains, the worn wooden floor, the white cloth upon the table, the little jars and vases that sat upon the mantel. It was a somewhat tired but not unacceptable private salon in a village inn, almost certainly the best such place within miles. Similarly, the young maid had been polite and efficient, and the tea hot and strong. It was exactly the sort of place he would have selected for her to wait. If only he had known, when he made the arrangement, how long that wait might be!

As she waited for the maid to return with her tea, her mind drifted to the events that had led her here, to this inn in a small village in Surrey, alone but for her maid and with no thought as to when she might return home.

The events had all begun, she supposed, when Colonel Forster of the —shire militia had announced that the entire regiment would be removing to Brighton for the summer. It was hardly a wonder, Mary supposed, after the shocking events of last autumn, but the unit would be missed by many in Meryton. The shopkeepers and tavern owners would miss the custom of the officers and men, and the young ladies of the town would miss the sight of so many smartly dressed young men in their scarlet coats and tall hats. For the autumn and winter, there had at last been enough men present to equal the number of ladies at the town assemblies, and many an evening at cards or musical events had been enlivened by some of the officers.

Colonel Forster himself was a garrulous and friendly man when not on duty, and the young wife he had introduced to Meryton's society was even more so. What basis there had been for a friendship between Harriet Forster and Lydia, Mary would never know, for the former was a married lady of three and twenty, and the latter not quite sixteen and scarcely out of the schoolroom, but both were full of high spirits and rather silly. This, it appeared, was sufficient for the colonel's wife to request that Lydia accompany her to Brighton as her special friend.

Papa had agreed almost without a thought, and somehow it was decided that Mary would accompany the party to Brighton and remain for a week with her sister and Mrs. Forster before returning alone to Hertfordshire.

This was where Mr. Darcy's role in the events had begun.

He and her sister Elizabeth had been returning to London from their estate in Derbyshire, and had broken their journey for some few days at Longbourn, the Bennets' estate. Lizzy was as radiant as any bride, having been married only a few short months, and Mr. Darcy was much improved in manner. He was as formal as ever he had been, but there was an ease in his movements and a lilt in his voice that had not been present when first they had met, and he had become very pleasant company. That he had all but saved Lizzy's life last autumn was yet one more point in his favour. She could not have asked for a better brother.

Thus it was that after dinner on that day that the Darcys arrived, when Lydia had announced her invitation from Harriet Forster and Papa had acquiesced to squeals of glee from Mama and wails of woe and anger from Kitty, that Mr. Darcy had sat back in his chair and rested his chin in his hand, as he was wont to do.

"That is most interesting, Bennet!" the great man exclaimed. "I have some business I wish to conduct in Surrey, part way between London and Brighton, near a small town called Highbury. There is an estate for sale in the area, and I promised to take a look at it for both Bingley," he mentioned Jane Bennet's future husband, "and my cousin, Colonel Fitzwilliam."

He turned his dark eyes to his wife and smiled a small secret smile just for her. "I had thought, at first, to ride down alone, but now I have an idea, if my wife will agree." Again he gave Lizzy his secret smile. Was that a flash of envy that Mary had felt upon seeing his face as he gazed upon his wife? What must it be like to be adored like that? She had little time to consider this, for he continued.

"If Mary will accompany Lydia on the journey to Brighton, I can assist her in returning home. Allow me to send my own carriage to meet you in Brighton, Mary. If it is acceptable, Elizabeth and I can drive down in my curricle if the weather is fine, and we can stay for some days in the area. I will then have more time to devote to examining the neighbourhood and the estate, and you and Elizabeth will be good company for each other whilst I am occupied. What think you, dearest?" He turned to his wife once more as if seeking a reason to gaze upon her again.

"It is a splendid idea! Mary. Do you like it?"

How could she not? She had never travelled past London before, and the idea of seeing the sea was enthralling! She was nineteen years of age, more than old enough to manage the return journey in a private carriage. Furthermore, she found she longed to spend some time with her sister. She and Lizzy had always shared a sisterly love, but it was not until the events of the autumn that they had formed a bond as close as the one between Lizzy and their oldest sister, Jane.

"Yes," she replied at once. "I like it very much!"

And so the plan was formed and settled. Mary would travel with her maid from Brighton to Highbury, where she would meet her sister and new brother, and from there they would drive the additional short distance to the cottage he had planned to take for his short stay in Surrey. It was a simple and foolproof plan.

The countryside between Brighton and Highbury was beautiful, but the drive was long, and the small party took several long breaks along the way to allow the horses to rest. It was well past seven o'clock in the evening, therefore, when at last they turned from the road towards the town where they were all to meet. The sun was still up and the sky bright, but it would begin to grow dark before another hour was out, and she hoped it was not too far from the inn to the cottage.

But even as the carriage had drawn up to the inn, and as the footman had leapt from the box to announce their arrival and ask after the Darcys, Mary could see that something was amiss. A man who must have been the innkeeper rushed up to the footman and driver and conferred with them in hushed tones, after which Mary was hustled into this small but comfortable salon and presented with a pot of tea and a tray of small sandwiches and this letter. She knew the handwriting well, for Mr. Darcy had a distinctive hand. But the presence of the letter meant that the man himself, and her sister with him, were not here.

Without reading a word, she could see that something was wrong. The usually smooth and crisp handwriting was jagged and uneven, the result of hurry and distress, a portent of the dreadful matter mentioned within. She read the content, and then in shock, read it again.

Dear Sister Mary,

I must write quickly, and will dispense with pleasantries, for which you may castigate me when next we meet. All your family are well, never fear. But some dire events have occurred in London which prevent your sister and me from meeting you in Highbury as planned, and which must necessitate your remaining in that town for some amount of time.

I had considered caution in relating this to you out of concern for your sensibilities, but I know you to be a reasonable and intelligent young woman who will not swoon at the news. I will not insult you by refusing to impart it.

London is all in an uproar tonight, for only minutes ago, from the time that I write, the Right Honourable Spencer Perceval, our Prime Minister, was shot and killed in front of Parliament. I was in the neighbourhood when it occurred and heard the outcry but not the shot, and came immediately home to write to you.

I have sent Elizabeth back to Longbourn. She is not pleased with me, but her safety is paramount and she may shout at me for all of her life should she wish. My only concern is her health and wellbeing. I will join her there as soon as I am able to conclude my affairs here, and we will remain there for several days until the City is brought back into order.

I must beg your forgiveness, Mary, for abandoning you in this way, and must entreat you not to return home, nor to travel anywhere near London, until such time as it is safe once more.

I will not forsake you altogether. I know a gentleman—as fine a man as I have met, and one of the few very sensible people of my acquaintance—who lives not far from Highbury. I have already written to him to request his assistance in providing for your security and comfort whilst we all await a return to order in our country. His name is George Knightley, of Donwell Abbey, and he will see you right.

I will send this message off at once with a fast rider, along with sufficient funds to see to your immediate comfort at the Crown Inn upon your arrival. (That explained the private salon and the tea and food.) *Enclosed please find five pounds for any further needs you might incur, with a promise for more should it be required.*

Your affectionate brother,

FD

The room seemed not quite in focus; the shock of the news and the surprise at being suddenly so completely alone and so far from home were making themselves known on her nerves, and for a moment, Mary dreaded becoming like her mother. Perhaps she ought to ask for some smelling salts. This was all rather troubling!

She was reading the letter for the third time, hoping it would impart different news on a subsequent perusal, when a tap at the door signalled the return of the maid. She carried with her a tray that held another pot of tea and a rather large plate of biscuits, which she set down on the table in the centre of the room.

"If you please, Miss, a gentleman is here to see you, asking after Miss Mary Bennet. May I show him in? It's Mr. Knightley, Miss. I know him well, we all do in the town. I will sit with you."

He was here already? Mr. Darcy's messenger was very efficient! "Yes, yes, of course." She raised a hand to her hair to ensure it retained something of its morning style and straightened her skirts and fichu. Almost at once an unknown man strode into the room and made his bow. His appearance was of some surprise to Mary, for she had expected a different sort of man. This gentleman must be nearer to forty than to thirty, and his clothing was sensible country attire rather than the elegant garb worn by the dandies in Town. He seemed to be of average height, and whilst his brown hair held no trace of grey, light wrinkles were beginning to adorn the corners of his mild brown eyes. He was not so much handsome as appealing in looks, and he carried with him the impression of a sensible, intelligent and decent sort of a man, and Mary liked him at once.

She rose to curtsey and waited as he introduced himself. "Forgive the impertinence, Miss Bennet. We must assume our mutual friend Darcy to have performed the honours through his missives. I normally would not presume, but these are strange times." His voice swam through the fog in her mind and she forced herself to focus upon him.

He seemed a straightforward person, not one to speak in circles around a topic, or to pad his meaning with extraneous verbiage as some dandies padded their thin legs and shoulders to better fit their clothing. She was a lady of simple meaning herself and appreciated his forthright manner.

"Yes, of course," she returned. Her voice sounded more normal in her ears now. "Please, I have a pot of tea, only now arrived. May I pour you a cup?" There was a second cup on the tray; the maid must have added it when Mr. Knightley asked after her.

He accepted the hot tea and asked briefly after her journey and general health before turning to matters of business. "I understand that the terrible events in London today will require you to stay with us for some time. I have taken the liberty of securing an invitation for you to stay with a friend of mine. He is a solid chap, leading family in town and all, and he has a daughter of about your own years. Emma Woodhouse is her name, and I hope you will become friends. Will that be satisfactory?"

Still half in a daze, Mary accepted. "Thank you indeed, sir. That would be most kind." She could not, after all, stay in the inn alone, even with her maid to accompany her. Although the Bennets were hardly of the circles that fed the daily gossip sheets, such an impropriety would nevertheless soon be known far and wide. It was much better to be the guest of a young woman of good standing.

Mr. Knightley proved as good as his word, and within half an hour, he stood with Mary at the front door to Hartfield, a large and elegant house just outside of the town. Miss Woodhouse herself answered the door and ushered the two inside.

"Oh Miss Bennet! You poor dear! What an ordeal you have suffered. Come in, come in. Mr. Knightley, how kind of you to bring Miss Bennet to us. Of course we have a room for you. Do you prefer pink or pale green? The pink room is larger, but the green has a nicer view of the gardens. I would take the green, but I shall leave it to you. Come in. Have you dined? It is eight o'clock, so you must be hungry. I'll call cook for a tray; there is always something ready at Hartfield, for just such occasions. We are expecting company momentarily, and you are so welcome to join us and meet some of our society, unless you would rather rest. But really, I believe some cheerful conversation would do you good after all you have endured. My friends will be only too happy to meet you. Do come and join us at tea and cards, Miss Bennet, I implore you!"

The deluge of words was too forceful to deny, and once more, Mary found herself accepting. Despite not waiting to hear Mary's thoughts on the matter, Miss Woodhouse was correct: an evening of company would be better for her spirits than fretting alone in her room. It was part of her nature to dwell on matters too seriously, and with the unsettled thoughts brought about by Mr. Darcy's news, and her sudden predicament of being alone in a strange town, she knew her mind would turn her troubles into something far greater if left alone.

Within moments, Miss Woodhouse called to a footman to have Mary's trunks brought to her room, and then led Mary up the elegant staircase that graced the centre of the large entrance. As they walked, Miss Woodhouse a few steps ahead of her, Mary had an opportunity to observe her hostess.

Emma Woodhouse was, indeed, about her own age, perhaps a year or two older, and very pretty, with an open face and sparkling light eyes that seemed to promise mischief. She had an elegant sort of figure and an upright carriage, and Mary believed she thought rather well of herself.

Of course, Mary mused, if she were pretty and rich and the centre of everybody's attention, she might think rather well of herself too. But this had never been her lot. Instead, she was the plainest of five sisters, and the right in the middle in terms of age. She had enjoyed neither the adoration due to the precocious and witty older sisters, Jane and Lizzy, nor the doting poured upon the younger and more spirited two, Kitty and Lydia, and instead was mostly ignored by everybody around her. Perhaps it suited her nature to be so easily forgotten, for she always felt awkward when everybody's eyes were upon her. Mama pressed her constantly to exhibit her meagre skills upon the pianoforte, but whatever talent she felt she might possess always fell victim to the discomfort of performing for strangers.

No, she was far better suited for quiet contemplation and the company of one or two good friends of excellent understanding and depth of character. People like Lizzy or Mr. Darcy or that annoying man from London whom she had vowed to think on no more. No more! She had better attend to Miss Woodhouse, who was talking once more about the house and the tray of food and the company to whom Mary would soon be introduced.

Hartfield boasted an excellent staff, for the tray of hot beef pie and roasted potatoes was already waiting in the sitting room off the bedroom she had been offered. Miss Woodhouse quickly showed her the room, which was not large but very beautiful, in delicate shades of green and eggshell white, with pale yellow ornaments and decoration all done most tastefully. The wide canopied bed promised a comfortable sleep, and soft yellow draperies hung over the window that was said to enjoy so lovely a vista.

What caught Mary's attention, however, was the gown that had been laid out on the bed.

"When Mr. Knightley came earlier to explain your situation, I took the prerogative of setting out something for you, should you wish to change. We are not a particularly elegant party and your current gown will suit well, but I thought you might wish to refresh yourself."

"Yes, thank you." Mary picked up the dress. It was a pale blue, not her best colour, but it looked like it might fit her nicely.

"It is the most easy of my frocks to adapt to different figures," Miss Woodhouse explained, "owing to the lacing at each side. I did not know your size and thought this the most likely to fit. If I have overstepped, please excuse me." But her face and bearing suggested she had no real such concerns. Miss Emma Woodhouse seemed very much a young woman who enjoyed taking charge of people and situations, albeit with a happy and benevolent heart.

Too tired and overcome by the day to refuse, Mary thanked her for her kindness and sat down to enjoy her tray of food before venturing to the salon to brave the members of local society. The food was simple and excellent, and no sooner had she finished her meal when Alice, her maid, slipped in through a door in the sitting room to help her mistress dress.

The servants, Alice reported, were kind and helpful, and she had been offered as comfortable a bed to sleep in as she had enjoyed anywhere. If they had to be stranded anywhere, Highbury seemed almost ideal. Perhaps, after the turmoil of last autumn and the ceaseless roiling of her mind in the aftermath, and after the exciting but exhausting week with Lydia at Brighton, a few days of peace would be what she needed. Mama would not be calling on her every five minutes to do some task that Jane or Lizzy had been accustomed to performing; Kitty would not be pestering her constantly for help with her bonnets or embroidery, and Lydia would not be nagging her to cease her practice at the pianoforte. Perhaps there would be sufficient pleasant diversion that she could succeed in spending a day without thinking of... A man of no importance.

Alice helped her dress and redid her hair and then called for a footman to show Mary the way to the salon where the company were gathered for their pleasant evening of cards and friendship. Yes, this would be a most welcome respite indeed.

The tall footman bowed smartly and led her down the grand staircase again and then through a maze of hallways to a wide doorway that stood just ajar. He pushed the door open and took a breath to announce her, but before he could speak, a voice ran through the quiet conversation of the room.

"What? Can it be true? Yet another man has died?"

Watch out for Death in Highbury at your favourite bookseller soon!

About the Author

Riana Everly was born in South Africa, but has called Canada home since she was eight years old. She has a Master's degree in Medieval Studies and is trained as a classical musician, specialising in Baroque and early Classical music. She first encountered Jane Austen when her father handed her a copy of *Emma* at age 11, and has never looked back.

Riana now lives in Toronto with her family. When she is not writing, she can often be found playing string quartets with friends, biking around the beautiful province of Ontario with her husband, trying to improve her photography, thinking about what to make for dinner, and, of course, reading!

If you enjoyed this novel, please consider posting a review at your favourite bookseller's website.

Riana Everly loves connecting with readers on Facebook at facebook.com/RianaEverly/

Also, be sure to check out her website at rianaeverly.com for sneak peeks at coming works and links to works in progress!

Also by Riana Everly

Teaching Eliza

The Assistant: Before Pride and Prejudice

Through a Different Lens: A Pride and Prejudice Variation

The Bennet Affair: A Pride and Prejudice Variation